Dark Asylum

Also by E. S. Thomson

Beloved Poison

Dark Asylum

E. S. Thomson

CONSTABLE • LONDON

CONSTABLE

First published in Great Britain in 2017 by Constable

1 3 5 7 9 10 8 6 4 2

A CIP catalogue record for this book is available from the British Library.

ISBN: 978-1-47212-231-5 (hardback)
ISBN: 978-1-47212-232-2 (trade paperback)

Typeset in ITC New Baskerville by SX Composing DTP, Rayleigh, Essex
Printed and bound in Great Britain by Clays Ltd, St Ives plc

Papers used by Constable are from well-managed forests
and other responsible sources.

Constable
An imprint of
Little, Brown Book Group
Carmelite House
50 Victoria Embankment
London EC4Y 0DZ

An Hachette UK Company
www.hachette.co.uk

www.littlebrown.co.uk

Angel Meadow Asylum, 18th September 1852

The first time I saw the devil I was six years old. The vicious thoughts that filled his head were etched upon his face in every line and shadow. I saw greed and malice in his grinning shrivelled lips, lust and death in his black, empty eyes. He gave me nightmares, and the others laughed at me for being so fearful. After all, it was only a crude woodcut on the back of one of the boys' penny bloods. Only Goblin understood. He didn't laugh. He said that I should put the image from my mind and that I would soon forget. But I never did. And when I saw the devil again, many years later, I knew exactly who he was.

Chapter One

He lay on his back in the centre of the floor, a dark crescent of blood about his head. Above the left ear a long metal object projected. His face – my God, I shall never forget it, nor would anyone else who looked on such a sight, for it was like nothing on earth I had ever seen. The eyes were blackened with blood, as if the sockets had been daubed with the stuff. The ears were missing, cruelly severed so that the wounds gaped in two dark gashes; the lips darned shut with six long, black stitches. They gave the face a crude death's-head appearance, like a child's drawing. Beside me, I heard Will give a faint moan, and fumble in his pockets for his salts. I was half tempted to ask for a whiff of them myself – and I with my years as St Saviour's apothecary too! Why, I had seen faces so eaten away by the pox that it was impossible to tell where mouth ended and eye socket began. I had seen flesh corroded by gangrene, cancers swollen and pustulant – those were the wounds nature inflicted upon humanity with wanton capriciousness. But this? This was nothing one would ever find in nature. This was vicious and calculated, brutal and terrifying. This was man's handiwork.

I leaned closer, until I was breathing in the iron reek of blood, the earthy odour of flesh and hair; so close that I could almost taste the fear that had broken from the skin as life left it. Between the blackened lips and beneath those taut strands of bloodied wool something pale protruded.

'The tongue?' whispered Will.

'The ears,' I said. 'I believe they have been cut off and stuffed into the mouth, the lips sewn closed over them.' The eyes too, I could see now, had been sutured with two crossed threads.

'Dear God,' said Will. 'Who would do such a thing?'

I had no answer. 'Have the police been summoned?'

Dr Hawkins, Angel Meadow's physician superintendent, shook his head. 'I thought it best to call you first,' he said. 'After what happened with Dr Bain at St Saviour's last year – without you the matter would never have been resolved. But I will be sending Pole out for them directly. Pole!' He waved a hand towards the shuffling attendant waiting in the hall. 'Go along. The watch passes down St Saviour's Street at twenty past five. Find the constable and tell him there's been a murder at Angel Meadow Asylum. A doctor. Hurry now!'

'And the body was found by whom?' I said.

'Mrs Lunge.'

'Is she here?'

Dr Hawkins shook his head. 'I sent her back to her room to lie down.'

'Is she sedated?'

'She refused. She said she did not wish to be sedated whilst a murderer was at large about the place.'

'Might she be prevailed upon to explain what she saw, how she came upon him?' I had met Mrs Lunge many times. She had always struck me as a hard sort of woman and I had the feeling she would not blench at being summoned back to so horrible a scene.

'I'm sure she will,' said Dr Hawkins. 'I'll fetch her myself.'

The moment the doctor had gone I set to work. We had to move quickly – when the police came they would be all over the place, touching things and making a mess. I pulled out my lens, and the rolled canvas pouch that contained my pocket collection of scalpels, probes and scissors.

'What's this?' said Will, pointing to the metal object that protruded from the head. He sniffed again at his bottle of sal volatile. 'It looks like some sort of measuring instrument.'

'It's a set of phrenological callipers,' I said. I crouched down to turn the head in my hands. I had seen those callipers – a long metal handle with a pair of blades projecting from one end like a pick-axe – and others like them, many times at Angel Meadow, though I had never imagined they might be used for such a purpose. I put my fingers to the wound. The handle hung down; the blades, closed so as to create a long spike, had been smashed through the left pterion – the thinnest part of the human skull. I almost vomited as my fingers felt the cold mush of blood and bone and hair. The blades had been driven into the head with a single blow.

'There's an artery directly below this point in the skull,' I said. 'Once ruptured, or severed, epidural haematoma is the only possible outcome.'

5

'I assume you mean death,' said Will. 'Death is the only possible outcome.'

'It is in this case. The blades of the callipers have been driven in right up to the hilt.'

'And was it a matter of luck or judgement that the blades landed where they did?'

'Impossible to say. Given how small the area is, it was possibly both. But look at the angle of the handle.'

'Pointing towards us a little,' said Will. 'The assailant was directly in front—'

'Anything else?'

'He was right-handed.'

'He?'

'Would a woman really be capable of so brutal a murder?'

'I think a woman might be capable of anything.'

'Is strength required?'

'No,' I said. 'Only determination. And luck. Any higher or lower and the result may well have been nothing more than a severe fracture.'

Will took a deep breath and turned away. 'God help me, Jem, but I cannot bear to look.'

'Then don't.' I was bent over the corpse, peering at the gashes at the side of the head and noting the precision and neatness of the stitching – this was no ragged, hasty butchery, that much was clear. From my set of knives I selected a scalpel. Leaning close, I snipped off a length of suture from the corner of the sewn mouth. I folded it carefully in a scrap of paper and slid it into my pocket book. The stitching, and the severing of the ears, had been inflicted post mortem – there would have been much more blood otherwise. What had pooled about the skull was from the head wound only. I put out a finger and dabbed at the surface. The edges were almost dried. Close to the head, however, where the blood was most abundant, the stuff was still sticky, though a satiny meniscus, thick and gluey, had started to form. The face, despite its stitches, had a rigidity to it, the lips straining against their threads as the muscles had contracted in the early stages of *rigor mortis*. I moved the right arm. Its nascent stiffness supported my thoughts: death had occurred no more than three hours earlier. Two o'clock. Little happened that was virtuous at such an hour of the night.

'Does the angle of the blades suggest anything?' said Will.

'Not really,' I said. 'But I would say that the assailant held the callipers like so.' I clenched my fist, my arm stretched out behind me, my hand low. 'And swung them up and through like this—' I brought my arm round in an arc. 'Plenty of momentum, plenty of force – a man, as much as an angry woman, could do it if they were quick enough.'

'Their height?' said Will.

'Hard to say. Anything from five feet to five feet eight – my height. When the body fell backwards onto the floor it jarred the callipers and mangled the wound, so it's impossible to be more accurate. There is one thing I'm reasonably certain about though. The attacker was known to the victim—'

'How can you be sure it was not an intruder?'

'In an asylum? People want to get out of a place like this, not into it. I think the blow was struck quickly, and hard, when least expected. Why would it not be expected? Because the assailant was known – and presumably considered unthreatening. Besides, the room is quite neat and orderly. There is no sign of struggle, no evidence of self-defence—'

'What d'you make of that, then?' said Will, pointing over my head.

Behind me, above the fireplace, the mirror was smashed into myriad shards. Knife-sharp, they radiated outward from a single point, a glittering spider's web of cracks and fissures. 'Mm,' I said, turning back to the corpse. I pulled out my magnifying lens and examined the fingers. 'No skin or hair beneath the nails. Scrubbed clean, in fact. In short, I'd say this attack was quite unforeseen.'

From somewhere outside I heard the bang of a door and the insistent jangling of keys. Dr Hawkins and Mrs Lunge? Pole and the constable? We would not be alone with the corpse for much longer.

Will was over at the fireplace. He reached forward and plucked something from the grate. 'Look,' he said. 'What's this?' He held up a small rectangle of card. It was no more than three inches wide and four inches tall. 'It looks like a calotype. A photograph. An old one too – hardly anyone uses the calotype method these days.'

I took the photograph from him. It showed a woman sitting alone on a high-backed chair. Her skirts were of a dark crumpled fabric, with the tight waist and fringed bodice that had been fashionable several years earlier. Behind her was a white sheet or curtain; beneath her feet were bare boards, and in her hands – what manner of horrible thing was it?

'Who can she be?' said Will, and then as if reading my mind, 'And what in God's name is she holding?'

I shook my head. There was no way of identifying who

she was for her face had been burned away, consumed by the fire so that there was nothing above her shoulders but a ragged-edged space. As for what she was holding – a tangle of rope and rags, all mixed up with long strips of a curious black, leathery-looking substance. It was the most bizarre posy I had ever seen.

I am not a suggestible person. I pride myself on my rational and logical approach to life, and yet even I could not suppress a shiver at that strange ruined image. The hands were loose, the fingers languid against that horrible nosegay. The woman's posture was half slumped, and yet erect, as though the only thing holding her up was the head-clamp photographers habitually used to keep the subject still whilst the image was forming. I opened my pocket book and slipped the picture inside.

Ten days earlier

Chapter Two

M y name is Jem Flockhart. My mother died as I was
born; my father hanged for a crime he did not
commit. I am their only surviving child – a daughter,
whose identity my father swapped at birth for my dead
twin brother's. Who I am is concealed beneath shirt
and britches – and behind a port-wine birthmark that
covers my eyes and nose like a Venetian courtesan's
mask. No one looks beyond such a stain and I am known
everywhere as Mr Flockhart the apothecary, formerly
of St Saviour's Infirmary. Since the infirmary was razed
to the ground I am also Mr Flockhart of Fishbait Lane,
supplier of fine herbs and quality remedies – for those
unable, or unwilling, to make the journey to St Saviour's
new location south of the river.

Do I regret not accompanying the infirmary when
it left? After all, there had been an apothecary named
Flockhart there for four generations. But they had allowed
my father to be sent to the gallows; they had turned their

faces away from the fact that one of their number had been responsible for the murder of my friend Dr Bain, and they had caused me to lose someone so dear to me that I still could not think of her without pain. St Saviour's had made me who I was, but I had no use for the place now. I took from it only what I needed: the memory of my father, the physic garden, and my most beloved friend and companion Will Quartermain. Will had come to work on the demolition of the old infirmary, and in those terrible last days had proved himself to be the very best of men. We shared lodgings, he and I, above the apothecary on Fishbait Lane, along with my apprentice Gabriel Locke.

We were still in the parish of St Saviour's: still close to the rookeries of Prior's Rents and still within sight of the high walls of Angel Meadow Asylum.

The asylum had been a part of my life for as long as I could remember. As an apprentice I had rarely gone up to the place as my work at St Saviour's kept me busy all day, but the building had been visible from the window of my bedroom and I looked out at it every morning, and every night. It was younger than St Saviour's with its medieval cellars and ancient chapel, and yet it looked older; a dark, square-shouldered hulk as fearful to me as a prison. Hunched in her chair before the apothecary stove, as the night drew in and the cold fogs of September rubbed against our window panes, Mrs Speedicut, St Saviour's fat old matron, had painted a vivid picture of its infernal interior: a warren of dingy corridors; the mad, affixed by chains to its walls, rending their clothes and gnawing like beasts on the straw they had pulled from their filthy mattresses.

'How d'you know such things?' I had asked. 'I've never seen you go near the place!'

She had boxed my ears. ''Ow dare you question me! Didn't my own dear Mr Speedicut end up in the place, his mind turned to mush by drink and intemp'rate be'aviour?' I had yet to learn that the fate of 'dear Mr Speedicut' changed depending on whatever fiction the woman was intent upon. I remembered Mrs Speedicut sitting back and sucking on her pipe, grinning like a gargoyle as she released a brimstone cloud. 'They got a ward for children too. Them's what's peculiar. Unnat'ral.' She had squinted through the smoke at my crimson birthmark, her expression stony. 'Ones like *you*.'

I considered this exchange as Will and I walked up the broad thoroughfare – wide enough to allow a padded carriage to plunge along it at speed – that led to the gates of the asylum. I would never have guessed back then that my uncle would die in the place and my father would end up a resident, both of them driven mad by a hereditary condition that made sleep impossible. Now, as we waited to see whether I might share my father's fate, I too had become a regular visitor. Dr Hawkins, the asylum's medical superintendent, had become my friend, as he had been my uncle's and my father's. He had been away in Paris for almost a year, and I had missed him greatly, for there were things I said to him – fears for my future, worries about how I might manage my own descent into the abyss, the strain of living with the unknown – with which I had not the heart to burden Will. I was glad to think that he would soon be back. His replacement at Angel Meadow was a Dr Rutherford, who had worked there for years as a consultant and was pleased to be offered the role as superintendent, even if it was only while Dr Hawkins was away.

Initially, Dr Rutherford's interest in my case had been rather oblique. If I was not actually mad, what purpose was there in discussing the matter? And yet his curiosity was evident, and he had agreed to continue with Dr Hawkins's inquiries: noting down my sleep patterns, listening to my heart rate, testing my reflexes. The results were recorded in a ledger, so that any changes, however slight, might be observed and monitored. Over time, his interest in me had grown, so that I had come to dislike these consultations. Only if Will came with me did I feel less on edge.

I looked up at the asylum's dark edifice of soot-blackened bricks. Here and there patches of moisture glimmered upon its anthracite surface, as if it were blotched with weeping sores. Above the entrance, two windows stared down the thoroughfare. At one of them a face looked out, pale and unsmiling. Mrs Lunge. The asylum's house-keeper, she was matron, turnkey and quartermaster all rolled into one. Buttoned up to the neck in stiff black crêpe, her hair drawn back tightly beneath her widow's cap, her keen grey eyes were fixed upon us. She would already have sent Pole down to let us in, would already have informed Dr Rutherford that I was on my way, and probably, somehow, would already know what was in the packet I had in my pocket and who it was for.

In fact, the packet contained a quality of *dawamesc* – a paste made from *Cannabis indica* – and it was destined for Dr Golspie, the asylum's youngest and most inquiring physician. Truth be told, I was not entirely certain I should be giving Dr Golspie the stuff at all, for there was something reckless and impulsive about him that, although it appealed to me, also filled me with disquiet.

16

And yet he was my friend and he had asked me, and his motives were both exploratory and scientific. He would surely treat the stuff with the respect it deserved.

'So how are you?' said Dr Rutherford. 'Are you sleeping?' The inquiry was perfunctory.

'Yes,' I said. In fact, I was not sleeping well at all, but I didn't want to tell him. I had resolved from the moment Dr Hawkins left for France that I would not succumb to my father's fatal flaw on Dr Rutherford's watch.

'Good, good. And we have Mr Quartermain today too. Again.' Dr Rutherford smirked as he motioned me towards a chair. 'I wonder how you would manage without him. Do take a seat, Flockhart. And you, Quartermain.'

He stared down at me in silence. He was popular with the ladies – those who came to see their relatives, as well as the lady philanthropists who brought flowers and read to the patients from the scriptures. I had seen him smile and simper at them, pursing his lips sweetly and crinkling his eyes. But I had also seen his face when their backs were turned, when the saccharine smile had dropped away and the artful twinkle of his eyes was extinguished. Then, he looked hollow-cheeked and morose, his eyes hard and cold beneath an angry brow. I could not make it out – did he like them or hate them? Perhaps he was not sure himself. 'Well,' he said, evidently tiring of watching me. 'I suppose we had better get on with it.'

And so, for Dr Hawkins's sake, for my dead father and uncle, and for my own hunger for life, I submitted while Dr Rutherford commenced his examination. His long

17

thin fingers were cold upon my wrist, and I could not help but shiver. I saw a smile twitch at the corner of his mouth. *Damn the man*, I thought. He made me feel uncomfortable and he knew it. The fact that my uneasiness brought him some amusement irritated me more than I could say.

'Have you enjoyed your time as superintendent?' I said. 'I believe Dr Hawkins is back soon.' Dr Rutherford did not reply. His fingers tightened about my wrist as he drew out his pocket watch. Seconds passed.

'Yes,' he said at last. 'There are some interesting cases here. I think you may benefit from my methods one day.'

'But I'm not mad,' I said.

'No, you are not. Not yet, at any rate.'

'Your methods hold no value for me, sir,' I said.

'No?' He smiled. 'You are thinking of Letty. And yet, her condition was remedied, you must allow that much.'

'But at what price?'

He bent his face close to mine. 'My dear Mr Flockhart,' he whispered. 'Life always comes at a price.'

Letty. She was often in my mind, though I tried hard not to think of her. She was one of Dr Rutherford's patients at Angel Meadow, and he was interested in her because she appeared to demonstrate the accuracy of his theories. Dr Rutherford made no secret of his devotion to phrenology, that study of the contours of the head that purported to reflect the aptitudes and characteristics of the person who possessed it. He owned a collection of two hundred human skulls and over fifty plaster death-masks, each of which belonged to those he termed 'deviants', who were either mad or criminals. He carried a pair of anthropometric callipers in his pocket at all times, just in case he might suddenly find himself in the company of someone with an especially interesting cranium. Some months earlier I had attended a lecture on phrenology that he had given to some medical students. The week after, I witnessed a new surgical procedure, based upon Dr Rutherford's work, which Rutherford himself carried out in his rooms at Angel Meadow. The patient Letty was the object of his attentions.

'There are those who are violent in their madness,' Dr Rutherford said as we waited for Letty to be brought up. 'In these people the organs of destructiveness are enlarged. Sometimes grotesquely so. The skull of the patient I have chosen clearly demonstrates this – be sure to observe the contours behind the ears once she is restrained. If we might excise the corresponding area of the brain, then it follows that there should be a diminution of violence. The subject will be rendered placid.'

'Or dead,' Dr Golspie muttered. 'At best a walking vegetable, we cannot be sure.' Dr Golspie was in attendance to administer a new drug, chloroform, which would keep the patient sedated. 'I've tried it on myself repeatedly,' he said, dripping a clear fluid onto a pad of gauze. 'And I can gauge the correct amount easily. It's imperative that the patient does not move – I'd hate Dr Rutherford to slice off her "organ of hope" instead of her "organ of destructiveness".'

'I don't imagine she has an organ of hope,' Will said. 'It will surely have withered away to nothing by now.'

'I can't think why *you* need to be here,' said Dr Rutherford.

Will did not answer. In truth, he was there because I was there. 'You, alone with Rutherford, a bottle of chloroform, and a knife?' he'd said. 'No, Jem. I'll come with you, no matter what.'

'Dr Golspie will be there,' I'd replied. 'It's surgery, Will. Brain surgery.'

'All the more reason for me to come.'

And I? I was there because Dr Rutherford had insisted. Were the job to prove a success, he said, I might like to consider a similar procedure for myself should my own hereditary malady appear.

Dr Rutherford had selected Letty because she was subject to violent fits of temper and was often put into the strait waistcoat. She had no relations – none that appeared to care what happened to her at any rate – and of course, once one entered a mad house all notions of *habeas corpus* were left at the asylum gates. It was only the humanity of Dr Hawkins that ensured that the inmates of Angel Meadow were, on the whole, treated with sensitivity and compassion. But Dr Hawkins was not there, and Dr Rutherford had very different ideas.

I shall never forget it: the bewildered babbling and sobbing of the patient as she was brought into the doctor's lamplit consulting room, row upon row of phrenology skulls and plaster death-masks peering down at us in a glimmering sightless audience. Then came the creak of leather as Dr Rutherford tightened the strap that held the woman's head against the operating table, the sweetish smell of chloroform, and the visceral tang of blood as Dr Rutherford sliced through the scalp. The room filled with the acrid reek of hot bone as the circular saw sliced through; and then we saw that pearlescent organ, the soul and centre of our very being, pale and glistening, exposed to the world. How little we knew of its mysteries, I thought, and how dare we assume we might change human nature by slicing it up like a piece of fruit.

Dr Rutherford took hold of a scalpel. He sliced away a sliver of brain. Then another. Then another, the way he might carve himself slices of brawn. He laid the slices on a saucer, as if about to add them to a sandwich. Beside me, Will's breathing became laboured.

'Struggling, Mr Quartermain?' Dr Rutherford said.

'I'm quite well, Dr Rutherford,' replied Will faintly. He took a surreptitious whiff from his bottle of salts. 'Let us hope your patient will soon be able to say the same.'

In fact, the patient said nothing of the kind. Indeed, she said nothing at all ever again. Certainly she recovered, which is to say that she did not die. And yet in my view she did not live either. From that day on she neither spoke, nor demonstrated any sign of intelligent thought whatsoever. She spent her days standing motionless, staring out at the grass of the quadrangle as if waiting for the return of her former self.

Dr Rutherford released my wrist and slipped his watch back out of sight. 'There was much in Letty that resonated with Gall's later work,' he said. He bent towards me again, his face inches from mine, and peered into first one eye, and then the other. 'More inquiries are needed, however. Experimentation. Observation. I have found the means to take things further.' Dr Rutherford stood up straight. 'Well, Mr Flockhart,' he said. 'Everything seems to be in order.'

'Good morning, gentlemen.'

A man stood in the doorway. He was tall and slim, with thin blond hair and pale blue eyes. His lashes were white, giving him a curious, squinting appearance. He stood with his hands in his pockets, his topcoat drawn back, a gold watch dangling from a chain looped across his waistcoat buttons.

'Good day, Christie,' said Dr Rutherford.

The man grinned. 'Has he measured your head with his callipers yet?' he said. 'I won't let him near me with them. I assume you've measured yourself, Rutherford?'

'Of course,' said Dr Rutherford, stiffly. 'My organ of benevolence is especially well developed.'

Dr Christie laughed. 'I'll wager that there's a few patients who might disagree. Hello there, Quartermain.'

'Good day to you, sir,' said Will, stepping forward to shake the fellow's hand. 'What a surprise! What on earth brings you here?'

'Me? I'm the consulting physician. I've been in the post for a month or two now – in addition to my duties at the House of Correction – and I must say I'm quite delighted by the appointment.' He grinned, and rubbed his hands together. 'I've not seen you here before, though that's perhaps not surprising as I'm kept busy in the custodial wards. Like Rutherford here I'm particularly interested in lunatics of a criminal disposition – women, obviously. But all that's as clear as day. What's more of a mystery is what on earth you might be doing here!'

'Why, we're practically neighbours,' said Will. 'My friend and I live not two streets away, at the apothecary on Fishbait Lane—'

'You're not an apothecary, Quartermain.'

'No, sir. But my friend Jem – Mr Flockhart – is. He and I are partners, so to speak, though our professions are quite different.'

'And is this your friend here?'

'If I might introduce you, sir,' said Will. 'Jem, this is Dr Christie. He's consulting physician at the Surrey House of Correction – my current employer, if you like!'

Like so many buildings in London, the Surrey House of Correction was in a sorry state of disrepair. In Will's view it needed to be demolished and rebuilt entirely. But the governors were unconvinced and the prison – for such it was – was to be altered and expanded as cheaply as possible. Will had been tasked with drawing up the plans for these modifications. The drains – and the sewers – were causing him particular problems. Drains and sewers were a problem for everyone in London. I saw a frown darken Will's face, and I knew he was thinking about the place.

'Jem Flockhart, sir,' I said. 'Apothecary – formerly of St Saviour's Infirmary.'

Dr Christie stepped forward to shake my hand. 'St Saviour's?' He looked at me so closely that for a moment I thought he was about to pull out his spectacles. Then, 'I was sorry to hear of your troubles,' he said. His voice was soft. 'Your father hanged for a crime he did not commit – it's enough to turn anyone mad. "In the world you will have tribulation." John, sixteen, thirty-three.' He shook his head. 'Never a truer word, eh?'

'Indeed,' I said.

'Still.' He smiled again. 'Let us hope for better things ahead. And you're friends with Mr Quartermain here?'

I nodded. 'Will's a fine draughtsman, sir,' I said. 'He has a keen eye for detail.'

Dr Christie's fingers were as cool and smooth as marble. He was staring at my birthmark, and I knew he had not heard a word of what I had just said. 'Well, well,' he murmured, releasing my hand at last. Then, 'Such a physiognomy! Rutherford, have you taken the fellow's likeness?'

'He will not allow it,' said Dr Rutherford. They spoke to one another as if I were not there, or as if I were too addle-pated to answer their questions myself.

Dr Christie took up his watch absently, and began turning it over and over between his fingers, his still gaze fixed upon my face. 'Such a pity,' he murmured. 'Perhaps he might permit me—' His lashes fluttered like moths. My eyes are sharp, and I could just make out the words engraved upon his watch as it slipped beneath his fingers: *To Dr John Forbes Christie, from the Association of Medical Officers of Asylums and Hospitals for the Insane.* The man was too young for the watch to be his own. Was it his father's perhaps? Might not the son follow in his parent's footsteps?

'Oh, he won't permit anyone,' said Dr Rutherford. His face was close too, now, his gaze sweeping over my birthmark, so that for a moment I thought he was going to touch it. 'Amazing, isn't it? This is the fellow I told you about—'

All at once it was as though Will was not there at all, as though there was no one in that asylum but Dr Rutherford, Dr Christie and me. Was it my imagination, or had there been something mocking about the way Rutherford had said the word 'fellow'? I felt as a bird must, caught in the stare of a pair of cobras: I could not flinch, could not blink, or all would be lost.

'I beg your pardon, sir?' said Will. He sounded flustered. Had he noticed it too?

'Oh, nothing, nothing, Mr Quartermain,' said Dr Rutherford. 'Just a little matter of interest to Christie and myself—'

'You must have found the tropics trying, Dr Rutherford,' I said suddenly. 'Those of a fair complexion often do. Some would call *that* madness – when a man is so afflicted by heatstroke that he hardly knows his own name. Others might say he is never the same—'

A look of surprise and confusion crossed Dr Rutherford's face. 'Why, yes,' he stammered. 'How did you—?'

'The skin about your eyes betrays your time abroad,' I said. 'The sun in the southern hemisphere leaves its mark – freckles, crow's feet – after only two or three summers. The scars about your forehead from a severe *erythema solare* confirm it. We seldom have the heat in England for such blisters. Did *you* go mad, sir?'

'*Erythema solare?*' said Will.

'Sunburn,' I said. 'Dr Rutherford once caught the sun quite badly. Such burns are likely to have been accompanied by delirium, at least.'

Dr Rutherford put a hand up to the patches of pale pink skin that mottled his hairline. 'I forgot my hat,' he said. 'I wasn't out for long, but the heat—' He shook his head. 'The sun almost killed me. I should have known better!'

'India?' I said.

He smiled at that. 'No, Mr Flockhart, there are places in the world where the sun is far hotter.'

'Amazing, Jem,' cried Will.

'Merely observation,' I said.

'Oh? And what do you observe from me?'

'Everything, Will,' I replied. 'I know you too well.'

'Christie then? What can you tell us about him?'

'I think you would be better off asking his sister.'

'A sister?' said Will. 'Really, Jem, you're guessing now—'

'I rarely guess,' I said. In fact, I had guessed a little. But I wished now I had kept my observations to myself for I did not want to explain – and yet Will was insistent—

'Very well then,' he said, laughing. 'How did you conclude it?'

'From the doctor's waistcoat. It's quite clear.'

'Then I must be very stupid, for I can't for the life of me see how. Can you, Dr Christie?'

The doctor's smile had vanished. 'Do illuminate, Mr Flockhart.'

'You wear an embroidered waistcoat,' I said. 'The work is – forgive me – poorly executed. There are missing stitches and the tension is all wrong. Would any man wear such a garment if he did not feel compelled to do so out of love or duty? You are not married – I see no wedding ring – and a fiancée or mother would surely make a better job of it. No, the work speaks of youth – inexperience and impatience. And yet it was completed, and completed for you. A sister is the most likely explanation. A young one, perhaps, but one old enough to attempt a fashionable garment. The cut and the colours are modish even if the implementation is—' I hesitated. Had I gone too far?

'Maladroit?' supplied Dr Christie.

I inclined my head in agreement. 'Inexpert.'

Dr Christie said nothing.

'Jem,' said Will quietly. 'The girl may be deceased—'

26

'The waistcoat is perhaps a year old, at most,' I said. 'Dr Christie is wearing no items of mourning. I would not have spoken otherwise, Will. I do have some sensitivity.'

'Very good,' said Dr Christie. 'Very interesting.' He was silent for a moment. Then, 'I also see that I shall have to watch you, Mr Flockhart. And watch myself – I would not want *all* my secrets to be uncovered so easily.' A smile tugged at the corner of his lips, but quickly fell away. 'Would you?'

I was glad to leave them, Dr Rutherford and Dr Christie. They made me uneasy, though I could not say why. The way they looked at me, and at each other, as though they shared some sort of delicious secret – how glad I would be when Dr Hawkins returned. But not everything was disquieting about Angel Meadow, and I had at least one friend in the place.

'Pole,' I said to the attendant who was escorting us back down the stairs. 'Is Dr Golspie in, d'you know?' Pole was a curious-looking individual with weathered skin textured by pockmarks and scars. His hair grew patchily upon his head and some sort of palsy pulled at the right side of his face, dragging his lip and the rim of his eye downwards. He gazed at me with his one good eye, his hanging lip quivering. I tut-tutted. Why one as ugly as he might stare me out of countenance was a mystery, and I had had enough of being looked at for one day. 'What is it, Pole?' I said. 'If you want an ugly face to look at you might well take a peek in a mirror. Is Dr Golspie here or not? We have a package for him.'

Pole nodded, leading us forward in silence, his hands thrust deep into the oily pockets of his shapeless coat. He kept close to the wall, moving noiselessly from one shadow to another so that it was as though we were guided forward by some hideous shambling apparition. At length we came to the door that led through to the men's wing. Pole put a hand on my arm.

'I'll tell you what turns a man mad, sir,' he said suddenly. 'It's cruelty and injustice, that's what does it.' He leaned in close, as if divulging a secret. The smell of dirt and stale tobacco from his coat made my gorge rise. 'All on us is mad at some time or other. And when we are, well, then we do things no man can explain, and no judge can forgive.'

He stepped back then, his face waxier than ever in the dim lamplight. All at once it seemed to be filled with sorrow, as if his eye was worn away by tears, his lip weighted down with misery and despair at the way we treated one another. And then he coughed and spat a blob of phlegm onto the stone floor and leered up at me, so that the effect was instantly dispelled, and there once more was the repulsive, palsy-faced turnkey.

'Thank you, Pole,' I said.

I could feel the man's eye watching us as we walked away, but when I looked back the door was closed. Perhaps there was a peephole in it through which he was regarding me. I would not be surprised. There had been all manner of changes since Dr Rutherford had assumed the role of superintendent.

Dr Golspie had a consulting room on the ground floor of the men's wing. Formerly a patient's bedroom,

Dr Golspie had done his best to make it his own. He had painted the walls a muddy green – a restful colour chosen for its soothing properties. These were adorned with calming watercolours depicting nebulous rural scenes. He deliberately avoided clutter, and the disturbing paraphernalia of his profession – skeleton, bottles and instruments, lurid anatomy books – were absent, the room minimally furnished with nothing but a table and two chairs, both bolted to the floor, and a heavy chaise longue. Anything else he brought with him in his bag and took away again at the end of the day. Dr Golspie had graduated from medical school some two years earlier and had decided to pursue a career amongst the mad.

'It's the future, Jem,' he had said to me on our first meeting. 'Look at the nation! In the last twenty years our land has changed beyond recognition. There are factories where once there were fields, chimneys and sewers in place of trees and streams. What effect might this have on our minds, our spirits? There are more of us mad than ever, and no wonder! Crowded together, one on top of the other, forever looking out at grimy walls and breathing in the stink of London. So many people, each of us passing amongst hordes of strangers every day! I see no sign that this'll change, and the number of those whose wits are turned by it grows apace with each year that passes. What are we to do with them all? How can we help?' He had smiled then, his face aglow with the optimism of youth. 'The profession is still crystallising. There is no consistent way of approaching the mad – should we chain them to the walls and hose them with water to frighten their demons into submission? Should we sedate them and hope that one day they won't wake up? Should we – God forbid – slice open their minds as Rutherford would have us do, gouging out the parts that make them objectionable? Or should we simply offer them the same humanity, the same care and consideration we would offer any other human being who was lost or troubled?' He flung his arms wide. 'Such opportunities! But I can help them, I'm sure of it. I have ideas. New ideas.'

Today, however, Tom Golspie was looking discouraged. He had kicked off his boots and was lying on his chaise. 'Hello, Jem. Will.' Dr Golspie made a limp gesture with his hand. His pipe lay on the hearth beside him and the room had a heavy, unpleasant smell to it, smoky and musty and thickly herbal. 'You don't require me to get up, do you? You're always welcome, both of you.' He sighed, and closed his red-rimmed eyes. 'But I cannot be bothered with such tedious pleasantries as standing.'

'Are you tired?' I said.

'Tired?' he laughed. 'Merely frustrated. By myself and the limitations of my own mind more than anything.' He sat up, his expression fierce. 'If I could at least understand the patients' experiences. I feel we stand on the outside and try to look in, which is simply impossible. We need actually to *be* inside. Only then can we truly know. And once we know,' he spread his hands, 'why, then we can help!'

'You mean that to understand the mad, we need to be mad ourselves?' said Will, sitting down on one of the stiff-backed chairs and stretching his legs out before him.

'Why not?'

'I don't think it's something one can step in and out of voluntarily.'

30

'But one can't leave everything to men like Rutherford. All that heroic stuff with saws and knives. This is the brain, the organ that houses our mind, our memories, our very being! We cannot just slice it up – such guesswork! It's not as though he might stitch a bit back on if he doesn't like the results.' He shook his head. 'I only attended that butchery last month out of curiosity – and to make sure old Rutherford didn't scoop out poor Letty's entire brain and have done with it.' Dr Golspie threw himself back onto his cushions and reached for his pipe. 'I need a brain. A whole one. Preferably in a head, and ideally with a spinal cord. But they are so hard to come by.'

'You can have mine,' said Will. 'Once I'm done with it.'

'I fear it will be quite empty,' said Dr Golspie. 'And therefore of little use.' He sucked in a lungful of smoke. 'I would like to feel what it's like to be mad, just for a little while. It would be a most instructive experiment.' He held up his pipe. 'Hashish,' he said. 'It's said to bring one close to the condition.'

'You'll need more than a pipeful for that,' I said. 'You must eat it, and in quantity.' I pulled the package out of my pocket and put it into his outstretched hand. 'The *dawamesc* I promised you.'

'What's that?' said Will.

'A soluble paste made from hashish,' I said. 'Rather a large quantity. Don't you dare take the stuff when you're alone, Golspie.'

'How much should I have?' he said.

'I'd suggest a quarter ounce in a single dose, perhaps a little more. Be sure to take a light meal first.'

'Do you really think you should be encouraging him,

Jem?' said Will. 'D'you really think he should flirt with madness?'

'If we are with him at the time—'

'What if he cannot regain his senses?'

'Then I'll end up in here for good.' Dr Golspie laughed. 'I won't be the only one. There are a few who should not be here.'

Will looked aghast. 'Who?'

'Edward Eden – there's one for a start. He's no madder than you and I, merely simple – harmless, naive, an innocent adrift in a world of wickedness.' Dr Golspie sighed and rubbed his eyes. 'Dr Hawkins would never have accepted him. But Dr Hawkins is not here, and Edward Eden's father was very generous. Edward Eden is one of our wealthiest patients. Rutherford signed him into Angel Meadow, and as he hardly concerns himself with the male patients – he's not been along here for weeks, you know – it's been left to me to manage the fellow.'

Edward Eden, Dr Golspie told us, was the heir to Eden's Mourning Warehouse, a large and successful drapery and funeral business at St Paul's Churchyard. Edward had been schooled by his father in all aspects of the business from an early age, but showed neither aptitude nor enthusiasm for any of it. One day – a day which was to prove his undoing – Edward was sent into the very heart of his father's retail empire: the basement cash office. Here he was given the task of checking the contents of the small boxes brought in by the cash-boys before they were sent back out to the waiting customers. These boxes were numbered according to the precise counter from which they had arrived, and each contained the customer's money along with a receipt filled in by the shop assistant. Although other, more capable, hands took the money from the boxes, examined the receipt and supplied the correct change, Edward was required to check everything before the boxes were sent back out onto the shop floor.

Things did not proceed smoothly. Bored with his task, Edward soon gave up counting pennies and peering at receipts. Cash boxes began to accumulate before him. Searching for a distraction, all at once he noticed a crack in the plasterwork beside his desk. Something moved behind it. Was a small creature trapped, trying to get out? A spider, perhaps, or a beetle? Perhaps it was a mouse! Edward liked spiders and beetles and mice, so he loosened the plaster with his fingertip. A bigger crack appeared. He stuck the nib of his pen into it and levered off a chunk of the wall the size and shape of a slice of bread. Behind it, kept warm and moist by a wraith of steam from the heating pipes below, a mass of cockroaches seethed. The wall appeared to be stuffed with them, he told Dr Golspie. Crammed full, as though the building itself were built not out of brick and stone at all, but out of wriggling, scuttling insects. Edward knew this because he had made another, smaller hole with his pen further along. A leg had appeared within the aperture, and a brown shiny carapace, like a huge dried date, had shifted within.

The cockroaches tried to get away from the light, pulsating in the manner of rotten leaves caught in a blocked drain. Excited, Edward jabbed at them. Would it not be nice to have a few insect companions while he went about his tedious work in the cash office? Cockroaches began to drop onto the blotter, plopping into his inkpot and racing across the table top. Edward's excavations grew larger. There appeared to be an inexhaustible supply of the creatures and soon they were everywhere, their little scratchy feet trailing spirals of ink as they danced across the growing pile of receipts. Beside him, the cash boxes continued to arrive. *Clack . . . Clack . . . Clack . . .* they went as they slipped through the chute onto his desk. He became dimly conscious of another sound too – the anxious murmur of a crowd of cash-boys, all awaiting their boxes. The cockroaches seethed and tumbled over his fingers. Perhaps they would enjoy a ride in a little box? 'I would,' said Edward. Soon, the hole in the wall was empty, and all the cash boxes had been passed out of the hatch to the waiting boys. The screams of the lady customers, and the shop assistants, could be heard outside in the street.

'Edward Eden is simple, that's all,' said Dr Golspie. 'He cannot be cured or changed, there is no physic that might "improve" him, no procedure that might turn him into the man his father wishes him to be—'

He had hardly finished his sentence when a terrible wail echoed up the corridor. Dr Golspie, who had been growing more and more languid and drowsy the more he talked, sprang to his feet as though stabbed by hot pins. The three of us rushed out into the hall. Further along, a door stood open. Dr Golspie barged past the two male lunatics who were standing outside, evidently enjoying whatever was taking place within, and plunged into the room. On the table stood a large cage, inside which a wriggling mass of mice teemed and squeaked. Against the wall, a young man with a round pale face was crouched in terror. Before him, Dr Rutherford loomed, his face furious. On the floor in front of them was a dead mouse, squashed.

'What in heaven's name is going on here?' cried Dr Golspie.

Edward Eden pointed a finger. 'It's him!' he cried. 'He came in just as I was about to put Francis back in his cage. He frightened me, and when I dropped Francis he, he . . .' Edward's chin trembled. 'He stamped on him!'

'What have you done, sir?' said Dr Golspie.

'What have *I* done?' cried Dr Rutherford. He gestured at the cage of mice, and the sack of oatmeal that had clearly been used as food for the creatures. 'We do not permit the patients' rooms to be used in this way. Cages of mice? What were you thinking?'

'These are Mr Eden's mice. He's been breeding them.'

'Breeding mice?' thundered Dr Rutherford. 'I find mice are excessively adept at breeding themselves. I cannot believe you have countenanced such an activity. More than that, you seem to have sanctioned it!'

'Why, yes I have, sir,' said Dr Golspie. 'It's been very calming to the patient to have things to care for, things that depend upon him for food and shelter. I'm most struck by the effect it's had upon his mind—'

'And so you permitted it?'

'I permitted the orderly husbandry of mice, yes, sir. For therapeutic purposes.'

'*The orderly husbandry of mice?*' It was clear that Dr Rutherford could hardly believe what he was hearing. I glanced at Will. I could see that he was trying not to laugh. Dr Rutherford saw it too and the sight enraged him further. 'Pole?' he screamed, looking about for his favourite henchman. 'Confound the man, where is he? Pole!' Clearly unwilling to wait for assistance, Dr Rutherford stalked over to the fireplace. He produced a bunch of keys and unlocked the cage that surrounded it. He picked up a poker from the hearth, and proceeded to ram it into the fire, levering the coals so that they roared and flamed.

'Oh, God, no,' murmured Will.

'Sir, I must protest.' Dr Golspie stepped forward.

Dr Rutherford pushed him aside and seized the mouse-filled cage. The mice inside began to whirl and leap, trying to scramble away, but it was no use. Dr Rutherford wrenched open the cage door. I heard Will and Dr Golspie cry out, and the sound of my own voice raised in outrage. The crowd that had gathered in the doorway began to scream and bellow, one or two of them laughing and clapping, as though they had no idea what they were watching, only that it was a spectacle and had therefore to be approved. And beneath the hubbub was a terrible high-pitched squealing as the mice tumbled onto the burning coals. They writhed and danced on the embers. Some of them managed to spring out, but Dr Rutherford was onto them, shovel now in hand, scooping them up and flinging them back onto the flames. And then it was over. Pole appeared, flanked by two burly attendants. One of them struck Edward Eden across the head with a leather truncheon, and they hauled him away.

'Where have they taken him?' said Will, visibly shocked.

'Downstairs,' said Dr Golspie. He shook his head. 'Poor fellow.'

'It's your fault if he suffers,' cried Dr Rutherford, the

shovel and poker still gripped in his hands. 'Your fault entirely.'

'What happens downstairs?'

I had been downstairs only once before. I found I could not reply.

Angel Meadow Asylum, 18th September 1852

The path that led me here began in the shadow of this very building. Prior's Rents: the name has become a byword for dirt and misery. Its walls conceal more secrets, have seen more pain and grief than anyone unacquainted with the place can possibly imagine. Once, it was the only home I knew. I slept with the chill of its stones creeping into my flesh. I awoke with the cries and groans of its wretched occupants ringing in my ears.

There is no beauty and no hope in Prior's Rents, no grass, no birdsong, and no sunshine. There are no broad airy thoroughfares, only a maze of passageways dominated by Prior's Row, a foul lane flanked by crumbling walls and blistered with patches of aged cobbles. Beyond the Row is a cluster of cottages – pale and peeling and crowded together like toadstools. Long ago the cottages skirted a pond. They looked out over fields and trees at the smoky haze of the distant metropolis. But the fields and trees are long gone, and the pond has become a pestilential pit.

Behind the cottages, a crooked line of chimneys point from the slumped roof of a large ugly building. Once, the building was a part of St Saviour's Priory. Later, it became the fine home of a lady and gentleman, who incorporated the cottages into a stable yard and had gardens full of fruit and flowers. But time, the city, and inheritance law, worked their shady magic. The place fell derelict, the gardens trampled beneath London's greedy expansion. The brick-men who fired the kilns for the building of St Saviour's Street made it their home, their masters dividing up rooms, slicing through moulded plaster and blocking up windows. Tenements rose up on either side to house those who could not fit into the old mansion's crowded chambers. And when the brick-men left, others of a more degraded hue took their place – road sweepers, bone collectors, rag pickers – the very dregs of the city's miserable poor. It became a place of noise and squalor, of crime and sorrow.

You'd think I would be glad to leave, that I'd seize the chance to put it far behind me. And so I was. So I did. But the devil was right about one thing: once you've been a part of the Rents, there's a piece of it that's always inside.

My earliest memory is of boots. Brown and black. Big and small. Caked, always, with filth. I was a child, perhaps no more than eight years old, curled up on a ragged blanket beneath my mother's bed. In front of me, every night, was a reeking chamber pot. Beside that were the boots. Above my head, the bed creaked rhythmically so that the wire beneath the thin mattress bowed and dipped, bowed and dipped, with such violence that it sometimes touched my shoulder. I was not allowed to sleep in the bed – it

was big enough only for my mother and my mother's gentlemen friends. So I lay beneath, feeling the bow and dip of the mattress, hearing the sounds that came from above. Every night I lay there. Every night I feared that the bed would break, and I would be crushed: crushed beneath my mother, who was crushed beneath a man. We would both die, I thought, me and my mother. The man, of course, would simply put on his boots, and walk away.

The room I shared with my mother was at the top of the old mansion. I thought I would never forget it, but time papers over even the worst of things and my memories now seem to be made up of fragments, like a miscellany of photographs pasted into an album. I can recall the floor – bare, but for a mat of sacking before the fire; the fire itself no more than a gaping black mouth, the ashes in the grate clustered against its lower lip like rotten teeth. In one corner was a washstand and pitcher, cracked and dirty and filled with brownish water drawn from the pump in the yard. In the other stood my mother's bed, its mattress stuffed with sawdust, rags and newspaper, its coverlet patched and darned. At the window was a table covered with oilcloth. I remember my mother at the window bent over her work, or sitting close to a tallow candle, sewing, sewing, sewing till her fingers were too cold to move and her eyes burned with tiredness. But that particular memory is dim and half-formed, for all those stitches were never enough to stop her life, and mine, from unravelling.

I remember the stairs, crooked and reeking of piss, winding up to the top of the house. I remember stepping carefully over the creaking boards, flitting across a bridge of planks that traversed the landing where the worm-eaten wood had given way. A man was killed there. He fell through the rotten floor when he was drunk and he lay there, down at the bottom of the hole, his limbs twisted, and his jaw broken wide. I knew the

man. *I knew what he did to my mother when she'd put away
her sewing.*

*Goblin and I moved the planks one night when we heard him
staggering up the stairs, so that he was forced to cross the rotten
floorboards in the darkness. His corpse lay there all night, and for
most of the next day. Then it was gone. Goblin said it had been
sold for cat's meat. Neither of us was sorry.*

*Goblin was my friend. We were almost the same age, he and I,
and born on the same day, a Monday – 'execution day' Goblin
called it, because that's the day when there are hangings at
Newgate. He said he would look after me, always.*

'Look after yourself,' I told him. 'No one else will.'

*When I was older, I liked to spend the mornings in town,
watching the fine ladies and gentlemen walking up and down. I
liked to listen to their fancy talk and I'd try it out on Goblin when
I got home. Goblin always laughed when I spoke like the ladies,
making my voice all high-pitched and bird-like. 'Oh!' I cried. 'My
dear child! Have you no shoes? There are Levant slippers for sale
at Checkall's. Very reasonably priced. Can you not buy a pair to
keep your toes warm?'*

'Slippahs?' said Goblin. 'Wot's slippahs?'

*I remember both of us laughing at that, at Goblin trying to
talk fancy. 'Slippers are something you'll never have,' I told him.
'But I will.'*

*'Bet slippers ain't as good as this,' he replied. And he tossed me
an apple pinched from the fruit market near St Saviour's. That
apple! I've never forgotten it. Crisp and sweet as nectar, red and
white where I had bitten into it, bright as a jewel while all about
us was black and dirty. Goblin let me eat it all. He did not ask for
any, but watched me, smiling.*

*It was hard to imagine a place crueller and more sorrowful
than the Rents, but there was. Oh, there was. The time soon came*

when I wished with all my heart that I was back beneath my mother's bed, my hands stopping my ears against the sound of the beast who rode her. But it is not so easy to shut out the devil once he has marked you for his own.

Chapter Three

We heard via Mrs Speedicut that Edward Eden had spent the rest of that week in the basement in a strait waistcoat. He had emerged, sullen and dejected, to a room without mice. Mrs Lunge, under strict instructions from Dr Rutherford, had supervised the removal of all animals from the patients' care. Dr Golspie had objected, of course. Edward's mice had been one of his 'therapeutic innovations' – along with a patient who had been allowed to keep a pair of canaries, and another who looked after a tank full of newts.

'That Mrs Lunge.' Mrs Speedicut was sitting before the stove in the apothecary, a mug of strong coffee in her hand. 'She 'ad Pole take everything away. She wrung the birds' necks, she said, as a kindness. A kindness! An' she made 'im tip them frogs into the drain.'

'Newts,' I said.

Mrs Speedicut wrinkled her nose. 'Can't say I ever liked 'em much, whatever they were. Nasty slimy things.

But Dr Golspie were furious. Not that 'e said much about it to anyone. Leastways not to Dr Rutherford, nor Dr Christie, not even to Mrs Lunge. 'E's afraid of 'er.' She took a swig of coffee and smacked her lips. 'Mind you, ain't we all? I don't never know when she's goin' to appear be'ind me. She puts on all those airs and graces, driftin' about the place like she's royalty.' She made an explosive sound indicative of deep disgust. 'She ain't no better than you an' I.'

'Thank you, Mrs Speedicut,' I said. 'I had no idea you valued me so highly.' I filled her mug again. She had refused to follow St Saviour's south of the river when it had moved, and instead had found herself a situation on the women's wards at Angel Meadow. I had little affection for her, but I knew she loved to come down to us and gossip. It reminded her of how things used to be – before St Saviour's was pulled down, before my father was hanged. She had always cared for him, in her way. I could forgive her a lot because of it. Mostly, her talk these days was of Mrs Lunge.

Mrs Lunge, it appeared, was a woman who – to Mrs Speedicut at least – possessed almost magical powers when it came to the sniffing out of laziness, pilfering, insubordination, and other forms of iniquity. For me, Mrs Lunge was little more than a purse-lipped female gaoler; a tall, upright shadow topped by a pale face, her tiny widow's cap balanced upon her scraped-back hair like a saucerful of cinders. She did not say much, but her appearance – always heralded by a jangling of keys – was enough to make patients fall silent and attendants turn diligently to their tasks. Her thin corseted body radiated disapproval – at the muddy footprints I left on the floor, at the way I went in and out of the asylum with confident regularity, at the way Will, Dr Golspie and I talked and laughed together. And yet her face registered no emotion, so that her eyes, shifting in her colourless face, were like live things in a waxen mask. She had been handsome, once, that much was evident. Her height and bearing set her apart from the other women who worked at Angel Meadow, and her voice, when she spoke, was without the coarse edge one usually heard amongst the asylum's attendants. Her eyes were fine, grey and intelligent. But something cruel glinted within them, and the lines about her mouth spoke of hardship and disappointment, so that I did not warm to the woman at all.

'She's the very devil,' muttered Mrs Speedicut. 'She took my gin!'

'Then you'll have to learn to hide it better,' said Will. He was seated at his drawing board at the back of the apothecary, poring over Halliwell's *Principles of Modern Drainage*. He tossed the book aside and ran his hands through his hair. 'My master says we might save money if we omit drainpipe shoes and hopper heads across the new building – it's only a prison, after all. But I cannot agree. The savings would be small and the consequences for the efficient removal of water during heavy rainfall would be disastrous.'

'It's Mrs Lunge what's disastrous,' said Mrs Speedicut, clearly unable to bear any change in the topic of conversation. 'Disastrous to me an' my gin.'

'What can be done?' I said, hoping the question might meet the needs of both of them, for I was hard-pressed to decide whether drains or cheap spirits was the more tedious subject.

45

'My dear Mrs Speedicut,' said Will. 'Can you think of nothing but your bottle of Mother's Ruin? Hide it in the coal scuttle, woman. Or under the floorboards. Use your imagination.'

'I ain't got no imagination.' Mrs Speedicut's teeth champed down hard on the stem of her pipe. 'Can't hide nothin' from Mrs Lunge. She knows where everythin' is. Always creepin' an' spyin' – it's no wonder there ain't no secrets about the place. They say she's made peep'oles – 'er and Dr Rutherford. If you asks me I'd say she were sweet on 'im, though Gawd knows why.'

'Peepholes?' said Will. 'To spy on you? I can't imagine the woman has the stomach for such an undertaking.'

'Peep'oles in the walls. In the doors! 'Ow else would she know?' She produced a bottle from her apron pocket and glugged a measure of gin into her coffee. 'That's why I keeps it in me pocket now.' She sighed heavily, blowing a blast of tobacco- and gin-sour breath into my face. 'She wants to get rid o' me. I can feel it. That Mrs Lunge!'

'Surely not,' I said. 'Your experience is invaluable. Any institution would be delighted to have you and I know for a fact that St Saviour's was sorry to see you go.'

'Mrs Lunge wouldn't be. She's sorry to see me stay.'

I murmured soothingly. It was a long time since Mrs Speedicut had knowingly taken orders from a woman and it was bound to rankle. At St Saviour's, once the ward rounds were done and the medical men had left, the place had been her kingdom. Things were very different now; at Angel Meadow the locked doors alone had taken her a while to get used to.

Mrs Speedicut sniffed, and commenced a lavish throat-clearing. I laid my pipe down on the mantel. Sometimes, the sight and sound of the woman – the long brown teeth, the constant coughing and hawking – made me wonder at the wisdom of tobacco.

Mrs Speedicut spat a lump of brown phlegm into the coal. 'Things ain't what they were,' she said. 'Even at Angel Meadow.'

'How so?'

'It were better with Dr 'Awkins in charge. That Mrs Lunge! She didn't used to follow 'im round like she does Dr Rutherford. Now it's all *Dr Rutherford said this an' Dr Rutherford said that . . .* It's not even like she's 'appy about it – I've 'eard her, crying at night when everyone's abed, though she said it were just Letty when I asked 'er about it.' Mrs Speedicut snorted. 'Letty!' she said, witheringly. 'Letty don't say nuthin'.'

'No,' I said.

'An' it's not even like the place is better because of it, neither. The patients is all at sixes and sevens, 'specially since Mr Eden's mice was got rid of.' She leaned forward, and added, 'It were Mrs Lunge what told Dr Rutherford about them mice. Mrs Lunge what got Mr Eden locked up and Dr Golspie into trouble.' She sucked on her pipe, her expression one of satisfaction. 'Well, Dr 'Awkins is back soon enough and things is bound to be different. Won't she get a surprise then?'

In fact, we all got a surprise when Dr Hawkins came back, because he came home with something no one – not even Mrs Lunge – could have guessed: he came home with a wife.

I had to confess I was rather taken aback. Dr Hawkins had always appeared uninterested in women. He claimed none of them as acquaintances, avoided the asylum's Ladies' Committee, and as far as I was aware had never frequented Mrs Roseplucker's brothel nor any other similar establishment. But if I had learned anything from my experiences during those final days at St Saviour's Infirmary it was that everyone has secrets, and that people behave in the most unexpected ways, especially when they think no one is watching.

I was keen to see him again, and to meet his new wife, and we did not have to wait long, for Dr and Mrs Hawkins had scarcely been back a week when Mrs Speedicut came down to the apothecary with an invitation for all of us – Will, my apprentice Gabriel, and myself – to attend the asylum the following evening.

'A soirée?' said Gabriel, peering at the invitation in alarm. He pronounced it 'SOY-ree'. 'What's that?'

'An evening of music, singing and dancing,' I said.

Gabriel looked appalled. 'Like a . . . a ball?'

'Don't worry, Gabriel,' said Will. 'Mrs Speedicut can run you up a gown and a crinoline in no time.'

Of course, it was nothing like a ball. Instead it was more like a gathering, with music, of those who wished to welcome the doctor home and congratulate the couple on their happiness. It turned out that the patients had also been told they were to meet the doctor's new wife – Dr Hawkins asked that they dress in their best clothes and be brought down to the atrium at the entrance to the asylum, where the auspicious encounter would take place, for eight o'clock that evening. The atrium was illuminated by pale lanterns, its panelled walls hung with paintings of various asylum worthies. I could see that a number of the patients were alarmed at the sight – the stern portraits, the great orbs of light – and their voices grew loud. Only those least likely to cause offence had been permitted to attend. I observed Edward Eden amongst their ranks, along with Letty, the silent girl whose brain Dr Rutherford had sliced up. Her gaze was vacant, her stitches hidden beneath her cap. Edward's face wore its usual expression of benignity, and I was glad to see he was looking calm. In my pocket I had a box containing a single white mouse – bought for a shilling from a boy out on St Saviour's Street. Perhaps, now that Dr Hawkins was back, Edward might be permitted to keep at least one. I beckoned him over, and pressed the box into his hands.

'Look after him for me,' I whispered. 'Every mouse needs a house.' I gave a wink, and put my finger to my lips. Edward's face lit up.

The patients grew excited as Mrs Hawkins passed amongst them. Some stood rocking from side to side, grinning and plucking at their lips, clearly with very little idea of what was going on. Others laughed and clapped, reacting to the celebratory atmosphere but completely uninterested in the tall dark-haired woman who was trying to shake their hand. Many appeared quite normal and behaved impeccably. As for Mrs Hawkins, not once did she flinch or look disgusted at the motley collection of individuals who had been chosen to represent her husband's professional interests. She smiled and murmured greetings to them all as Dr Hawkins escorted her from one patient to the next. In the background, the attendants prowled up and down. I saw Mrs Speedicut, starched, ironed and corseted into a semblance of respectability.

Her bulldog face was set in an expression of controlled pain – she hated to stand, and I could tell that her stays were too tight and her shoes pinched. On the other side of the room was Mrs Lunge. She looked no different to usual, tall and slim, one hand pressed to the high collar at her throat. Her face was impassive, her lips pressed together in a thin line. She watched Mrs Hawkins passing amongst the assembled multitude with grave indifference. The dim light accentuated the hollows and lines on her face giving her a weary, unhappy appearance. Beside her, Pole waited in silence, his one good eye fixed upon Mrs Hawkins. It was watering horribly, and I saw him dab at it with the edge of his filthy cuff, his giant bunch of keys swinging in his fist.

After the patients completed their welcome we made our way up to the Governors' Hall. A handful of the most quiescent inmates were permitted to follow, though the majority were herded back to their rooms. Upstairs was crowded with benefactors and subscribers, friends of Dr Hawkins and others associated with the asylum. There were some faces that I knew, but many I did not. I was not feeling particularly sociable, and hoped I might simply saunter through the crowd with Will, observing and eavesdropping on different conversations. I was about to suggest as much when a man stepped out of the crowd.

'Jem,' he said. 'My dear fellow, how delightful to see you! Don't you recognise me? Surely you do! Has it been so long?' He shook his head. 'I fear it is. But you must remember me—'

'I do, sir,' I said, pumping his hand up and down. 'Of course I do. How could I possibly forget?'

It was impossible to forget Dr Stiven. I first met him when I was little more than a child. For the most part, my upbringing had been a joyless one: my mother died at my birth, and my father was unable to forgive me for it. Born a daughter but raised a son, heir to an illness that had left my father mad, my life was bounded by secrets and silence. I was a serious child, duty-bound to conceal my true nature from the world even as I hid my ugly blighted face behind jars and beakers and books on physic.

Into this life of silent rebuke came Dr Stiven. He was a friend of my father's, though how they were acquainted I had never been told. I was recovering from scarlet fever, in bed for over a week and looked after by my father and Mrs Speedicut, then the matron of St Saviour's. One afternoon, after the fever broke, I awoke to find a man sitting on the end of my bed. He said that my father had gone out to a meeting of the St Saviour's Medical Committee, but had asked him to look in on me to make sure I was comfortable. He was one of the most unusual men I had ever seen. I was used to a world where men dressed in drab colours, as befitted the ominous nature of their profession – a physician was just as likely to kill as to cure. And yet here was a man in a waistcoat of turquoise watered silk beneath a topcoat of midnight blue. His shoes were black patent leather with gold buckles, his legs sheathed in navy britches and white stockings. He carried a walking stick topped with a silver knob in the shape of a cat's head. Most unexpected of all was his wig, a grey mass of tight curls. Beneath this his cheeks were powdered like a doxy's above a regency-style neckerchief as pale and thick as clotted cream. He called his head of false hair 'a peruke', and stroked it fondly with the flat of his hand, as though it were an old family pet. It was of the very highest quality, he said, and made from real human hair.

'Which humans?' I asked, intrigued.

'I don't know them personally,' replied Dr Stiven. 'One can only hope they were sufficiently hirsute to bear the loss with dignity.'

Dr Stiven came to see me every day for the rest of the week. He never stayed longer than fifteen minutes – a length of time accurately measured by the gold pocket watch he set out on the counterpane where he sat. On the first day he reeked strongly of lavender and witch hazel – two smells with which I was comfortingly familiar. The lavender came from Norfolk, he said, the witch hazel from Kent.

The following day he abandoned these homely aromas in favour of something more exotic: a heavy mixture of attar of roses, sandalwood, and lemon verbena. 'These,' he said, 'are the perfumes of the East, the costly scents of kings and princes from mysterious and faraway lands – Persia, Babylon, Arabia. D'you know,' he added, 'it takes one hundred freshly picked rose petals to form a drop of rose oil. The oil is squeezed out by the trunks of elephants. The rose bushes grow in fields, stretching out beneath the azure skies as far as the eye can see. They are tended by teams of rose-men, each in charge of a particular group of bushes. The colour of a rose-man's turban is precisely matched to the colour of the flowers he tends.'

'Have you seen them?' I said. 'Have you seen the endless fields and the elephants and the rose-men in their coloured turbans?'

'Oh no,' replied Dr Stiven. 'But I have read about them.' He sighed. 'And yet, you are right to ask, for the whole thing may well be a fairy tale, and reading is not quite enough for you and me, is it, Jem?'

I shook my head, uncertain where my acquiescence might lead. 'No,' I said.

'No indeed. For one must see for oneself, one must observe, Master Flockhart, to know the truth.'

The following day Dr Stiven smelled of cherry pie. He told me that the cherry pie smell was 'heliotrope', and that he did not wear it often because its aroma made him want to nibble his own shirt sleeves. He showed me where a button was missing from his coat, and said that he had eaten it during a meeting with the Lunacy Commission that very morning.

I laughed. I loved his talk of Persia and princes and pies, even though I knew it was nothing but fancy. I peeped at the watch as it ticked off the seconds, and asked him to tell me again about the rose fields, and the elephants that squeezed out the oil with their trunks.

And then, he was gone. I knew straight away that he had made me see life in a more colourful and fascinating way. I had discovered my imagination, but, as befitted the rational daughter of a punctilious apothecary, I applied it in the most scientific manner. I began to look at the commonplace happenings around me and consider what desires, what motivations and ambitions might lie behind them. I tried to think beyond the obvious; to evaluate the possibilities of the singular, to hazard a guess at what I did not know based on what might be probable or improbable. It was a means of observing and interpreting the world that was to stay with me for ever.

I did not see Mr Stiven again for a long time after that first week. Then, one day, I came back from out-patients to find him sitting in the wing-backed chair before the apothecary fire.

He took me to the pleasure gardens down by the river. Ahead, at the heart of the crowd, I saw vast diamonds of green and red and yellow, girdled by a tasselled fringe of gold. I caught sight of a roaring flame. Before it, a man in a red coat and a tall black hat was shouting to the crowd. *No man has ever attempted such a feat . . . five thousand feet above your heads . . . I alone am so valiant, so daring . . . I alone am the Great Goddard . . .* The spectators cheered as the balloon, and the basket, inched into the air. The man made a sweeping gesture with his arms and the golden ropes that tethered the thing miraculously fell away, dropping to the ground like burning snakes. In no time at all the Great Goddard and his hot air balloon had become a tiny blot of colour on a blue sheet of sky.

Soon afterwards, Dr Stiven and I left the pleasure gardens. As we walked home the balloon reappeared above us. It was low now, the basket almost brushing the chimney pots, the bulbous harlequinade coat bright against the grey roofs of the city.

I seized Dr Stiven's arm and pointed to the spire of St Saviour's Parish Church, as sharp as a fish-hook, towards which the Great Goddard was heading with unstoppable momentum. The basket hurtled forward to slam against the spire. A rope snapped. The balloon jerked, and the figure tumbled out of the basket. He bounced once, twice, his red coat as bright as blood against the slates, and then he was gone.

Dr Stiven and I ran into the churchyard. Beneath the nave window the Great Goddard lay smashed into the earth. Overhead, the balloon billowed and flapped.

'There are two lessons to be learned from this,' said Dr Stiven. 'The second is that arrogance is the curse of the age.'

'Yes, sir,' I said. I closed my eyes to shut out the horrible sight before us. 'And the first?'

'The first is that death always catches up with us, often when we least expect it.'

And now here he was once again, in the main hall at Angel Meadow Asylum, shaking my hand as if he never wanted to leave go of it. I had not seen him since we had witnessed the death of the Great Goddard. The thought of it made me shiver, for I had never forgotten the sight of that mangled body, those twisted and broken legs. *Death always catches up with us, often when we least expect it.* The words were commonplace enough, though I had never forgotten them.

I introduced Dr Stiven to Will and Gabriel. Gabriel stared in amazement, until I jabbed him in the ribs and told him to find Dr Stiven a glass of punch, and to be sure not to drink any of it himself as he brought it over. Will shook the fellow's hand. He hid his surprise well, for although Dr Stiven's appearance was less colourful than when I had first met him – his use of powder less copious, his waistcoat less garish – his appearance was unique nonetheless. I could never understand why he chose to attract attention so ostentatiously – if he removed his wig and powder he might pass down the street unremarked and unnoticed.

'A pleasure to meet you, sir,' said Will. 'Are you well acquainted with Dr Hawkins?'

'I'm not sure I would say that,' said Dr Stiven. 'Though we are certainly acquainted and he has been kind enough to offer me, and my ward, accommodation here this evening. His rooms are commodious enough, and Mrs Hawkins no doubt prefers the town house on St Saviour's Street—'

'Your ward?' I could not keep the surprise out of my voice. 'I had no idea you had such a thing.'

'My dear sir,' the voice that came from beside Dr Stiven was low and melodious, and playful in its rebuke. 'I can assure you I am most definitely not a thing.'

'Ah,' said Dr Stiven. He smiled. 'There you are, my dear. Come along, come along and meet my friends.'

She was small, no taller than five feet, and wore a tightly fitted dress of green silk. She had a small, heart-shaped face, out of which peered a pair of eyes as black and glittering as the jet buttons on her dress. She did not quite look like a lady – her gaze was too direct, too amused, for that – certainly she did not walk like one, and she stepped forward in a strange rolling, bobbing manner.

'Susan Chance,' she said. Her grip was as strong as a man's, but soft, her fingers small and slim. 'Dr Stiven is my guardian.' And then, before I had a chance to say anything, she added, 'You are no doubt wondering why I have the walk of a seasoned sea captain.'

'No, ma'am—' I began.

'It's because I have a crippled foot, which is encased in an ugly boot of hardened leather and braced with a metal calliper.'

56

'I see—'

'Most people perceive my gait and wonder. I find it easiest to state the fact of the matter openly so that we might . . . ' Her eyes twinkled. 'Get off on the right foot, as it were.'

'And yet it is the left foot, I think?'

'Yes it is.' She grinned at me then, and I felt myself blush with pleasure that I had made her smile.

'Susan, my dear,' said Dr Stiven, tut-tutting. 'You are too . . . *arch*.'

'Oh no,' said Will and I together.

'I am always telling her,' said Dr Stiven. 'Ladies are not forward. Nor are they witty.'

'There was a time when you would've considered both of those things a virtue,' I said.

'And so I do. And yet I fear I have made you rather too unique, my dear. I am hoping to introduce Susan to society,' Dr Stiven said. 'Dances, soirées, calling round for tea and such like. I thought here might be a good start. I have a slender acquaintance with Dr Hawkins, who is fully aware of the case.'

'The case?' I said.

'Oh yes. It makes me hesitate to bring Susan out. Here at Angel Meadow all is well. And yet I fear what might happen if I were to take her to less understanding places.'

'I'm sure Miss Chance would be a credit to any society,' said Will. He had not taken his eyes off the girl. 'How could anything untoward possibly happen?'

'My past precedes me,' said Susan.

'Now, now, my dear,' said Dr Stiven.

'I'm from the Rookeries.' Susan Chance stood as tall as her stature would allow. 'I was born in Prior's Rents.'

'We know the Rents, don't we, Mr Jem?' cried Gabriel, who had suddenly appeared at my elbow. He handed a sticky-looking glass of rum punch to Dr Stiven.

'Oh?' Susan's face betrayed a polite interest.

'Mr Jem and me takes stuff up there sometimes,' said Gabriel. 'Prescriptions an' remedies and such. Mr Jem says there's no chance for anyone in a place like Prior's Rents, and most of 'em's likely to end up dead o' the cholera, or twitchin' on the end of a rope or like as not a whore and none of those is a fit choice for anyone to make.'

'They are not fit choices at all,' said Susan.

But Gabriel wasn't listening. He screwed up his face thoughtfully. 'We don't go there much, but when we do—' He shivered. 'The place don't half get into your bones, don't it, miss? Them dark, dripping walls.' He drew his arms about himself. 'No one could ever forget them. And the sounds, the cries and groans o' the place.' His voice sank to a whisper. 'Why, miss, sometimes if I'm awake at night, if I can't sleep and the wind's a-blowin', I feel like it's callin' to me. *Callin'*—'

'That's enough, Gabriel,' I said sharply. 'You're not reading one of your penny bloods now.' Susan's face had turned sickly.

'I were just sayin',' said Gabriel, his expression sulky.

Susan forced a smile. 'You're quite right, young man. Your impression of the place is most . . . exact. I remember it well. Perhaps a little too well at times.'

'Nonsense,' said Dr Stiven. 'You are quite free of the place now. Books, tranquillity, friendship, hard work, these are universals. These can be learned in the same way that vice can be learned. Prior's Rents has been excised from your heart and soul, just as I have excised it from your lips. She speaks just like a lady, don't you think, Jem?'

'Yes, sir,' I said, though I had noticed something rather wooden in Susan Chance's elocution, as though she wore her new-found respectability with some awkwardness.

As for the girl herself, her face had darkened.

'See that clock?' she said, nodding towards the mantel–piece. 'Along with them candlesticks and that lamp? Fetch two guineas fenced at Finch's shop in the Rents, that lot would—'

'Not now, my dear,' said Dr Stiven. 'Not here—'

'You think it's behind me, sir? You think the place is gone from my heart and soul? Perhaps it is. But what about my mind? I've not forgotten what I know. I'll never forget.'

'Knowledge is never wasted,' he answered. 'I have always taught you that.'

'And you include knowledge of the lusts and vices of men, or the inside of a Newgate cell?'

Dr Stiven seized Susan's hands. 'Of course I do. We none of us judge you here.'

'Newgate?' I could not help but draw breath.

'For sure!' chided Dr Stiven. 'Miss Chance is quite familiar with the inside of Newgate.'

'She visits?' I asked, though I could not imagine that tiny bobbing figure in the midst of a band of Bible-reading lady philanthropists.

Dr Stiven chafed the girl's fingers fondly. 'Oh no, Jem. Miss Chance does not visit. She was once a resident. She is a murderer.'

Angel Meadow Asylum, 18th September 1852

I helped my mother as best I could, sewing and mending night after night, though we could hardly see to make our stitches. She was a proud woman, not born into Prior's Rents but forced there by hardship. Her own mother and father had been respectable people, she said – weavers from the north. But they had died of the cholera, my father too, so there was no one but her to keep us both alive.

Downstairs from our lodgings, in the basement of the old mansion, there was a kitchen. It was the home of a woman who called herself Mrs Kindly, though I doubt that was her real name. The kitchen was a long, low-ceilinged dungeon, festooned with lines of damp clothes, and cluttered with benches and chairs, upon which men and women would gather to talk about the day's activities. Mrs Kindly kept a generous pot of broth boiling on the fire. It was little more than watery slop glistening with fat and lumped with bits of soft turnip, gristle and bone, though it was hot and filled your belly, and a plate of the stuff might be had for a penny. I suppose it was horrible down there – the air close and stinking, the people dirty and drunk. And yet it was warm and – to Goblin and me at least – as safe and familiar a place as we were likely to find in such a neighbourhood. It was peopled by all sorts, though none of them anything but poor – thieves and whores, mostly, bit fakers, housebreakers and pickpockets.

At the back of the kitchen, far from the fire and wrapped in layers of old coats and blankets, a student sat huddled over his books. We all knew him, and as he wanted nothing from us and caused us no trouble, we left him alone. He had no money, being from humble origins with little to support him, and in that regard was no different to the rest of us. He lived somewhere in the Rents, but spent time, as so many of us did, in the basement kitchen whenever he needed warmth and the company of others. He earned his money as a screever, writing letters for pennies, though he told me he was a medical student, and that one day he would be a doctor riding in a fine carriage and looking after the health of rich ladies and gentlemen. I watched him poring over his books and scribbling on bits of paper. His voice was soft and kind, his writing as neat and beautiful as lace across the page.

One day I asked if he would teach me to read and write, to add and subtract. I was willing to learn, I said, and like him I wanted a better life. I spoke in my most clear and polished voice – the voice I had learned from the ladies and gentlemen who strolled up and down on Oxford Street. He laughed at first; no doubt it amused him that this girl from the Rents should be so adept, should have schooled herself to talk like a lady. Perhaps it would be more amusing still to see whether she could master reading and writing too. What a narrow life we lead! For all that we might travel the seas, cross continents, change our lives or faces, we inhabit a narrow compass when all is said and done, and I was to meet this kind gentleman again, though his circumstances were to have proved just as capricious as my own. He taught me well, sitting beside me in that steaming kitchen, surrounded by dirty washing, dirty faces, noise and laughter. He taught Goblin too, sometimes, though Goblin could not see the advantages as well as I.

But any improvement in my situation would not come without money, and after a time I took my fancy accent, and my neat handwriting, and found employment in a boot and shoe repair workshop and blacking factory owned by a pair of gentlemen named Mr Knight and Mr Day. Goblin came too. He worked in the polish factory and the boot and shoe workshop, but I was put in the 'office', a small stuffy room above the workshop, filled with the fumes of old leather, ink and boot blacking. I was to be trained in book-keeping. Mr Day was to teach me himself. He paid me a shilling a week.

'A shilling?' I said. 'Is that all?'

'It's a fair price for a girl from Prior's Rents,' he replied. 'It's a job for boys, usually, not girls. You're lucky.'

The boot and shoe workshop had a number of functions. All manner of repairs were attended to. Boots and shoes in varying states of decrepitude – dancing pumps, top boots, lace-up shoes, walking boots, brogues – all were welcomed at Knight and Day's. If they had life left in them, Day's repair workshop would find it. Aside from this, Mr Day collected and reconditioned old boots and shoes, refurbished them and offered them for sale. Finally, Knight and Day's gathered exhausted and useless boots and shoes for pulverisation at the dye works.

Keen to offer a product as well as a service to his customers, Mr Knight heated up giant vats of boot blacking next door. These were continually on the boil, and Knight and Day's factory was begrimed with the substances of their trade – soot, turpentine, beeswax, tallow. The place reeked. It was insufferably warm, as the wax had to be melted until liquid without evaporating the turpentine. Mr Knight regulated the steam that heated the vats, whilst men and boys brought in the ingredients from the yard; others added the lampblack once the mixture had cooled, ladling the stuff into bottles or sticking labels. Goblin was to be a polish ladler, but he was also asked to carry sacks of lampblack from the yard into the factory and add them to the mixture. One day Mr Knight discovered that Goblin had mistakenly poured a sack of soot into the polish at the wrong moment in the process. He lashed Goblin with a strip of leather from the workshop to teach him a lesson.

I worked in the office every day under Mr Day's watchful eye. When I had finished with his account books, I was tasked with writing advertisements. Mr Day fancied himself a literary man, and wanted verses penned that might emphasise the qualities of his and Mr Knight's products as well as of his own literary pretentions. I gave him my work and asked for an increase in pay. I can still remember the verses, written by the light of the grimy window in Mr Day's office, the stink of blacking so heavy in the air that my head ached. He read out my work in his high-pitched mincing voice.

Out in St James's I met a young lady
'Mongst crocus and daffodil, dancing and gay.
Wind-whipped, her hair was in frightful confusion,
Sable locks streaming, like night tossed with day.

'O find me a mirror to pin back my tresses,
A surface with lustre and polish, I pray,
A mirror,' she pleaded, 'a glass whose reflection
Shines bright as the sun once the night turns to day.'

With cries of delight at my feet fell the lady,
And crouched o'er my boots (she would brook no delay)
The reflection she found there of looking-glass brightness,
From peerless jet-blacking, the best KNIGHT and DAY.

'Oh, Miss Devlin,' he said, grinning. His teeth were as brown as the shoe leather he reconditioned. 'This is quite the thing. Can you write others?' And so I did, though he never gave me a penny more and he did not hesitate to put his own name to my work. He said he had other ways of thanking me, that I would soon find out what they were, and that I would enjoy what he had to give me far more than a few extra pennies every week.

Every day Goblin and I trailed in from Prior's Rents. As we walked through the factory we passed lines of men toiling over lasts, and benches of women stitching leather, all surrounded by shoes and boots in various stages of repair. Beneath the windows of Mr Day's office were the polishing benches, where lustreless leather was transformed into something that gleamed like polished jet. Some of the men and women had been there all their lives. Was that to be my fate too?

'It's a good business,' said Mr Day, stroking my shoulder as he looked out at his workers. 'And, if now and again I can save a girl from filth and squalor, is that not a good and noble service? A philanthropic act?' He settled his hand on my shoulder. 'I've brought a number of girls here,' he said. 'Some from Prior's Rents. Once they are cleaned up they can be quite pretty. And they are so grateful. I allow them to demonstrate their gratitude in a variety of ways. I assume I can count on your gratitude too?'

I said nothing.

Mr Day sighed then, and moved round to stand beside my chair. His hand was heavy on my shoulder, his fingers hot against my neck, smooth and soft from years of beeswax and tallow. I sat without moving, my eyes focused upon the account sheet before me.

'You, my dear, are not like most of those who come from the Rents.' He put a hand to the back of my head. 'You are something of a lady, and a pretty one too.' I could hear his voice tremble, hear his excited heartbeat echo in his breathing. He pulled my face closer, both hands pushing my head down towards the bulging buttons of his trousers. Inches from my nose, they were pungent with a smell like fish oil and rancid animal fat. 'Perhaps you would like a pair of dancing pumps,' he said. 'I have a spare pair, just newly cleaned. They would look so dainty.'

'I cannot afford dancing pumps,' I said. My neck ached from resisting the pressure of hands.

'Oh the price is quite affordable.' Mr Day smiled again, and let me go.

Chapter Four

At length I found myself alone in the crowd with Dr Hawkins. Love seemed to agree with him, and he looked younger – and happier – than before he left for France. The rose in his lapel was ruby red. 'Good to see you, Jem,' he said, shaking my hand warmly. 'Thank you for coming. I realise you dislike these sorts of gatherings – your father was just the same.'

'You know me too well, sir,' I said.

'How are you? Are you sleeping?'

'I'm in good health, sir,' I said. 'But I must congratulate you—'

'Yes, yes, Jem, we will come to that in good time. But what of your Mr Quartermain? Young Gabriel? They're both here, I think?'

'Yes, they are, and we are all of us glad to have you back amongst us.' I meant it, truly, and I could not keep the relief out of my voice.

Dr Hawkins heard it and he looked at me sharply. 'Rutherford treating you well, I hope?'

'Well enough,' I said.

Dr Hawkins rubbed his chin as the crowd surged and ebbed about us. 'Yes,' he said. 'Stiven dislikes the fellow too. I saw you talking to him just now. D'you know him?'

'An old friend of my father's, sir,' I said. 'You say he knows Dr Rutherford?'

'He and Rutherford have crossed swords in the past. You know Stiven has a ward?'

'Miss Susan Chance. Dr Stiven says she is a felon.'

Dr Hawkins nodded. 'She was only a child at the time so one might be able to forgive her, though the law made no such distinction. The girl was ten years old – old enough to know what she was about, some might say.' He shrugged. 'She has certainly landed on her feet, though her start in life was not so fortunate.'

'What happened?'

'It's not clear what her origins are precisely, only that she comes from Prior's Rents, and that her mother was a whore who set her daughter to the same profession. Not that the girl was ever used in that way, but that was the beginning of it. Her mother sent a man to her – a so-called gentleman from a respectable family who enjoyed visiting the less salubrious brothels. The night was cold; the girl was put into a bed and told by her mother that she would soon be warmed up good and proper, and that she must do anything that was asked of her to please the nice gentleman. But Susan Chance was having none of it. When the man climbed into bed with her she fought him off, seized the poker and dashed his brains out.

'As you can imagine, the girl was sentenced to hang. But Stiven argued that she was rendered temporarily insane, driven out of her wits by hunger, cold, neglect, poverty and lack of moral guidance. All the usual things, I suppose. Plus the shock of realising that her mother had sold her for sixpence. According to Stiven, anyone forced to live in those conditions and treated in such a way by their own mother could scarcely be responsible for their actions.'

'One might excuse the behaviour of any number of children in Prior's Rents on similar grounds,' I said.

'Perhaps we should,' said Dr Hawkins. 'Perhaps we should be looking elsewhere for the guilty rather than sending such unfortunates to prison. And yet, in this case, there was a little more to it. It appears that the girl Susan went on battering the man long after he was dead. The first blow may well have been fatal – we must assume it incapacitated him as what chance would a ten-year-old ragamuffin have against a well-fed man? And yet when they found them the fellow was unrecognisable. His pocket book proclaimed his identity, for his head was completely pulped. "Human jam" were the words used by the constable. How she had the strength to commit such violence for so long I don't know, as the sustained ferocity required would, in normal circumstances, be beyond the capabilities of a child.'

'An accomplice?'

He shook his head. 'There was no evidence that anyone had aided her, for the door had been locked from the inside and the key was found in the fellow's pocket. Anyway, Stiven used the violence of the act as evidence in the girl's favour. He suggested that the whole event indicated a complete but temporary derangement. If she had felled her assailant with one blow, that would have been a different matter. And yet she went on and on and on beating him. How else might she have managed so prolonged an attack – why else would she have done it – had she not been insane? And if she were insane when she committed the deed, then she could not be hanged for it.'

'The McNaughton Rule?' I said.

'Precisely. A recent addition to the statute books, and one which has already proved controversial, but it was central to the girl's defence: at the moment of the crime Susan Chance was suffering from a disease of the mind. Of course there were those who were not so generous. Rutherford was a witness for the prosecution. He said the girl was clearly guilty, knew exactly what she was about and should hang. He made life very uncomfortable for her – she was weeks in Newgate. But they followed McNaughton to the letter. She could not be hanged once insanity had been established. Two medical men agreed to it: I was one – the girl deserved a chance and I could not condemn one so young to the gallows – and Stiven was the other. I can't account for his motives, though he is known to be a good man, from what I hear – a clever one too, and not to be underestimated despite his penchant for coloured silks and face powder.'

'My father always had the highest regard for him,' I said.

Dr Hawkins looked at me kindly. 'Then that is all the approval the fellow needs to make him my friend.'

'And yet Susan Chance is not a resident of Angel Meadow?'

'Oh no. She never has been. Stiven was determined to help the child and has done all he can to change her life for the better. Once the matter of her sanity – or insanity

– was settled Stiven insisted that he could take care of her – keep her safe from harm and prevent her from harming others. There was a precedent for the domestic management of a homicidal lunatic – a woman who, like Susan, could be said to have acted quite out of character – though it had been some years earlier. And, of course, Susan had age on her side, for she was young and her mind malleable. I'm still not sure quite how he managed it but Stiven was permitted to look after the girl if he guaranteed to take charge of her upbringing and custody himself. It was an experiment, he said, to demonstrate that with the right instruction, the right care and attention, the right environment, it is possible to take command of a person's sanity. There were those who said it couldn't be done. To batter a man to death so violently was a crime that showed something deeply corrupt within the heart and soul—'

'But she was only a child,' I said.

'Even so, the point remains the same. If the assault – attempted assault – turned her wits then it might be argued that her mind is inherently unstable. Mania could erupt at any time. Stiven always carries a strait waistcoat when he is out with her – just as a precaution – though as far as I am aware he has had no cause to use it.'

I thought of the diminutive Susan Chance with her club foot and jaunty walk, her tiny hands and black, laughing eyes, and I could not imagine anyone less likely to erupt into mania.

'Anyway,' said Dr Hawkins, 'she seems to have recognised it for what it was – an opportunity for a life that was better than anything anyone else had to offer. Certainly it was better than what might await her in the Rents, never mind in prison, or the madhouse. And yet, one ought not to underestimate the tug of the old ways – of habit. Heredity too.' He hesitated. 'She's not quite cast Prior's Rents off. You've met the girl. Didn't you notice?'

'Yes,' I said.

Dr Hawkins raised an eyebrow. 'I think you like her already, Jem. Just a little? Or are my senses so old and dull that I can no longer detect such things? And Mr Quartermain too, perhaps?'

I followed Dr Hawkins's gaze. Will stood beside the fireplace, a glass of punch to his lips. He was staring at Susan Chance – who was now being introduced to one of the Fellows of the Mind and Brain Society by Dr Stiven. Gabriel was chattering in Will's ear, but he was clearly oblivious. He watched Susan as she moved away, his expression rapturous. I saw her look over at him, and I felt a twinge in my heart.

'Good luck to you both, Jem.' Dr Hawkins clapped me on the shoulder. 'But, to other matters. Come and meet my wife.'

I had seen Mrs Hawkins as she passed through the crowds, shaking hands with the lunatics and greeting her husband's friends, and I knew already that she was a beauty – not the pale sort usually so prized by men, but dark and tall with a fearless gaze.

'Mr Flockhart,' she said, taking my hand. 'My husband speaks of you, and your father, very warmly.' Mrs Hawkins smiled as she spoke. And yet, as she uttered the usual welcoming platitudes, I became certain that she was thinking something quite different – the way she glanced at me, the way her eyes sparked.

'And the weather has been so warm,' she was saying. 'But I think the heat only affects ladies. Our costume is so cumbersome and impractical, one might almost hope for a day when we can all dress as freely as men.' She looked into my eyes and grinned, as broad as any street urchin. I felt a flash of fear and excitement. She knew! She knew that I was no man, that my shirt and britches, my neckerchief and waistcoat, my long stride and firm handshake, all were affectations and beneath them I was as much a woman as she. It was a moment only, a second when Dr Hawkins turned away, but I read in her face, in the pressure of her hand and the flash of her smile a surge of joy and a silent cheer for the act I sustained. *Go on!* She seemed to say, *go on, Jem!* I grinned back at her. I could not help myself.

I spoke with her for only a few more minutes. I could see she was tired – so many people to meet, so many hands to shake. She was faultless in her manners and her conversation. 'Do tell me about the physic garden,' she said. And, 'You must bring Mr Quartermain up for dinner.' But something, I knew, had passed between us. What, exactly? I could not fathom it and my mind whirled as I tried to make sense of my impressions. Of one thing, however, I was certain. I am a skilled and practised dissembler. All my life I have played a game, deceiving the world about who and what I am, and I have become adept. I liked Mrs Hawkins very much, but I could recognise a fellow impostor when I met one.

The evening wore on. I came across Gabriel, who was looking bored so I sent him off to Mrs Speedicut, who was sure to have a seed cake in her room that she would be glad to share with the lad. Soon after that I found Will standing against the wall.

'You look about as comfortable as a suit of armour,' I said. 'Perhaps we should go soon.'

'Where did you get to?' he said. 'Did you speak to Mrs Hawkins? You might have introduced me.'

I saw Dr Golspie approaching through the crowd. 'Hello, Tom,' I said. 'I wondered where you were.'

'Have you met Mrs Hawkins, Tom?' said Will.

'Not yet.' He looked about. 'Is that her over there? I see she's stuck with Christie. Poor woman.'

'What's that in your pocket?' said Will, pointing to a large bulge in Dr Golspie's coat.

Dr Golspie drew out a potato. 'Thought I might as well take it home for my tea.' He sounded dejected. 'It's not been much use for anything else.'

'What other use did you have in mind?' I said. 'Apart from eating it.'

'Was it one of your "stimuli"?' Will grinned. 'For Mrs Fitzwilliam? The woman who hears voices in her head?'

I laughed. 'This one of your new ideas, Tom?'

'I believe that the unspoken – thoughts, feelings, dreams, fears – may build up in the mind like . . . like matter in a drain,' said Dr Golspie. 'If we can unblock the drain, as it were, if we can call forth these deeply embedded emotions, then the effect must surely be relief. I thought that if I could tap into Mrs Fitzwilliam's thoughts and fears from when she was a girl in Ireland, perhaps we might come to understand the voices.' He shrugged. 'But the woman could not empty her mind, could not dwell on the stimulus—' He stared at the potato gloomily. 'Perhaps it is the wrong stimulus.'

'Perhaps some other vegetable,' said Will.

'Or fruit?' I said.

'You mock me, sirs,' said Dr Golspie. 'I simply need to find the correct stimulus and ask the correct questions. My views on the matter are still developing.'

'You think you can effect a cure by making our lunatics talk about themselves?' Dr Rutherford's voice was a sneer. I had not seen him approach, had not noticed him standing so close, but he had clearly heard everything.

'In some cases, sir, yes,' insisted Dr Golspie. 'I believe it may well be possible. Or at least instructive.'

'But the voices of the insane are exactly that: insane and as such not worth listening to. They have no insights into their own condition.'

'Surely we must try. We owe it to them as fellow human beings, and there are so many different types of madness, we must develop different ways of treating its causes and symptoms. But if you're looking for quackery you might look no further than your own approach. Photographs and head-measurings? What cure do they offer? What real science are they are grounded in?'

'Dr Gall of Vienna—' cried Dr Rutherford.

'Is easily dismissed by one simple fact,' said Dr Golspie, raising his voice to match Dr Rutherford's. Those around us began to fall silent, listening. 'The brain is a soft organ. It conforms itself to the shape of the skull, the skull does not shape itself around the contours of the brain.'

'You cannot deny the success of my methods,' said Dr Rutherford. 'The patient Letty is no longer violent.'

'She is no longer anything! Phrenology is dismissed by all but the most dim-witted of our profession, those who adhere to it are no more than quacks – charlatans, and fairground entertainers. You might as well pull out a crystal ball and have done with it!'

'Tom—' I said. But Dr Golspie shook off my hand.

'I might also add that you have no empathy, sir,' he cried. 'You make no effort to understand those in your care, no effort to meet their individual needs. You expect the same from every one of our female charges – obedience, docility, silence. And I fear you will slice and chop till you get it.'

Dr Golspie turned on his heel and vanished into the crowd. Dr Rutherford remained where he was, his face white with rage. But it was clear that those around us – mostly doctors and benefactors – were in complete agreement about the need for obedience, docility and silence amongst women, for they looked after Dr Golspie in some surprise.

'Impudent fellow!' said a bald, round-shouldered man I recognised as the President of the Mind and Brain Society.

'Empathy?' said another. 'A gentleman in this profession must be strong, not weeping into his tea over the plight of his patients.'

Dr Rutherford's frown eased. The buzz of conversation started up once more.

A string quartet struck up a waltz, the music echoing upward, mingling with the sooty wraiths that guttered from the lamps. The conversations around us grew louder; a big fat man bore down upon Dr and Mrs Hawkins, his wife and daughter following in his wake.

'Mothersole, ma'am,' he cried, bowing low over Mrs Hawkins's hand. Not only had I never seen so tall a man, but I had also never seen one as obese as he. His upper arms looked to be thicker than his daughter's waist; his bald head a mound of dough into which someone had pushed two raisins, his eyes small and beady above the rosy quivering folds of his cheeks.

'Dr Mothersole is a visiting physician,' I heard Dr Hawkins say. 'He is with us for a few weeks, taking notes and helping out and so forth. He is a well-known philanthropist and an advocate of what might be termed hygienic methods of care – exercise, music, recreation.'

'My daughter is writing my life story,' boomed Dr Mothersole. He indicated the girl standing at his side. She was as thin as her father was wide, her shoulders so narrow and drooping that it was a wonder her dress did not slide off them onto the ground. 'It is most educational for her.'

'My father feels it will improve his chances with St Peter if he has a coherent biography,' murmured Miss Mothersole, a notebook and pencil clutched in her ink-spotted fingers.

'I am patron of many charitable enterprises, in addition to my celebrated commitment to the lunatics of the city,' said her father. 'The Ear Dispensary. The Truss Society for the Relief of the Ruptured Poor. The Limbless Costermongers Benevolent Fund. In the eyes of God we are all men.' He leaned forward. 'Mind you, Mrs Hawkins, we may well all be men, but such as they are as akin to me as a stray cat is to a lion. And whereas one would be tempted to kick a stray cat, one has only respect and reverence for a lion.' I saw Mrs Hawkins suppress a shudder, perhaps at the nearness of the man, whose face was so close to hers that his breath disturbed a curl of her hair. Dr Mothersole turned to his wife. 'Is that not so, my dear?'

Mrs Mothersole had been standing beside her husband, looking up at him adoringly. 'Yes, my dear,' she crooned. She put out a hand and pawed at his sleeve. 'Oh, it is so!'

Dr Mothersole beamed and turned to his daughter. 'Write that down, my dear: "there are few lions and far too many stray cats".'

The crowd swelled and shifted. I saw Mrs Hawkins and Susan Chance standing side by side, their heads close together as they talked. Beside me, Will was looking troubled. I knew he hated crowds – especially ones indoors. He was a country boy at heart and the close atmosphere, warmed by bodies and breath and poisoned by smoke and coal dust, made him uncomfortable. Perhaps we should leave, I thought. We might take an evening stroll to the physic garden. He would like that, I was sure.

'This place is far too hot,' he muttered. 'How long do we have to stay here? Can't we go to Sorley's for something to eat? I'm starving.' Then he spotted Susan, and his face brightened. Mrs Hawkins had disappeared. I looked about and saw her being escorted from the room by Dr Hawkins, her hand to her brow. Will was about to weave his way through the crowd towards Susan when Dr Christie hailed us.

'Good evening, gentlemen,' he said. 'Mr Flockhart, I must apologise for my conduct last time we met. To scrutinise you in such a way.' His pale eyelashes caught the light like cobwebs. 'Unforgivable.' He followed my gaze to Susan, and the corners of his mouth twitched. 'There's a curious specimen,' he said. 'No wonder she's caught your interest. She manages well enough, I suppose, though her own nature is sure to catch up with her one day. You know of her background?'

'Yes,' I said.

'At first glance she might appear to be as much a lady as one might hope to find anywhere.'

'She seems quite perfect to me,' agreed Will.

'And yet she is not,' murmured Dr Christie. He pulled out his pocket watch and regarded it, open like an oyster, in the centre of his palm. It was as though he were counting down the seconds until Susan Chance went mad once more. 'The temporary sickness of an otherwise lucid mind is quite fascinating. Especially in the female – a creature already at the mercy of her own bodily weaknesses. The womb, gentlemen. Need I say more?' He snapped the watch closed, and looked again at Susan Chance. He shook his head. 'What might we do with her if she may not be hanged? Rehabilitation is an unpredictable approach. I fear we will find that out soon enough. That leaves us with incarceration, and yet incarceration changes nothing if the confinement is merely custodial—'

At that moment there was a commotion on the far side of the room. The musicians came to a caterwauling halt as a voice cried out: 'Rutherford! Rutherford! Where are you?'

We pushed our way through the crowd. Dr Golspie was standing in the doorway, his coat missing and his collar awry. His hair stood up from his head, the face beneath it pale and sweaty-looking. His eyes were red-rimmed, the pupils dilated, giving him a wild, nocturnal appearance.

'Rutherford!' He lurched forward, his arms wide. 'Christie! Oh this is glorious! Glorious!' He seized hold of Letty and swung her around in a crazy, lopsided polka.

'What's happened to him?' hissed Will. 'Jem, what's wrong with him? What's he doing?'

'*Dawamesc*,' I muttered. 'That's what's happened.'

'Has he lost his wits?'

'In a manner of speaking.'

Will clicked his tongue. 'For God's sake, Jem, you're not making any sense.' He looked about at the ring of faces that had turned to see what all the noise was about. 'Help me get him away.' He stepped forward and took Dr Golspie's arm, but the doctor shook him off. He had become distracted by something in the air above Letty's head, and he pointed upwards, his face ecstatic.

'Oh!' he cried. 'Look! Look there! It's Mary. Mary, my dear sister, d'you not see her? Floating above us in a circle of light! She's an angel now. I knew she would be!'

'Tom,' I said gently. 'Come back to your rooms.'

'You!' Dr Golspie grabbed me by the shoulders and peered into my face. 'You're the devil! The very devil himself! I see it in your crimson face. And look! Look!' He put his hands up and seized two handfuls of my hair. 'Horns!'

'Tom.' I pulled his hands away. 'Stop this.'

'Shh!' He held a finger to his lips. 'Shh! The mice will hear you. They will hear you and they will come for me.' His eyes grew wide and fearful and his voice sank to a whisper. 'Oh, but the mice are gone! I saw them! I saw their faces in the fire!' He put his hands to his head in an attitude of despair, and then drew them away again with a cry. 'Ugh!' he shouted. He held out his fingers. 'Insects! Thousands and thousands of them!'

'Tom!' I cried. 'Listen to me. Concentrate.'

He looked at me, and for a moment I knew he was quite lucid. 'I cannot,' he said. 'I *will* not.' And he began laughing, laughing as if he would never stop.

Dr Rutherford and Dr Christie appeared at my side. They surveyed Dr Golspie's grinning red face with disgust. 'What's going on?' said Rutherford.

'Perhaps Mr Pole ought to bring the strait waistcoat,' said Dr Christie.

'Dr Golspie has consumed *dawamesc*,' I said. 'It's a paste made from cannabis. Taken in excess it's said to produce a state akin to mania. The condition is intense, but it is usually self-conscious and – fortunately – only temporary.' I watched Dr Golspie trying to wipe the 'insects' off his hands, and I cursed myself for not being more insistent that he exercise caution – and for not bringing my notebook. I looked about and was glad to see that Miss Mothersole was scribbling away – someone at least was taking notes. Then I saw the expression of glee on Dr Rutherford's face and I wished with all my heart that Dr Golspie had waited until we were alone before he consumed the hashish paste I had so carelessly given him.

'And how much has the fellow taken?' said Dr Christie.

I shrugged. 'A drachm, I would say.'

'Is that a lot?'

'Undoubtedly.'

'And you supplied it?' He sounded incredulous.

I blushed. 'I did, sir. The effect will last some hours yet, though he will recover.'

Beside me, Dr Golspie was now on his knees, his hands over his face. 'I am down a well!' he cried. 'Down a deep, dark well! Oh, help me! Mary! Mary!'

'For God's sake, man,' bellowed Dr Rutherford suddenly. 'Pull yourself together.'

Dr Golspie looked up at him, his mind suddenly clearing. 'Can you not see how this can benefit our noble profession?'

'I cannot, sir. I would not treat the mad with madness. No one would!' There was a murmur of approval from the assembled doctors.

Out of the corner of my eye I saw Dr Christie nod to someone in the crowd, and then there was Pole, flanked by two attendants, a strait waistcoat in his hands.

Oblivious to his fate, Dr Golspie threw back his head. 'Oh Rutherford,' he cried. 'I don't refer to the patient. I refer to the physician! Can't you see? This allows us direct access to the abnormal mental states we spend our lives trying to treat. To comprehend the ravings of a mad man it is necessary to have raved oneself.' He flung his arms wide. 'I am travelling deep into the realms of delusion, mapping the very landscape of madness. Such insights! My dear Rutherford. My dear Christie, can you not see? Oh, you dolts, you utter fools!' And he burst out laughing once more.

Angel Meadow Asylum, 18th September 1852

We worked at Knight and Day's blacking factory six days a week, for fifteen hours a day. It was easy for me to see that Mr Day made more money than he admitted. The advertisements I wrote had increased his takings too, though I noticed he said nothing about it to Mr Knight. Mr Day kept his extra money at home. His wife and his daughter spent it on fine clothes and gowns; I had seen them with Mr Day on Oxford Street. Mr Day ignored me then, though when he was alone with me in the office above the boot and shoe repair workshop he was not so aloof. He stroked my cheek with his pale soft fingers.

'You learn fast and you are good with words and figures, Miss Devlin. But there is so much more I can teach you. Will you sit on my knee so I can show you?'

'No, sir,' I said. Goblin had given me his knife, and in my pocket my fingers curled around its worn wooden handle.

'Come, come,' said Mr Day. 'I will send you down to the polishing bench if you do not.' He slipped a hand into his trouser pocket. His breath was hot and stale, heavy with the smell of tobacco, boot blacking and dirty leather. At that moment the office

boys returned from the fool's errand Mr Day had sent them on. I had never been so glad to see their grubby smirking faces.

Mr Day caught me off guard. He told me that he needed me to work late, that he wanted me to stay for a little while after my shift. He said he had decided to pay me more for my work on his advertisements, but that he did not wish to reward me in front of the office boys or other staff. How naive I was! I thought I could manage him, that I could deal with his advances. I was soon to find how much I had underestimated him.

I had been watching him all day out of the corner of my eye for he was more bothersome and excited than ever. He wiped his sweaty hands continually on his waistcoat and prowled the office, passing up and down before the shelves of brown ledgers. At last, the two office boys were sent home for the evening. Their presence so far had proved useful as it had stopped Mr Day from making his advances more open and insistent. The boys were eagle-eyed. They did not talk to me, but only watched me, before wiping their noses on their sleeves and turning back to their ledgers. But it was clear to us all that they made Mr Day self-conscious, and he could only lay a hand on my shoulder or steal a caress of my cheek when they were not looking.

And then the boys were gone. As I turned to dip my pen in the inkpot, all at once he was upon me.

Mr Day was stronger than he looked, his wiry frame taut as a harp string with expectation, his whole body quivering with lust and determination. In an instant he had my hands pinned behind my back. His pants and grunts sounded in my ear, and he had clearly planned his moment, for as I opened my mouth to scream he reached round and stuffed a polishing rag into it. My mouth was filled with the acrid taste of boot blacking – soot and fat and turpentine. I thrashed beneath him, revolted, filled with fury at my own stupidity, and damp with fear at what he was about to do.

Astride me, as though riding a beast to market, Mr Day was jubilant. His voice was high-pitched with excitement.

'You'll earn your pay tonight, my dear. You'll make good on all those promises you made and find what kind of a master I really am.' From somewhere to my right, far off amongst the vats of melted tallow, a bell rang. It was the bell that summoned Mr Knight to the office. My flesh turned cold. Were there to be two of them? After a moment I heard the sound of hurrying footsteps, and then Mr Knight was there too. Perhaps they will boil my body afterwards, *I thought, as they pulled at my clothes and pushed their faces against my neck,* so that I might be rendered down to fat, mixed with lampblack and turpentine and smeared onto the boots of men.

Mr Knight's breath smelled of tallow – did he eat the stuff too? 'Hold her, Mr Day,' he cried. 'Tightly now!'

I coughed, gagging on the foul rag that stopped my throat. I had only one trick. I was sure they would not fall for it, but what choice did I have? I moaned, and fell limp beneath their hands. And then, as Mr Day's grip loosened, I burst once more into movement. Before they could hold my arms again I had ripped out the dirty rag and screamed with all the breath left in me. 'GOBLIN!' I felt a blow to my head, and I fell forward on top of the ledger.

'Shh!' hissed Mr Day. They stopped and listened, but the workshop, and the factory, were silent.

Mr Knight laughed. 'Your little friend will be half way to Prior's Rents by now. You may scream all you like, he will not hear you.'

But Goblin would not have left the workshop without me, and I knew he would come. They stuffed the rag back in, ramming it down my throat so far that I feared I would choke to death, and shoved me onto the desk. Ink seeped from beneath me in a dark pool.

'Careful, Mr Day,' said Mr Knight. 'You're messing up the accounts.'

Mr Knight and Mr Day argued as they held me down. 'I caught her,' said Mr Day. 'I should be first.'

'But my name is first on the labels, and on the business,' replied Mr Knight. 'I am always first.'

At that moment, the door burst open. I saw Goblin standing on the threshold. In his hands was a cobbler's last. His face was streaked with tears and lampblack. He lurched forward, and before either man could move or cry out, he swung the last at Mr Knight's head. I heard a moist crunch, and then a scream from Mr Day as Mr Knight crashed to the ground. Mr Day leaped off me. He could not get to the door as Goblin was barring his way, so he scuttled past the office boys' desks to the back of the room. There, he ran up and down like a rat trapped in a sewer, babbling and crying out, his hands clawing at the air as though he hoped to tear a door in it with his fingernails. Before us Mr Knight stared up, a pool of red seeping from his head. Goblin dropped the bloodied last and pulled from his pocket a variety of boot-mending tools: a button hook, a hammer, a shoemaker's awl, a bodkin.

I spat out the rag and snatched the sharp-spiked awl from Goblin's hand. Suddenly I was blind with rage: rage against Mr Knight and Mr Day, rage against the father who had died and left me and my mother to make our way alone in the world, and rage against all the men who had used my mother in any way they pleased and who sought to do the same with me. I hardly know what happened next, but I came to to find myself crouched over the corpse of Mr Day. My fingers were bloody, and a cobbler's awl projected from his right eye. The left eye, and his mouth, had been stitched closed using thread from the mending bench.

Chapter Five

The crowd about me was unmoving, frozen, like figures in a painting. I could listen to their thoughts, hear everything that passed through their minds, but I could make no sense of it. Dr Stiven banged on the mantelpiece with the silver head of his walking stick. *Bang bang bang!* We were no better than the mad with our noisy jabbering. Could we not be quiet and let a man think? The sound of it dinned in my ears so that I turned my head this way and that, this way and that . . . and all at once I saw that I was not at Angel Meadow at all. I was in my bed in the small whitewashed room above the apothecary and the hammering I could hear was at my bedroom door. *Bang bang bang!* My candle was out and the place was as dark as Hades.

'What is it?' I said, my voice sticky with sleep. 'It's the middle of the night!' I struggled into my clothes in he pitch black.

Downstairs in the apothecary Pole stood beside the

door. His one good eye regarded me balefully. The other, pale and moist in its melted eye socket, shifted from side to side, unseeing. He brought with him a breath of outside, an invisible shroud of cold damp air that reeked of sulphur and decay. He refused to say anything, only that we should come. Both of us, Will and I, should come immediately. Beside him the skeleton of Dr Bain that had once graced the out-patients' waiting room at St Saviour's grinned down at me in wicked delight. The game, I could sense it, was about to begin.

Outside, a thick pall of brown fog enveloped everything. When we had walked down from Angel Meadow Asylum some five hours earlier the air held nothing more than the usual taste of soot and effluent. Now, it was as though we were lost at sea, Pole's lantern a dim beacon glowing in the depths of a muddy ocean. My own flame seemed cowed by the gloom, crouching low in its glass casing as the fog pressed in upon us. The apothecary clock had told me it was five o'clock in the morning. The sun, I knew, should be a dull glow against the eastern sky. And yet there was nothing. Nothing but a blank world hulking with dim shapes. Will took my arm, and I was glad of the warmth and pressure of his hand. We knew the way up to the asylum well enough, even on such a morning as this, and we walked quickly and in silence, the scarves across our noses and mouths muffling our breath and protecting our lungs from the choking fog. Ahead of us, a smudge of dirty yellow told us where the lamp blazed beside the entrance to the asylum. The door squealed on its hinges, the hallway within no more welcoming than the street where we stood.

Dr Hawkins awaited us, standing beside the corpse of

Dr Rutherford though it was clear that he was trying not to look at the mutilated face of his former colleague. His fingers moved restlessly against one another, his hands clasping and unclasping, 'Thank you, Pole.' He addressed the bunched shadow still lurking behind me. 'If you would see that no one else comes up.'

While Dr Hawkins went to fetch Mrs Lunge, and Pole was out in search of a constable, Will and I had examined the body as best we could in the dim lamplight of Dr Rutherford's room. A post-mortem would reveal more about the inside of the body, but I could not help but think that we had already gleaned as much as would be useful. This crime was about what was visible to the eye, I was sure: the stitching, the position of the weapon, the place where Dr Rutherford's corpse lay – all would tell us far more about who had done this, and why, than the state of his heart or what he had eaten for dinner. I slid the charred photograph of the faceless girl into my pocket book, alongside the fold of paper containing the fragment of suture I had snipped from the bloody stitches at the corner of the corpse's mouth.

'Shouldn't we give that picture to the police?' said Will.

'Probably,' I said. 'Though I can't think what they'll do with it. Far better that we should keep it for now. But we have very little time before they're here. Look about, Will. What of the room? Does it tell us anything useful?'

I had been in Dr Rutherford's room many times – for it was here that he had conducted his monthly examinations while Dr Hawkins had been away. It was set out in the most orderly fashion, the fireplace flanked by a pair of wing-backed chairs, the desk at the shuttered window piled with books and papers. The books were arranged with their spines all facing the same way; the papers held still with paperweights, each one sitting in the centre of the sheaf. To the right, a pen and a pewter inkstand, blotter, and sealing wax were laid out side by side. On either side of the fire there were shelves of books, neatly ordered and dusted. On the opposite wall hung frame after frame of beetles and butterflies, gassed and pinned and set out in labelled ranks. Beside these stood display cases containing the skulls of birds and beasts set out in ascending order of size. On the lower shelves bottles of preserving fluid held worms, fish, macabre crustaceans, and lizards, all in silent suspension, alongside polished seeds and nuts of the most extraordinary kinds, so that even I, with my knowledge of botany, could not but be impressed.

'Nothing,' said Will. 'It tells us nothing – other than the fact that Dr Rutherford was neat – meticulously so.'

'Mmm,' I said. I held up my lantern. At the back of the room, tiers of white-painted shelves covered the entire wall from floor to ceiling – a distance of some twelve feet or more. They stretched from one side of the room to the other, uninterrupted by window, door or fireplace. Each shelf was crammed with faces, men, women and children, row upon row of them – skulls of all sizes and white plaster death-masks, a ghostly sightless jury of long-dead criminals and lunatics.

Dr Rutherford had been fascinated by the shapes and contours of heads. He had made no secret of his obsession, and was proud, more than proud, of his extensive collection of real human skulls. He was pleased to declare

that he knew the provenance of each one in his possession, that he had met many of them in person, and that
he had boiled the flesh off them himself in copper cauldrons. Once, I arrived to find him with his shelves bare,
his skulls laid out upon the floor in front of him in neat
ranks. Dr Rutherford was kneeling before them. A soft
chamois-leather in his hand and a bowl of water at his
side, he wiped each skull tenderly, before drying it off
with a muslin cloth and buffing it to a gleaming lustre
with a mitt of finest kid.

'Look,' he crooned when he saw me. He held up a
large, yellowish cranium with a broad, flat forehead. 'This
is Maria Seldon of Spitalfields. She cut her husband's
throat and hid his body beneath the cellar floor. See the
sloping forehead?' He ran his fingers over the gleaming
bone. 'Close eyes, pronounced jaw and a marked
protuberance precisely where her organ of deviousness
is located. It is unmistakable. Her crimes were entirely
true to her character, her character entirely readable
from her cranium.' He laid the skull down and picked
up another. 'And here's Moll Caraway. She murdered
her mother and had her lover dress up as the old woman
to fool the neighbours. The organ of deceit is singularly
well developed, the organ of wit a pronounced bulge, the
tendency to violence clearly evident. Miss Caraway was
considered something of a humorist and did a regular
turn as a laughing artiste at the Cat and Barrel on Fenwick
Lane, Whitechapel.

'And look here! Dorcas Gilmour. A quite infamous
prostitute from Seven Dials. Murdered at least six men
before she was caught.' He closed his eyes and threw
his head back, his face radiant as his hands traced the

90

contours of the girl's skull more gently than any of her customers would ever have done.

'Amativeness,' he said with a sigh. 'Oh, it was strong in this one. And greed. And violence too. I could pick her out with my eyes closed.' He opened his eyes and dabbed the cheekbone with his wash-cloth. 'She was transported but died on the journey. I made sure to get my hands on such a prize specimen.'

'And the others?'

He shrugged. 'The poor house. The gallows. The resur– rectionists – they know my tastes.' He picked up a small skull no bigger than an apple. 'Left for dead beside the pump in Prior's Rents. Newborn. Even in the womb the personality is set. See the indentations here, the elongated cranium? The child would have grown into a sot, and a whore, there is no doubt about it.' He held the tiny head close to his face and peered into its empty eye sockets. 'Well my precious, shall we wash you now? Shall we make you nice and clean?'

Now, looking up at that wall of skulls, I had the impres– sion that they were glad that Dr Rutherford was dead, each one of them relieved to be free from his urgent caresses, his lascivious sponging and polishing. Death had granted them peace and obscurity. Dr Rutherford had denied them even that.

I caught a movement on a high shelf and almost dropped my lamp. But it was only a mouse, its white tail vanishing between the broken teeth of a large mottled skull.

'What is it?' said Will. 'Is there something wrong?' He shuddered beneath the gaze of so many leering faces. 'Not that there's very much right about a wall adorned with two hundred skulls. Sometimes I wonder who's really mad at Angel Meadow. Compared to this, Edward Eden seems the sanest man here!'

'Look,' I said. 'Up there. What do you see?'

'Faces,' said Will. 'That's all.'

'You said yourself that Rutherford was neat.'

'So he was.'

'Then what's happened to those two skulls on the top shelf?'

Will squinted up. His breath grew sharp, and I knew that he had seen it too. 'They're crooked.' He looked at me. 'And there's a space.'

I lowered my lantern. 'One of them is missing.'

I could hear footsteps approaching from the hallway behind me. 'We must be quick,' I said. 'There's one last thing—' I peered again at the body of Dr Rutherford stretched out on the hearthrug, its feet towards the door, its head pointing to the fireplace. The phrenology callipers projecting from the side of the head glinted dully in the lamplight; the darned face more waxen and grotesque than ever as the skin paled and grew firm, the stitches lengthening over the lips as they were pulled taut by a growing *rigor mortis*. I looked at the door, at the corpse, at the mirror – broken into long shards so that the room was reflected in a kaleidoscope of fragments. I lifted my lantern and scanned the floor, the hearth, along the skirting boards. I clicked my tongue. 'It has to be in here—'

'What?'

I grabbed the heavy iron poker and stirred the cinders in the grate, the heart of the fire glowing angrily as I shifted the coals. And then I saw it. I could not pluck it out from amongst the embers with my bare fingers as the fire was still hot, nor could I pocket it without burning myself.

'Your handkerchief, Will,' I said. 'Quickly!' Between the claws of the coal tongs I held an object – ovoid in shape and no bigger than a lemon; hard, but slightly yielding to the touch, and as black as coal. I slipped the tongs onto the hearth and plunged what I had found into my pocket.

The sound of footsteps grew louder, and all at once Dr Hawkins was back. Beside him was Mrs Lunge, as white as a ghost in her nightdress and dressing gown, her hair hanging in dark waves about her shoulders. She carried a candle, the shivering flame making the shadows behind her rear and leap. Her face was paler and haughtier than ever, and she loomed over the doctor the way a medieval queen might stand over a peasant.

'Good morning, Mrs Lunge,' I said. 'How are you feeling?'

'As you might expect, Mr Flockhart, sir,' she said.

'I believe it was you who came upon him?'

'Yes, sir. I was restless and couldn't sleep. I was going to go down to the kitchens to make myself a cup of tea. It took me past Dr Rutherford's door—'

'You have a room on this floor?'

'At the other end of the corridor. I saw that there was a light in here.'

'Was the door open?'

'No, sir. It was closed.'

'Locked?'

'No, sir.'

'And so you came in?'

'I assumed Dr Rutherford had gone home, but had left the lamp burning by mistake as he sometimes does. I came in to extinguish it and I saw—' She dabbed her lips with a handkerchief and mopped her eyes, though they looked dry to me. 'I saw him.'

'And what time was this?'

'Some half an hour before you arrived, sir.'

'Did you hear anything that evening? You say you couldn't sleep?'

'No, sir.'

'Did you touch anything when you came in?'

'No, sir.'

'Did you see anything? Anything unusual or out of place?'

'Save for Dr Rutherford's murdered and mutilated body?' I had the feeling she was mocking me. 'No, sir.'

'I wonder you are not more upset to find your employer so brutally murdered,' Will said.

She fell silent then. I had the impression that there was something she wanted to say, some rejoinder she wished to make – then Pole arrived, and with him the constable, and I decided I would save what further questions I had for another time. The constable stepped into the room and I heard him draw a gasp of breath. He crouched down to peer into Dr Rutherford's face, his handkerchief clamped across his mouth.

'Here,' said Will, handing the fellow his salts.

Dr Hawkins turned to me. 'Take these,' he said in a hushed voice. He held out a bunch of keys. 'You may come and go as you please, Jem. Do what you can. Find out who did this.' He shook his head. 'I can't think why this has happened. Can the man have had such an enemy?'

I put the keys in my pocket. I did not know what to say. Angel Meadow had changed profoundly since Dr Hawkins's incumbency – for sure, he had returned as medical superintendent, but he had been away for almost a year, what did he really know of the conflicts and tensions that might exist between its current inmates? He had come back to a very different place to the one he had left behind. He looked bemused, stunned even, by what had taken place, and seemed hardly able to tear his eyes away from the corpse.

'Who would do such a thing?' he whispered. 'Have I come home to this? Perhaps I would have been better to have stayed away.'

'How is Mrs Hawkins?' I said.

'She was unwell last night. I took her home early. I think it was the excitement and the warmth of the room. I have not seen her this morning, though I assume a night's rest will have restored her. Jem.' Dr Hawkins took my arm. 'Just be sure that every door you unlock is locked again after you have passed through it.'

'Yes, sir.'

'Do not be remiss – either of you. There are dangers here—' He gestured to the body, his face tense. 'You must look after yourselves. And each other.'

'You think this is the work of a mad man, sir?' said Will.

Dr Hawkins looked at him strangely. 'You think it is the work of a sane one?'

I did not venture an opinion. Pole, standing in the doorway, regarded me in silence. His palsied features were as unreadable as ever but there was something in his drooping eye that gave me pause. I did not know the man; he was no more than a turnkey to me, but I recalled what he had said the week before as he ushered me into the asylum's main corridor: *All on us is mad at some time or other. And when we are, we do things no man can explain, and no judge can forgive.*

Chapter Six

We went back downstairs. 'I've had enough of this place for one morning,' said Will. He pulled out his watch. 'And it's not even six o'clock.'

'What do you say to a pot of coffee and a plate of kippers at Sorley's?' I said.

'How can you even think about food?'

'Because I'm hungry. If a bloody face and a dead body put me off my breakfast, I would have starved to death long ago.'

We were passing a heavy panelled oak door, discoloured with age and scuffed and gouged, I presumed, from the violent resistance of the lunatics who had been dragged through it. From the other side, I heard the slow stumping approach of heavy ill-fitting boots, the guttural sound of a muttered oath and a rich tubercular coughing. Keys jangled, and the door swung open. An attendant peered out into the corridor where we stood. He looked exactly as I remembered him, his skin etiolated from a life spent underground, his eyes watery and blinking in the light from the candle he held aloft. His coat was a greasy-looking verdigris, the high shawl collar glistening and oily and scattered with flakes of dry skin. The breath of the basement billowed out around him, damp and stale. When he saw me, he froze, the hand that clutched the keys a bony pointing claw. 'I know you!'

'Hardly, sir,' said Will, clearly appalled that such a fearful apparition could claim me as an acquaintance.

'Not you,' said the attendant. '*Him.*' He jangled his keys in my face. I noticed a yellowish excrescence on the sleeve of the fellow's coat, like mould or mildew of some kind. Really, I would not have been surprised if he had had mushrooms sprouting from his pockets. 'Quick!' he beckoned us into his lair. 'Come see!'

We followed the man down a narrow flight of stairs and along a low-ceilinged passage. The stone floor beneath our feet struck cold through the soles of our shoes and I shivered. There were doors on either side. From behind each came the familiar sounds of the incarcerated mad – cries and groans, the sound of sobbing and a perpetual rhythmic moaning.

'Locked 'im in meself last night. Then this mornin' I goes to see 'im and 'e's disappeared. Vanished! I've been 'ere, man and boy. I've seed 'em die in there – bite through their own tongues, some of 'em, or swallow it, whole! I seed 'em scream till they kilt themselves with it and choke on straw like they was beasts. But I ain't never seen one disappear.'

The lock was well oiled and the key turned smoothly and silently. The cell inside was eight-feet square, the walls and floor covered with a stained and slimy-looking oilcloth. Inside, crumpled upon the floor, lay a strait jacket. In a corner, as if flung aside in fury, was a leather bridle. The last time I had seen it, it was being forced between Dr Golspie's lips. And yet the sight of the empty strait jacket and the discarded bridle meant only one thing: that Tom Golspie had not spent the night brutally confined after all. Yet if he was not here, then where was he? How had he escaped? As I looked about that tiny cell, breathing in that hot, stale air, the questions in my mind wavered and grew confused, engulfed by a familiar dread. My uncle had spent his final days here, my father had been destined to follow him. Would I, too, live to call this tiny chamber with its padded walls my home? I could almost taste the stale and leathery tongue of the bridle.

'I must get out of here,' I said thickly. 'Take a closer look, Will. I . . . I cannot.'

I took the steps two at a time, my stride growing longer, the flame in my lantern shrinking and guttering. And then it went out. The darkness drowned me, pouring into my eye sockets like black water. My fingers clawed at the door, my fists banging and banging—

And then all at once the door opened and I tumbled out to lie asprawl on the floor of the main hallway. In front of my nose I saw the shiny toes of a pair of well-polished boots; beneath my elbow I felt the grasp of a helpful hand.

'You're safe now,' said a voice. I looked up into the round expressionless face of Edward Eden.

'You!' I said. 'Did you open that door?'

'Yes, sir,' he said.

'How? With what?' And then, 'Aren't you locked in at night, like everyone else?'

'Yes.'

'Then how are you out of your room?'

'Because I have these.' Edward held up a bunch of keys identical to the ones I had in my own pocket.

'Where did you get them?'

'From Dr Golspie.'

'But he is – was – locked up in the basement.'

'I let him out.'

'But when? How?'

'Dr Hawkins said some of us could be out last night. We were to meet his wife. When Pole put Dr Golspie in the basement I went to Dr Golspie's room and found his keys.'

I knew that the lunatics were not locked into their rooms during the day, not in the private wards anyway, and last night a number of them had been at large during half of the night too. Given what had happened since, it now seemed the most careless and incautious of decisions. 'You have many freedoms here,' I said. 'Some asylums would not allow you half so much liberty.'

'We don't have liberty at night. Not usually.' Edward looked at the door I had just emerged from. 'And we don't have any at all in the basement. I've been down there,' he whispered. 'I didn't like it one bit. I hated knowing that Dr Golspie was down there, that's why I took his keys. I had a plan to let him out. It was a good plan, wasn't it?'

'I don't know,' I said. 'Perhaps you should tell me more about it.'

Edward grinned, and leaned in close. 'Later, when they locked me in my room for the night I waited for a bit and then came out again. I used Dr Golspie's keys. I came down here and I crept downstairs to the basement and I let him out too. I like Dr Golspie. He's kind.'

'When? When did you let him out?'

Edward shrugged. 'Don't know.'

'And where is he now?'

'Don't know.'

'Did you see where he went?'

'He ran away.'

'Where? Did he say where he was going?'

'He said he had to see Dr Rutherford.'

'Did he say why?'

'No.'

'Did you see Dr Rutherford?'

Edward chewed his fingernail. His face had taken on a worried look. 'I lost Albion,' he said after a moment.

'Albion?'

'My new mouse. The mouse you gave me.'

'The white mouse?'

'Yes,' said Edward. 'That's right. You remember him!'

'Of course,' I said. 'And I have seen him too. Just this morning.'

'Oh!' cried Edward, clapping his hands. 'Where?'

'In Dr Rutherford's room,' I said. 'Is that where you lost him?'

Edward fell silent. He wound his hands together and pressed them to his cheek as if in search of comfort.

'Well?' I said.

Tears filled Edward's eyes, and he looked about, his expression fearful. 'You mustn't ask,' he said. 'I cannot tell. I mustn't.' He began blubbering, wiping his eyes and nose on his coat sleeve and refusing to say anything more.

'Do you not have a handkerchief, Mr Eden?' I said with a sigh.

He nodded, and pulled a large square of crumpled silk

from his inside pocket. Like the dawn that was now visible outside the asylum's high windows it was streaked and clotted with scarlet.

We went to Sorley's for breakfast. The place was busy despite the early hour but we managed to find a booth at the back beside the fire. Will ordered two plates of cutlets and a pot of coffee. We ate in silence, both of us preoccupied with what we had seen and heard that morning. When we had finished we pulled out our pipes and sat back, regarding one another through a haze of blue smoke. In the course of one night Angel Meadow had descended into misrule – doctors strait-jacketed and imprisoned underground, patients roaming the hallways unlocking doors – and in the midst of it all was a dead man.

In particular I feared for Dr Golspie – for we had found him soon after, lying upon the chaise in his consulting room. He had opened a vein in his arm with a scalpel 'to let the madness out', and his sleeves and furnishings were soaked in blood. He was raving and incoherent; muttering about angels and voices, about Rutherford, about wanting to stop the madness for he was too tired to manage it any longer . . . It had taken Pole and two burly attendants to hold the man down while Dr Hawkins and I bandaged his arm. Dr Hawkins had wanted to give him a dose of laudanum, but I was uncertain how it would react with the hashish he had taken, and so we had forced him into the strait waistcoat instead. There he was to remain until he recovered his senses.

I was relieved to be away, I could see that Will was too, though I knew we had to go back. We had to talk to Tom Golspie. Where had he been? Did he have any memory of his deeds? I could not believe so kind and gentle a man had been transformed into a murderer. And yet there was more to hashish than might be guessed – and he had eaten such quantities! Beside his chaise I had found the package I had brought up from the apothecary. It was quite empty. As far as I was aware he had consumed a massive twelve drachms of the sticky green paste in less than six hours. The stuff was so bitter I could not imagine how he had managed to ingest so much without being sick.

'How long before Dr Golspie is lucid?' said Will.

'A while yet. He gravely underestimated the stuff, though I told him what to expect.'

'Did you tell him he would go raving mad? That he would not even know his friends?'

'I said it was imperative that he approach it with extreme caution, perhaps taking a little more each time until he had achieved the effect he was looking for. And I told him always to take it when someone was with him. The first time we saw him, when Rutherford had him confined, I think his wits were quite within reach. When we found him in his room with his vein sliced open he had clearly taken a much larger dose – on top of what he had already ingested. The effects speak for themselves.

'Hashish has an interesting providence. Its excessive ingestion is associated with states of extreme violence in some eastern cultures, though I suspect there's much that's apocryphal in the interpretation. Of course, there are other variables – whether alcohol had been taken, the body weight of the patient – the usual things one might consider whether trying to ascertain the correct dose of anything. All these might make its effects more unpredictable.'

'It's an oriental concoction?'

'No more so than opium. Culpeper mentions cannabis as a remedy for inflammations and as a general analgesic. The seeds can be beneficial for headaches.' I put my hand to my brow. 'I could do with some now.'

Will looked at me askance. 'I hardly think so, Jem!' He drained his coffee cup. 'We have to go back. We have to talk to Tom. Oh Jem, I wish you'd never given him that package.'

'Yes, well, what's done cannot be undone.'

'Do you think he murdered Dr Rutherford?'

'I cannot say. You spoke to the basement attendant, I suppose? You spent the devil of a time down there.'

'Yes,' said Will. 'Though what he said amounts to very little. Edward Eden spent three days in the same cell last week. Without the gag. It seems he had plenty to say against Dr Rutherford for killing his mice and putting him down there.'

'There are many fingers pointing to Edward Eden. He hated Rutherford. He had a set of keys and could have gone wherever he pleased. He was, by his own admission, at large about the asylum all evening.' I sighed. 'I saw his mouse creeping into the mouth of one of Rutherford's phrenology skulls.'

'Not forgetting the fact that his handkerchief was covered in blood.'

'Yes. But to kill a man? To mutilate the body? I cannot believe it of him any more than I can believe it of Tom Golspie.'

'Some might say that both of those actions are more likely to be the work of a mad man than a sane one. Dr Hawkins intimated as much, and as the crime took place in an asylum, well, that in itself suggests an inmate as the most likely perpetrator.'

I said nothing.

'You think it unlikely?'

'I think it seems rather simple,' I said. 'Perhaps too simple, and because of that I think solving this riddle will, in all likelihood, be extremely difficult. But there are elements of all this that are so singularly grotesque that we do at least have some hope of uncovering the truth. It's the unusual that sets a thing apart and makes it notable, and easier to explain. The commonplace, by its very ordinariness, is the most perplexing. But perhaps we might start with some obvious questions. How many people were involved, for example?'

'You think this is the work of more than one?'

'I'm not sure. Not yet. Perhaps there were two people. One who killed him, and one who mutilated his body.'

'So we can't assume them to be one and the same?'

'Certainly, we can't,' I said. 'Though the fact that the body was set out so neatly would lead me to assume that either one person is responsible for everything, or that the murder and the mutilation were carried out by individuals closely associated in some way.'

'Once the fellow was dead one might assume that the main objective – his death – had been achieved. And yet—'

'Exactly!' I sat forward. 'You have put your finger right upon it, Will, for in this case death was not enough. Instead, someone felt moved to disfigure the corpse, and to do so in an elaborate and systematic way. Is there a message here? A warning, perhaps? Or a sign of justice completed? Is it a ritual? If so, then at whom is it aimed? At one person? A group? And why kill Dr Rutherford at all? Was it something he did? Something he heard or saw? What do we know of the man? For the sake of Edward Eden, we must also ask whether anyone would really do such a thing to avenge the death of some pet mice.'

'If they were a lunatic they might.'

'But Edward Eden is not mad, he is simple. A more kindly fellow one is unlikely to meet with. Oh, it would be easy to blame him. But whoever it was who stitched and sliced made sure to remove all traces – there were no scissors, no needles, no thread. Are the mad so inclined to orderliness?'

'Some of them,' said Will. 'Edward is fastidious.'

'So was Dr Rutherford.' I shrugged.

'And we must not forget that . . . that thing, whatever it was, that you took from the fire.'

'Yes,' I said. I could feel it, still warm in my pocket, though I was reluctant to discuss what it might signify – at least, not until we had seen Dr Golspie again.

'And the photograph—'

I took the image from my pocket book and passed it over. I could tell he was intrigued, puzzled. 'Is there something—?' I said.

'I'm not sure.' He stared at that curious ruined picture – at the awkward half-slumped posture, the grotesque tangled posy – 'I'm certain I have never seen this before – who would forget if they had? And yet there is something—' He shook his head. 'Perhaps it will come to me. May I keep it?'

'Of course.' I sat back and watched the smoke from my pipe coil upward in a tall blue question mark. 'Our reasoning should be based around what we know already – the real and concrete facts of the matter. We must be logical. And yet as the motivations that make human beings act in extreme ways are rarely rational, we must also bring our imaginations into play.' I rubbed my hands together. I could not help it. I had no love for Dr Rutherford, and although I could not applaud the manner and circumstances of his death it presented me with an opportunity for thinking and reasoning, for detection and inquiry that suited my inquisitive mind. 'We can leave nothing to chance. We can make no assumptions about anything or anyone. Whoever did this must be supremely confident – brazen almost. And clever. We should be in no doubt at all about that.'

'But we will catch him,' said Will. 'For we are cleverer still.'

I said nothing. It was a mistake I had made before – allowing my arrogance to cloud my judgement, assuming that I would always be one step ahead of my adversary. My conceit had led me to the foot of the gallows. '"Him"?' I said at last. I shook my head. 'Nothing is certain, Will. Not even that.'

Angel Meadow Asylum, 18th September 1852

There was lampblack and tallow in sacks and barrels, and kegs of turpentine the size of hogsheads sitting in the yard. Goblin dragged these into the factory and positioned them about the hot cauldrons of boiling polish. I gathered shoes and boots – collecting the most dried-out specimens I could find – and dumped them about the floor as mounds of kindling. Upstairs, in the office, Mr Knight and Mr Day lay where they had fallen. Mr Knight with the cobbler's last beside his head, Mr Day with the sharp spike of the boot-maker's awl projecting from his eye. A row of long black stitches sealed his mouth closed.

The factory and the workshop were dried out with years of warmth from the steam-heated blacking vats and they caught fire in an instant, the flames roaring and crackling. We watched the spectacle from the other side of the river, crouching out of sight as the place exploded. The smell – of burning fat and scorched leather – was fierce. The smoke was thick and black, acrid, and reeking of charred flesh.

Soon, small crafts appeared on the river, and shouts could be heard across the water. We saw men running along the bank

– nightwatchmen from nearby warehouses. Would the flames devour the whole of the waterfront? But then there were plumes of water spraying onto the inferno. There was another explosion, and a ball of flame rose into the heavens, reflected like a gigantic red moon in the river's dark waters. Inflamed by our night's activities, the two of us danced like demons, our shadows black as devils on the ground behind us.

But the night was not over yet and we had more work to do. Mr Day lived in a terrace of brown flat-fronted buildings not far from his factory. The street had once been fashionable, its simple façade admired for its classical elegance. But fashions change and it had become outmoded, an undesirable location, the long row of houses as plain as a workhouse. For a while Goblin and I stood at the street corner watching. We were looking and listening for signs of life but Mr Day's wife and daughter were away – he had told me as much himself and given it as the reason why he could stay late. I knew too that his servants had been given the night off – had he planned to take me home? The thought made me feel sick.

Equipped with Mr Day's keys, which I had taken from the chain about his neck, we entered his house. Inside, everything felt as though it was coated in a film of grease, as if each evening Mr Day brought home a miasma of boot blacking from the factory. I rubbed my hands on my dress. I could not get the smell and the stickiness off my fingers, and in my mouth the oiliness of the rag still coated my tongue, so that I felt as though I would taste the stuff for ever. If I closed my eyes I could still see the dancing flames of the burning blacking factory against my eyelids. If I screwed them closed tightly, so that the flames were obliterated, I saw the face of Mr Day instead, his mouth stitched shut, the awl sticking from his eye like a spoon from a grapefruit. I still see him now, in my nightmares.

The drawing room was crammed with objects: small spindly-legged side tables, sideboards, embroidery frames, work baskets and chests of drawers. On every surface there were ornaments – vases, figurines, candlesticks, clocks. The mantel was cluttered with more of the same, the walls hung about with paintings and mirrors and murky examples of needlepoint – the ham-fisted handiwork of Mr Day's wife and daughter. Beside the door a tall clock chipped away sullenly at the time, whilst a small yellow bird sat silent in a cage at the window. Goblin and I had never seen such opulence before, and it was as though we had entered a magical cave filled with treasures. And yet we had to be cautious.

'Take only what is small and valuable,' I whispered. 'Coin and jewels. No plate, no candlesticks. They are too heavy to carry and too difficult to get rid of.'

'I knows a fella that can get rid o' stuff,' Goblin said.

I took his hand. 'No,' I said. 'No one must know. It is our secret. You must promise, or all is lost.'

In Mr Day's bedroom we found a chest. It was easily opened using the smallest key on Mr Day's chain, and it was filled with coins stuffed into bags and tied with string. We emptied as much of it as we could into our pockets. Next, we visited Miss Day's room and examined her wardrobe. I took two dresses, both of them new.

Only when we had left, when we had locked the door behind us and flung the keys into a drain, did I feel safe. Once we were back in the streets leading to the Prior's I stopped. I took Goblin by the shoulders and looked into his eyes. 'You and I are bound together by blood and fire,' I said. 'They will hold us together for ever,' and I flung my arms about his neck.

'I'll always look after you, Kitty,' he said, his cheek pressed against mine. 'Always.' I squeezed him tight. I was crying,

though I would not let him see it. But Goblin could not save me from the thoughts that filled my head: I could still hear Mr Day's scream echoing there, could still feel the warm spurt of his blood against my hand. His eyeball had put up no more resistance than a poached plum.

Chapter Seven

Despite Dr Rutherford's death, the mundane commitments of our lives continued. I had prescriptions that demanded my attention and a batch of poke root ointment to make. Will had work to do too, for the plans for the House of Correction could not be avoided for ever. He sat at his drawing board while Gabriel and I worked at the bench. Customers came in and out. We had plenty of them, for the Flockharts had been well respected at St Saviour's and there were many who were pleased that I had stayed in the neighbourhood after the infirmary had gone. That morning they were more numerous than ever. They knew that I supplied Angel Meadow with remedies, and that I was friends with Dr Hawkins, and the news of Dr Rutherford's death was common currency about the neighbourhood already. I blamed Mrs Speedicut, aided and abetted by Gabriel, for we had seen the two of them whispering together outside the bakery as we came home. But I was not a gossip, even if my apprentice was, and I spent the morning shrugging off even the most persistent of inquirers. Most of them felt obliged to buy something trifling to cover up their nosiness, and we sold more peppermint lozenges and dandelion cough mixture in an hour than I usually sold in a month.

Will groaned as the door slammed closed for the umpteenth time. 'This place is worse than a fairground this morning,' he said. 'I cannot concentrate.'

'Gabriel?' I said. 'This is your doing?'

Gabriel's face, rosy with the heat from the stove, appeared round the door to the storeroom. 'Everyone knows that doctor's dead. That tall one from Angel Meadow.'

'Really?' said Will. 'And what've you heard, exactly?'

'That he died horrible.' His voice was a whisper and he covered his mouth with his hand. 'We oughtn't speak of it. I told Mrs Speedicut she shouldn't speak of it neither, but she don't listen to no one.'

'She certainly shouldn't have spoken of it to you,' I said.

'I'll not peach.' Gabriel looked from right to left in a theatrical manner, though there was no one in the apothecary but us. 'Don't want to be next!'

'Why on earth would Dr Rutherford's murderer be interested in you?' said Will. He reached for his hat. 'These matters are no concern of yours.'

Gabriel fell silent, his lips pressed together in a stubborn line. 'It's jus' like *Vicious Dick an' the Accursed Stranger*,' he said. 'In *Tales of Violence and Blight*—'

I clipped the back of his head with the flat of my hand. I had enough to think about without Gabriel's foolish prattling. 'You and your penny bloods,' I said. 'You should spend your money on something else. And your time.'

'Where are you going?' I said to Will as he pulled on his coat.

'The House of Correction.'

I took up my bag. 'I'll come with you as far as the Rents. I have some errands to run, and if I get asked once more whether I have been up to Angel Meadow this morning I shall go mad myself.' I turned to my apprentice. 'Gabriel, since you're partly the reason why so many people wish to come in and see us today, I will leave you here to attend to them.'

I had some preparations to take up to Prior's Rents – mallow and chickweed salve for itchy skin conditions, some wormwood and black walnut powder against worms, and my own special preparation for scabies. Not that I could achieve much lasting improvement with anyone there. If the conditions of their lives remained mired in squalor, filth and hunger, what use were salves and tinctures? Will disliked me going into the Rents on my own, and when he knew that's where I was heading he insisted on coming with me.

We entered the place via a dismal, blackened street called Prior's Fields. Foul alleyways branched off it, giving out onto small pestilent courts, or vanishing, ever deeper, into the crooked and teeming houses. The ground underfoot was a mire of straw, ordure, and muddy earth, scabbed with cobbles but devoid of paving. Pools of stagnant water lumped with refuse and shimmering with flies blotched the thoroughfare. Of lighting there was none, and they were not streets I would ever venture into after dark. Even during daylight the place was dim and murky, the sky overhead squeezed into a narrow grey ribbon. How anyone might live a life of cleanliness and decency here it was impossible to imagine. And yet those who made it their home were people, just as I was, just as Will or Dr Hawkins. Many of those to whom I gave my mixtures would share them randomly with others: any bottle of 'medicine' was seen as a panacea, as good for worms as it might be for the palsy, for the pains of childbirth or the hopeless agony of the cholera.

We toiled up steep rickety staircases, past damp walls and rotten doors, stepping over huddled groups of ragged children and piles of refuse. I gave a bottle of iron tonic to a tiny, cross-faced old woman so mounded with scarves and raggedy blankets and bits of ancient sacking that it was hard to tell where she ended and her bedding began. She had been in bed for a week already, enfeebled by a lifetime of bad diet, pestilent air and gin. She snatched the remedy with dirty fingers and yanked out the stopper with her hard wet gums. Sniffing the mixture cautiously, she pulled a face. She would have preferred a bottle of spirits. Perhaps it would have been more of a kindness to have provided one.

To a woman who appeared to be the mother of ten half-naked children I gave a specialist mixture of wormwood, chincona and back cohosh, a remedy designed to purge all manner of internal parasites. The children were listless and silent, bundled in rags like badly wrapped parcels, their little faces pinched and hollow. In the next room a woman was tearing up the pages of a Bible and using it for tinder.

'Got it from them wimmin,' she said when I asked.

'Them visitin' wimmin.' She screwed up another page and fed it into the small pyramid of sticks and clinker she had assembled in the fireplace. 'Said they was from some society or other. I weren't listenin'.' She coughed explosively.

We were on our way back to St Saviour's Street when we heard the shouts of men and women and the barking of dogs. I had heard sounds like that before, when I used to come to Prior's Rents with my father, or Dr Bain, and I knew what it heralded. As outsiders we would not be welcomed, though I was aware there would be at least one man who would be glad to see me.

I could tell from the way the ground was churned and mashed that many feet had passed that way not long before. From up ahead came the roar of an unruly crowd. I gripped my bag tightly. 'This way,' I said to Will, and I plunged down a vile thoroughfare flanked by oozing walls.

At the end of the passage the houses gave out onto a space formed by a collapsed building. Here and there makeshift pigsties had been erected out of the rubble. The space was confined on all sides by tall tenements, faces peering from the gaping windows. No sunlight reached us, and no breeze, so that as an arena it was dim and shaded, the press of bodies that filled it a stinking sea of unwashed clothes and flesh.

'Ugh!' said Will. 'What's this stuff on the ground? It looks like paste, rust-coloured paste. And the smell!' He sniffed, his face disgusted. 'I thought my nostrils had been assaulted by every stench the city had to offer but that . . . that *tang*. What in God's name is it?'

'The place is used as an impromptu butcher's yard,'

I said. 'When it's not filled with people.' Around us, the roar and scream of voices echoed off the walls in a dizzying pandemonium. A fat bluebottle droned back and forth before my nose in search of a ripe carcass. 'Stick with me,' I said.

'Where are we going?'

I took his arm. 'To the ringside.'

In front of us, two burly men were standing shoulder to shoulder, looking over the heads of the crowd. 'Excuse me, gentlemen,' I said as I tried to shove between them.

One of the men seized my collar. But the other punched his hand away, jabbing a dirt-blackened finger at my bag – a leather one with a rich oxblood patina that Dr Bain had given me years ago. 'Doctor, ain't 'e? Let 'im through.'

The bag, as I had expected, was the key with which I might unlock the crowd, and I flourished it before me as I pushed my way forward. 'Excuse me,' I cried. 'The doctors!' We encountered no hostility. Most strangers, no matter how well intentioned, could expect to be treated as fair game – worth robbing, at the very least – in such a crowd as this. I put my hand to my pocket book. It was still there. From up ahead I heard the dull, meaty slap of a fist striking flesh.

We emerged, gasping for fresh air but finding none, into a circle of faces – men, mostly, but women also. 'Who is it?' I shouted to the man standing beside me.

'Big Brendan O'Dowd,' he screamed in my ear. 'No one beats 'im!' His gaze was fixed on the scene before us. 'Go on, Brendan!' he shouted. 'Get in there!'

In the middle of the circle made by the crowd, two men stripped to the waist faced one another. The smaller of the two danced back and forth, his bald head glistening in the vaporous light, his fists held up. The other – bigger, taller and more thickset – stood motionless. His shoulders were covered in pimples and scars, streaked with dirt and matted with curly black hair. His face was blotched with the bruises of previous battles. His teeth appeared to be entirely absent and the bridge of his nose had collapsed – though whether this was due to fighting, from being poisoned in the womb by his mother's drinking, or from congenital syphilis, it was, from the ringside, impossible to say. He swung a thick hairy arm. The smaller man bobbed backward and the fist swept past without impact. The crowd roared.

Beside me, Will could only gape at the spectacle before us – not least because on the other side of the ring, between a pair of burly bellowing men, stood the last person either of us expected to see. Susan Chance's face was crimson with excitement, her mouth open in a yell. I could not hear what she was saying – for some reason I was grateful for it – though her intention was clear. The big Irish man was the one she had put money on. She had not caught sight of us, but like Will I could not take my eyes off her. Gone was the spry, upright young lady, Dr Stiven's cosseted darling, and in her place was a tiny, screaming, devil-faced figure. Her hands, now gloveless, were balled into fists, her hat was trampled in the mud at her feet. Her stance was pugnacious, crouched as if to dart away or spring forward as the occasion required, her eyes bright as she shouted – What? Blandishments? Oaths? Encouragement? She jabbed at the air twice with her left fist, bobbed sideways and then punched the air with her right. She moved with such speed that I could hardly believe what I had seen. Until she did it again, this time punching with the right and swinging a sharp left hook. And all the while she was shouting, her gaze fixed upon the big prizefighter.

The smaller of the two men bobbed back once more, out of the range of Big Brendan's giant fist. He had been forced to the edge of the crowd, his back to Susan who was standing almost directly behind him. And then, to my amazement, Susan Chance lifted the hem of her skirts. I caught sight of a stockinged leg, a red garter and a flash of white underthings as she kicked the fellow's arse with her steel-callipered boot. The crowd roared with laughter as the smaller prizefighter staggered forward, into the waiting arms of his huge opponent. Brendan grinned, revealing that he was not toothless after all, but was in fact the proud owner of a mouthful of shattered yellow stumps. He released his victim and drew back his right hand – just as the other fellow smashed his left fist hard up against the big Irishman's jaw. Brendan dropped to the ground like a giant lump of masonry and lay prone in the dust. There was a moment's stunned silence, and then the place exploded in uproar: from one half of the crowd a groan of disappointment, from the other a roar of delight, followed by a general hullaballoo as they turned to one another and began settling their debts.

The victor, his face cut and bloodied, was carried off – I presumed to the Six Bells, a hideous drinking den not far from the arena. The vanquished lay where he had fallen, recumbent in the mud. Someone seized me by the arm and began to drag me towards him, but at that moment something else caught my eye, something bright in that sea of dark clothing and dirty faces. I could not see what it was, though somehow it was familiar. I pulled my arm away. 'Wait—'

I glimpsed him for a moment only, but a moment was all I needed. A pale face with fair hair and white lashes. Dr Christie. His face was set in a half-smile, his gaze fixed, unwavering and unblinking, on Susan Chance. He was not accompanying her, that much was clear, for he appeared intent on hanging back, keeping her in sight even as he avoided her line of vision. His expression was a mixture of satisfaction and disgust, as if he was pleased to find her back in the Rents in so violent a location, and also that he was unsurprised by it. Had he followed her there? I would not have been surprised. Was he spying on her? I wondered whether to accost him, to ask what he meant by it, but it was too late. The crowd heaved and surged and he vanished amongst it.

Someone yelled into my face that if I had come to see to Brendan, I had better get on with it, and I was pushed forward onto my knees at the side of the fallen giant.

'What do you have for him?' said Will.

'Not much,' I said. 'Witch hazel and alcohol.' I dabbed at the man's cuts.

'Poor fellow,' said Will. 'From the stink of him he's already full of the stuff. He'd probably achieve much the same benefit if he licked his own wounds.'

'Look at his face,' I said. 'Today's pounding was no worse than he's received in the past.' I smeared some arnica balm onto the black and purple bruises beneath his eyes and examined his fists.

'Did you see her?' said Will, unable to keep his thoughts to himself any longer. 'She was here. She was watching! What an adventuress!'

I was tempted to point out that I regularly came to Prior's Rents alone, and had seen many such street fights. But I didn't. I tied a bandage around the knuckles of the unconscious man, and held a bottle of salts beneath his nose. He groaned, and opened bloodshot eyes. Around us the crowd was swirling like refuse in a drain, the press of bodies diminishing as people sought egress through alleys, lanes, passages I had not even noticed.

'Quite extraordinary,' said Will. 'Did you see her, Jem? She was right opposite us!'

'Yes, I saw her.' I couldn't say more. Susan Chance had been in my mind more than I cared to admit. I was used to a lonely life, but I could still remember how it felt to touch and be touched by someone I loved with my whole physical being, whose nearness made my skin prickle and my blood sing in my veins. And yet, as much as I longed again for love, I knew I could never have it. For who would want me? I could not be a husband any more than I could be a wife. But what about Will? Why should Will endure a similar loneliness? I watched him searching the crowd for Susan Chance, his face aglow, and felt sadness flood through me like salt water.

Chapter Eight

I arrived home to find Dr Mothersole rapping on the door to the apothecary with the head of his stick. 'My dear fellow.' He seized my fingers between his meaty paws. 'Such a tragedy. Such a loss to the profession and to Angel Meadow.' His skin was smooth and soft and slightly tacky to the touch, as if he were wearing a pair of flesh-coloured kid gloves.

'You knew Dr Rutherford well?'

'No,' said he. 'But I have only the highest praise for him and his work.' He swabbed at his face with a giant hand-kerchief. 'Forgive me, sir.' His eyes glistened with tears. 'I have a good deal of heart. Too much, some would say, and I am generous in my regard for others, especially when they are dead. It behoves us to remember Dr Rutherford with the profoundest respect.'

Dr Mothersole turned to his daughter, who waited at his side like a pilot fish. 'Write that down, Constance, my dear. *His bounty was as boundless as the sea.*' When she made no move to obey he added, 'Come along, my dear, write it down. It captures my largesse with admirable restraint.'

'But it is not your own, sir.' Constance Mothersole licked the tip of her pencil.

Dr Mothersole blinked. 'Not my own? What do you mean, not my own? I have just uttered it, have I not?'

'Those are Shakespeare's words.'

'Further evidence, if indeed it were needed, of my felicity of expression.' He waved a hand. 'My eloquence finds its equal!' He stuffed his handkerchief back into the bosom pocket of his coat, and stared down at me expectantly.

'After you, sir,' I said. 'And you, Miss Mothersole.'

Dr Mothersole eased his giant bulk through the apothecary door. Will had left me on St Saviour's Street and gone up to the House of Correction. Gabriel – who had regarded Dr Mothersole's appearance with alarm – seized an apple from the basket, snatched up his penny blood and disappeared into the yard. I would have Dr Mothersole and his daughter to myself.

A fold of paper was propped against the clock on the mantel – a note from Dr Hawkins – and I snatched it up and tore it open as Dr Mothersole removed his hat and lowered himself into my father's wing-backed chair before the fire. The contents were brief: *Edward Eden has been arrested.* I was not surprised. Would we be able to prove he was innocent before he ended up on the gallows?

Dr Mothersole sat with his ankles and feet daintily pressed together. His face was smooth as a pebble, his mouth a crimson rosebud between porcelain cheeks. His head had not a single hair upon it, and his lashes and brows were entirely absent, giving him a curious appearance, doll-like, and yet half complete, as if he had escaped from his maker before the finishing touches had been applied. He blinked his tiny eyes, his gaze darting to the pocket in which I had pushed Dr Hawkins's crumpled note.

'I realise that we are scarcely acquainted, you and I, though I assume you know who I am,' he said. 'My reputation generally precedes me.'

'I'm afraid I don't know you, sir,' I said. 'But then I don't claim to have made the acquaintance of every medical man in London.'

'Well, well,' he chuckled. 'I flatter myself, clearly. I am a guest at Angel Meadow, though I have known Dr Christie for many years in one way or another. Think of me as a visitor come to assist, a kindly uncle happy to help those who are less fortunate.' His eyes vanished into the folds of his cheeks as he gave what he presumably considered an avuncular smile. 'Dr Hawkins approved. My approach is not unknown to him, and he was only too pleased to have me come amongst the poor benighted souls in his care. Like so many of our asylums, there are more who are mad than there are doctors to treat them.'

'Dr Mothersole specialises in women's minds,' said his daughter.

'Quite so,' he said. 'And I have put my principles into action in my own life, for what use would a man be if he advised others to do one thing when he himself did another?'

'What indeed,' I said.

'My wife is a jewel of quiescent womanliness.' He held up his fat hands in a gesture that spoke of simplicity and obviousness. 'With her there has been no need to improve upon perfection. Constance, of course, is a very different matter. Take a look at her, Flockhart.'

'Sir, I—'

'Go on! Don't be shy, man, she's quite used to it. As you can see she is flat-chested, dull-complexioned, lank-haired, excessively tall, excessively angular and generally awkward.' He spoke as if the girl were not present, and I blushed for shame at how she must feel to have her private worth so publicly judged. 'The menses are absent too,' he went on. 'Intriguing, don't you agree? She has no role as a woman – she cannot be a mother, she cannot be an ornament. I'm afraid she is entirely redundant as no man would have her. I make use of her as best I can without inflicting her upon the world and she makes an admirable secretary.'

'I'm sure she is grateful for the opportunity to assist,' I murmured.

'Do you mock me, sir?' Dr Mothersole's mouth tightened into an angry button, all trace of medical bonhomie vanishing like smoke in a gale. I became aware of the numerous feminine touches visible here and there about the apothecary – the bowls of dried rose petals and orange peel I used to scent my room upstairs and which I had refreshed only that morning; the shawl I draped about my shoulders when the nights were cold; the raspberry leaf and valerian mixture I used for menstrual cramps which stood on the table beside him.

'Not in the least,' I said. I fumbled for something to say that might pacify him and, at the same time, reassure him of my manly self-belief. 'But don't you . . . don't you worry about the balance of her mind? With so much work to do, so many . . . words to write—' Miss Mothersole stared at me, her expression as cold as I deserved. 'I refer, of course, to her role as your biographer—'

'The richness and complexity of my thoughts are meat and drink to her.' Dr Mothersole laughed. 'They are so much more than *words*, sir, they are *ideas*. As a well-bred woman she is unlikely to get any of her own. And so I give her mine. It is a gift like no other.'

I glanced at Constance Mothersole, standing still and erect beside her father. She had not moved, or spoken. I noticed a muscle flexing in her jaw.

'And yet perhaps she does have ideas,' I said. 'Ideas of her own. How could she not, with you as her guardian and guide, with your own thoughts constantly before her? Perhaps she just chooses to keep silent – out of respect for you, sir.'

'I have schooled her never to venture an opinion.'

'And she does you credit. Yet you say she is an admirable secretary. Perhaps you *should* inflict her on the world – if I might be so bold as to use your own expression. After so intelligent and rigorous a training she can only be of value to others.' I glanced up at Constance as her father looked away, and winked. Her expression remained impassive.

Dr Mothersole smiled. 'You should marry, sir,' he boomed suddenly. 'Every man should marry, you know, and do it to advantage.' He eyed his daughter. 'Note it down, my dear. We are to have a section on aphorisms, I think, in our first volume? That's a good one. It is sage advice for all men.' Then to me he said, 'I must speak as I find, for my wife brought me twelve thousand a year and I have benefited from it greatly.' He looked about at the apothecary, its shelves crowded with bottles and jars, its table scuffed and stained and littered with apparatus. He wrinkled his nose. The place certainly had a sulphurous reek to it that day. 'You could do better, Flockhart,' he said. 'A man of your abilities.'

'I must sharpen my pencil,' said Constance.

'Allow me,' I said, stepping forward.

'Leave her, sir!' cried Dr Mothersole. 'What use would she be if she forever needed help with her utensils? Constance can whittle a point faster than you can say "cat".'

I stepped back. I had hoped to take a peek in her notebook – had she not been scribbling away for the entire evening on the night that Dr Rutherford was murdered? I could not help but wonder what she had written about me in it too.

'The madness of women,' mused Dr Mothersole. 'There is not an aspect of it that I am unfamiliar with – causes, manifestations, prognosis, treatment . . . all fall within my purview.'

'Dr Rutherford claimed a similar expertise,' I said.

'And Dr Christie also – though it is the criminal mind that most intrigues the two of them.' He chuckled again. 'There are so many mad, bad women! I have known Christie for a long time, though my methods are more cultured, more addressed to the soul of the patient than the mind.'

'Dr Christie's father was an asylum doctor too?' I said, thinking of the name I had seen on Dr Christie's watch.

'Yes indeed.' He shook his massive head. 'It is a sorry story indeed. Christie's father died . . . precipitately, in his own asylum. I'm certain I can rely on your sympathy and understanding, as well as your professional discretion. Besides, it is a tale not unlike that of your own father—'

'Quite,' I said sharply. I would not discuss my father's fate with this bloated stranger.

Dr Mothersole regarded me with amusement. 'I see I am correct in my assessment.' He whispered the words, as if he sought to tiptoe from a sickroom he had inadvertently entered. 'I am rarely, if ever, mistaken. I should be careful, if I were you, Mr Flockhart,' he added, 'if you do not wish to give yourself away.'

'I don't know what you mean, sir,' I said.

'Most people don't observe. They see, I grant you. They see enough to allow them to get by, enough to allow them to feed and clothe themselves, to eat and work, and to manage their affairs with others. But there are things before them that they do *not* see: the unconscious gesture, the involuntary hesitation, the hasty rebuttal. These things give us away, show who we really are. There are few who can master these tricks of the body, few who can read them as well as me. And yet I can read you as easily as I can read Constance here.'

'Can you?'

'You are ashamed, sir,' he said. 'Ashamed of who you are, I can see it quite clearly.'

He fell silent. His tiny eyes glittered, though whether this was due to mirth or craftiness I could not tell, for his face was so bloated with fat that all meaningful expression was obliterated from it. But I have been scrutinised all my life, pitied for my looks, my ugly face and tall thin figure. I have hidden who I am from the world for over twenty years, and I was not afraid of Dr Mothersole with his oblique threats and guesses.

'I confess I am still at a loss as to what you mean,' I said, more loudly than I had intended.

'There is no shame in madness, Mr Flockhart, for it cannot be helped. But there!' He slapped his legs. 'To the purpose, Mothersole! Mr Flockhart, I am here because I believe Dr Hawkins has asked you to . . . to make inquiries concerning the death of our dear colleague Dr Rutherford.'

I waited.

'The arrest of Edward Eden, which I'm quite sure you know about, is most likely mistaken and ill advised – his father will be furious, which is most unfortunate as the fellow is one of Angel Meadow's chief benefactors – not to mention the fees he pays for his son's accommodation—'

'More to the point is the fact that Edward Eden has no history whatsoever of violence. Why would he suddenly start now?'

'Quite so, quite so,' said Dr Mothersole. 'Well, he is bound to be released at any moment and then where will we be? Is there another likely suspect? I think there is, Mr Flockhart, I think there most definitely is.'

'You do?'

'Yes. You see there is . . . there is something about dear Dr Rutherford – I would remain silent, but I fear it is now germane to our current sad circumstances. You are aware that Dr Rutherford was well acquainted with Mr Stiven's ward, Miss Susan Chance?'

'Yes, Dr Hawkins told me.'

'He told you too, no doubt, that Rutherford wished to condemn the girl to the gallows? That he was convinced of her guilt?'

'Yes.'

'Did you also know that Rutherford had met the girl

before? That he had reason, and experience, to believe that she was capable of the most monstrous of crimes?'

'No,' I said. 'No, I did not.'

'Well, Mr Flockhart, I shall be brief, as it is brevity that suits such a tale as this.' He cleared his throat, and held a knuckle to his lips as if overcome with nausea at the prospect of further exposition. 'I understand that Rutherford originally met the girl some years earlier in the most benign of circumstances,' he said. 'Her mother was a seamstress, and the child Susan her helpmeet. Rutherford began intimate relations with the mother. It was against his better judgement, he said, but she was well known as a prostitute and such women make temptation their business. Besides, a man has urges and we must forgive what cannot be helped or undone. The girl was indifferent to her mother's casual affairs, or so it appeared, and was happy to continue with her needlework while Rutherford disported himself with the mother in the next room.

'But one morning, Rutherford was awakened by a sudden feeling of draughtiness about his person. He opened his eyes to find the bed clothes pulled back. Susan Chance was standing over him with a pair of scissors in one hand and his manhood in the other, and an expression on her face of such murderous fury that he scarcely knew her for her mother's child.' Dr Mothersole's porcelain cheeks had turned a dull crimson. He licked his lips. 'Dr Rutherford sprang from the bed and, to his lasting good fortune, the girl's blades snapped closed upon nothing but the bed sheet.

'There was no sign of the mother; it appeared that she had gone out to get breakfast, so Rutherford and Susan

Chance were quite alone. What happened next is most unfortunate, though perhaps no more than the girl deserved.'

'What happened next?' I said.

'It seems that, after a tussle, Rutherford seized the scissors. Then – as he put it, "so that she might learn a little respect for the organ she had been about to cut off", he gave the girl a beating, and a vigorous taste of what her mother had been enjoying for the past seven nights.'

All at once the air in the room had become heavy, stifling and still. The scratching of Constance's pencil stopped. She and I exchanged a glance. She looked appalled, and I could feel my cheeks flaming, but Dr Mothersole was talking once more. He had not noticed the horror on our faces, despite his much vaunted powers of observation.

'As you can imagine,' he said, 'Dr Rutherford never went back to the place, and it is no fault of his that the girl's mother sank so deep into degradation and infamy that a few years later she put her own daughter out to tender. The consequences of that are well known to us all.'

I said nothing. Why had Dr Hawkins not told me this? Perhaps he had not known of it if it had taken place some years before Susan's trial. 'Is it true?' I said at last. 'Can you be sure? Has Susan Chance corroborated it?'

'There is no reason to think it is *not* true. Whether Susan Chance has spoken of it or not is hardly relevant now – who would listen to such a one even if she did? But now that Dr Rutherford is dead, and under such circumstances, it seems only right that the matter should be revealed. And I am the one to reveal it! It was Christie who told me the tale, though he was reluctant to come to you himself.' He shook his head. 'Christie is a man of circumspection, but *I am a man to seize the moment where others fear to act.* Constance, write that down!'

'Why did Rutherford not mention this at her trial?'

'He told Christie that the girl should be judged on the facts of the case in hand, and not by her previous actions.'

'How magnanimous of him,' I murmured. 'I imagine he was also reluctant to reveal himself as someone who sees fit to violate a child and turn her mother into a whore. But why are you telling me, sir? Would it not be more prudent to tell the police?'

'I feel you are a far more useful repository for the information I have just divulged than any police inspector might be. When the facts of the matter pertaining to Dr Rutherford's death are finally discovered I will be sure to testify as to the truth of its account. Dr Christie and I are in full agreement.' Dr Mothersole rose to his feet. The seams of his waistcoat creaked like the timbers of a galleon as he drew himself up. 'I have said what I came to say, and you may do as you see fit with the information. I'm sure you see it as Dr Christie and I do, Mr Flockhart.' He shook my hand. 'Good day to you, sir.'

Chapter Nine

Will came back from the House of Correction in the afternoon just as I was making a pot of tea. I could tell straight away that he had something to tell me, but I was too full of my own news, too eager to have his opinion on what Dr Mothersole had said to let him speak. When I came to the part about the scissors, and Dr Rutherford, I saw him blanch.

'If what Mothersole says is true,' I said when I had finished, 'it gives Susan Chance an even stronger motive. Especially as Dr Stiven and Susan Chance were both staying in Dr Hawkins's old rooms at Angel Meadow that evening.' I shook my head. 'I cannot believe it of her. She has too much to lose.'

'And yet, she has been diagnosed as insane already. There's every chance the malady might come upon her again. Dr Stiven always carries a strait waistcoat when he is out with her, but what of those times when she slips away from him? She was alone in Prior's Rents this morning.

How many other times might she have been at large and unattended?'

'So you think she is mad?' I said.

'I think it might come and go. Is such a thing possible? With the evidence placed before us in this way it's hard to think otherwise. And yet,' he flung himself back in his chair. 'Perhaps it is just that she defies convention. We saw her today in a place no lady should ever be seen – the front row of a bare knuckle fight. Some might say she looked wild – ungoverned and devilish – a vision of madness. But that's only because we expect her to be demure and ladylike. Perhaps we just saw someone who was happy, excited and uninhibited. Someone who was already sufficiently familiar with that milieu to derive pleasure from the spectacle.' He sat forward again. 'There is something about the girl that intrigues me, Jem, I admit it. I've no love for the vain and cosseted women of London. I'm drawn to those who speak their mind, those who show spirit, who resist the harness others would put upon them, those who are not like everyone else—'

'Goodness, Will!' I said. 'I think you might actually be a little bit in love with her!' My voice sounded shrill in my ears.

He grew still at that. His face was in shadow, so I could not make out his expression, but I could sense he was looking at me. 'If I am it is only because she is something like you,' he said. He sighed, and looked away.

I could not think what to say. I *had* thought he was falling in love with Susan Chance. And yet here he was telling me . . . what, exactly? That he loved me? He had said as much once before – back when St Saviour's was still standing, when my father was alive and my heart was owned

134

by Eliza Magorian. I closed my eyes at the thought of her. I knew I could not offer Will more that my friendship, but I could also not bear to have less than his love.

'This is not the time for a conversation such as this,' I muttered.

'No,' he said. 'I suppose it isn't.'

For a moment there was a pause, a heaviness between us. I took a searing mouthful of tea and said, 'Well then, are you going to acquaint me with what happened to you today, or not? There's something on your mind, I can tell.'

'Can you?' He sat back in his chair, putting his boots up onto the stove to warm his feet. 'Why, Jem, we are just like an old married couple, whether you like it or not!'

I grinned. 'Well?'

'I had been wondering about this.' He put his hand into his pocket and drew out the ruined photograph, the burnt edges still flaked with ash, turning his fingers black. 'You remember I said there was something that was familiar about it, but I could not place what it was? Today, I found out. Look at it closely. What do you see?'

I stared at the burnt-away face, the ragged dress, the tangled bouquet. I turned the picture over. The back was blank. 'I see nothing,' I said.

'And yet there is something,' said Will. 'Something about this that is unique and revealing.'

I sat forward. All at once I sensed we were about to make progress.

Will told me that he had gone to the House of Correction for a meeting with the prison governors. He had arrived

early because he wanted to examine the roof space and
the top floor of the building with a view to arguing against
the expansion of the existing structure. One of the
wardens was sent to accompany him – she had a full set
of keys, and was familiar with the quickest ways about the
place. She took Will up a winding staircase that emerged
at the topmost corridor, and along a narrow passage that
traversed the length of the main building. Windows on
the right-hand side looked out over the flat roof of the
floor below; on the left-hand side a row of doors gave out
into various attic storerooms and cupboards. Will climbed
out onto the flat roof, peering down into the dirty patch of
mud and cinders that was the women's exercise yard, and
made his examination. He climbed back inside, and then
went in and out of the various rooms, opening windows
where he could, investigating the quality of the brickwork
and the pointing, and measuring the width and breadth
of the walls. Mostly the rooms were used for storage. In
one of them they came across contraptions of restraint –
gyves, bridles, manacles, heavy chains and straps – so cruel
and wicked-looking that Will could not look at them. The
warden laughed at his squeamishness.

'You think we don't use them things now?' she said.
'Course we do! We got plenty more downstairs. These was
for them what was bound for Van Diemen's. And them
what misbe'aves.' She chuckled. 'They don't misbe'ave
for long once they've got the bridle on! It don't take long
to make 'em quiet in this place.'

Another room contained numerous chests of small
wooden drawers. Will had seen drawers just like them
downstairs in the administration wing when he was first
shown around the place. 'Files,' said Will's guide. 'Old

uns.' Something stirred in the back of his mind, but it was gone again before he could place it.

It was the next room, however, that gave Will pause. A bright, airy chamber, north facing, it had two windows that looked out across the city, and two skylights that stared up at the ochre-coloured clouds of the London morning. Behind the door there was a table, littered with bottles, photographic plates, cloths, and sheaves of paper curling at the edges. In the centre, beneath the skylights, was a chair – straight backed, un-cushioned and, on closer inspection, bolted to the floor. Facing the chair was a large mahogany camera on a tall tripod of wood and tarnished brass. To one side, a small darkroom had been erected, walls of cheap wood partitioning off the dimmest corner.

He asked the attendant about it, but she had no idea who had used it and why. Of course, the sight of the camera, the chair, the darkroom, reminded him of the photograph we had found that morning. He still had it in his pocket and he took it out. Had it been taken in that room? He thought it unlikely. The image was a simple one without any background to distinguish it. Besides, what remained of the image was so charred, so partial that it was impossible to see very much at all, apart from the hands and body of the subject. And yet there was something, Will said, something familiar about it that still bothered him.

The warden didn't seem to mind the length of time Will was spending looking about the place, and she sank onto the chair in front of the camera with all the grace of a dropped laundry bag. Looking at the woman sitting there with her hands in her lap, the camera's inscrutable eye trained upon her, gave Will an idea: What if he took her likeness? Might that curious feeling of familiarity crystallise into something real, something useful? He had some knowledge of the calotype process, though he had not undertaken any photography for a long time. Could he do it? Once the idea had gripped him it would not let him go. He used his handkerchief to clean the lens and the plates, checked that he had everything set out correctly in the darkroom, and began.

His subject was the most unprepossessing of women – short and fat, a stranger to any form of corsetry, her clothing so patched and stained that it was a wonder she was not more often mistaken for one of the inmates herself. She proved most adept at sitting quite motionless and staring vacantly into space, which was exactly what was required.

'The result,' he said now, 'is not without merit.' And he pulled from his pocket a small calotype the size and shape of a *carte de visite*. It showed a fat woman sitting in a chair, her bulldog looks and grubby dress just as Will had described.

'Well?' I said. 'I see nothing that might connect the two.'

Will clicked his tongue. 'For one so observant you are exceptionally blind today. Look here,' and he pointed to the bottom of the image. 'You see?' I snatched my magnifying glass off the table. There, unmistakable in the lower right-hand corner, just where the prison attendant's dress ended and the background began, there was a blurring, a greyish smear as if a finger had smudged a small portion of the image into indistinctness. It was plain to see, once it had been pointed out, an indelible flaw embedded in the picture as irrevocably as the image itself.

'The lens is cracked,' he said. 'It shows up as a blur when a photograph is taken.' He handed me the image he had culled from Dr Rutherford's fire. Burnt and ruined as it was, the right-hand corner remained untouched by the flames. 'And on this one?'

'It is the same!' I cried. 'The very same!'

'Of course I remembered then,' said Will. 'I had seen a box of old records, months ago, in a storeroom downstairs at the House of Correction. Each of them had a photograph attached, and each of the images had that blurred flaw across the corner. I knew there was something about it that I had seen before.'

'Well done,' I said. I grinned at him and clapped my hands. 'Well done indeed. And was this image in the old files too? Did you have a look?'

'Yes, I did,' said Will, 'And no it isn't.'

'Oh.' I sounded disappointed. I could not help it.

'At the governor's meeting I asked about the camera. The superintendent said he knew nothing of it. Then, one of the others who had been there some twenty years or more said that they had only used photographs for a while as it was too time-consuming, but remembered the chap who took them.'

'Was it Rutherford?' I said. My heart was suddenly racing. 'Did Rutherford take the pictures?'

'No,' said Will. 'Apparently it was a chap named Gunn. He's dead now. Afterwards no one bothered to find a replacement, though it seems Dr Christie is quite interested in the approach.'

'Oh,' I said. I held up the burnt fragment. I could feel my excitement draining away. 'So this is the image of a convict? Why would Dr Rutherford keep such a thing?'

'No,' said Will again. 'She is not wearing a convict's dress. This is a different image altogether.'

'Whose?'

'That, I cannot say.'

'Oh. Oh well.'

'Actually I quite enjoyed taking the woman's likeness. I'm going to ask the governors whether I can have that old camera—'

'I think you should,' I said. I could not help but feel frustrated.

Angel Meadow Asylum, 18th September 1852

But Goblin and I hardly knew how to live when we were not in the Rents and it was not long before we drifted back to the world we knew – back to that thieves' kitchen. We sat on either side of the fire and we laughed to find ourselves back where we had started. I had a fine dress, dainty shoes and bangles on my wrists, but Goblin had nothing, nothing but bruises from the fights he had got into, for there were plenty of crooks who wanted me for their own – a clever girl who had learned to speak like a lady would be useful to anyone wanting to gull the quality out of a few sovereigns. How Goblin suffered because of it! But he never complained, and he never asked me for anything.

It wasn't long before they found us. There is no honour among thieves, no matter what the penny bloods say. We were betrayed by our own kind, for there was a reward upon our heads paid for by Mrs Day, and what comradeship we thought we had found amongst those we had known all our lives was illusory. The remains of Mr Knight and Mr Day were never found, for the heat of that fire had turned their remains to cinders and blown them away on the wind. Whether they had been murdered or not was impossible to prove; whether the fire had been set could not be wholly established. But I had taken Mr Day's keys and we had burgled his house. Our complicity was indisputable – and, when they came for us, I was sitting before the fire wearing Miss Day's dress and Mrs Day's jewellery.

It is said that the air of Newgate was enough to kill a man, and that those inside it numbered the worst, the most degraded and wicked men and women in all England. They are wrong. The worst men in England make up judge and jury, are masters and property owners who crush the rest of us and drive their carriages over our bones. My fellow prisoners might be vicious and selfish, but it was life that had made them so. Capricious and unfair, it was a life that put some men above others, made some rich and some poor, that forced those with nothing to seek comfort in the only way they knew how – by taking from those who had more than enough. I had only sympathy for the wretches who surrounded me, though they tore the ribbons from my hair and left me with nothing but the clothes I stood up in. We women were kept together in long airless wards, the windows high in the walls and thickly barred, so that the light that entered was dim and tainted. Inside there was such a crying and wailing – some had children with them, though how these fared in that hideous place I had no idea, for they must surely have suffocated, or else died of misery and want before their mothers were released. Many of the women were barely clothed, but covered themselves as best they could with whatever rags they could lay their hands on. We slept – if such an activity might be called sleep – laid out side by side, like bodies in a plague pit, though the noise raged all night. The air was thick with our own stink, and we were afforded no

dignity whatever, obliged to manage ourselves, and all that made us women, with miserable fortitude.

I denied the murder of Mr Knight and Mr Day. I denied setting alight to the blacking factory. I admitted only the theft. The deaths of the two men and the destruction of their premises could not be proved to be my handiwork, but I had clearly profited from the death of my employer. I said he had tried to rape me, that I had been assaulted and molested. No one listened – I was the daughter of a whore, what more might be expected but that I would turn to similar pursuits? I was sentenced to hang. Goblin – younger, and therefore clearly led stray – received seven years' transportation. I saw him in the courthouse. Only a few weeks had passed, but he was not the boy I had known. He had grown hard and fierce. His face bore the marks of ill-usage – a black eye, another missing tooth, a part of his ear lobe torn away. Poor Goblin. I never saw him again after that, and I can only hope that he found happiness; that he succeeded where I have failed.

I was to be hanged on 13th July. My mother did not come to see me. I heard she had died, and I was glad she had been spared the spectacle of watching her only child standing on the scaffold. I remembered how she had stitched and stitched as the light faded around us, the men's feet heavy on the stair. She had left me with one certainty in my heart: that I would do all I could to keep from living a life like hers. Now, I would not even have the chance to try. The only person who did come to see me was the Ordinary, as was the right of all of us who were to spend our last night on earth in the condemned cell. But there was nothing I wanted from him. What had God ever done for me? How might he help me now? And so I sent the man away. Alone, I watched the evening bleed

143

into the night, the night seep into a crimson dawn. The window was small and double barred, the room itself a foetid dungeon hardly fit for a dog. My ankles were chained, though where I might run to was a mystery for the door was triple locked. I lay upon my narrow plank bed and felt the lice crawling on my skin, though I would be free of such petty torments soon enough. The crowd, I knew, expected a good death. I was to give them one they would never forget.

Chapter Ten

The following day Will and I went up to Angel Meadow. The day had turned grim; the clouds barely cleared the tops of the houses but lay, brown and unmoving, as if weighted down by the city's pestilence. The asylum windows stared out at the city. At the door, I did not ring the bell to summon Pole, but unlocked it myself, Dr Hawkins's iron keys cold and heavy in my hand.

Downstairs in the men's wing the inmates were agitated. No one had told them that Dr Rutherford had been murdered – Dr Hawkins had given express instructions that the matter should not be mentioned by anyone – but all the same they could sense that something was wrong. A number of idiots with whom Edward had been particularly friendly were gathered at the door to his room. They surged towards Will and me as we approached and the babble of voices grew in volume. *Where's Edward? Has he gone? Is Dr Rutherford angry again?* Some of them were crying, others moaning and rocking from side to side, though I was certain that most of them had no idea what all the emotion was about.

'I brought him this.' A fist was thrust into my face. Its owner opened it to reveal an earthworm writhing upon his palm. Two others had caught mice and were holding them up by their tails. 'Presents!' shouted one. 'For Edward!'

Pole was waiting for us outside Dr Golspie's room. 'I've told 'em you was coming, sir,' he said. 'You'll be wanting to see him for yourself, sir?' He jangled his keys. But I had my own keys now and I did not need a chaperone. I jangled mine back.

'Thank you, Pole,' I said. 'You may go now. Or at least—' I gestured at the patients milling about outside Edward's room. 'Perhaps you might see that everyone is settled?'

Dr Golspie's room was rather crowded. Dr Christie and Dr Hawkins stood side by side looking down at Dr Golspie, who had evidently just been released from his strait jacket. He was sitting on his chair running his hands through his hair. His skin was as pale as suet, with a sickly sweaty sheen to it. The room was warm and close, and stank like a rabbit hutch on a summer's day.

'For God's sake, Tom,' I said. 'Look at the state of you! And the smell of the place!' I marched across the room and threw open a window. In fact, I was surprised his mania had not lasted longer, though I did not mention it.

Dr Golspie looked up at me ruefully. 'I believe apologies are required, Jem. Will. I have behaved abominably.' He shook his head. 'And Dr Hawkins tells me that Dr Rutherford is dead.' His shaking fingers plucked at his pale dry lips.

'You find Dr Golspie somewhat recovered, Jem,' said Dr Hawkins.

'A reckless experiment, sir,' said Dr Christie. He looked tired, the black circles of a sleepless night that ringed his eyes making his lashes look like gossamer. He was watching Dr Golspie closely. 'And yet one that is not without merit.' He looked at Dr Hawkins. 'The patient is yours, sir. But, may I?'

'Yes, yes, of course.' Dr Hawkins waved a hand.

'I'm no one's patient,' snapped Dr Golspie, recoiling. 'Get away from me, Christie.'

'Come along, sir,' said Dr Hawkins. 'We cannot let you out of this room until you demonstrate that you are master of your own senses.'

'I am quite in charge of myself,' said Dr Golspie.

'In which case, you will demonstrate this by submitting to the ministrations of your colleague.'

Dr Golspie remained silent while Dr Christie took his pulse and temperature, peered into his eyes, tested his reflexes. 'I would recommend rest and a lowering diet,' he said. 'Custards and other milk-based foods in particular.'

Dr Golspie snorted.

'I concur, Dr Christie,' said Dr Hawkins. 'Were you in your right mind, Golspie, you would see the value of the diagnosis. I might also add, sir, that I am not entirely certain that you are suited to a career in medicine. This reckless approach—'

'It was a mistake, sir,' said Dr Golspie. 'I see that.'

'Well, it hardly matters now. What matters is what has happened. Edward Eden has been arrested and charged with the murder of Dr Rutherford—'

'Edward?' said Dr Golspie. 'He would no more hurt Rutherford than—'

'We are all aware of that,' said Dr Hawkins. 'And yet as far as the police are concerned he is a lunatic, he hated Dr Rutherford and – thanks to you – he had a set of keys in his possession and was at large about the asylum all night.' He sighed. 'We must correct this injustice as soon as possible. Can you remember what you did? Where you went? What, if anything, you saw?'

'I cannot,' whispered Dr Golspie. 'My mind is empty of any recollection of what happened after . . . after I . . .' He looked in dismay at his bloodied sleeves. 'Oh, God. Oh, God!'

'Indeed, sir,' said Dr Hawkins. 'You attempted to bleed yourself – had it not been for the timely intervention of Mr Flockhart and Mr Quartermain I daren't think what might have become of you. Dr Golspie, you *must* remember. We must prove that it was not Edward Eden, but we must also prove that it was not you.'

Dr Golspie put his head in his hands. 'I remember leaving that evening, sir, shortly after I'd had a disagreement with Dr Rutherford. I went to my room and I prepared the hashish paste as Mr Flockhart had instructed. It was horrible and bitter. I thought I would be sick so I washed it down with a few slugs of brandy.'

'Inadvisable,' I muttered.

Dr Golspie pressed his palms against his eyes. 'I remember wondering when it would happen, when the doors in my mind that lead from sanity to insanity would open. And then all at once I was laughing, laughing uncontrollably. I looked at my hands. They looked huge, as though they were no longer a part of my body but somehow were the hands of someone else. I sat staring at them. It felt like a long time. Perhaps it wasn't. The candle was bright, so bright that I felt I could hear the sound it made, a high-pitched singing as it gave off its luminescence, like the sound of angels—'

While he was talking Dr Golspie's face had taken on a rapturous expression. But then he paused, and dabbed at his lips with his handkerchief. When he continued, his voice was low and cautious, and I had the feeling that he was struggling to remain his own master.

'I could hear the roar of the fire in the grate. It was loud, the loudest thing in the room and I was amazed I had never noticed it before. I had the impression that I could hear . . . I could hear the voice of the devil himself roaring. The longer I stared at the fire the more acute the impression became, so I ran out into the corridor. It was cooler there, and I forgot about the fire completely. All at once I felt full of life and strength. My mind was . . . was altered, my senses perceiving sensations that had been hidden from me – it was then that I went back to the party.'

'Do you remember being restrained?' asked Dr Christie.

'Yes,' said Dr Golspie. 'I remember that it was you who pulled my arms tight and forced that bridle between my lips, Christie.'

'You were deranged,' said Dr Christie. 'There was a room full of witnesses who will testify to it.'

'Pole took you downstairs,' said Will. 'Do you remember that too?'

'He put me in a cell. I could not move. The hashish made me feel sick and I thought I would vomit. I was dizzy too and I lay still, very still, and hoped it would pass. The next thing I remember was Edward Eden bending over me. He set me free, I assume, for I cannot remember that either, and yet you tell me that's what happened. I don't know what happened next, or where I went.'

'Next, you went up to see Dr Rutherford,' I said.

'Did I?'

I drew my handkerchief from my pocket, and unwrapped the charred oval object I had culled from the cinders of Dr Rutherford's fire. 'Do you know what this is?'

'No,' said Dr Golspie.

'It is a potato,' I said. 'Your potato.'

'Mine?'

'It is a stimulus. For Mrs Fitzwilliam.'

'Oh,' said Dr Golspie. All at once his face cleared. 'Yes,' he said eagerly. 'Yes, it is. I *did* go to see Dr Rutherford. He was surprised to see me.'

'I'm sure he was,' muttered Dr Christie.

'He looked . . . It was as if he was expecting someone else.'

'Well,' said Dr Christie. 'I'm quite certain that whoever he might have been expecting it certainly wasn't you.'

'What happened next?' I said.

'He mocked me.' Dr Golspie took the potato in his hand. He turned it over and over until his fingers were black with soot, as if the feel of the thing awoke the memories of what he had done with it. 'He mocked my ideas, my approach to medicine – my attempts to understand madness. He was holding one of his damned phrenology skulls. Caressing it. Telling me its characteristics.' Dr Golspie looked at his fingers, as if seeing them properly for the first time. 'I threw my potato at his head as hard as I could.'

'It smashed the mirror?'

'Yes,' Dr Golspie's face cleared, so that he looked just like his old self. 'Yes,' he said again, this time with more confidence. 'I was frightened then. I thought he would ring for Pole, or some of the attendants, to take me away again, but he didn't.' He frowned. 'He didn't. I wondered why.'

'So what did he do?'

'He laughed. He said, "Is hurling vegetables the best you can do? Go away, Golspie. Go away and rave at the moon. It is all you are fit for."' Dr Golspie put his hand to his head. 'I began to feel dizzy. The noise, the hot room, the skulls, Dr Rutherford's grinning face.' He wrung his hands together and his voice rose in agitation. 'The light was too bright. It dazzled me, blinded me as if I had knives in my eyes, and I had the most peculiar image flash into my mind, a face but not a face, eyes and lips and noses, but not put together properly, not as it should be.' Dr Golspie's cheeks were suddenly paler than ever, and a sheen of sweat gleamed on his forehead. His lips had drained of blood, and his expression was now so fearful that I could hardly bear to look at him. He swallowed, and took a ragged breath. 'It was the face of a demon, Jem, of a monster.' He put his hands over his eyes. 'It was looking straight at me, and yet not at me. I knew its name, and yet I did not know it. It knew me, I could tell. I could sense it. Oh!' Dr Golspie lurched to his feet and seized me by the shoulders. 'Jem,' he whispered, 'I can see it even now, in my mind's eye. Have I gone mad? Tell me I have not gone mad.' His breath was sour, his eyes wild and darting.

'You killed Dr Rutherford!' Dr Christie shouted. 'That's what you remember!'

'No!' cried Dr Golspie. 'He was alive when I left.'

'Yes! These are fragments of memory – eyes, lips, monstrous faces – these are the fragments that speak of your own murderous act.'

'Christie,' said Dr Hawkins. His voice was calm, authoritative. He shook his head.

'Fragments,' whispered Dr Golspie. 'Like knives in my eyes.' He looked from me, to Dr Hawkins, and back again. And then all at once his face cleared, and I knew that Dr Golspie was as sane as any of us.

Chapter Eleven

Dr Golspie sank back onto his chair. 'I didn't kill Rutherford.'

'But you have as good as admitted—' cried Dr Christie.

'Dr Christie,' I said. 'Let us not be hasty. If Dr Golspie had murdered Dr Rutherford then he would surely have been covered in blood. Did he commit the crime, then change his clothes and wash himself? Of course he didn't. When Will and I found him the blood we could see was on the furnishings, on his own hands, and on his shirt sleeves. Surely it would have been daubed on the door handle if he had entered his own rooms after murdering Dr Rutherford. It would be on his shoes and trousers. Dr Rutherford's room was neat and tidy; would Dr Golspie, in his madness, really have cleared away scissors, needle, thread – all the evidence of his handiwork?'

I was thinking quickly. Even to my own ears my

arguments sounded weak and desperate. Dr Golspie *had* been covered in blood, there was no mistaking it.

'Besides,' said Will quickly. 'Dr Hawkins, you saw Rutherford's corpse – those neatly stitched lips and eyes. Could that really have been the work of someone as deranged as Dr Golspie was that night?'

Dr Hawkins did not answer.

'He managed to open his own vein with surprising accuracy,' said Dr Christie. 'He might equally have stitched up Rutherford's face. And to kill a man with one of his own instruments? Is that not the work of one who is insane?'

It was true, I could not deny it. Was Dr Golspie guilty of such a crime? I could not believe it of him.

Dr Hawkins shook his head. 'I hardly know what to think,' he said. 'Dr Golspie, you must remember what you did, what you saw.'

But Dr Golspie was staring at the ground, and he did not reply. It was as though he had retreated into his own mind, was so absorbed by his thoughts that he could not attend to anything else. And yet, as I watched him, I sensed that he was quite aware of what was going on around him, and entirely certain of what he was being asked. Dr Hawkins sighed, and turned away. Dr Christie shook his head and plucked out his pocket watch to check the time. At that moment, unnoticed by the others, Tom Golspie glanced up at Will, then at me, and I knew instantly that he had something he wanted to tell us.

Dr Hawkins opened the door. Pole was standing on the other side of it. The turnkey's melted face looked moist and yellow above the grubby folds of his neckerchief. The watery sunlight, filtered by the half-closed window blinds, glanced off his scars and pockmarks and gave his skin the texture of grated cheese. I had the impression that he had been listening, and his gaze – what one could see of it – searched the room hungrily, looking from one face to another before settling on Dr Golspie. And yet Pole always looked shifty. It was not his fault that his appearance was so hideous, and I did my best never to judge a man's character by his looks.

'What is it, Pole?' I said.

'Nuthin'.'

'You realise that those who listen at doors seldom hear things that are meant for them?'

The man scowled. 'Weren't list'nin',' he said. 'Were standin'. Helpful like.'

'Pole,' Dr Hawkins said, 'could you see that a bath is brought up for Dr Golspie. He will take it here, in his room. And find him a change of clothes too. Ask Mrs Lunge. I'm sure some can be procured.' He turned to Dr Christie. 'I think he might as well go home, Christie. He needs rest – and some lowering foods, of course. His own bed is the best place for him. He will not run away – where might he go? I can send Mrs Lunge round with a custard later.'

Dr Christie looked down in disgust at the blood-stained and dishevelled figure of Dr Golspie. His watch was still open in his fingers and he snapped it closed, seeming gratified to note that the sound made Dr Golspie flinch. 'Very well,' he said. 'Though I think you would be wise to keep him here.'

'He's not under arrest,' said Will. 'And you're not the police inspector.'

Dr Hawkins raised a hand. 'I am sending him home and

that's an end to it. He lives not far from the apothecary, Jem. Perhaps you might call in on him now and again, just to make sure all's well. And you, Quartermain. But no more hashish. The man's mind has been through enough. And we want him to remember.'

The lunatics who had been clustered around Edward Eden's doorway were nowhere to be seen. Dr Hawkins looked relieved. He chivvied us out of the room and shut the door, leaving Dr Golspie stretched out on his chaise longue, his hands over his face.

The four of us walked down the passage in the direction of the gentlemen's sitting room. A curious sound echoed along the hallway, a discordant wailing and moaning that, despite its unpleasantness on the ear, had a peculiar familiarity. Dr Hawkins cocked his head. 'What the devil is that?'

'It's Lead Kindly Light,' said Will. 'I think.' It grew in volume as we listened, a mixture of singing, strumming and a curious draughty fluting sound. The singing had been joined by other voices, ones that gave no thought to tune or melody but sought only to add noise. Gradually, the bellowing accompaniment grew louder, the singing and fluting sinking beneath the cacophony like an orchestra swallowed up by a tempest.

'The Ladies' Committee,' muttered Pole. 'Mrs Lunge let 'em in.'

I had never met the Angel Meadow Ladies' Committee before – something I congratulated myself upon. Every medical institution in the city had one, a gaggle of interfering women eager to get out of their drawing rooms and into the lives of those less fortunate than themselves. At St Saviour's, the Ladies' Committee had been the bane of my life. Reading the Scriptures to those too sick and infirm to object or escape was their principal activity. On Monday, Wednesday and Friday afternoon they had filed through the wards in a bustling gang, their skirts sweeping aside spittoons, their dismal bunches of ragged chrysanthemums cluttering up table-tops, their shrill voices the murderers of sleep. Here at Angel Meadow, however, it appeared that Bibles had been set aside in favour of hymn books. That morning the ladies were in the gentlemen's sitting room, a large bright chamber at the far end of the corridor. The place was full to bursting with patients and attendants, their attention upon the fireplace and the group of women stationed before it. Most of the ladies were unknown to me, though that morning I recognised Mrs Hawkins and Mrs Mothersole in their midst. In the centre of the group, most unexpected of all, loomed Dr Mothersole, his pencil-wielding daughter at his side. Standing at his left hand, Mrs Mothersole was strumming on a lute and warbling in a shrill tremulous soprano. Dr Mothersole had a set of pan pipes to his lips. The other ladies were singing; the patients were joining in and the place was in uproar.

Dr Hawkins pulled a whistle from his waistcoat pocket and blew a single blast upon it. The noise came to a caterwauling halt. 'May I ask what on earth is going on?' he said. 'Mrs Lunge?'

Mrs Lunge had been standing against the wall, tall and impassive. She glided forward. 'It's Tuesday, sir,' she said.

'And this means what, pray?'

'Tuesday is the day the ladies come, sir. Had you forgotten?'

'I try to,' he said.

'My dear Dr Hawkins,' thundered Dr Mothersole. 'I fear I may be at fault here. I have joined the Ladies' Committee today as I was sure I might find the experience beneficial. I'm sure they find my presence enlightening – many have said as much to me – as I have a deal of experience in matters of what I like to call "the environment of madness". Music, sir, is the key to tranquillity. Need I say more?'

'I think you do, Dr Mothersole,' said Dr Hawkins. 'Your music, if that is what we can call it, sounds anything but tranquil to me.'

'Music, sir, quells the savage beast and soothes the heart and soul.' Dr Mothersole raised his pan pipes to his lips and blew a quavering note. 'I sing too,' he added. 'Counter-tenor, of course, though I cannot sing and play my pipes at the same time, more's the pity.'

Will and I looked at one another and grinned. Dr Mothersole was standing on the hearth, and looked more gigantic than ever. He was dressed in a coat of royal blue boiled wool, and still wore his tall hat, so that I was reminded, briefly, of a ringmaster I had once seen at Cremorne Gardens. His pan pipes looked tiny in his enormous hands and he moved them back and forth across his pursed lips piping a draughty bar of Lead Kindly Light. Many of the patients were laughing. Even Dr Christie could hardly keep his face straight.

'Of course, it was my specific intention that our music would attract the patients.' Dr Mothersole threw his arms wide. 'And they came unto us. You hear how they join in? Such a balm!'

'I did not find it to be a balm, sir,' said Dr Hawkins.

'In the light of the recent tragic happenings here at Angel Meadow I thought it might provide solace, as well as a welcome distraction from melancholia.'

'Well,' said Dr Hawkins. 'I can see that you mean well, Dr Mothersole, but—'

'And how is Dr Golspie,' boomed Dr Mothersole. 'Perhaps he might join us?'

'I think not.'

'He has recovered his senses?'

'Most of them.'

'And he remembers the evening? He recalls his time about the asylum? I believe he was free, despite his initial incarceration? Might he be able to cast some light on the terrible events? Perhaps if *I* were to talk to him—'

Dr Hawkins looked uncomfortable. The eyes of the entire room were upon him now. 'His memory of last night is returning,' he said quickly. 'He will make a full recovery, I'm quite certain. He is to go home to rest, that is all the physic he requires.'

'And might he—'

'I am not at liberty to say more, Dr Mothersole,' interrupted Dr Hawkins sharply. 'By all means continue with your . . . your music if you wish. I can see that the patients appear to be enjoying it.' He looked at his wife and raised his eyebrows. 'I trust you are too, my dear.'

With Dr Golspie incapacitated and Dr Rutherford dead, I knew Dr Hawkins would have many matters to attend to. He asked Dr Christie to accompany him to the women's wing, where he was already late for his rounds, and the two men left together. Although I did not take to Dr Christie I was glad to see that he had agreed to help

Dr Hawkins, glad also that the two of them got along well enough, for I could not help but think that Dr Christie's manner, and approach, would be improved by the acquaintance. As for Will and me, we stayed a little longer to watch the spectacle. Mrs Hawkins was enjoying herself, and she caught my eye more than once and laughed. She was tall and slender, a handsome woman, with the hair piled up on her head thick and dark. The grey streaks I had noticed on our earlier acquaintance were artfully concealed, the jet beads she wore about her neck were adorned that day with a large jade stone that matched the colour of her skirts. She sang well, and had the only melodious voice to be heard above the noise. Even Pole was affected, and he stared at her as if he had never heard anything so beautiful. Mrs Lunge appeared to be the only person who was not enjoying herself. She stood against the wall, her fingers plucking at the high collar of her dress as if the skin below burned. She jabbed Pole in the ribs, and motioned to him to open a window, for the room was growing warm and stuffy with so many crammed into it.

At length, the recital was over, and the ladies went about the room handing out sprigs of herbs and flowers.

'How bizarre,' I muttered to Will. I watched a lunatic staring in bewilderment at the tuft of rosemary one of the ladies had given him.

'Inspired by Shakespeare,' boomed out Dr Mothersole, by way of explanation.

'Dr Mothersole draws upon the same well-spring of poetic inspiration as the Bard,' said Mrs Mothersole. She stroked her husband's sleeve and peered up rapturously into his giant moon of a face.

'Quite so, my dear. "Rue for remembrance",' he laughed.

'It's "rosemary for remembrance", Father,' said Miss Mothersole.

Her father waved a hand. 'That too!' he cried. 'Mr Flockhart, perhaps I might be permitted to hand a sprig to dear Dr Golspie? As an *aide memoire*, so to speak?'

'I believe he is to be left alone,' I said.

'So be it.' He smiled. I thought I saw something I did not like at the back of his eyes, something hard and vigilant, but then his smile grew wider, so that his eyes, and whatever expression might have been hiding within them, vanished into the folds of his cheeks. 'Constance,' he cried. 'Do you have something for Mr Flockhart? And Mr Quartermain?'

Constance Mothersole came forward with a shallow basket. Her notebook was clamped beneath her arm, her pencil lay amongst the flowers. She handed me a tangled hank of chickweed, whilst to Will she gave a large green leaf with a small yellow flower.

'Thank you, Ophelia,' I said. Miss Mothersole looked at me fiercely, and stalked off with her basket.

'If rosemary is for remembrance,' said Will, twirling his leaf, 'then what's this for?'

'Gonorrhoea,' I said. 'It's a corchorus leaf. We use it for the clap, for loose stools and for worms.'

Will blinked. The corners of his mouth twitched. 'And yours?'

'For itchiness.'

Soon, the floor of the gentlemen's sitting room was strewn with trampled flowers and foliage. I saw Mrs Lunge purse her lips at the sight, and despatch Pole to get a broom. Mrs Hawkins came over to us.

'I trust you enjoyed our recital, gentlemen?'

161

'Very much, Mrs Hawkins,' I said.

'The pan pipes were most affecting,' added Will. 'And as for the lute—'

'The instruments of the angels,' said Mrs Hawkins. Her eyes twinkled. 'I'm glad to hear Dr Golspie is recovering. My husband told me what had occurred.' She shook her head, and said gravely, 'Such terrible happenings. The ways of an asylum are new to me. I am trying to learn what I can about Angel Meadow, for my husband's sake, but it is a most peculiar place.'

Pole appeared beside us, rasping at the floor with a broom. 'Watch yer crabshells, miss,' he muttered. Mrs Hawkins stepped aside neatly as the broom whisked past her feet.

'Can you not sweep up somewhere else for the moment, Pole,' I said.

'Got to clean, don't I, sir?' muttered Pole. He glared at the greenery he had gathered at the head of his broom and moved away, his yellow face drooping.

'There's as good an example of the peculiarity of Angel Meadow as any you might hope to find,' said Will, watching Pole shuffle towards the fireplace.

'And yet I was thinking of Dr Mothersole.' Mrs Hawkins smiled. 'His approach is unusual, but seems most wholesome. He was also talking of dancing, gardening and countryside walks.'

'They are methods Dr Golspie at least would have some sympathy with,' said Will.

'My husband speaks very highly of Dr Golspie,' said Mrs Hawkins.

'He's a good man,' said Will. 'And a good friend. He just acts too impulsively.'

'I am impulsive myself,' she said.

'It is a most becoming trait in a lady,' offered Will gallantly.

'Were you away from London for many years, Mrs Hawkins?' I asked.

'Twelve years, Mr Flockhart.'

At that moment Pole reappeared beside me. 'Beggin' yer pardon, sir,' he said. 'But I'm to tell you that Dr Graves has arrived.'

'Dr Graves,' said Mrs Hawkins. 'I don't believe my husband has mentioned him. Is he a physician here too?'

'No, ma'am,' I said. 'He's an anatomist.'

'I see.' She looked alarmed. 'And he's here for—?'

'He is here to perform a post-mortem on Dr Rutherford.'

'What an unpleasant thought. Still, I suppose it has to be done.' Mrs Hawkins's face had turned as white and luminous as a pearl.

'Are you quite well, ma'am?' Mrs Lunge appeared like an apparition at Mrs Hawkins's side. Her expression was as stony as ever despite the solicitousness of her question. 'Perhaps you might care to sit down – if these gentlemen have finished?'

We watched as the two women walked away. 'That was rather odd,' said Will. 'I admit that the very idea of Dr Graves makes me nauseous, but she's surely never met the fellow.'

'Well,' I said. 'Either his reputation precedes him, or Mrs Hawkins is pregnant.'

Chapter Twelve

Up ahead, descending the stairs that led to the mortuary, I recognised a small figure, dressed all in black and wearing a stovepipe hat almost as tall as Will's. He carried a doctor's bag, and moved with a curious crouching gait, as if he carried an invisible sack of bones over his shoulder.

'Look,' I said. 'Our visitor from St Saviour's. Dr Hawkins asked for Dr Graves, I believe, as it is best if the post-mortem be conducted by someone unconnected with Dr Rutherford.' I put my hand on Will's arm. 'Don't let's catch him up. I see no need to endure his company any earlier than we have to.'

Dr Graves was a wiry man, not tall, but strong, with long sinewy arms. He radiated a nervous energy, moving quickly with his curious creeping gait. He stank of decay due to the amount of time he spent in the company of putrefying corpses and formaldehyde. The man had been no friend of mine, though I could not but admire his speed and skill at the dissecting table.

'Must I come?' said Will. 'I will swoon like a woman and humiliate myself.'

'You will swoon like a man,' I said. 'The effect will be just as diverting. Take your salts. Come on, Will, you've attended brain surgery and remained on your feet. The days when you slipped to the ground in a dead faint are far behind you. Besides,' I added, 'I cannot go without you. I do not *want* to go without you. It is Dr Graves—'

The last post-mortem I had attended had been conducted by Dr Graves at St Saviour's Infirmary. It had been the final dissection to take place there, for the old infirmary was demolished soon after. The body we had anatomised had belonged to my dear friend, Dr Bain. Dr Graves was a zealous and speedy worker, and he had eviscerated Dr Bain for the edification of his students with a gusto it still pained me to recall. In no time at all he had sawed off Dr Bain's head, removed his brain and internal organs and peeled back the skin of the legs and arms to reveal the crimson musculature below. Once the body had been emptied of its various organs – the medical students had taken these away for the benefit of their own collections – Dr Bain's body was boiled in the giant copper cauldron Dr Graves kept for the purpose. Finally, stripped of every shred of skin and tendon, Dr Bain's bones had been wired together and placed in the Out-Patients' Waiting Room, a grim memento mori of what might happen to those who did not take their medicines as they ought. When the infirmary was torn down I had saved my friend's skeleton from the rubbish heap, and brought him home to the apothecary. Now, his bones warmed before the fire, watching over Gabriel, Will and me. I had often wondered what he would have made of his fate – poisoned, anatomised, boiled and displayed. It was immortality – of a kind – and Dr Bain had been vain enough to crave such a thing.

In the event, the dissection of Dr Rutherford was far less of an occasion than the dissection of Dr Bain had been. For a start, the mortuary at Angel Meadow where the business was to take place was a far more intimate location than the glass-roofed wooden amphitheatre we had had at St Saviour's. Dr Graves's anatomy room had reeked of putrefying flesh and boiled corpses, the mortuary at Angel Meadow stank only of drains and sewers – both of which were fierce that day. Dr Graves wielded the knife, assisted by me and watched only by Will and Dr Hawkins.

I had not seen Dr Rutherford's body since the morning it had been discovered. The image of that ruined face had, I thought, been etched for ever onto my mind. But nothing could prepare me for the changes twenty-four hours had wrought, nor for the sight of Dr Rutherford, naked and laid out for all of us to see. Rutherford's face was now a terrible greyish white, the skin had the texture of any piece of butcher's meat – firm to the touch, cold and dampish and yielding to the pressure of fingertips so that indentations remained, faint but unmistakable, as if beneath the skin was nothing but soft and pliable wax. His eyes beneath the black stitches were partly open, the eyeballs rolled back in his head, the greyish pearlescence of the sclera glimmering between taut lids. He was now without the dignity of clothing too, and with the dark suit of his profession stripped away he looked thin and weak and pale as a flounder, the skin loose over his thin chest and arms, his abdomen sunken, his legs knotted and sinewy.

We stood in silence and looked down upon him. The blood that had leaked from the place where his ears had been had hardened into crusts. It was evident, as it had been that first morning, that the stitches had been inflicted post mortem, and for all that I disliked Dr Rutherford, for all that I had learned nothing recently to cause me to alter my view of him as a cruel and vicious man, I was glad he had not had to endure such torture as that. There was no bruising, only the stab marks where the bodkin had passed through the flesh. The thread itself had absorbed the blood in thick clumps.

The fatal blow was to the left-hand side of Dr Rutherford's head. As I had already ascertained, it had been struck at his temple where the skull was thinnest, the bone quite bashed in, forced against the brain which was impaled upon the phrenological callipers. It would have killed him instantly. After that the blood would have drained out slowly onto the carpet.

As I had also suspected, Dr Rutherford's mouth contained his severed ears. 'Sliced off with a surgeon's knife, I think, sir?' I said to Dr Graves.

'The wounds are clean, certainly,' he replied. 'Though if the knife is sharp anyone might cut smoothly.'

Dr Graves slit through the skin across the brow and around the head, and peeled back Dr Rutherford's scalp. He reached for a saw, bracing himself and putting his hand on the corpse's head to keep it still. His rolled-up shirt sleeves exposed long, muscular forearms. I heard a harsh, grating rasp, and hot bone-dust stung my nostrils. At length, the top of the head came away and Dr Graves began to ease the brain from its membranous moorings.

'I believe Dr Golspie wanted a brain,' murmured Will thickly. 'And a spinal cord.'

'Dr Golspie is not in a position to have any such thing at the moment,' replied Dr Hawkins. I saw Will cover his mouth with his handkerchief as Dr Graves dumped Dr Rutherford's brain into a bowl. I could hardly blame him. The squelching of blood and flesh echoed about the place horribly.

'The thread used is a surgical suture,' I said. 'It looks to be no different to the one Dr Rutherford kept for his own use.'

'It is a standard fine-gauge suture,' barked Dr Graves without looking up. He was focused on the innards now, slitting open the belly and hauling out handfuls of glistening entrails. The stomach he removed and flopped into another bowl. 'Perhaps you might examine the contents, Mr Flockhart?'

'Yes, sir,' I said. I hated stomach contents. I slit open that crimson muscular bag while Dr Graves stood with his hands plunged into Dr Rutherford's body cavity.

'What do you find?'

'Nothing unexpected,' I said. What had I hoped to find there? Nothing. Whereas I realised the need for a post-mortem examination, I had not expected to find anything useful for our quest. I was sure we had uncovered everything that Dr Rutherford's body might tell us about what had happened that night simply by observing externals. It was the outside of the corpse that would provide us with clues – the neatness of the stitching, the choice of weapon, the nature of the mutilation itself – not the inside. Nonetheless, we had started so we must finish, and I remained with Dr Graves until he deemed the job complete.

Afterwards, he was taken to the visitors' parlour, where Mrs Lunge had laid out some refreshment – cold meats and potatoes, and an iced fruit cake.

'Thank you, madam,' he said. He seized her hand – his fingers still damp and glistening from the hasty wipe he had given them with the mortuary towel, and touched it to his lips. He loaded his plate with chicken legs and slices of boiled ham, and took it away to eat in the silent company of Dr Rutherford.

Will and I walked home in silence, weighted down by our own thoughts and too preoccupied by them to say much. I knew Will was still trying to put from his mind the images from the post-mortem. I thought the noise and bustle of the world would do much to achieve that, but when I looked at him I saw that he was paler than ever, as if the city was sucking the life from him.

'Come on.' I took his arm. 'Let's go this way.'

The physic garden was mine. It was a gift, the governors said, for the two centuries the Flockharts had spent, man and boy, as apothecaries to St Saviour's Infirmary. They said they had hoped I would accompany the infirmary when it moved to its new location south of the river, but I knew they were lying. And so, when I gave up my post there I asked for the physic garden in recompense. The governors were glad to have no more to do with the place, and they consented instantly to my proposal – with the tacit agreement that I would never approach them again, and that I would never allude to the crimes that had taken place in or near their precincts. I wondered how they could pretend that those events had not happened, events that had ruined lives and seen innocent people die. I could not think of St Saviour's without disgust, so that when they had asked me to remove the ironwork above the physic garden gate that bore the words 'St Saviour's Infirmary' I was only too happy to oblige. Now, instead, I had a brass plaque that read Flockhart and Quartermain, est. 1849. Beneath this, connoting the garden's principal contents, was a skull and crossbones – the suggestion of Gabriel, and influenced, I had no doubt, by his reading of the penny bloods.

Along the garden's south-facing wall I had grown a Virginia creeper – green and lush in summer, vermilion and crimson in autumn. Its berries had healing properties, reducing septicaemia; the leaves, as an infusion, act as an aperient. As a decoction it destroyed head lice in an instant – Gabriel could testify as to its efficacy. Alongside was a pear tree, planted years ago by my father. The pear helped colic, constipation, fluid retention and nausea, as well as working on a hardened liver, easing spasms and calming a fever. Like many of the plants I grew it also had a more sinister application: in common with its sisters from the *Prunus* genus – cherry, apricot, peach, plum and almond – it contained cyanide within its seeds.

Will sank down onto a bench and closed his eyes, the bees of early autumn buzzing about his head. We sat side by side in silence, our faces warmed by the sun. I tried to empty my mind, but I could not, and when I closed my eyes I could see Dr Rutherford's face, Dr Graves crouched over him, knife in hand.

'I think I'll gather some herbs for Mrs Hawkins,' I said. 'I feel better when my hands are occupied.'

Will stretched himself out on the bench as I stood up, his coat folded beneath his head. 'I feel better when I'm dozing in the sun,' he said. 'Wake me when you've finished.'

Most ladies want roses and lilies, and it was not something I would have done for many women – in the main because my plants are not mere ornaments. They have utility and in that, for me, their beauty lies. If she were feeling poorly – and she had looked most unwell as Mrs Lunge escorted her away from us – then what better way to stimulate the system than with fragrant herbs? Mrs Hawkins struck me as an intelligent and unaffected woman – had she not greeted the lunatics with kindness and compassion? Did she not join in with Dr Mothersole's 'hygienic methods' with gracious good humour? I felt sure she would recognise the earthy, healthful qualities of such a gift, freshly picked from my own garden.

I took my gardening scissors from my satchel. Was she pregnant, I wondered, as I strolled through the beds? Certainly she had looked nauseous and dizzy, her complexion almost green she had turned so pale, and I was rarely wrong about such things. And yet somehow with her I was not so sure. I thought also of Mrs Lunge as she took Mrs Hawkins's arm – the way she had plucked and worried at the collar of her dress as though the skin beneath itched and burned. Constance Mothersole should perhaps have given her a handful of chickweed, for the stuff was excellent against the itch. I wondered whether it would be importunate of me to offer her a salve next time we met.

I picked only the most tall and stately of herbs: rosemary – woody and astringent; fennel – sweet and fragrant. I cut a few stems of Chinese skullcap, a useful herb and one of my favourites, their long bracts of purple flowers hanging in rows like bells of embroidered silk. I gathered bay and lemon balm, meadowsweet, hyssop and goldenrod, humming to myself as I made my choices. The summer had been late that year, and for all that it was September many of my plants were still at their best. I took them to my workbench in the hot house and tied their stems together with string – the way I do when I am hanging them up to dry. I wrapped my handiwork in brown paper.

I was startled in my labours by the sound of a throat being cleared. I looked up to see Dr Stiven watching me. His face, shaded by the leaves of the fig tree, looked grey and tired. I was surprised to find that I was not best pleased to see him.

'Good morning, Jem, please forgive the intrusion. Miss Chance and I were walking down St Saviour's Street when we saw you coming in. Susan begged me let her see the garden.'

'We rarely have visitors,' I said. 'Many of my plants are poisonous and I cannot have the uninitiated roaming at will plucking at this and that.' I glanced up the garden. I could hear voices – Will's and Susan's.

'Quite, quite,' said Dr Stiven. 'But I also wanted to ask you whether you had heard anything?' Despite his powder, I could see he was anxious. His smile was strained, and fell away before it had reached his eyes.

'No, sir,' I said. We were walking towards the spot where Will and Susan were sitting, concealed behind the rose bushes. I could hear them laughing.

'Have you seen Dr Golspie?'

'He's much better,' I replied. 'Dr Hawkins has sent him home.'

'And Dr Graves? I saw him arrive. Did he find anything?'

'No, sir.'

'And do you have any further thoughts?'

'Other than the fact that Edward Eden has been wrongly accused?'

'And who do you think—'

But I did not want to talk about it, did not want to have talk of murder follow me wherever I went, and I strode on ahead.

'Jem!' Will sprang up. 'There you are. I see Dr Stiven found you.'

Susan and I exchanged some bland pleasantries about the warmth of the day and the pleasing absence of fog. She was animated, smiling and chattering about the beauties of the garden, plucking at the leaves of the lavender and rubbing it between her fingers. The four of us sauntered around the garden. I showed her the poison beds, the hot house, the rock garden. My words seemed to please her, and she listened intently, asking about this and that, how it grew, what it was used for. Her hand rested on my arm and I felt the uneven pressure of her gait as she moved. But I was not in the mood for either of them, and my stride grew long as I tried to hasten their departure.

'If I were you I would never leave this place,' she said.

'I don't intend to,' I replied.

Over the wall, she caught a glimpse of the villa next door. 'Who lives there?'

'It belonged to Dr Magorian. No one lives there now.'

'How I wish I could live there,' she said. 'And be near your garden. I might climb over the wall.'

I said nothing. Eliza Magorian had climbed over the wall. She had loved the physic garden as much as I.

They left, not long after that. I think Dr Stiven sensed my mood and he hurried Susan away. I was not sorry to see them go. I felt tired, and there were few whose company I could bear when I was not in the vein to talk. Will seemed to be of the same mind, for we both turned back towards the garden the moment we had closed the gate upon them.

We stayed for a few hours more. I told Will where to hoe and weed, what to cut and what to tie back, and he followed my instructions with evident pleasure, his sleeves rolled up, his hat cast aside, his collar undone. The garden worked its magic, as I knew it would, and by the time we left to return to the apothecary our cheeks were rosy and we were both smiling.

Gabriel was working resentfully at the pestle and mortar. 'You can't leave me all alone like this,' he said. 'People coming in and out and wanting things and askin' after you, and I've got no idea when you're coming back, if you're ever coming back, or even where you are. You might be dead and stitched up horrid or anything and I'd be the last to know—'

'Who came asking after me?' I said.

'That doctor from Angel Meadow. Dr Golspie.'

'When?'

'About an hour ago. Longer, p'raps. Waited a good

while too. Sat in that chair, said he'd wait for you. I asked if he'd like to help for a bit seein' as he was intent on stayin' but he said "no". He drank some tea. Then he read *Tales of Violence and Blight*. I knew doctors liked blood, but I din't know they liked the penny bloods.' Gabriel laughed, and looked at us expectantly. I wondered how long he had been formulating his joke.

'And?' I said.

'Didn't stay after that. Left quick as you like, actually. Rather rude if you ask me, and me givin' 'im me paper an' all. Took it with 'im too. Well you can get it back off 'im 'cause I'd not finished readin' it a third time. I always reads 'em three times. That way you *really* know.'

'Dr Golspie took *Tales of Violence and Blight?*' I said.

'He wants you to go over there as soon as you can. And you can tell him to give it back. I ain't read it proper. I ain't had time.'

Dr Golspie lived on the top storey of a tall, decaying town house. His landlady was a slatternly-looking woman with many children. The older ones roved the streets with gangs of other urchins, the younger ones gathered in clusters on the stairs or crawled about the hallway. Dr Golspie was without the benefit of inherited wealth, and his entry into the medical profession was slow and not at all lucrative. He hoped to move into better appointed accommodation once his work at Angel Meadow improved his connections, and therefore his patients and his income, but until then he had to be content with the attic room of number 6 Cuttlefish Lane.

The landlady's front door was always open, and we went in and up the stairs without anyone seeing us or asking what we were about. Usually, I found this ease of access rather convenient. That evening, however, mounting those creaking rickety stairs in the darkening afternoon light without anyone noticing or caring made me feel uneasy. I looked back at Will. I could see by his face that he shared my disquiet.

We knocked on Dr Golspie's door but there was no answer. We tried to open it, but it was locked. I put my eye to the key hole and found it to be unobstructed – whoever had locked the door had taken the key away with them – though I could see nothing.

'And yet he is supposed to be in there,' said Will. 'Something is wrong. Can you open the door without the key, Jem?'

'No,' I said. 'Not unless we break it down.'

'Then there is only one option left,' and he bounded back down the stairs to fetch a key off the landlady.

The woman insisted on following Will back up the stairs, talking continually as she did so. 'I've not seen much of him these past few weeks. Seems as though he's always up at Angel Meadow, though Lord knows what he does there, nor how he stands it what with all those lunatics about the place. And now there's that terrible murder. Oh yes, sir, we've all heard about it. I were goin' to ask Dr Golspie about it myself but, well, I ain't seen him to ask, have I? Not yesterday, an' not today, though I did hear him come in earlier. He ran straight up the stairs even when I called out and asked whether he'd like kippers or chops for his tea. Didn't stop. Didn't say, "Chops please, Mrs Slater" or "No thank you Mrs Slater, I'll not 'ave anythin'," just went straight up. No, I've not seen anyone on the stairs, sir. Nor heard 'em. You say he's in there? Yes, here's the key—'

She was still talking when I unlocked the door and we stepped into the room, and still talking when I dragged open the curtains. Her talking only stopped when she saw Dr Golspie's body stretched out in front of the fireplace. When she saw that his head had been stabbed, and that a pool of his blood was on the carpet beside his corpse, she began screaming.

Will sprang past me and fell to his knees. There were not many in the city that he called friend – other than myself I knew only of Dr Golspie – and his sobs were wretched. Beside him the landlady still shrieked and babbled. I seized her by the arm and propelled her back out onto the landing. I heard her footsteps skittering down the stairs, her screams and cries echoing out into the street, a banshee-like wailing starting up from her terrified children.

I crouched at Will's side and put my arms about him. He had buried his face in his hands, unable to look at what lay before us. But I could not allow my emotions to overwhelm me. I had to think clearly, to try to understand what had happened. I forced myself to look at Dr Golspie, at the blood that pooled about his head, at the way his features had been obliterated, turned into a hideous mockery of a face by a clumsy and cold-blooded hand. Like Dr Rutherford, he had been stabbed through the head with a medical instrument – in this case I recognised the ebony handle of a curved double-edged amputation knife. Why would Dr Golspie have such a thing? He was not a surgeon. I looked closer. Was it engraved? Some of the more egotistical surgeons liked to stamp their presence on their equipment. I pulled out my handkerchief and wiped the handle. Three letters. R.J.G. I knew that knife, and I knew those initials. Richard John Graves. The knife must have been stolen from Dr Graves's bag. Also like Dr Rutherford, Dr Golspie's ears had been cut from his head and stuffed into his mouth, his eyes and lips darned shut with long black stitches. The crime was the same – in its manner and presentation. And yet there was something wrong, I knew it.

'Will,' I said. 'We have just spent the afternoon contemplating the death and mutilation of Dr Rutherford. Can you see any difference between this . . . this needlework and the other?'

'No,' said Will. His face was wet with tears.

'Will, look. Think. You must help me.'

'I cannot look, Jem.'

I took from my pocket the rolled-up canvas pouch full of knives and blades Dr Bain had once given me. I snipped a piece of the bloody thread from Dr Golspie's eyes, and another from his mouth.

'Dr Rutherford was stitched using his own suture,' I said. 'There's no doubt that the stuff was close to hand – Dr Rutherford had some on his desk, as he had used it to stitch up Letty's scalp not three weeks earlier. But this? This is different.' I took a fold of paper from my notebook and wrapped the scrap of thread inside it. 'The job is not half as neat,' I added. 'In fact it is quite a mess. Was it done in haste, or was there some other reason?' I looked about. The walls were streaked and stained with damp, the sagging curtains and dirty windows blackened by the soot that belched from the ancient stove. It was untidy, though whether this was due to Dr Golspie's slatternly domestic habits, or because the murderer had ransacked the place in search of something I was not sure. 'Is the place always this disordered?' I said. 'You've been here more often than I.'

'Yes,' said Will. 'Yes, it always looks like this.'

I pulled out my lens and examined Dr Golspie's fingernails. They were dirty, but they appeared to contain no visible trace of skin or blood. 'The room was locked. There was no sign of forced entry, no evidence of a struggle. We can only assume that Tom let his murderer in, just as Dr Rutherford did. That he knew him, and did not think of him as a threat.

'I am quite certain that there was something Dr Golspie wanted to tell us,' I continued. 'But what?' I thought back over Tom Golspie's words earlier that afternoon. *The light was too bright. It dazzled me, blinded me as if I had knives in my eyes . . . I saw a face but not a face, eyes and lips and noses, but not put together properly, not as it should be.* 'Was he simply raving?' I said. '"It was the face of a demon," he said. "It was looking straight at me, and yet not at me. I knew its name, and yet I did not know it. It knew me . . ."' I stared down at Dr Golspie, at that hideous bloody mask, his youthful features obliterated beneath dark criss-crossed stitches. 'It was after Dr Christie spoke that his manner changed,' I said. 'Something Christie said had triggered a thought. A recollection. Something.'

'What did Christie say?'

'He said, "These are fragments of memory – eyes, lips, monstrous faces – these are the fragments that speak of your own murderous act."'

'Yes,' said Will. 'Tom repeated the word. "Fragments," he said. "Like knives."'

And then all at once it was as clear to me as it had been to Dr Golspie. What a fool I had been. 'The mirror!' I said. 'Dr Golspie smashed the mirror that was above the fireplace. Those are the fragments he is talking about, Christie just supplied the word. The broken shards were sharp as knives. Did he see someone? A face glimpsed in a broken mirror is not a face at all, it is nose, lips and eyes but not as it should be. But who did he see?'

'The person Dr Rutherford was waiting for. The person who killed them both.'

'But why would he not tell us straight away? Why did he wait, for it is the delay that has killed him, I am sure of that. Did he not want Dr Christie or Dr Hawkins to hear?'

'Perhaps the face he saw was one of theirs.' We fell silent. 'It cannot be,' said Will.

'What other explanation do we have?'

'There must be other possibilities. Who knew that Dr Golspie had been sent home from Angel Meadow? That his memory was returning'

'Thanks to Dr Mothersole, every single person listening to the Ladies' Committee's recital.'

Will groaned. 'This is impossible.'

'And there is still the question of why Dr Golspie took Gabriel's penny blood.'

'To read, I assume. I believe they're compelling.'

'Dr Golspie is an educated man. He would not choose to read a penny blood for his own entertainment. And yet, when faced with sitting still and waiting for us to return to the apothecary he did the one thing that any intelligent, inquiring and impatient person would do.'

'What?'

'He read something. Anything! Probably the first

thing that came to hand. Look at all these books!'
I gestured to the shelves that covered the walls. They
were filled with novels, medical books, plays, volumes
of essays. 'Dr Golspie is addicted to reading. If he sees
words, he reads them. If he cannot see words, he tries
to find some. So while he awaits us he picks up Gabriel's
penny blood—'

'I hardly think it matters—'

'But of course it matters! Why would he take it away?
Was he really so enthralled by its contents that he could
not bear to leave it?'

'It does seem unlikely—'

'Then why—?'

I was looking about the room as I talked, searching
the floor, the desk, the mantel. And then I saw it, *Tales of
Violence and Blight*, lying open on the arm of Dr Golspie's
fireside chair. I snatched it up, and flicked through its
grubby pages. On the cover was a woodcut, painted
black and red, and depicting a young lad in a tricorn hat
pointing a pistol at an evil-faced man. It was stained with
fingerprints, coal dust and grease smuts from Gabriel's
fervid readings, and the cheap paper was already almost
coming apart in my hands. The main story was *Vicious
Dick and the Accursed Stranger*. Something snagged at the
back of my mind. It was something Gabriel had said,
when he had said he knew that Dr Rutherford was dead.
Dr Rutherford had been 'cut ugly' Gabriel had said, and
'stitched up somethin' bad . . . just like *Vicious Dick and
the Accursed Stranger*.' I had told the lad to be quiet. I had
told him to shut up and not to repeat the tittle-tattle of
others. Had he had something useful to say all along? I
skimmed the first page of *Vicious Dick*. Such overblown

rambling prose! I had read the bloods myself when I was young, but I did not remember them being as lurid and tedious as this. And then I found what I was looking for.

Angel Meadow Asylum, 18th September 1852

The day was fair. Not for me a stage draped with London's fogs and vapours: I would have a blazing arc of summer sky for my theatre. I had seen the spectacle of a hanging many times, felt the excitement of the crowds. I had seen the way the condemned wept and shouted, though even the most brazen were cowed into silence at the sight of that broad cross-beam, the noose a black teardrop silhouetted against the heavens. As I mounted the scaffold on that warm and sunny day I could not help but wonder how many felons had climbed those steps before me, for the wood was lustrous and smooth, the treads worn and bowed from so many shuffling feet. But my thoughts were not my own for long. Even inside Newgate I had heard the roar of the crowd, and now that we were outside, standing before our audience, the noise was deafening. The smell in my nostrils was the smell of the fair: of bodies crammed together, ale and onions and sweat.

There were three of us to be hanged that morning. Three women. One was a fat old beldam from Seven Dials. Married to a bit faker, she had been caught with a purse full of false sovereigns. The other was as young as I. She had been in service, had killed her baby and hidden its body under her bed. The coiner's wife appeared unconcerned, but so drunk was she that I wondered whether she comprehended what was about to take place. The younger one was so pitiful I could not look at her. She hung off the Ordinary's hand as if he might somehow lead her to glory, poor wretch. But my real sympathy was for myself, and I had little to spare for my sisters upon the scaffold. We were not united by the death we were about to share, and I knew nothing about these women other than the crimes of which they were accused.

At the foot of the gallows I saw a boy selling chestnuts, and a man hawking sheets of printed paper – presumably an account of the bloodthirsty crimes we were said to have committed. Closer still, and practically standing beneath the gallows itself, the anatomists were clustered. Dressed in black coats with tall hats and golden watch chains looped across their chests, they looked up at us with hungry eyes, their long pale fingers steepled thoughtfully before their mouths. They nodded and pointed and frowned as they talked to each other. I wondered whether they had already sharpened their knives, whether my young flesh would slice open any easier than the tough old woman standing next to me – and then a hood was thrust over my head. It stank of bile and vomit. I heard my companions – a piteous wailing from the ruined servant to my right, to my left the drunken weeping of the coiner's wife. The reek of urine – from which of them it came I do not know – stung the air. I was manhandled backwards, and the rope pulled over my head. It was heavy against my neck, and as warm as a lover's arm from the heat of the sun.

You might think that we would fall silent, cowed by a sudden terror at what was about to take place. Two of us did, but the girl to my left continued to weep and babble, to cry for 'dear Everett', who I assumed was the rake who had ruined her. But the crowd was quiet now too and her voice rang out, thin and piteous.

The stillness of a crowd is a silence that chills the soul, that stops the heart and turns the mind mad. Beneath that black hood I could hear only the sound of my own breathing, my own muttered prayer and the thumping of my heart. My life was over before it had begun. I had committed crimes, but had I not been driven to it by my persecutors? I had wanted to escape the life I had been born to, but how was it possible in a world that was so clearly weighted in favour of those who had everything?

Then all at once there was a loud, clattering bang to my left and the ground beneath me dropped away. My heart abandoned me, jumping from my chest as I fell. There was a jolt and a searing pain at my neck as if the rope were scalding hot and twisted tight and cruel against my skin. My mouth filled with a foul metallic taste; the blood in my head raging as if it would burst. I felt my eyes bulge and throb, my lips grow thick and livid, pulsing in time with the pounding of my heart. My breath rasped, squeezing through the smallest of openings in my throat. My lungs burned within me as though what air remained to them had turned into acid. Lights burst before my eyes, blinding lights that joined with the blazing pain in my neck and throat and lungs until I was consumed by it entirely.

Chapter Thirteen

What more could we do? Will pulled a sheet from Dr Golspie's bed and covered up his body. Should I take one more look round? I would not get the chance again.

'Was he cautious with visitors?' I said. 'Was he a private man?'

'Not really,' said Will. 'He never locked the door when he was in. I was always telling him he should be more careful. The landlady's children used to come in sometimes – more than once I came up to find one of them in here. The eldest was always hanging about. He used to take away the ashes, and bring up the water but I'm not sure his intentions were always honest—'

'What's his name?'

'Billy Slater.'

I went to the window and threw it open. 'Billy!' I yelled. 'Billy Slater!'

'Who wants to know?' A lad of about twelve years old

was standing in the street, his hands on his hips, looking up at me.

'Come up,' I cried. I flung out a penny. 'Come up and I'll give you another!'

A minute later I heard his boots upon the stair. I met him at the door. I did not want to let him in, did not want him to see Dr Golspie's body, even though it was now concealed by a bed sheet. 'What's she on about?' he said, gesturing with his head back down the stairs to where his mother could be heard still shrieking and wailing.

'Did Dr Golspie have any visitors this afternoon?' I said.

'Yes,' came the reply. A cunning look stole into the boy's eyes. 'Want to know who?'

'Yes,' I said.

'Cost you a shillin'.'

'Sixpence.' I tossed him a coin. 'Who came to see him?'

'A lady.'

'Did you see her coming up the stairs or going down?'

'Shillin',' said the lad. I passed him a penny. 'Going down,' he said. 'What's this all about anyhow?'

'What time?'

'Dunno,' he said. 'Ain't got a watch, have I?'

'Then what did she look like?'

He shrugged. 'Like a lady.'

'Is that the best you can do?'

'It's all you'll get for a penny.'

'Well, was she tall? Was she small?' I flipped another sixpence at him. I was running out of change.

'She were neither.'

'What colour was her hair?'

'A shillin'!' I clicked my tongue and tossed him my last ha'penny. 'I didn't see,' he said. 'She were wearing a cloak.'

'Well what *can* you tell me?'

'She were pretty. That worth anythin'?'

'Not much,' I said. To a lad like Billy Slater any woman who might be considered a lady would be pretty. 'What else?'

He thought for a moment, his fingers to his chin, his eyes looking me up and down as though he were evaluating how much more he might be able to extort. He grinned. 'How about her name?' He jangled his cache of coins. 'That's definitely worth a shillin'.'

'Will,' I said. 'Have you got—?'

'For goodness' sake!' Will rooted in his pocket and pulled out a coin. 'You tell us the name or this goes back in my pocket and you get nothing but my boot against your arse.'

The boy snatched the coin and plunged back down the stairs. As he went, he shouted a name over his shoulder. 'Susan,' he cried. 'Her name was Susan.'

The police came and took Dr Golspie's body to Angel Meadow. Dr Graves's hansom had hardly reached the gates of St Saviour's before he had to return to the asylum to conduct another post-mortem. There was little to report: the blow to the head was given by someone right-handed, delivered in all likelihood while Dr Golspie was facing his attacker. The assault was swift and hard, so that Dr Golspie had neither shied away nor sought to defend himself. The wound to the head had been made by a surgical knife that – to his surprise – belonged to Dr Graves himself. All this, I already knew. And yet Dr Golspie was hiding one last secret: inside his stomach was a quantity of custard tart.

'Dr Hawkins said he would send Mrs Lunge up with a custard,' I said to Will. 'Clearly, Tom was alive at that point. We must speak to Mrs Lunge.'

'We must also speak to Susan Chance.'

Dr Graves seemed rather bored by the whole procedure. 'How many more post-mortems will you be needing today, gentlemen?' he said. 'I do have other things to do with my time.' He sounded irritable. He washed his double-bladed knife and dried it with a soft cloth. He stroked the blade fondly, as if reassuring it that its ordeal as a murder weapon was now over, before stowing it away in his bag. When he found that Dr Golspie had no relatives to bury the body, he packed Dr Golspie's organs back into the corpse, sent for a wagon, and had it trundled off to the anatomy school at St Saviour's. 'Two cadavers in one week?' he said as he sprang up beside the driver. 'You don't deserve such a boon.'

That evening, Will and I were silent as we sat before the fire. We had not the heart to talk about the murder, and there was much to do the following day. I examined the strand of thread I had taken from Dr Golspie's stitched eye socket and compared it to the suture I had taken from Dr Rutherford. They were both the same, though I remained convinced that there was something different this time. 'The stitches were inelegantly executed,' I said.

'Perhaps there was no time to be neat,' said Will.

'Or perhaps this person was clumsy. Inexperienced.'

Will shrugged. 'Perhaps.'

What more might we do that night? I prepared the

apothecary bench for the next morning's work and tried to clear my head.

The office of *Tales of Violence and Blight* was at the top of a dilapidated building in Blinker's Lane, a dingy thoroughfare not far from Prior's Rents. The stairs groaned with every step, the windows rattling as we passed, as though someone outside were trying to get in. The owner was a small red-haired man with ink-stained fingers and a woollen waistcoat worn almost to the threads. He introduced himself as 'Ravelston Dykes, sole proprietor of London's most pop'lar penny weekly'. Mr Dykes's eyes were rimmed with red, his gaze forever sliding back to his desk or darting to look over our shoulders as if he expected a bailiff to march in at any moment – clearly, running London's most popular penny weekly was a precarious and exhausting business. The room where he worked was small and stuffy, warmed by a pot-bellied stove and hung about with washing. Mr Dykes lit a long-stemmed pipe, and sat back in his chair. '*Vicious Dick and the Accursed Stranger,*' he said. 'Came out only the other day, that one. A good un. We get a lot from that particular writer. Feller named McLuker. He's got a real feel for the slums. Tells it likex 'e was there.'

'Do you have an address for Mr McLuker?' I said.

'I do. But I don't want you disturbing my writers. They've got enough to do. Mind you.' He smirked. 'They might take one look at you and decide to put you in a story.' He peered at my crimson face. "The Curse of the Bloody Mask". Might write than one myself.'

He scribbled a few lines onto a scrap of paper. Cost you,' he said. 'A quid.'

'One pound for the address of your worst hack writer? I hardly think so. Especially as I've already inspired your next piece.'

'Oh well.' He held out the ink-scratched words. 'Worth a try. Make it two shillings and we'll call it quits.'

'Here?' said Will in disbelief. '22 Wicke Street? Really?' He seized the bit of paper Mr Dykes had given us and checked the address.

There was no fog that day, not even a brown fuzziness in the air to blur the sight of the hideous street before us. Once a graceful curving terrace of tall and elegant town houses, in my lifetime they had never been anything but ramshackle. Even so, the place was far more decrepit than I remembered its once white stucco now a streaked and blotchy ochre, like a row of rotten teeth. One building drew the eyes, however, for it was the worst of all. Here, chunks of plaster had dropped away entirely, revealing the brickwork beneath in ugly dark welts. Green streaks smeared the edifice from gutters to ground, like curtains of translucent seaweed pasted to a rock at low tide. Dr Bain had come here often. Dr Graves had come too, and so had I, though I had despised myself for doing so. Since St Saviour's had been demolished and the doctors and medical students moved across the river to the new building, the place had fallen on hard times. The curtains were more ragged and dirty than ever, a pipe protruding from the wall seeped a sticky brown fluid, and one of the lower windows was clumsily boarded over.

As we stared, the door opened and a man appeared. He was big and flabby, his coat shiny with grease, his face as round and expressionless as a turnip. Mr Jobber. He stood on the top step, his arms swinging. Mrs Roseplucker always said that he never forgot a face, though as the man scarcely said a word I was not entirely sure how she knew. She also used to say that he 'never forgot an arse, neither', for those who outstayed their welcome at Mrs Roseplucker's Home for Young Ladies of an Energetic Disposition were likely to be pulled from between the legs of their hired companion and jettisoned, naked, into the street by Mr Jobber himself.

Will and I climbed the steps. We scraped our boots, and entered the hall in silence. Inside, the place was as warm and damp as a laundry. The decor was just as I remembered – the walls ox-blood, the cornice as purple as entrails, the ceiling daubed in mottled crimson. Dusty curtains of red damask draped the windows. Mr Jobber closed the door behind us, and pointed silently to the entrance to Mrs Roseplucker's lair.

The woman herself was sitting behind a desk at the back of the room. The curtains were drawn so that daylight was excluded, and the room had the musty odour of long occupancy – sweat, breath, dirty linen and cheap coal. Mrs Roseplucker was stationed, as she always was, behind an oak desk in the far corner of the room. Her face was a sagging ruin, the features daubed on with a lurid palette. The décolletage exposed above the rim of her bodice was wrinkled and liver-spotted, the fingers that rooted in her box of coins yellow and scaly, like the talons of a chicken. She looked up at me.

'Well then,' she said. 'Mr Flock'art, ain't it? One gentleman I ain't seen for a while.' She cackled. 'And your
virgin friend with the tall 'at, o' course. Got to bring 'im
along too. Well, you're early. None of the girls is up yet.'
She slammed her box of coins closed and scratched her
head, moving her wig of auburn curls back and forth, her
expression a mixture of irritation and ecstasy. All at once
she snatched it off. 'Damn this thing,' she said. 'It itches
like the devil. I thought you was some gent'men wanting
one o' me girls, but since it's only you.' She tossed the wig
onto the desktop and sat back with her pale scabby scalp
lewdly exposed. 'You ain't gent'men. Leastways not ones
what wants any o' my sort o' business, I knows that much,
at least!'

'Good morning Mrs Roseplucker,' I said smoothly.
'How nice to see you so well.'

'Got any salve?'

'Salve?'

'For me sores.'

'Why, yes I do,' I said. I rooted in my satchel and
produced some calendula balm – essence of marigold
mixed with beeswax, olive oil and tallow, plus a little
lavender to make it more appealing to the nose. Mrs
Roseplucker sniffed at the pot.

'Oh,' she said, grinning like a death's head. 'Lavender,
ain't it? Reminds me o' when I were a girl. The Prince o'
Wales always smelled o' lavender.'

'So I believe, ma'am,' I said. 'He was known to favour it.
It deters the moths, you know.'

Mrs Roseplucker dipped a black fingernail into the pot,
extracted a blob of salve and smeared it across her scalp.
I saw Will's expression resolve into one of such disgust

I could hardly stop myself from laughing. 'Well?' The salve vanished into a secret pocket in Mrs Roseplucker's voluminous crimson costume. She pulled her shawl tight and peered up at us belligerently. 'What is it? Can't you see I'm busy?'

'I was sent here by Mr Dykes, of *Tales of Violence and Blight*,' I said. 'He said I might find one of his authors here. A Mr McLuker.'

'Prosser McLuker?'

'I believe so. Is he here?'

'Yes,' said Mrs Roseplucker.

'May I see him?'

'Yes.'

'May I see him now? This very moment?'

'You is doin'.'

'I beg your pardon?'

'Oh!' Will groaned. 'Of course. Jem, "Prosser McLuker". It's her. It's an anagram—'

'You?'

Mrs Roseplucker gave a fiendish laugh. 'Course! "Prosser McLuker" is "Mrs Roseplucker" but all mixed up. Me an' one o' the girls worked it out. You remember Annie? Clever girl, our Annie.'

I smiled. I could not help but admire her. I knew Mrs Roseplucker to be a shrewd old hag, but her opportunities in life had been limited. I was surprised to hear that she could write at all, never mind complete one lurid story after another for publication. And yet she had always been an avid reader of the stuff, and she was something of an expert in sensation. Her position behind the table in the front parlour had always been adrift in a sea of penny papers. There was a mound of them beside her chair even now.

'Since when?' I said.

'Year or more.' Her voice took on a tired, complaining tone. 'Business ain't what it was, 'specially since St Saviour's were pulled down. And the girls! Too picky by half, though I told 'em they must do whatever a gent'man asks and pretend it's the best sport they'd ever 'ad.' She shook her head. 'Ain't nearly as obligin' as they used to be. An' then last year we weren't even in Bartleby's *Book o' Gent'men's London Pleasures.* Mrs Roseplucker's Home for Young Ladies of an Energetic Disposition 'as always been in Bartleby's *Book o' Pleasures.*' She sighed and sucked absently on one of her teeth. 'Then one day Mr Jobber ups and says, "Now then, Mrs Roseplucker, ain't you always bin one for tellin' tales? Ain't you always readin' them there penny bloods? Why bless us, Mrs R, why don't you go and write one yourself?"'

I looked over my shoulder at the silent man-mountain sitting it the hall. I had never heard Mr Jobber utter more than three words at a time. No doubt the fellow saved his eloquence for the intimacy of the private realm. But Mrs Roseplucker was still talking: 'An' I thought "You're right, Mr Jobber, yes I will!" And so I writes 'em up and I sends 'em to Mr Dykes and 'e prints 'em.' She laughed again, that deep sepulchral rattle like the shifting of chains in a dungeon. Her sputum was sure to be as thick and brown as treacle. 'I get paid by the column inch, Mr Dykes says. Us girls'd not make much of a livin' if that's 'ow we asked our gent'men to pay,' and her face split like a rotten apple as she cackled.

'So you wrote *Vicious Dick and The Accursed Stranger?*'

'Bless you, sir, yes I did.' She grinned again. 'Straight from Prior's Rents is that one.'

'You didn't make it up?'

'Didn't have to. Leastways not all of it.'

I pulled out my crumpled copy of *Tales of Violence and Blight*. "'Young Jack the boy highwayman grabbed Vicious Dick by the wrist and dragged him down the steps to the cellar,"' I read. "'I won't scream," said Vicious Dick. "As sure as my name's Vicious Dick, I won't." "That's the truth, Dick," said young Jack. "For if you do you know what will happen. Bodkin Bess will find you. And when she finds you she'll cut you up – cut you up straight, she will!"' I paused to miss out a few lines of repetitive dialogue, before resuming. "'You'll get cut ugly, cut ugly and stitched up like a worn petticoat. She'll cut your ears off. You won't hear nothing then, will you? She'll stitch up your lips. You won't say nothing then, will you? She'll stitch up your eyes. You won't see nothing then, will you? She'll stitch you up good and proper, will Old Mother Bodkin. I can't stop her once she finds you. No one can, though it ain't no more than you deserve for what you've done."'

Mrs Roseplucker was rocking back and forth and nodding. 'Oh,' she crooned. 'But you read it jus' lovely.'

'Thank you,' I said.

She grinned up at me. 'What's it you want to know?'

'Where did you get this story?'

'I made it up. Vicious Dick ain't real, you know.'

'But the stitching?' said Will. Up till then he had been standing beside me in silence. I had sensed his agitation, and out of the corner of my eye I had seen him turning his hat in his hands, running his finger around his collar. The sticky warmth, and sulphur reek of the fire, the sight of Mrs Roseplucker's bald and scabrous head above her costume of ragged crimson flounces – evidently he could bear it no longer. 'Where did you get the idea for the stitching, woman? Can you not just get on and tell us, so that we might leave this hellish place? Good God, Jem,' he muttered. 'It is like the ante-chamber to Hades in here and she's the very devil.'

'Is this about that doctor?' said Mrs Roseplucker. 'That dead one at Angel Meadow? The one that got stitched?'

'Yes,' I said. 'He was killed before your story was printed. Gabriel buys *Tales of Violence* as soon as it comes out, and he got it the night the doctor was murdered, so it's not as though the murderer was copying your story. Perhaps he was copying the crime. But how might he know of it? Where does it come from? Is it common knowledge?'

'Not unless yer from Prior's Rents.'

'What does that mean?' I clicked my tongue. 'Come along, woman. I came here for help, not riddles.'

'Help?' she laughed. 'There's nuffin' fer nuffin' at Mrs Roseplucker's.'

'I know that,' I said. Were we never to find someone who didn't want money just for passing on a bit of information? But times were hard, I could see that. I bounced her a half crown. She caught it deftly in her left hand, bit it – Lord knows how such rotten dentition could test the validity of anything – and stowed it away in some secret nest beneath her skirts. 'Now get on and tell us.'

'I used to live in the Rents,' she said. 'Long time ago now. The place were bad, even then – p'raps worse than now, some might say. Too many people, nowhere for 'em to live, no work . . . It were full o' gangs. Gangs o' boys, gangs o' men. Thieves, they were, robbers an' cutthroats, gibbet dodgers and wanted men the lot of 'em, and those what weren't were boys learnin' the trade. Rob anyone for sixpence, all of us would.' She shrugged. 'Most of 'em are dead now. Most of 'em was caught and hanged.

'But the gangs kept each other close. They had to, see, to keep others from knowin' their business, and to keep them what was in the gang loyal. And quiet. They had their own language so as to keep what they was up to a secret. They 'ad punishments too, and warnin's all rolled into one so's you'd not cross 'em and they'd not cross each other.'

'Yes, yes,' I said. 'Come along, woman, get to the point.'

'I'm tellin' you, ain't I?' she snapped. 'Interrupt me again and it's another shillin'.'

'For God's sake, Jem, let the woman finish,' muttered Will. 'My dear lady,' he addressed Mrs Roseplucker. 'Pray continue. But to the purpose, if you please. Punishments and warnings, all rolled into one?'

'That's what I said, ain't it? That's what you wants to know. Cause what they did back then, some of 'em who was partic'lar vicious and cruel, what they did was cut you up, and stitch you. Cut your face up – ears off mostly, then stitch up your eyes an' mouth. "Stitched up", that's what they called it, just like what I put in *Vicious Dick*.'

'What for?' I said.

'What for? Weren't you listenin'? It was fer doin' what's wrong and deservin' it!' She shrugged. 'Most o' them what was in the gangs was got rid of – hanged or sent to the hulks an' put on a transport. More 'n one of 'em were dissected by your Dr Graves, as I recall.

'My stitched up eyes will never see
My sewn mouth cannot speak of thee,
Cut both my ears to 'scape the fee
Of one last jig on Tyburn's Tree.

'That were the rhyme. All the children knowed it.' She looked up at me, her face hideous and sunken. '"Bodkin Bess will get you", that's what my mother used to say.' She chuckled.

Will and I exchanged a glance. It was hard to imagine Mrs Roseplucker having a mother. Looking round at the spongy red walls and ragged crimson curtains it was as though the woman had emerged fully formed from the very fabric of the room.

''orrible times, 'orrible doin's, Mr Flock'art,' she said. 'But 'orrible times and 'orrible doin's is what people wants to read about. Mr Dykes says they can't get enough o' blood an' murder an' suchlike.' She pulled out a pen knife and began whittling on an old yellow goose feather. 'Can't hardly keep up,' she muttered. 'There'll always be gangs, and robbin' and stealin' and murder. But bein' cut and stitched? That's somethin' from Prior's Rents.'

Chapter Fourteen

Will needed the garden more than I, I realised now, and I had hardly put the keys back into my pocket after locking the gate behind us before he pushed past me and vanished behind the lavender bushes. I hoped we would be alone this time, for I wanted no other company but his.

'Thank God the sun is out, for once,' I heard him say. I looked at the sky. I could tell that the fog was coming, even if it was not yet with us, for there was a dampness to the air that was unmistakable. I had noticed it at Mrs Roseplucker's. We would have a couple of hours and then the world would be lost to us.

Will was on his back in the middle of the camomile lawn. I considered a lawn to be a waste of space in a garden, especially a working, productive one. But Will had persuaded me, and for him I had sown a square of fragrant low-growing camomile mixed with zesty lemon thyme. Will loved to lie on it, staring up at the sky through half-closed eyes. He had discovered that if he lay at a certain angle he was unable to see any walls, spires, or windows, and so could indulge his fantasy about being back in the country. It was only the reek from the middens beyond the haven of our walls that threatened to destroy the illusion, though the herbs where he lay did something to sweeten the air.

I had bought a jug of ale from Sorley's, a piece of pie each and a bag of apples. Will took a swig from the flagon and bit into his pie. Already he was looking better. He crushed some lemon thyme between his fingers and held it to his nose. 'I didn't think we'd ever see Mrs Roseplucker again,' he said. 'The place hadn't changed much, had it? It was worse, certainly, but other than that—'

'Mm,' I said.

He pulled out his knife and sliced his apple into quarters. 'What are you thinking?'

'I'm wondering how the murderer knew about the cutting and stitching. Mrs Roseplucker said it was from the Rents. From the gangs of thieves and footpads, but I've never heard of such a thing.'

'Why should you have heard of it? It's from a thieves' code. The customs and rules of Prior's Rents are a mystery to outsiders. We're not supposed to know.'

'Then how did the murderer know about it? We can only assume he – or she – comes from Prior's Rents. More than that, we must assume it's someone who is familiar with the codes and habits of its most vicious residents. Perhaps Rutherford was cut and stitched as some sort of retribution?'

'For what? He surely wasn't in a criminal gang. Dr Golspie certainly wasn't.'

'No, but perhaps he knew people who were. I am minded to think that the two murders are linked, but separate,' I said. 'Designed to look the same, but in fact perpetrated by two quite different hands. I believe Dr Golspie was killed because he saw someone in Dr Rutherford's mirror. Dr Golspie also said that he thought Dr Rutherford was waiting for someone. Whoever he saw in the mirror was, in all likelihood, that person. But who was it and why had they come? Was that person the murderer?'

'And what is the connection between all this and Prior's Rents?' Will munched on his apple.

'We must look at Rutherford's past to find that out, to discover what connections he had to that place.'

'We know one already,' said Will. We looked at one another, but neither of us spoke. I saw Will shiver. 'There's a fog coming in.' He sat up and drew his coat back on. A name hung between us, unspoken, in the dampening air: Susan Chance.

We walked back to the apothecary. I was not sure what to do next. We did not know who had murdered Dr Rutherford and Dr Golspie. We did not know who the woman in the photograph was, nor did we know who Dr Golspie had seen in the mirror. Was it Susan Chance? She had been staying in the asylum. For all I knew she might have even pickpocketed some keys and gained access to every room in the place. And had she not attempted to maim Dr Rutherford when she was a child; had she not beaten a man to death with a poker? Was violent cruelty a part of her nature? She was familiar with Prior's Rents where such things were commonplace. She was also the daughter of a seamstress. Was she not adept with the needle herself? And Billy Slater said he has seen her on Dr Golspie's stairs. But Susan Chance was small; she was a cripple, ungainly and lacking agility. Surely she would be no threat to men like Rutherford and Golspie? Both of them might have batted her aside with one swipe. And yet she was quick and strong. Had I not seen her lash out at Big Brendan's opponent with her metal boot?

My mind was seething with thoughts that I could neither order nor control, so that when we first heard the noise echoing down St Saviour's Street I did not realise what it was. It grew louder, coming closer, the sound of shouting, of something hard striking against stone and the rattle of wheels and hooves. And then all at once it was as if my thoughts had conjured her out of the deep, for at that moment, Susan Chance burst out of St Saviour's Lane and began racing down the Street towards us. People looked over their shoulders, or stopped and stared, as the clear discordant blast of a police whistle shrilled on the air. The girl's eyes were wild and staring, her mouth open in a gasping 'O' of horror. Her metal calliper clunked rhythmically on the pavement, drawing golden sparks as it struck again, and again. Her hat was missing, her hair loose and flying about her shoulders in black snakes.

Ahead of her, down the street, a narrow passageway squeezed between the bookseller's and the ironmonger's. It was known as Hangman's Bolt, and it plunged from St Saviour's Street directly into Prior's Rents. If she reached it, she would vanish into another world. Why was she running? Was the police whistle for her? And then around the corner behind her burst a Black Maria. It was pulled by a mare as black as the wagon she hauled and lashed onwards by a tall dark figure in a tall dark hat. I felt my skin grow cold at the sight of that lustreless creaking box – little more than a wooden prison strung between four rattling wheels. It had a small grille to the front, so that the driver might slash at the fingers of any occupant desperate enough to seize the bars, and a small grille at the back, so that those inside might be scrutinised and those outside might make ready their chains and cudgels. The fog was rising quickly now, blowing up the street in a brown shadow as if the Maria were borne along upon it. I had been in such a vehicle once, and the sight and sound of it brought back feelings of horror and fear that I had hoped never to experience again. It was one such wagon that had taken me to Newgate. I had travelled alone, gyved and fettered like a criminal. Inside, the stink of fear, of piss and sweat and the breath of screaming oaths had been as thick and heavy as brine in my nostrils. For a moment, a single second, as the sound of the thing rattled against my ears I thought it was coming for me, and my heart turned to stone in my chest. But it was not coming for me. Not today. Today it was coming for Susan Chance.

She did not look over her shoulder – to do so would slow her down, fear at the sight of the thing turning her legs to jelly. Instead, her gaze was fixed upon Hangman's Bolt; her legs punching the ground, her callipered boot striking the pavement with a sound like a quarryman's hammer. But the Maria was upon her, the driver's cape billowing about his shoulders, his tall hat a black chimney above his white face. The whip in his hand cracked above his horse's head and the mare plunged forward. The wheels, metal rimmed, roared over the cobbles, throwing up plumes of filth.

Susan did not stand a chance. The wagon raced past the girl and halted at Hangman's Bolt, blocking the passageway completely. Two policeman, who had been clinging to the back, jumped down and flung open the doors. They leaped upon Susan and grabbed her around the waist. But oh, how she fought! She spat. She bit. She kicked. She swore and railed and tossed her head. She writhed and punched and lashed out with her iron boot. I heard one of the policemen curse as she struck his arm a stinging blow with her foot.

'She's broke my arm,' came his pitiful voice. The driver climbed down and bade his colleague hold her arms, and then, as she turned to twist free, he punched her – once, twice – in the face.

They flung the small limp body into the van and locked the door. And then, just as quickly as they had appeared, they were gone.

Chapter Fifteen

Neither of us spoke. The sight of Susan being flung into the police vehicle was imprinted on my mind like a series of photographs. Amongst them was an image of her face twisted in fury, her sharp little teeth had cut her lip and blood mixed with spittle had gathered at the corners of her mouth. I saw her disordered hair, her fingers scratching at the policemen's eyes. Gone were her demurely folded white-gloved hands, the smooth hair tucked in at the nape of her neck. And the way she had swung her callipered foot! I would not be surprised to learn that she had indeed broken the fellow's arm, as I was sure I had heard the crack of it from across the street.

Will spoke first. 'I suppose it was not unexpected.' He shook his head. 'And yet the manner of it. Three burly constables against one terrified girl.'

'That's not how they'll see it. I'm afraid it won't be in her favour that she resisted so fiercely.'

'And so many things already point to her—'

'Almost everything, in fact.'

'Who else might it be? She has a history of violence, she has every reason to want revenge – have you forgotten what Dr Mothersole told us?'

'On the contrary,' I said, 'I remember it very well. I'm only surprised that Dr Christie didn't tell us himself, but sent Dr Mothersole as his emissary.'

'Who is there, other than Susan, who might choose so distinctive a form of mutilation? She's from the Rents – you've seen her there yourself and she's quite at home in the place.'

'Well,' I said. 'I wouldn't be surprised to learn that Pole also knew about being "stitched up".'

'You think there's room for doubt? You think Susan is innocent?'

'I think there's every possibility,' I said.

We were walking down St Saviour's Street now, past the site of the old Infirmary. It had taken hardly any time at all to knock the place down. Some of it had been taken away to be used in other buildings, the rest had been pounded to rubble and packed into the earth to provide a base for the foundations of the bridge that replaced it. When I had lived there with my father, in our rooms above the apothecary, it had felt permanent, strong and impregnable. All day people had come in and out – doctors, patients, nurses, medical students – all of them talking, arguing, laughing, complaining, so much noise and bustle, so much life and purpose. In its place now there was nothing but the silent colossal legs of a railway viaduct. The infirmary building had always looked so large and imposing, with its tall, high-roofed façade, its courtyards and ward buildings, its sturdy medieval chapel.

Now, I could see that it had been small and cramped, a vestige of the city's ancient past – adapted, certainly, and modernised in a piecemeal kind of way to accommodate the needs of later centuries. But it was a building that had looked to history for its worth and belonging. St Saviour's, like the past, had become unfashionable. Obsolete and irrelevant, it had been stamped into the ground, obliterated to make way for the future. Yet was it really so easy to blot out what once had been? The city's history was embedded in its very fabric, in the plague pits that pocked its soil, the streams and rivers that flowed beneath its streets, in the lives of its citizens, some of whom still remembered when there were orchards and fields where engine sheds, slaughter houses and gin shops now stood. Time moved forward and change was inevitable, but the past had long fingers and would not let go of us so easily.

'I think we need to discover who Dr Rutherford really was,' I said. 'Where did he come from? Why was he here at Angel Meadow?' We were standing beneath the railway bridge. Its span was incomplete, and its ragged half-finished end jutted out precariously, a mass of scaffolding, wooden spars, ropes and tarpaulin leading only to the abyss. 'Dr Golspie thought progress was turning some of us mad. D'you remember?'

'Yes,' said Will. We looked up at the looming half-structure overhead. 'Perhaps he was right.'

Crouched at the foot of the half-finished bridge, in the shadow of its massive arch, was St Saviour's Parish Church. Its ancient spire, whose weather vane had once pricked the heavens, was dwarfed by the new structure that reared beside it.

'I once saw a man in a balloon get caught on that

208

weather vane,' I said. 'His name was the Great Goddard. His balloon snagged and he fell to his death. If he got caught on it now he could just step out of his basket and onto the bridge. Dr Stiven was with me. He said it was a lesson I should never forget – that death could come in the most macabre and unexpected of ways.'

Will was staring over the lych-gate at what remained of St Saviour's churchyard – that part of it that had not been eradicated by one of the railway bridge's giant feet. He had supervised the removal of the bodies before the bridge was built, but there was a small section of humped greensward that remained. 'Shall we go in?' he said.

I hesitated. My parents' graves were against the southern wall of the old church but I had not visited them for a while. They had each other, now, which was what they had always wanted, and that last time I had visited I had felt unwelcome – a stranger almost.

'Come on,' said Will. He took my hand and pushed open the gate.

My parents' graves looked out over the mounded plots of their fellow incumbents, towards the ivy-covered wall and the tumbledown hovel where Old Dick the sexton lived. Theirs was a well-tended spot, neatly laid out, weeded and hoed, with the roses that grew on it in late summer bright and blowsy against the grim sooty walls of the old church.

'I keeps it lookin' nice,' said a rough voice at my elbow. 'I do it for her, o' course.'

'Hello Dick,' I said.

'*Old* Dick,' he said. 'There's many a Dick, but none's as old as me.'

Will grinned. 'How's your dog?'

'I ain't got no dog, young feller,' said Old Dick. 'Dog died years ago. Only got meself now.' He looked at Will closely, and a scowl wrinkled his walnut brow. 'I know you. You built that thing.' He jabbed a stubby tortoiseshell fingernail in the direction of the railway bridge. 'Whatever it is. Can't see why we need it. Can't see where it's goin'. Nowhere, by the looks o' things!'

I rummaged in my satchel. 'Would you like some balm, Dick? For your fingers? I've got some comfrey here – comfrey and arnica. It's my mother's recipe.'

'Yesm.' Old Dick put out a hand. It was wrapped in black, greasy bandages, the fingers beneath twisted and gnarled as tree roots. I passed him the pot. He sniffed it and grunted, then thrust it into the pocket of his coat. 'I got summat fer you, an' all,' he said. 'It's in me cottage.'

Will and I exchanged a glance. There was not a more repulsive dwelling in all London, and I could not begin to imagine what on earth he might have for me hidden inside it. But he was already walking away, stumping through the graves with his ancient tricorn hat pulled down low over his eyes, and we had no choice but to follow.

Old Dick's hovel was smaller and meaner than I remembered. The table had vanished altogether – perhaps he had used it for firewood at last, for it had been fit for little else. A kettle so furred with soot that for a moment in the gloom I mistook it for a crouching cat, sat in the hearth. The fire smouldered meanly, a thin stream of black smoke issuing from a mound of sticky-looking coals. There was nowhere to sit, and so we stood. Will and I were equal in height, and our heads brushed against the grimy beams of the ceiling. Will carried his beloved stove-pipe hat under his arm, mine dangled from my fingertips.

Old Dick vanished into the shadows that gathered thickly in a corner of the room. I could make out an old box, and a mound of filthy rags – I assumed this wretched nest was the old sexton's bed. He re-emerged a few moments later with something in his hand. He spat on it, and rubbed it on his coat, and as he stepped forward I could see that the thing he held was pale and roundish, and the size of a small grapefruit – I felt my stomach lurch.

'Thought I should give it you 'cause o' what 'appened that time,' said Old Dick. 'That time afore we buried yer father.'

'The resurrectionists?'

'That's it. Well, they done brought this 'n last night. Not much of a one, but that's all there were,' and he handed me a small pale skull. 'Baby,' he said.

'Someone buried this?' I said. 'One little skull, all on its own?'

'Queer, ain't it?' whispered Old Dick, peering at the skull with his one sharp eye. 'But that's what I seed. It were two o'clock. I 'eard the chimes. I seed the lantern.'

'How many were there?' said Will. 'Was it a man?'

'Yis,' said Dick. Then, 'Naw!'

'Yes and no?' said Will. He sighed. 'Which is it, sir?'

'Dunno.' Old Dick shuffled over to the fire. He jammed the kettle onto the soot-caked trivet and hunkered down, his rag-wrapped hands outstretched to the dismal coals. He seemed to have forgotten we were there.

Outside the fog was now so thick that we could hardly see our way to the gate. The crooked gravestones, so forlorn and neglected in the light, assumed almost human form, hunched like silent beggars, lost in the gloom. The arch of the railway bridge was nothing but a dim shadow overhead. Will's eyes looked huge and dark beneath his tall black hat, his whole appearance ghostly, as if he were receding into another time and place. It was clear that he had the same impression of me, for he took my arm and said, 'Thank God you're here, Jem. This fog sets my nerves on edge.' The skull in my pocket felt cold beneath my fingers.

At the apothecary, Gabriel was asleep before the fire. I shoved him awake with my foot and put on a pot of tea to brew. 'Well, Jem,' said Will as he set down the skull before us on the stove top. 'What do you make if it?'

'Where did you find that?' said Gabriel. He wrinkled his nose. 'Stinks.'

'It's from St Saviour's churchyard,' said Will. 'Of course it stinks. The ground is little more than a mush of decomposed flesh. I had hoped never to touch the contents of the place ever again.'

'Who'd bury a head on its own?' said Gabriel. 'Who does it belong to?'

'We don't know,' said Will.

'Yes, we do.' I said. On the underside of the skull, at the base of the occipital bone a number had been scratched and inked: 260442. 'It belongs to Dr Rutherford.'

Chapter Sixteen

Dr Stiven came to see us at the apothecary. Susan Chance had been locked up in the female criminal lunatic ward at Angel Meadow and he was distraught at the news.

'I tried,' he said. 'I tried my very best. I thought I could help her. I never left the house without the strait jacket – and yet she would escape. She was so wilful, no matter what I said, always returning to the places she was familiar with.' He shook his head. I had never seen him so impassioned, so distressed. 'None of us can predict how we will act when pushed to the edge of human endurance by circumstances beyond our control, but should we be held to account for it for all eternity? Is there no atonement? No rehabilitation? I cannot believe it. I will not believe it. What one can learn one can unlearn. And if the evil is inside it can be winkled out, confronted and banished by kindness and charity.' He was crying now, and he sank down into my father's chair, his powdered cheeks streaked with grey rivulets where the tears had run. 'We are all capable of wickedness. We are all capable of murder, but not this, not Susan. Oh Jem, Mr Quartermain, surely she would never do such a thing again, no matter what.'

I hardly knew what to say. I had been brought up by my father, a taciturn man who had his own secrets and sorrows to bear, and I was used to finding my own comfort. I looked at Will. He pulled his chair forward. 'Have you seen her?' he said, putting his hand on the man's shoulder. 'Since she was taken?'

'She will not speak to me. She will not speak to any man. She says we are all to blame, that she is the victim of us all, one way or another. She says she is innocent and that it is men who are guilty, guilty of the cares of the world, of brutality and violence and all that is wicked.' Dr Stiven sat back in his chair. 'Perhaps she is right. It is I who should be locked away.'

'You tried to help—' said Will. 'You can't blame yourself.'

'But I have *not* helped. And now . . . now . . . ' he looked up, first at Will and then at me, his expression aghast. 'There is more to this than you realise, either of you.' The light from the candle lit up his face in a terrible mask, his eyes black and hollow, his cheeks lined and sunken. All at once the man I had known since I was a child, whose good opinion I had sought and whose eccentricities I had never questioned, was unknown to me.

'What is it, sir?' I said.

'Jem.' Even his voice had changed. It was deeper and softer, and wretched with sadness. 'Mr Quartermain. I can trust both of you I know and I must, for I cannot go on . . . I cannot be without her.' He closed his eyes, and we waited – what else could we do? – while he mastered himself. He took a breath.

'There is something I've carried with me for many years,' he said. 'Something I bear every day with a sorrow that bows my shoulders and makes me into an old man. Guilt and remorse are constants. Fear, at being discovered, accused and condemned have lessened as the years pass, but they are with me always.' He reached up and pulled the wig from his head. The hair beneath was grey and stubbly, but thick. He went over to the sink and worked the pump so that the water gushed over his hands. He washed his face, splashing water over his cheeks again and again so that his powder vanished down the drain. When he turned back to me, the Dr Stiven I had always known had vanished. Instead, there was a slim, clean-shaven man with keen brown eyes and careworn cheeks scored from mouth to nose with deep lines. Most noticeable of all was a long smooth scar across his right cheek. It was as wide as an earthworm, but smooth and flat, glowing a pale pinky-white against the sallow skin of his face as if it had been darned onto it with silken thread. He removed his luminous cobalt waistcoat and turned it inside out so that the dark lining was on the outside. He did the same to his topcoat, both of which I now noticed had been made so that this transformation might be possible. Dr Stiven had disappeared entirely.

I had always known that there must be some reason why he chose to dress as he did. His costume and contrived appearance were so ostentatious, so vivid – in the same way that my hideous red birthmark drew attention away from the person behind it, I recognised a disguise when I saw one. And yet he had always been so kind, so gentle and so fond of me, that I had respected his privacy and had never asked his reasons. Now, when he sat down, he was a different man. Unsmiling and watchful, he was a man I had never met before.

'My name is Joshua Milner,' he said. 'I was only a young man when I ended up in Angel Meadow. My story is, perhaps, not an uncommon one. I was not from the city, but from a village in Northamptonshire. I was taught by a man called Bickerstaff, a retired medical man who saw something in me that was worth encouraging and gave me an education that neither my parents, nor the schoolmaster, could ever have provided. He saw me every day, gave me the use of his library, and encouraged my love of learning, my curiosity about the world and man's place within it. It was the making of me, and yet also my undoing, for he also schooled me to expect more from life than the hand fate had dealt me at birth. My parents could neither read nor write and were content to scrape out a miserable cottagers' existence.' He sighed. 'I should have respected their contentment with their lot, but I could not. Instead, I despised them for it.

'Thanks to Dr Bickerstaff I gained a place at medical school, here in London. I left for the city as soon as I could and I never saw either of my parents again.' He was silent for a moment, his face filled with sorrow. But the deep lines in it had softened. 'I was at St Saviour's for a while, Jem. I knew your father—'

'My father?' I said. 'Back then?'

'Yes. I think he felt sorry for me. I hid my sense of inferiority behind a blustering self-importance that served only to make my fellow students spurn me. Your father saw through it straight away. He used to help me with my *materia medica* for he knew more about physic than anyone. That's how I met him, Jem. I knew you then too, though you don't remember me. To you I was just another arrogant student.'

'My father knew who you were?'

'He knew me as Joshua Milner, and as Dr Stiven. He was the only person who knew that those two people were one and the same. He was a good man, Jem. He never judged me, not for what I'd done or who I was – but I am getting ahead of myself. I want you to understand – you too, Mr Quartermain, for I know you to be a kind-hearted man and one I would trust with my life—'

'Let us hope it won't come to that, sir,' said Will. 'Pray, continue.'

'I worked hard as a medical student – too hard, it turned out – as I had to prove myself as well as earn my keep, and at the end of my third year I became sick, brought on, they said, by overexertion, the heat and pestilence of the city and ill-ventilated and verminous lodgings. For days I raved and sweated. No one visited me, and I was sure they would find me dead and cold only when they came to collect the rent. Of course, I did not die, for here I am before you, though since then there have been many times when I wished that I had.

'I was still recovering when I received a letter. It was from my old benefactor, informing me that my father had been caught poaching for the third time, and this time had been hanged at the summer assizes. My mother – alone now and unable to pay the rent – had been evicted from the cottage she had lived in all her life. In grief and despair she had drowned herself.' He put his head in his hands. 'I can hardly recall the events that followed, but what I do know is that I bought a pistol, and I went to the home of the landowner who had evicted my mother and condemned my father with the full intention of shooting him through the heart. When the time came, however, I could not do it. And so instead I . . . I turned the pistol upon myself.'

'Self-murder?' whispered Will. 'You?'

Joshua Milner raised his hand to touch the long pink scar at his cheek. 'The fellow's gamekeeper had other ideas, for he set his dog upon me at the very moment I pulled the trigger. You see here the result of his intervention. I have no idea what happened next, though I'm told I tried to end my life again, by slashing at my wrists with a pen knife.'

Will handed the man his handkerchief. 'And yet you are still here, sir,' he said gently. 'And you are amongst friends now.'

Tears ran down Joshua Milner's cheeks. 'I refused to eat. I refused to speak. I was in the depths of the most profound melancholia. I was aggressive too, attacking those who came near me, even those who tried to help.' He closed his eyes. 'Angry, full of loathing for myself and for the world, I was sent to live out my days as a criminal lunatic at Angel Meadow Asylum.'

'You knew Dr Hawkins then too?' I said.

He nodded. 'I have much to thank him for. Dr Hawkins had new ideas. Humane ideas, and I was a beneficiary of them. But I was put in the criminal ward. I had attacked a man and threatened him with a pistol. I had tried to murder myself and been violent to any number of others. And so I was restrained, and quartered with the very worst of them. The asylum superintendent at the time insisted upon it.

'The criminal ward was a terrible place. If one was not mad before one entered such a hell there was every chance one would become so before long. Once inside any chance of recovery, or improvement, was impossible. We were treated worse than beasts. We had no liberty, no air, no comfort. Sleep was unattainable – the cold, the dirt, the smell of the place. The noise.' He closed his eyes and dabbed at his lips with Will's handkerchief. 'You remember Newgate, Jem. I tell you to add to that the screams and violence of those who are without reason or logic; those who are rendered madder still by cruelty and fear. I could not bear it. I knew I would die if I remained in such a place. And yet I was fortunate – God help those who are not – for Dr Hawkins was interested in my case. Suicide interested him. Like Dr Golspie he saw it as one of the consequences of the age, and my own case – a clever lad from the country forced to live amongst strangers, weakened by hard work, want, grief and loneliness – seemed to bear this out. He knew that whatever had driven me to act as I did was temporary, that I might be cured – so long as I had food and rest and quiet.

'And so he put me in a cell on my own. He gave me a wooden bed, rather than the straw the others were obliged to sleep on. The asylum was busy – too many lunatics, not enough doctors or attendants. I was his project, he said. An experiment to prove that those condemned as violently insane might make a complete recovery. He gave me books – his own, mostly – on philosophy and theology, on physiology and anatomy. I learned all I could, and I remain convinced that it stopped me from going truly mad.'

'You were released?' said Will.

219

Joshua Milner shook his head. 'Over time I was granted privileges. Dr Hawkins persuaded the superintendent that I was no longer a risk, and I was released into the men's ward, away from those of a truly violent and criminal nature. He and I became friends. I helped him in the mortuary, dissecting and preserving brains and organs, and in the infirmary, looking after those who were sick. But no matter how many books I had, no matter how well treated I was, the fact remained that I was a prisoner. I was locked in my cell every night, and the violent acts I had committed – against myself and others – meant that I would never be permitted to go free. I could not bear it. I was young, was this to be my life? Dr Hawkins said that he would do his best to have me released, but always there were objections and I grew impatient.

'One day Dr Hawkins and I were in the gardens. Gardening was a part of the therapeutic regime Dr Hawkins was attempting to develop at Angel Meadow, and allowing the patients access to the grounds rather than simply having them shambling around in a cinder-strewn yard was a humane exercise not everyone was in favour of. God forgive me for it, for I cannot forgive myself, but when we were out of sight of the main buildings I . . . I attacked him. I knocked him down and left him bloody and unconscious. I took his coat, his pocket book and his keys. Escape, after that, was simple. And it is easy to hide in London – so many lodging houses, so many streets teeming with so many people. With a good coat and a little money it was not difficult to find work. And you must remember that I was no average felon. Yes, I had been mad and I had been violent, but I was mad and violent no longer. And so I became Dr Stiven. I had three years of medical school behind me, and Dr Hawkins had taught me well. I knew as much about physic as any doctor – and I knew more than many about madness.

'I could never show my face, of course. The scar I bore revealed my identity to anyone who cared to look. I must confess that I did not like to look at it either, for it reminded me of who I once was, and what I had once done. And so I covered it up. Time passed. I travelled, I prospered, I became the man you know, not the man I used to be. And yet I had wanted to kill a fellow human being – that had been my intention when I spent my last shillings on a pistol. I had tried to end my own life, and I had assaulted my only friend, Dr Hawkins, and left him, bleeding, upon the grass.' He covered his face with his hands. 'What could I do to make reparation?'

'So you saved Susan from the gallows, and the asylum?'

'Yes.' He looked up then, his eyes shining. 'In so many ways she was my salvation. My life was transformed by her. Susan Chance made me want to confront my past, as much as she was trying to come to terms with her own. I always hoped I could tell Dr Hawkins, I wanted to ask his forgiveness, to show him that I had become the man he always said I could be. Though she does not know it, Susan made me think that such an atonement was possible. When I came to Angel Meadow I hoped I might . . . I wanted to . . . But I did not tell him. I *could* not. And now . . . now Susan is locked away in that terrible bedlam and it is my fault. I brought her to it. I knew of her past. If only I had stayed away.'

'I don't think she killed Dr Rutherford—'

'How can you be sure? She had every chance to take my keys. She was in the asylum. She hated him. She blamed him for her mother's degradation, for her own violation, everything—'

'I know all that. But she's no murderer. At least, not this time. Have you seen her? Talked to her?'

'She will not talk to me. She will not talk to any man. Jem,' he seized my arm. 'She may not talk to a man, but I think she will talk to . . . someone like you.'

'You know?' I whispered. 'You know who I am?'

'You're your father's child,' he replied. 'That is what I know. Who I am, who *you* are, these are not the mysteries here. You must find the truth, Jem. You must find it before it is too late.'

Angel Meadow Asylum, 18th September 1852

I learned later that had I kicked and thrashed things might have turned out differently. I learned too that when the hood was pulled from my head I looked indistinguishable from my sister felons – black faced and bloody lipped, my skirts soaked with my own fear and shame. The three of us were loaded onto the anatomists' wagon and trundled through the streets to St Saviour's Infirmary.

I awoke in a curious place. The air was cold as the grave and there was a horrible smell in the air. Putrid and sickly, but sweetish too – not a pleasant sweetness, but nasty and cloying. I heard the murmur of voices, and then all at once I was awake and gasping, my eyes streaming. My eyeballs stung, throbbing in their sockets as if they were two sizes too big. My throat smarted, the skin on my neck stinging as if it had been burned away. I raised my hands. It felt moist to the touch and hurt like the devil from where the noose had chafed and burned, and when I took my fingers away they were wet with blood.

I reared up from the cold hard slab upon which I lay. Hands pushed me back down. But they were not rough hands, not the hands of thieves or gaolers. Instead, their fingers were soft and

223

cool. I could not see who they belonged to, for my sight was dim and clouded, though I could make out the movement of dark shapes, could see that the place I was in was bright, and lit from above by patches of ochre-coloured London sky.

'Salts,' said a voice. 'But carefully this time.'

There were six of them, their leader an older, smallish man with long yellow teeth set in a grimace, and a curious half-crouching posture like a creeping burglar about to spring. He was in his shirt sleeves, and he moved quickly about the table where I lay, staring down at me hungrily, though with disappointment in his eyes once he saw that I was not dead after all. The other five gentlemen wore old overcoats and caps, against the cold, I was sure, but also against the terrible stink of decay that pervaded the place.

I struggled to sit up once more, then slipped off the table and onto my feet, the gentlemen so shocked by my movement that they hardly knew what to do.

'Shall we catch her, Dr Graves?' said one of the younger men.

'What'll we do, sir?' said another.

'Get her back!' snapped the small man in the shirt sleeves.

'Quick,' said a third. 'Dr Graves, sir, she's taken your coat!'

Dr Graves's coat stank of sweat and death. Its pockets were full of sugar lumps, which scattered to the floor and crunched painfully under my feet as I turned about looking for a means of escape. On all sides there were jars and bottles of sparking glass, inside each an object so monstrous that I was sure I must have woken up in hell itself. A double-headed baby, pale as fat, its eyes two pairs of sightless milky orbs. Beside it was a lizard with its stomach slit open and pinned wide, the delicate bags of its innards on display like a purse full of jewels. To my right I saw a pair of filthy mottled feet and ankles, and the hem of a soiled chemise, and even in my delirium I knew that beneath the *winding cloth lay the coiner's wife; the skinny bruised ankles on the slab beside her those of the wronged maid. Worst of all, next to them both gleamed an array of knives and blades. I heard a scream and my throat stung, so I knew at once that it had been mine. I staggered back, into the arms of an anatomist.*

My knees buckled, and I screamed again as the arms around me grew tighter. 'Kitty,' whispered a voice. 'Kitty!' I looked up. I could hardly speak. My neck burned and my voice was as barbs in my throat. Tears filled my eyes, tears of relief and surprise for there was my old teacher, the medical student from the thieves' kitchen in Prior's Rents.

And that is how I became once again briefly acquainted with Joshua Milner. It was he who had taught me to read and write; how to add and subtract, and how to speak with the easy confidence of his adopted class. And yet fate had more in store for Mr Milner than he or I could ever have guessed. That evening at Angel Meadow, when we met again, I recognised him instantly. He had a powdered face and was dressed in fine clothes, but he could not hide his kindly eyes and smile, and when he spoke to me it was in the voice I had known and learned from so many years ago. I knew that Joshua Milner recognised me too that evening – why else had he spoken to me in his own voice – and it was all we could do not to embrace each other like lost lovers, sobbing out our tales of torment and sorrow, tales we were obliged to keep hidden from the world. Miss Mothersole noted our conversation down, I suspect, though whatever words she overheard can have meant little to her, or to anyone, so extraordinary were our interconnected lives.

Once he heard what I had to say Joshua Milner – Dr Stiven, whatever you wish to call him – said he would help me in any way he could. I have had many enemies, but I have also had many friends, and I have found the latter in the most unlikely of places. It was Joshua Milner who educated me, Joshua Milner who helped me to get well after I was hanged, and Joshua Milner who helped me get back what was rightfully mine. He helped me because he felt sorry for me. And because he knew it was right.

Chapter Seventeen

The façade of the female criminal ward was laced with cracks and fissures, the whole structure shored up at its eastern and western ends with heavy beams of wood. As we approached we could hear howls and cries coming from within, along with a high-pitched screaming and a fearful anguished sobbing sound, as if someone's heart had broken in two. Did one of those terrible demented voices belong to Susan Chance? I thought of the last time we had seen her, running down St Saviour's Street, her hair wild about her terrified face. I would never forget it, though it was the noise – the sound of the Black Maria's iron wheels upon the road, the rhythmic strike of her cripple's boot upon the pavement, the screaming and kicking as she was bundled into the van – that troubled me the most. And now she was locked in here? She did not deserve such a fate. In my satchel I had some witch hazel and distilled water, some iodine, gauze and bandages. I had little else I could offer.

The heavy wooden door was marked with the letter 'C'. From the bunch of keys in my hand I selected a pair similarly marked, one long and thick, the other longer still, but narrow, like a witch's finger. The thin key fitted a lock at the top, the other fitted a lock in the middle.

In a cramped parlour adjacent to the door two grubby-faced women were sitting on either side of a mean fire. The room was furnished with two armchairs of a stained and degraded appearance and a rickety table that would have been better suited as kindling. Against the far wall a cupboard stood open, upon a shelf inside I could see blue poison bottles: bromide and laudanum – the clumsy staples of asylum treatment. Two pairs of bloodshot eyes turned to look at us.

'We are here to see the lunatic Susan Chance,' I said, trusting in my red-masked appearance and imperious manner to get what I wanted.

'Not you as well,' muttered the thin red-faced one.

'Who else wished to see her?'

'Mrs Hawkins.' The women laughed. 'She didn't get far. Went down that passage an' came straight back again. Didn't like the look o' the place, I imagine.'

'Dr Christie said no one were to see Susan Chance,' said the bigger of the two, who had not taken her eyes off my face.

'Stand up when you address me,' I snapped. 'Both of you.'

The women hauled themselves to their feet, their expressions mutinous. But I had met their like before – had I not worked all my life at St Saviour's? I could see straight away what manner of woman I was dealing with: fat, lazy, drunken and cruel, their best friend the gin bottle, their

228

worst enemies the mop, the bucket and the scrubbing brush. Both of them were relics from a miserable past when lunatics had been lashed into spinning chairs and hosed down with freezing water. They would treat their charges with, at best, indifference, and at worst a cruel and wanton vindictiveness. I jangled my keys. 'Don't just stand there,' I said. 'Can't you see we're in a hurry? We wish to see Susan Chance.'

'Sez who?'

'Dr Hawkins,' I said.

'Dr Hawkins ain't got no authority here,' said the fat one. 'It's only Dr Rutherford what had that, an' since 'e's dead it's bin Dr Christie. Told us so, 'e did. Straight.'

'Dr Hawkins is medical superintendent,' I said. 'He has authority everywhere at Angel Meadow.'

The women looked at one another and smirked. 'He don't never come here,' said the fat one. 'He's not been here since before 'e went away. It's Dr Rutherford and Dr Christie what comes these days—'

'Take us to Susan Chance,' I repeated. At the sound of my raised voice, a terrible caterwauling started up behind me.

'You've upset 'em now,' the red-faced one said. She grinned at me, exposing broken teeth. 'They'll need to be punished.'

I lost my patience. On the wall beside the fire a leather strap hung down, like a long brown tongue. I sprang forward and seized it. 'Is this what you use?'

'It is, sir.'

'May I try it?' I snatched the strap from its hook and leaped across the room towards them. The least drunken and most insolent lurched away from me, falling heavily back into her chair. An empty gin bottle rolled out from under her skirts.

'Jem,' said Will from the door. But my mind was whirling: might these cruel, drunken harpies one day govern me with the strap too? Why had the criminal wards degenerated into violence and brutality the moment Dr Hawkins had gone abroad? I heard Will say my name again, but still I ignored him. I raised my hand over my head. Should this woman not feel the same stinging pain she inflicted upon the miserable wretches locked away behind those dark forgotten doors?

'Jem,' said Will again. His voice was soft in my ear now, his hands gentle upon my arm. 'Stop this. This is not who you are.'

I felt the tears running down my face. The leather strap was sticky in my hand as I dashed it into the fire.

'We are here to see Susan Chance,' said Will. His voice was loud, where mine had been piercing. 'Did you not hear what Mr Flockhart said? Tell us where she is!'

'It's number twenty-nine. On the second floor.'

'Give me the keys,' said Will.

By now we were as desperate to get out of the place as they were to see us leave. The noise and heat in so enclosed a space, the stink of sweat, dirt and exhaled gin fumes was making my head hurt. Will ushered me into the corridor and slammed the door behind us. Judging correctly that the longest and stickiest of the keys might be the one to fit the lock, he locked the women into their own malodorous parlour.

The whole building was now in uproar. The air was close, rank with the breath of screaming lunatics, and my skin felt clammy, as though the noise and sorrow were somehow tangible, like dirty hands wiped upon me. From behind one door came a rhythmic thumping, as if from a head beating against a padded wall; from behind another I could hear a high-pitched wailing sound, a third muffled an incoherent bellowing voice, urgent and vexed. The door of each cell bore a small shutter at its centre. Did I dare look inside? I did not.

'Twenty-nine,' said Will. His eyes were wide and he looked about fearfully. 'This way.' A lantern hung from a rusty hook on the wall, its glow dirty and yellowish from the stump of tallow candle that flickered inside. Will took hold of the thing, seized my hand and plunged forward into the gloom.

We passed door after door, only the sounds that came from behind them – screams, groans, a plangent silence – distinguishing one from another. I could not help but think of what Dr Stiven had said: if one was not mad on entering the criminal wards at Angel Meadow, one would become so before long. And yet I did not feel mad – I felt excited, my senses sharpened and keen. Perhaps it was because I belonged here, I thought. Was not madness my destiny? Was it not in my blood and bones? I heard a curious laughing sound, and felt Will's hand on my arm.

'Jem!' He was looking at me strangely, his lantern held high so that he might see my face. 'Stop that!' he said. 'Stop that now!' The shadows loomed around us, swallowing my laughter. 'We must get on,' he said. 'We must do what we came to do and then leave this place. It's not good for you to be here. It's not good for anyone.'

At last, we found door number twenty-nine. I took a deep breath, and slid open the hatch to peer inside. A draught of foul air gusted into my face. The room beyond was no more than six feet by four, the window in the back wall a small aperture set too high to afford a view. It was criss-crossed with double bars as thick as two fingers. Something moved upon the floor. I heard the rustle of straw and saw a dim shape crouched in one corner; a small human form, pale as a ghost in the shadows. A white face stared up at me out of a tangle of black hair, the lips moving in a low, furious mutter. She had lost a tooth, and the face above the stained yellow canvas of her strait jacket was mottled with dirt and bruises, so that for a moment I hardly recognised her. I unlocked the door and stepped inside. 'Susan—'

She fell silent then, her pinched face a mask of wariness. She began rocking back and forth, shaking her head like a dog attacked by flies. All at once she started rubbing it against the cell wall with a frenzied and repetitive motion. I reached forward to stop her. Beneath my hand I could feel her hair crawling with lice. 'Susan,' I said gently. 'It's Jem. Jem Flockhart.'

'You!' she said without looking at me. 'You're no different to all the others, no matter what you say.'

'Dr Stiven is worried about you. *I* am worried. You are accused of the most monstrous crimes—'

'Jem,' said Will, setting down the lantern. 'Can you do nothing for her? Such bruises!'

I opened my satchel. 'There's some arnica in here somewhere,' I said. My hands were shaking, my breathing shallow. I felt as though the walls of Susan's cell were closing in on me.

Will took the satchel from me. 'This?'

I nodded.

He smeared some of the balm on a pad of gauze and

bent to touch it to Susan's face. 'If you would allow me, Miss Chance,' he said gently.

Susan looked up at him warily. 'You're Mr Quartermain.' She tried to smile, her gaze, for a moment, quite sane. Then she said, 'Don't you have any flowers for me? From your garden?'

Will hesitated, the balm still in his hand. 'Why, yes I do,' he said. He put the gauze down on the pot of salve, and slipped his hand into his pocket. In that dark and stinking dungeon what he drew out glowed like a handful of jewels. Susan Chance gasped, and leaned forward.

I knew Will was a countryman, that he had been brought up far to the west of the city, and had come to London only a few years earlier. I knew he missed the fields and open spaces of the village where he had grown up, and for him I had planted the everlasting flower, *Helichrysum bracteatum*. Its oil acts as a stimulant to the liver, gallbladder and spleen, and can be used as an expectorant, and so it is welcome to a place in my garden. But it was their brightly coloured flowers that Will adored – a vivid sunshine yellow, rich purple or violet, glowing scarlet. They flowered from summer to mid-autumn, and for him I had planted them in masses beside the camomile lawn. I had never seen him pick them, and I wondered how long he had carried that secret pocketful. Perhaps he always kept some there – there was no other flower that could survive such a location – so that he might look at them when times were dark, and innocence and beauty dim and distant things.

For a moment I thought Susan was going to smile, but she didn't.

'Shall I put them in your hair, Miss Chance?'

She nodded, her expression pleased. And so I sat

233

in silence, while Will laced his flowers through Susan Chance's tangled locks.

After that, she let him dab at her face with the salve. 'I didn't do anything,' she said. 'But I know who it was.' Her voice was a whisper. 'That's why I'm here. I'm here because I know. I saw.'

'Who?' he said. He stroked her forehead. 'Who did you see?'

'Both of them. I didn't do the things they said I did. I didn't touch Dr Rutherford.'

'But you knew him?'

'I knew him for a brutal and cold-hearted beast.' She glanced up at Will from beneath her garlands, but there was something half-hearted in her look, and her gaze slid away. 'I'm glad he's dead,' she said. 'But I didn't kill him. You have someone else to thank for that.'

'But you were in Dr Rutherford's room that evening?'

'I stole Dr Stiven's keys. It was easy enough. I knew they were the keys to the asylum.'

'But why?' Will paused in his ministrations. 'Why did you go to see Rutherford?'

'I wanted to . . . to know that I could get to him if I wished. Could I stand over him as he slept and hold a knife to his throat? Could I kill him if I chose? But I didn't. I couldn't.'

'Why not? After what he did to you. The way he treated your mother. What stopped you?'

Her expression became scornful. 'I cannot tell *you*,' she said. 'I will not talk to men.' She jerked away from him then, her eyes searching the shadows in the corners of the room for silent listeners. Suddenly she caught sight of the still-open grille in the cell door and her face assumed a look of complete terror. 'They listen at that little door,' she said. 'I see it open, slowly, in the night. I see eyes staring at me, eyes in the door. They are the eyes of an angel, pale and fringed with silver, but there are no angels in here.' She turned to look at me, but it was clearly an effort to do so and a moment later she was staring at the open grille once more. 'You saw what they did to Dr Rutherford,' she whispered.

'So he was already dead,' said Will. 'When you went to his rooms he was already dead.'

'Not you.' She spat onto the floor. 'I won't speak to men!'

'Then speak to me,' I said. 'I am neither man, nor woman.' The riddle appeared to please her, and her agitation subsided. 'You saw his corpse. The way it looked, cut and stitched—'

'It's a warning,' she said. 'A punishment. And so I tell you now that I saw no one, I heard nothing, and I will say not a word.' Her face was as white as bone, her eyes ringed by shadows, her hair straggling rats' tails about her face. 'Bodkin Bess will come!'

'You're not in the Rents now, Susan,' I said gently.

'Dr Rutherford wasn't in the Rents either, but they still found him.' She laughed. High-pitched and wild, it echoed about the cell, joining with the howls and cries from outside. When she spoke her voice was a curious sing-song.

> 'My stitched up eyes will never see,
> My sewn mouth cannot speak of thee,
> Cut both my ears to 'scape the fee
> Of one last jig on Tyburn's Tree.'

235

'Who did you see?' I seized her by the shoulder. 'Susan, who was it?'

'Don't you understand?' she screamed. 'You mustn't ask. I cannot tell.'

They were the same words Edward Eden had used. *You mustn't ask. I cannot tell.* Surely Edward Eden, with his cosseted life within his father's drapery emporium knew nothing of the Rents? From outside the cell I could hear footsteps advancing, the sound of raised voices and keys rattling in locks. Our time with Susan was done, but what had we learned that might help? Nothing at all – other than the fact that the girl was out of her wits with fear. And then the door opened and there was Dr Christie. Behind him in the shadows I saw the hunched and shambling figure of Pole, and the tall silhouette of Mrs Lunge.

'Oh!' Susan fell back, her mad gaze fixed upon the three figures standing before us, the flowers in her hair tumbling into the straw. 'Even my thoughts are not safe. But I can get you out! Out! Out! Out!' with each cry she banged her head against the wall with such violence that I could do nothing to restrain her. She fell silent and slid, unmoving, to the ground.

I gathered her into my arms. How small and thin she was. I could feel her skinny limbs and narrow shoulders beneath the thick canvas of her strait jacket. Which of them had she been referring to? Which of them had she wanted out of her head? Had she seen one of them that night as she wandered the asylum? I looked from Pole, to Dr Christie to Mrs Lunge and I could not tell.

'What are you doing in here, Mr Flockhart? Mr Quartermain?' Dr Christie's voice was low and quiet. Behind him, behind Pole and Mrs Lunge, I could hear doors opening and closing, the sound of muted screams and stifled yells; I could hear gurgling and sobbing.

'We wished to talk to Miss Chance,' said Will.

'You have no right,' said Dr Christie. 'Susan Chance has been judged to be insane by four medical men – myself, Dr Mothersole, Dr Hawkins and Dr Stiven. She is awaiting trial for murder. She is guilty, of that there can be no doubt.'

'There is plenty of doubt, sir.' I laid Susan down gently. 'Two of your colleagues have been murdered. The answers lie in this asylum.'

'The answers lie in this room,' he snapped. 'They lie with Susan Chance.'

I looked down at the small figure crumpled in the straw. 'How the mighty medical profession quails before this formidable woman,' I said.

'How dare you speak to me with such contempt,' cried Dr Christie. 'You treat my attendants disrespectfully; you cause uproar amongst the most fractious, disobedient and violent members of our asylum community; you enter the cell of one of our criminal lunatics. I can think of nothing you have done that is not disruptive, impertinent, discourteous and meddlesome. I will not *ask* you to leave, sir, I will *tell* you to do so. And if you will not, then you leave me no choice but to have you removed.' He turned his head. 'Pole!' Pole shambled forward, his coat flapping about this legs like folds of damp flesh.

'There's no need for your henchman, Dr Christie,' said Will, stepping forward. 'We can manage well enough.'

Dr Christie pushed him aside. 'You have even less reason to be here, Quartermain. You are interfering in matters you know nothing about. Stick to your drawing board, sir, and stay at home. But you,' he stepped up to me, his face so close that only I could hear him. 'Who are you that you come and go as you please? You have no jurisdiction here. You are not at St Saviour's now and I do not recognise you or your authority.' I saw his nostrils flare, almost as though he were scenting me. Then he said, 'There is something about you, Mr Flockhart, that I do not trust. Something that is not right. I have always thought it, and Dr Rutherford was in complete agreement.' His gaze was fixed upon me – not upon my hideous birthmark, but upon my eyes, so that I had the feeling that the man was peering into my heart and soul. 'Dr Hawkins says that you are one of us, but I don't think so. I don't believe that you have any place here – unless it is in one of our wards. I am minded to look up the origins of your birth, and your history, so that I might be sure before I act. And when I do act—' he snapped his fingers in my face, the sound as sharp and sudden as a mousetrap. I flinched. 'Well, then we will see what you are really made of.'

We walked across the stretch of muddy grass that lay between the women's criminal wards and the main asylum building. I moved quickly, filling my lungs with what passed for fresh air. Compared to the close stench of Susan's cell, the smell of effluent and coal smoke was the sweetest of zephyrs. At length we could no longer hear the sounds of the place either, and I took solace from the movement of my limbs and the easy rhythm of my feet across the grass. It was hard to believe that I might one day be similarly confined, my arms bound to my sides by long canvas sleeves, my stride measuring no more than a single pace from one side of my cell to the other. Would I still be able to recognise Will? Would I recognise myself? But I would not think of it now. I would not think of it ever. I walked faster, Will at my side. I could feel his hand brush against mine and was glad he was there. Had we been alone I would have stopped and put my arms around him. But we were not alone.

'What is it, Pole?' I said without turning my head. He had not made a sound, and yet I knew he was there. 'We can make our way perfectly well without you.'

'I'm to help you, sir,' muttered Pole. 'Dr Christie said—'

'We don't need help,' I said. I increased my pace. Behind us there was silence, though when I turned Pole was still at our back. 'Allow me, Mr Flockhart, sir,' he said, plunging forward to open the door. I stalked past him. I wanted to talk to Will, but I could not do so with Pole hanging about. Susan Chance had said little; we could not act upon what she had said – not yet, at any rate. And yet we had other mysteries still to deal with, and I was not quite ready to leave Angel Meadow.

Dr Hawkins was standing in the doorway to the dispensary, a ledger open in his hands. 'Sir,' I said, more relieved than I cared to admit at finding him there, 'we have just seen Susan Chance.'

Dr Hawkins held up a hand. 'I know what you are going to say, Jem, but there is nothing to be done about it. Edward Eden may well have discovered the body, his idiocy preventing him from alerting anyone to the situation – clearly the fellow was overcome with horror at what he had found – but everything points to Susan Chance's guilt. And she was found with keys in her pocket

– I can't think where she got them, but the girl is most likely able to pick any pocket she fancies. All I could do to help her was to agree that she had lost her wits. You have seen her. It was not a difficult diagnosis to reach.'

'But the criminal wards—'

'Dr Christie is responsible for that place, now that Rutherford is gone. I must trust to his professional integrity.'

'Can you not step in, sir? As superintendent—'

'I have worked with the criminal element before, Jem. I tried to treat them with humanity but the results were – disappointing. I prefer to leave their care to others.'

'You refer to Joshua Milner, sir?'

'Milner? How did you know?' He frowned. 'Yes. I vowed after that to help those who were more deserving. I've long since left the care of the criminally insane to those whose expectations are more realistic than mine.' He patted me on the shoulder. 'At least Susan Chance is safe – safe from herself, and from the gallows. It is as good an outcome as she might hope for at the moment.' He pulled out his watch. 'I must attend to the ward rounds. We're stretched more thinly than ever now that Golspie and Rutherford are—'

'Sirs!' A troupe of women had emerged from the committee room. Amongst them I recognised Mrs Hawkins, Mrs Mothersole and Miss Mothersole. At their head, and the owner of the voice, was Dr Mothersole. 'Sirs!' he cried again. He spread his arms wide as he came towards us. 'How providential! Will you join us, Mr Quartermain, Mr Flockhart, Dr Hawkins? The Ladies' Committee and I have new and interesting plans afoot. It's not for everyone, of course, but I cannot but feel that

240

art – music, painting, literature, drama – have much to offer our afflicted brothers and sisters.' He was dressed in a costume of voluminous buff-coloured canvas smock and a pair of blue cotton drill pantaloons. His calves were sheathed in white stockings, and on his feet were a pair of soft leather slippers embroidered with gold flowers and studded with glass beads. They were pointed at the toes, and turned up, like the shoes of an elf. On his bald head he wore a large black beret. The ladies were dressed normally, though they wore aprons over their dresses. Dr Mothersole, as usual, was the only man in the group. He towered over his companions like some fantastic ogre from an outlandish fairy tale. 'Today we will be engaged in creating works of art – paint, dried flowers, paper and card. It will be most calming.'

'I have no doubt you mean well, Dr Mothersole.' Dr Hawkins sighed. The rose in his lapel that day was red, its petals tight about a centre trembling with pale filaments, each topped with a powdery saffron-coloured blob. The stamens had scattered down the front of his coat in a trail of yellow fibres. He dusted them off absently and examined his fingers for pollen, as if anxious to avoid the other man's gaze. 'But there are many other matters to attend to at present. The recreational needs of the patients can surely wait.'

'Oh but they *cannot* wait,' said Dr Mothersole. He laid a fat hand on Dr Hawkins's arm. 'It is of the utmost importance. The patients are anxious. The tension is palpable – have you not perceived it? The murder of two of our most eminent doctors has not gone unnoticed.'

'Let us hope you're not next, Father,' said Miss Mothersole.

'Constance!' cried Mrs Mothersole. She clung to her husband's arm. 'How can you even think such a thing?'

'Ah,' Dr Mothersole beamed. 'It was merely a jest, my dear. Humour is the antidote to all manner of ills; it lifts the mind and the heart. Indeed, I have been thinking of trying my hand as a "laughing artiste", to raise the spirits of the patients – especially those of a more melancholy disposition. Laughter is the best medicine. Write that down, Constance, my dear.'

Constance produced her notebook and pencil and scrawled across the page.

Dr Mothersole breathed deeply, as though filling his lungs with artistic inspiration. 'Well, gentlemen,' he said, 'you will find us in the hall if you care to join us.' The group moved off, trailing into the large airy room where the dance had taken place on the evening of Dr Rutherford's death. Through the open door I could see that attendants had set up trestle tables, upon which were paints and paintbrushes, pots of glue, pieces of card and bowls of dried flowers. The door that led through to the men's wing opened and an attendant entered leading a group of the more biddable male lunatics. Amongst them I noticed Edward Eden. A stream of women patients was led towards the hall from the door opposite.

'Are you a member of the Ladies' Committee?' I said to Mrs Hawkins, who had remained beside her husband.

'It is a good way of getting to know more about my husband's work,' she replied.

'I believe you went to see Susan Chance.'

'Yes,' she said. 'I felt so sorry for the girl. I couldn't bear to think of her locked away like that. I wanted her to know that her friends are thinking about her. That she'll be amongst them again very soon.'

'There's every chance that she'll not be amongst us ever again,' said Dr Hawkins. 'You shouldn't make such promises, my dear. The mad often take things literally – if they understand what you are saying at all.'

'I think Mrs Hawkins didn't actually see the girl,' I said.

'That's right.' Mrs Hawkins's face was bloodless, the jet beads at her throat glinting as black as oil. 'I couldn't bear it. Those awful cackling women with their incessant jangling of keys and slamming of doors. They gave me a candle and sent me along the corridor; and bade me look through the hatch in the door. There were groans and sobs echoing from . . . I don't know where. And the darkness. And the smell—' She closed her eyes. 'I came away without even seeing her.'

'You have a generous nature, my dear.' Dr Hawkins smiled. He unfastened the flower from his lapel and affixed it to his wife's bodice. He kissed her fingers. 'There are many who would not dream of doing such a thing. But in all honesty you are best advised to stay away. For the time being at least.' Dr Hawkins watched Dr Mothersole setting up an easel. 'The governors will be here at any moment. I suppose Mothersole's demonstration will show them what a model madhouse we are, despite our recent troubles.' He sighed. 'I must admire the man's optimism. If you will excuse me, Jem? My dear?' And then he was gone.

Mrs Hawkins, Will and I wandered into the hall. We stood side by side in silence for a moment, looking out as the ladies set out paintbrushes and adjusted their aprons.

'I suppose I should join in,' said Mrs Hawkins.

'Why did you go to see Susan Chance?' I said. 'The real reason, I mean.'

'I've told you the reason, Mr Flockhart.'

'Did you know Miss Chance before you met her here at Angel Meadow?'

'That was hardly possible, Mr Flockhart. If you recall I am only recently arrived in London.'

'But you are from here, I think?'

'Yes. Like so many others.'

'Oughtn't you to be goin' now, sir?' Now that Dr Hawkins had disappeared, Pole reasserted himself.

'We are not ready to leave yet, thank you, Pole,' said Will.

'Are you to assist us amongst the lunatics, Mr Quartermain? And you, Mr Flockhart?' said Mrs Hawkins mildly. I saw Pole smirk. 'We would be glad of your experience as well as your assistance.'

'Still here, gentlemen?' I had not heard Dr Christie enter the room, but there he was beside me. The smell of the criminal asylum – dirty straw, sour breath, and fear, still hung about him. Beside him, Mrs Lunge looked out at Dr Mothersole's art lesson and pursed her lips. An attendant bustled past, muttering under her breath. Mrs Speedicut. I stepped forward and took her arm.

'Good afternoon, madam, might I have a word?' I steered her away from the others. I knew they were watching me – Dr Christie, Mrs Lunge, Pole; Mrs Hawkins and Dr Mothersole too – but I did not care. What made me so reckless? One of them was responsible for all that had happened, for the death of Dr Rutherford, and of Dr Golspie, for the false imprisonment of Susan Chance and Edward Eden. Was I hoping to provoke a response of some kind from one of them? It was a dangerous game to play

– I knew it then, though how badly I was to underestimate my adversary was still unclear.

'Mrs Speedicut,' I said. I kept my voice low, for fear of being overheard, though given what happened later I might well have shouted it from the rooftop. 'I need you to do something for me.'

'Yes, yes,' she muttered. 'There's always something someone's wanting from me.'

'There's supper waiting for you at the apothecary if you can do it without complaining,' I said.

'What is it?'

'I need you to go upstairs—'

'What's for supper,' she growled. 'That's what I'm askin'.'

'Pheasant pie,' I said. 'And a quart of Sorley's best ale. You can go with Gabriel.' I clicked my tongue. 'Come along, woman. You'll not get a better offer.'

'My poor feet,' she whined. 'Why can't you go – wherever it is?'

I did not want to go because, for a start, Pole was watching me and was sure to follow. Besides, I wanted to speak to Miss Mothersole. A crowded room was as good a place as any.

'Go upstairs to Dr Rutherford's rooms and bring back one of his phrenology ledgers. It's important you pick the right one. The one that has "1842" on the spine. They are on the shelf beside the desk.'

'What's it look like?'

'It's like the prescription ledger we used to use at St Saviour's – same colour, but a few inches shorter. Remember, it must be 1842. Bring it to me here.' I slipped the key to Dr Rutherford's rooms into her apron pocket. I hoped no one had seen me. 'Hurry now.'

'Hurry?' she muttered. 'On these feet?'

'An ounce of best shag says you can be there and back in ten minutes.' I pulled out my watch. 'Turkish.'

'Virginian,' she snapped.

I shuddered. Virginian tobacco was truly vile. Her tastes were as repulsive as they were cheap. 'As you wish,' I said. 'Just get on with it. We'll wait for you here.'

I watched the Ladies' Committee bustling about amongst the assembled lunatics. The scene before me had all the appearance of order and tranquillity. I recognised many of the faces I had seen at the dance on the night Dr Rutherford was murdered, though now they were seated on either side of long trestle tables, all of them wearing brown aprons over their clothes. In their hands they held brushes and bits of coloured paper. They painted and glued, not talking to one another but bent over their work, their mouths hanging open in concentration. One or two of them, presumably finding themselves unequal to the task, were staring vacantly at nothing, their hands plucking absently at their lips. Others rocked back and forth, smiling and shaking their heads and feebly dabbing their brushes against the paper. Dr Mothersole opened his arms wide. 'I call it "art physic",' he cried. 'Look, Christie, you see how contented they are?'

Dr Christie was standing in a patch of afternoon sunshine and his colourless hair and face dazzling white against the dark shoulders of his frock coat. 'You have no more than two score of them here, Mothersole,' he said. 'What of the many who are absent? What treatment might we offer them?'

Dr Mothersole smiled sweetly and pulled out his pan pipes. He blew a hollow, quavering blast upon them. His wife stood at his side, looking up at him. There was a movement to my left. I turned to see their daughter. 'Miss Mothersole, I must speak with you.' I kept my voice low.

'Oh?'

'Your notebooks.'

'Well, I do not have them here, sir.'

'Constance,' snapped Mrs Mothersole from the other side of the room.

'Will you not join us amongst the patients, sir?' Constance raised her voice, so that it might catch her mother's ears. 'There are many cards to choose from, as well as paints and flowers. My mother has provided the words.' And she handed me a small card, no bigger than a *carte de visite*, upon which were printed the words 'Trust in the Lord'. Beneath these were pasted three flowers in a row.

'I must see them,' I said. 'Your notebooks, madam.'

'I cannot give you something for nothing, sir,' she said in a low voice. She raised an eyebrow and gave me a look I could not decipher. 'I shall name my price soon enough.'

I opened my mouth to ask what she meant, but she was gone. I glanced up to see her mother staring at me crossly. I pursed my lips. How unwelcome the place had become – nothing but frowning faces and angry voices. At least the patients wished me no harm.

I saw Letty sitting still and silent, staring off into the distance as if absorbed by something that no one else could see. With one hand she held a knitted doll to her breast as if it were a baby, with the other she held a paintbrush, though she had not put it anywhere near her paper. She rocked gently from side to side. Opposite her, Edward Eden was gluing dried flowers onto a card in a painstaking, meticulous fashion. Every now and then, when he thought no one was looking, he slipped his hand into his pocket. At length, he pulled out a white mouse – how he had got it back from Dr Rutherford's room I had no idea. He held it close to his face and stroked it gently, whispering into its tiny pink ear. Suddenly, the expression on his face resolved into a look of alarm. He crouched down, as if anxious to avoid being seen. I saw him whisper something to his mouse, and point across the room.

Mrs Lunge was standing against the wall, one hand plucking at the high collar of her dress, the other resting on her bunch of keys. She watched Pole sweeping up paper and dried flowers from the floor; she looked at Mrs Hawkins assisting a patient with the glue pot; she turned her gaze to glance at Dr Mothersole and his warbling wife. And then she looked at Edward Eden. Edward scrambled to his feet, spilling paint and water onto the floor and knocking over his chair with a sound like a pistol shot.

'I would like to return to my room, please.' His voice echoed through the muttering silence. Mrs Lunge fixed him with a cold stare. 'Please,' he whined. 'I want to go.'

Mrs Lunge looked cross. 'Mr Eden, you have only just arrived.'

Edward shook his head, his gaze averted. 'Want to go.'

Mrs Lunge pursed her lips and nodded to an attendant. There came the familiar sound of keys and locks, and Edward was gone. Only Letty had not looked up. She was still nursing her doll, but dipped her paintbrush in the paint and drew it slowly down the page. She did it again, then again, until she had painted six crooked black lines, side by side across the paper like six burnt-out matchsticks.

248

At that moment the door burst open and Mrs Speedicut exploded into the hall in the manner of a bull bursting into a bullring. 'Nine minutes,' she bellowed, pointing at the clock above the mantel. 'That's a quarter of best Virginian!' But her thunderous entrance was set to become still more spectacular, for as the woman bustled forward she stepped in the slippery mess that Edward had spilled upon the floor. She gave an ear-splitting shriek, grabbing at a table as she went down, dragging more paint, dried flowers and water with her in a blizzard of noise and chaos.

The patients lurched to their feet, laughing and clapping and grinning at the sight of Mrs Speedicut's tubby legs sticking out from her stained petticoats. The phrenology ledger shot from her fingers and spun out across the floor, its pages splayed wide. In a moment that might have brought the house down in any supper room, Pole and Dr Mothersole leaped forward to snatch the ledger up, their heads knocking together like two coconuts, just as Will stepped in and neatly plucked the book from the floor. Not waiting to see what happened next (though at our backs we had heard the sound of Dr Christie's whistle and the continuing hubbub of confused and excited patients) we vanished into the corridor and headed out through the main entrance.

Chapter Eighteen

How relieved I was to get away from the place. I was
sure I could feel its cold shadow at my back, hear
the faint echoing howls of the mad in the air. But
this could only have been in my imagination, for once
outside those walls we were in a different world entirely; a
world so unlike the one we had just left that it was almost
impossible to comprehend the nearness of the two.
Inside, for all that the criminal wards resonated with the
shouts and screams of lunatics, much of Angel Meadow
was curiously hushed. Patients stood or wandered about,
their gazes directed at nothing; their fingers plucking at
lips or clothes, or twisted together and held against their
faces as if in search of comfort. Some sat listlessly on chairs
or beds; whilst those employed outside in the gardens
jabbed at the mean soil in silent indifference. Laughter
was rare; when it came it had a curiously resonant and
repetitive sound that was at once doltish and empty. And
yet separated from that world by no more than a few feet

of bricks and mortar was all the riot and turbulence of London. At the gates a girl hawked watercress from a wet basket, a whistling man carried a tray piled with pies to the chop house on the corner, and a pair of prattling women wheeled a tumbrel filled with dirty washing past a group of men idling outside an alehouse. A blast of singing and raucous laughter issued from its half-open doors to mix with the rattle of passing hansoms. Drays rumbled past laden with kegs of beer, with sacks of coal, and the pale carcasses of pigs. Lads destined for Smithfield drove their cattle bellowing by, as barefoot boys in ragged caps ran pell-mell past chattering wide-skirted women. No one looked up at the asylum. Silent and impassive in their midst it was seen but unseen, a great black rock against which the city foamed, and broke, like the sea.

The hair at the back of my neck prickled. I was in no doubt that eyes were watching us as we hurried away. Should I look back?

'Don't,' said Will, seizing my arm. 'Have we not had enough of the place today that we must look over our shoulders at it too?'

'I must,' I said. 'I must see who watches us go,' and I turned to gaze up at the building. Was there a movement at a window? The shadow of a face recoiling into the shadows? I saw no one. I did not know whether to be relieved or disappointed.

The apothecary was as warm as summer, the stove was burning cheerily, the afternoon sun illuminating the jars of tincture that lined our window ledges. The air was thick

251

with the scent of drying hops and liquorice root, fennel, rosemary and camomile. I took a deep breath of those beloved herby scents and felt all the better for it. Before we went out I had tasked Gabriel with making a gross of worming lozenges and I could see that he had completed the task and cleared everything away. The pills lay on the work bench in a box, their sugar coats drying. Beside this, the condenser had been set up, and a distillation of St John's Wort, newly extracted, gleamed red-orange in the flask.

'Well done, Gabriel,' I said. I handed him an orange I had bought as we came down from the asylum. A spray of oil burst from it as the lad ruptured the peel and tore the segments apart. Juice ran down his chin.

Will made a cup of tea and unwrapped a cherry cake he had bought from the bakery at the end of the lane, and we settled down on either side of the stove, our boots warming on the hearth. I had seen Dr Rutherford's phrenology ledgers before. He was proud of his position as collector and curator of so large a museum of human skulls, and in his ledgers he had a description, and an illustration, of each one of them. Measurements – of jaw, brow, depth of cranium, width of eye sockets – were recorded precisely, and any interesting aspects noted down. What he knew of the subject – their origins, life history and manner of death – was faithfully recorded alongside in a cramped hand. I knew the content and layout of the ledgers because he had once explained it to me. He was pleased with what he believed his collection had taught him about human nature, what it suggested for the study of behaviour, criminality and madness and he was keen to share it with anyone who would listen.

A number was recorded in the top right-hand corner of each page, beneath which, in a short paragraph, were the doctor's observations.

'How meticulous he was,' said Will.

'It was an obsession,' I said.

'And Letty?'

'I've no reason to doubt the man's intention to make Letty well again. And chloroform has done much to open men's imaginations as to what might be possible. Physic is all very well; theory, too – about physiology, about anatomy, about how the mind works. But surgery – physically intervening in the mechanics of the body – that becomes at once a place of such potential. Risks have to be taken if progress is to be made.'

'You sound as though you approve.'

'In general, I suppose I do,' I said. 'Given my own situation, how could I not? Would I allow myself to be cut if I thought it would save me from my father's malady? Only if all else were lost. But who we are is inside our heads. It is not something others should have the power to excise if they do not like the sort of human being we are. Should we not accept those who are different – cherish them and care for them rather than seek to make them "better"? Should we put Edward Eden under the knife merely because he's simple?'

'No,' said Will.

'No,' I said. 'And yet what might be cured, and what must be endured, are sometimes one and the same thing.'

We fell silent then, both of us thinking of my father, of my own future, of Letty staring blankly and hopelessly at nothing.

'Pass me the skull,' I said.

It was small, no bigger than a baby's. The number at its base, 260442, was etched onto the bone with a sharp knife and stained with ink. 'The numbers are not chronological,' Will said. 'Look. They start with 181136, then 110137, then 020237. Did Rutherford explain his filing system?'

'No,' I said. 'But these are dates. Day, month and year. The skull we have here was recorded in the ledger on 26th April 1842. There is no code, no mystery here. He recorded them as they came into his possession.'

Will was turning the pages. '17th November 1840, 3rd January 1841, 3rd June 1842—'

'Go back,' I said. 'You must have missed it out.'

'No,' said Will. He turned the pages rapidly. 'It goes from 3rd January 1841 to 3rd June 1842.' He ran a finger down the seam between the two pages. 'There's a page missing.'

I sighed. 'Of course. It would be too easy otherwise. Very well, but what can we learn from the surrounding cases? I will not be defeated by this.' I sat back in my chair and took a mouthful of boiling tea. 'Read out the two entries that fall before that missing page.'

'"Subject",' read Will. '"Jane Calloway. Twenty-five-year-old woman of low origins. Born: London. Died: Norfolk. History: theft, drunkenness, licentiousness, association with known criminals. Syphilitic: notched incisors, flattened bridge of nose—". It goes on in much the same vein.'

'And the one after?'

'"Subject: Mary Gillies. Fifty-(approx.) year-old woman of low origins. Born: London. Died: Norfolk. History: violence, forgery, attempted murder. Drunkenness. Pugnacious appearance. Had to be restrained"—'

'What picture emerges?' I said. 'There are similarities.

All Dr Rutherford's skulls are female, all belonged to criminals. What else do they have in common?'

'They all died in Norfolk.'

'How many in total?' I said.

Will flicked through the pages. 'Three,' he said.

'And before that where did they die?'

'London.'

'And after the missing page?'

'"29th April 1842. Subject: Mary Hale. Eighteen-year-old woman. Born: Bristol. Died: Newcastle. History: theft, robbery, infanticide."'

'Newcastle?' I blinked. 'Really?'

'Yes. The four that fall after the missing page all died in Newcastle.'

'And after that?'

'London again.'

We fell silent. The clock on the mantel ticked. It sounded like the disappointed clicking of a tongue, so that I was reminded suddenly of my father, and in my mind's eye I saw him shaking his head at me. 'Is this the best you can do, Jem? Is there nothing else you might learn?'

I jumped up. 'There is something here, Will, something important. London, Norfolk, Newcastle, London. Did he work in these places?'

'I think we can assume so,' said Will. 'What other conclusion might we draw?'

'I think we must empty our minds of this piece of the puzzle for now,' I said. 'We must take up another unanswered question.'

'Who is the woman in the photograph?'

'Exactly,' I said. 'And I think the House of Correction is our next destination.'

Gabriel had listened to all this in silence, sucking noisily on his orange. Now, he spoke up. 'Not again,' he said tearfully. 'You've hardly been here this past week, Mr Jem. You've been up at Angel Meadow every day and given me no help down here at all. There's remedies to be made and customers comin' in and out all day and you don't see none of them any more, though they're always askin' where you are and whether you know who killed them doctors. I don't know what to tell 'em about where you are or what's goin' on. But ain't this place our livelihood? Ain't I got my apothc'ry examinations to think about? What if something happens to you? Who's goin' to teach me then?'

'Nothing will happen—'

'How d'you know? There's two of 'em murdered already. Murdered, Mr Jem, and cut and stitched and I don't know what else.'

'Nothing else.'

'Ain't it enough? Ain't you scared?'

'Gabriel—'

'You should be! 'Specially now there's this.' He pointed to the skull. I had placed it on the stove top, its eye sockets mournful shadows above the small toothless jaws. I had seen dead babies aplenty – infants didn't stand much of a chance in the city. Diarrhoea, typhus and cholera saw to that. Had this one met a similar fate? Or should we be thinking about its beginnings rather than its end?

'Well then,' I said. 'Let me put it out of sight.' I placed the skull in one of the drawers of the cabinet that was marked with a skull – a drawer where I usually kept the poisonous substances – arsenic, or digitalis. The phrenology ledger I put on the shelf above, amongst my own recipe books and prescription ledgers. 'Just get on with your work,' I said, 'and don't think about it.'

'Can't he have a few hours off?' said Will. 'What's the worst that may come of it?'

'Very well.' I sighed. 'I suppose Mrs Speedicut will be along soon. They can both— talk of the devil!' A round podgy face had appeared at the window, its nose pressed against the pane. 'She leaves a greasy blob on the window pane every time she comes,' I muttered. 'Why she insists on pressing her nose to the glass before she enters I have no idea.' The woman's panted breath misted the window. She caught my eye and vanished. A moment later the door was kicked open. The bell jangled violently, before falling suddenly silent, the clapper ricocheting across the apothecary to vanish between two bushels of lavender. 'For heaven's sake, Mrs Speedicut,' I cried. 'Can you not just open the door using the knob like everyone else? You have broken my bell – again! Gabriel, see if you can find the clapper.'

'I've come for my tea and my shag,' she said, her expression belligerent. 'They made me clear everythin' up,' she added. She scowled. '*Everythin*'. And it were all your fault!'

I handed her a poke of tobacco I had bought on the way down from Angel Meadow. She pulled out her pipe and rammed a tufted plug of the stuff into the blackened bowl.

'Allow me, madam.' Will lit a taper from the stove and passed it over. She sucked hungrily on the yellow-stained stem, a cloud of acrid smoke billowing around her, and gave a grunt of satisfaction.

'Gabriel is coming with you to Sorley's,' I said. 'Tell Mr

Sorley to send me the bill. And no more than four pints of beer, mind.'

'Each?' said Gabriel.

'Between you.' I shook my head. Mrs Speedicut was no lover of restraint when someone else was paying the bill. I wondered at the wisdom of my decision to send them both together. What mayhem would Will and I return to? But I had other things to think about and we left them to it.

'What do you hope to find?' said Will as we walked.

'I don't know,' I said. 'There are links here. Between the present and the past – not the recent past either, but something further away, something Rutherford thought he had escaped. I don't know what we are looking for, exactly, but the skull, the phrenology ledger, the image from that camera, they are all connected – to each other and to Rutherford's death, as well as the manner of it.'

'And what about Tom?'

'Poor Tom Golspie is a different matter,' I said. 'I think we have a different murderer, though there is no doubt that the two are linked. How could they not be?'

'And what links them is Susan Chance?'

I hesitated. Susan Chance had given me little cause for confidence. Even Dr Stiven was beginning to doubt her. And yet . . . 'I think not,' I said.

'Then what—?'

'I don't know, Will. I truly don't know.'

I had never been to the House of Correction before, though I knew well enough where the place was. It was a long, low fortress of a building, not unlike Newgate in the heaviness of its walls and the tiny windows, thickly barred, that blighted its face like scabs.

'Extending the gaol will mean that more women can be housed here,' said Will. 'Whether or not the conditions within the place are any better remains to be seen. Any improvements will, I fear, prove to be brief, and illusory.'

'Who's kept here?'

'Women convicts – those who are not to be transported. They used to keep those who were to be transported as well, but not any more. Their terms are usually no more than a few months, a few years at most.'

'Are any of them lunatics?'

'Not any longer. I believe they go to Angel Meadow. They tended to disrupt the other prisoners if they were all quartered together.'

'All women?'

'Yes.' He laughed. 'I can't believe I know something about the city that you don't, Jem.'

'And Christie works here?'

'He has a consultant position here.'

The doors to the prison were massive, dark with soot and mud and studded with thick iron rivets. I could smell the place even before we were inside it – but then every place in London had its own stink – the brewery, the slaughterhouse, the meat market all reeked of the industries that took place within. But at the hospital, the workhouse and the prison it was human beings that were crushed, ground, and rendered. The smell from these places was the same – it was the smell of poverty and despair, of hopelessness and misery. I had grown up with the stink of it in my nostrils, though I had never become accustomed to it.

Will rapped upon the door – a small portal large enough for only one person to enter at a time that was cut into the tall arched gates. The superintendent obviously recognised him, for although the man looked at me askance, he gave Will a surly nod and motioned us inside. He beckoned one of the wardens, the blank-faced woman with the dirty neck that I had seen in the picture Will had taken with the prison camera. She scratched a flea bite on her wrist, plucked something from her skin and cracked it between blackened fingernails.

'Where's it to be today, then, sirs?' she said.

She led us across a courtyard paved with crooked, slime-covered flagstones and unlocked a narrow side door, scuffed with the kickings of a million prison wardens and worn where their shoulders had heaved against it. I found myself wondering how many times I would hear the jangling of keys and the scraping of locks before we were done, before we had uncovered the truth and might return to our lives. Would we ever be able to put from our minds the memory of those terrible stabbed heads, the stitches at their mouths and eyes? I knew I never would. The door wailed on its hinges. I closed my eyes against the sound. Had Will not been watching me I might have stopped my ears too. But I could not show my weakness, could not let him see the fear that the place awoke in me. I took a breath, nodded to him grimly, and followed the woman inside.

'Want to see around, sir? Them what's from the buildin' committee usually do.'

'No,' I said. I had no wish to look around the place. I knew that many of the women who found themselves there had already endured far worse – Newgate was the

260

first destination for most. 'Did Dr Rutherford work here?'
I asked Will as we mounted the stairs. 'You asked, did you?'

'I did ask,' he said. 'He did not work here. Perhaps
we might assume he worked in Norfolk, though how we
might find out where, exactly, is another matter.'

Something, some faint memory stirred at the back of
my mind, uncoiling, like a snake moving silently through
the grass. What was it? I could not place it. But we were
climbing stairs now, winding around and around, and
the noise from the wards was harsh upon my ears and
disturbing to my thoughts. The convict women were kept
in wards, long rooms where they were herded together
and left to fight over what straw and bedding might
be available. I could hear the crying of babies and the
sobbing of their wretched mothers, a dismal rhythm
beneath the oaths and raised voices of those with fight
still inside them.

'D'you want to see the wards, sir?' the warden asked.
I shook my head. In truth I was feeling sick and dizzy.
My heart was racing and my hands felt sticky. I had been
sleeping badly, though I had not told Will. I had not told
Dr Hawkins either. I could not bear to have them worry,
for Will to watch me with sad vigilant eyes, wringing his
hands and asking me over and over how I was, for Dr
Hawkins to test and prod me, to think of new ways I might
be saved. But I could not be saved, I knew that much.
There had been no developments in medical science to
help me. The noise from the prisoners grew louder. My
head reeled. Was this how it began, I wondered? Was this
the start of my descent into sleeplessness and the madness
that would so cruelly, so inevitably follow? I felt something
cold beneath my hands, the sound of voices shouting, my

261

name being called, and a curious sensation in my head, as if I were shaking it from side to side.

'Jem,' cried the voice again. 'Jem.'

The warden loomed against the whitewashed walls, her face impassive. She cracked the back of another flea between her nails and drilled her ear with a forefinger. Who was she? Where was I? I scrabbled about on the floor. 'Jem,' the voice cried again. And then there was Will. He put his arm about me and held me close. 'I'm here,' he said. He peered anxiously into my face. 'You fainted.'

I wanted to cry, to lean into him and tell him – how badly I slept, how worried I was for my future, for all of our futures, for how would Gabriel manage without me, where would Will live if there were no apothecary? How, when I did sleep I dreamed of dead men – my father on the rope, Dr Bain, his lips red with poison, Dr Rutherford and Golspie, cold and white against their blackened and bloody sutures. But instead I just nodded, shook my head impatiently at my own weakness, and struggled to my feet.

'Lots of folk is taken over peculiar-like when they're first here,' said the warden. 'Everyone gets used to it in the end.' She grinned. 'They 'ave to. An' there's always worse places if they don't be'ave.'

'Perhaps you should wait here,' said Will. 'I'll get the camera.'

'Camera?' said the woman. 'That box what's upstairs? That's been took.'

'Took?'

'Took downstairs to the infirmary. All that stuff's been took down.'

We followed the warden through another locked door

and along an echoing corridor. I could tell by the familiar smell of the place that the infirmary was not far away.
Ahead of us a door opened, and a fat woman emerged
carrying a brimming chamber pot. The sounds of hawking, sobbing and moaning drifted up to meet us.

'Where is it?' said Will. 'Not in there, surely?' He held a
handkerchief to his nose.

The woman pointed. 'In there.'

We found the camera, its boxes of plates and bottles, in
a small room filled with other mementoes of the building's
past: a tangle of manacles and fetters, and shelves of dusty
and discoloured ledgers. I opened one of them. Each
page bore the details of a single woman convict – age,
profession, details of her crime. 'You still think the woman
in the photograph is a convict?' said Will.

'Yes,' I said. 'Though I admit she was not wearing a
convict's dress.'

'Well, she's not in those ledgers.'

'Have you checked?'

'I have.'

I flicked through the pages nonetheless. Given how long
it took to take even one photograph using the calotype
method, I was amazed by how many images there were.
Page after page showed women's faces – young and old,
their expressions devoid of hope or happiness, so that it felt
perverse to look at them, to stare at the misery etched upon
each countenance. I wondered how many of them were still
alive, how many had worn out their lives on the treadwheel,
or gone mad with months in solitary confinement.

'Don't you believe me?' said Will. He sounded impatient.

'Oh, yes,' I said. 'It's just that – I don't know. Look at their
faces. I pass women like this on the street every day. These

are not criminals, Will, these are ordinary women whose lives are hard and desperate.' We fell silent as we turned the pages. Their faces all had a curious flat expression to them, a countenance I recognised as the face of the gin drinker. What hope did they have? I noted the crimes they were accused of – stealing a cloak, stealing two candlesticks, pickpocketing, being caught with a counterfeit note . . . Such paltry things. The photographs stopped as I went back in time, and from 1840 we were left with only names and numbers, dates and descriptions of crimes. But the faces, I knew, would have been the same. I was about to turn away, when all at once there was a name I recognised. 'Look,' I said. 'Look what it says about this woman.'

'Elizabeth Brodie? What of her? She's not the one we are looking for. She was here long before the camera was used.'

'But listen,' I said. '"Elizabeth Brodie. Aliases, Liz Greasly; Eliza Sanders, Bodkin Bess".'

'Bodkin Bess?' said Will, 'why, that's—'

'Mrs Roseplucker's old friend. Susan Chance's child-hood nightmare. Let's see – "Height: 5 feet 2 inches. Hair: grey. Eyes, blue . . ."' I jumped down the page, for her entry was extensive. '"Trade or occupation: seamstress . . . " Oh! Listen to this, "Offence for which convicted: Murder. 14th March 1828 prisoner found guilty of bludgeoning known felon James Hardwicke of Prior's Lane to death and subjecting his corpse to post mortem assault. To wit: The slicing off of the ears and the stitching closed of the mouth and eyes. Sentence: Hanging. Admitted three prior counts of assault upon a corpse: 1827 J. Wheeler, known felon of 26 Prior's Street, St Saviours; 1827 T. Costello, known felon, Prior's Street, St Saviours; 1826, T. O'Dowd, known Felon, Prior's Rents." I need to think,' I said. 'But I can't do that here.'

'Take these photographic plates,' said Will, handing me a canvas bag, clinking and heavy. 'I'll take this camera.'

We emerged from the room into the arms of a tall slim man carrying a jar of leeches. 'Hello, Quartermain,' he said. 'I see you've found it, then?'

'The camera? Yes, sir.' Will shook the medical officer's hand. He made the usual courteous inquiries about the man's health and introduced me to the fellow, though I was anxious to get out of the place and my responses were more sullen than they should have been. He shook my hand the way a washerwoman might shake out a wet stocking.

'Yes, I heard you were interested in it,' he said, addressing Will. 'There's been a lot of clearing out, as you can imagine, so I had it brought down for you. I thought Christie might be interested in it but no one's seen him for days. His head's full of Angel Meadow.' He lowered his voice. 'Terrible business, what? You can see how difficult and unpredictable the mad can be, can't you? Even those who seem docile. No wonder we don't want them here. Things are difficult enough without having lunatics in amongst the women too.'

'Quite so,' murmured Will.

'I heard there was an arrest?'

'A lunatic named Susan Chance,' I said.

'Yes,' the man said. 'Yes, I think I've heard the name before—'

'She was convicted of murder some years ago. Dr Stiven—'

'Ah, yes,' said the man. 'I remember now. Rehabilitation.

Said he could change the girl.' He shrugged. 'Oh well. Can't change 'em, you see. If the girl's locked up as a criminal lunatic I dare say that's where she should have been all along.'

'That certainly seems to be Dr Christie's view,' said Will.

'Yes, well, it would be, wouldn't it? Those deemed mad are transferred to whatever asylum seems appropriate. Angel Meadow takes a fair few. Of course, there was a time when such individuals would be sent out with the fleet.'

'Transported?'

'Yes. But what use is an idiot or a lunatic in such a place? None at all. And so, if they are out of their wits when they commit a crime then they cannot be hanged for it, and yet they cannot be released either. To send them away causes trouble, but to put them in here with the others, well, that's no use either. They're disruptive, you see. Fear, lack of comprehension of their situation, naivety about the wickedness of those with whom they're quartered.' He shook his head. 'It leads only to more violence, more cruelty, and there's enough of those things in here already. There's no special place for them – not yet at any rate, though there's talk of something out at Broadmoor.'

'How long has Dr Christie been here, sir?' I asked.

'Oh, three years or so.'

'And you, sir?'

He smiled. 'Too long. Years, in fact.'

'D'you remember when the camera was used here?'

'Oh yes. We'd never seen anything like it, of course. Pictures made of light and chemicals? We were all photographed, you know, all the doctors and governors, as well as the head warden. It was an excellent idea of Gunn's to photograph the prisoners. Far too time consuming and expensive, of course, though the governors were prepared to give it a try. But there are so many other things to spend money on, and the prisoners were uncooperative, and the photographic process took so long. They wouldn't sit still. And then Gunn was dismissed, of course. Got caught with one of the female inmates. He wasn't the only one, but he was the one who got caught. Left his camera here. They said he made a bad marriage sometime after, though I pity the woman who married him, if I'm quite honest with you. Well,' the man shook my hand and Will's. 'Good luck,' he said. 'I'm something of a photographer myself and it can become rather an addiction. Of course, there are faster methods of developing now—'

'Yes,' I said, anxious not to be drawn into a discussion about the merits of different photographic techniques. And then, on an impulse I asked, 'Before we go, sir, might I ask whether you can tell us anything more about Dr Gunn?'

'Ship's surgeon out to Van Diemen's Land before he came here, I believe. Deuteronomy Octavius Mandlebury Gunn.' He smiled. 'You never forget a name like that. The fellow always used the whole thing too.'

Will gave a polite laugh. 'I imagine they struggled to fit it all onto his headstone.'

'His headstone?' said the man. 'Why would he have one of those?'

'Because he's dead. The governors said—'

'Oh, what do they know? The fellow's not dead at all. Not yet, anyway.'

We found Deuteronomy Octavius Mandlebury Gunn easily enough. It turned out he had recently been the medical superintendent at the Workhouse in Seven Dials, but was now in the Lock Hospital, not far from the House of Correction.

'Are you sure you want to come in here?' I said. 'This place is for those with the pox—'

'Of course,' said Will. 'I remember St Saviour's foul wards well enough. How bad can it be?'

But out of all St Saviour's manifold awful places, the foul ward was the one I had most abhorred. There we had treated those with venereal diseases, their sores red and weeping, their faces consumed by the most repellent chancres, their mouths drooling and black from the medicine we had given them – if the pox did not kill them then the mercury might well do the job instead. The sight and smell of the place was indescribable. I remembered it well. I checked my pockets for my salts.

'Don't worry,' said Will. He patted his own pocket. 'I have some right here. I never leave home without them – especially if I'm coming with you.'

At first, I thought Dr Deuteronomy Octavius Mandlebury Gunn was working at the Lock Hospital. But when we asked after him, it turned out that he was one of the patients. We found him holding a spittoon, while another patient, too weak to spit alone, disgorged a mouthful of glistening grey saliva into it. Dr Gunn looked unkempt. His head was bald of hair, though here and there long grey wisps proclaimed where it once had been. What remained of his teeth were long and black-stained, his cheeks sunken, his eyes pale and deep set with hooded membranous lids. His coat was dirty, his neckerchief a slippery rag. He patted the hand of the man he was helping, and added a thin stream of his own saliva to the pot.

'Gentlemen,' he said. His voice was deep, the low vowels of the north of England roughened by drink and tobacco. 'I assume you come from Finch. Well you can tell him I don't have his money—'

'Dr Gunn,' I said. 'My name is Flockhart. I've come to tell you that Dr John Rutherford is dead.'

'Is he?' He shrugged. 'Why should I care?'

'Dr Rutherford was murdered.'

'I'm not surprised. Was it a woman?'

'Perhaps,' I said.

'He deserved it.' He eased himself back to lie on his bed, a mean straw-stuffed palliasse resting on a crooked pallet. 'No doubt I'll meet the old bastard soon enough for the pox'll see me off before much longer.'

'What can you tell us about Dr Rutherford?'

He closed his eyes. 'Rutherford was a coward and a bully. He was second rate, ambitious, cruel and ruthless. Is that enough?'

'Well,' said Will, 'those are our impressions of the man, certainly. But how did you know him? And perhaps—' he pulled out the photograph of the girl. 'Do you know who this is?'

Gunn opened his eyes again and took the ragged picture. He pulled out a pair of wire-rimmed spectacles and we waited while he fiddled them into position. He peered at the girl in silence. Then, 'No,' he said at last. 'I've never seen this before, though I can tell you it was taken with my camera. Why do you ask?'

'We found it near his body,' said Will.

'Oh.' Gunn removed his spectacles and closed his eyes again, sinking back into his stained and lumpy pillow. 'I can't tell you much, but I can tell you what I know. I met Rutherford years ago. Phrenology was his obsession. It was quite the fashion, for a while, though no one takes it seriously these days.' He chuckled. 'Some of us didn't take it seriously then either, but Rutherford loved it. He was very meticulous about it. Took photographs, measurements, everything. The camera was his before it was mine. He adored the thing.'

'It was Rutherford's?'

Dr Gunn opened an eye. 'That's what I said. But he lost it in a game of cards. He was furious, but he'd lost fair and square and there was nothing he could do about it. He's not the good doctor, you know, despite his exalted position at Angel Meadow. He had a past, did old Rutherford. He worked hard, and was a hard man too. He took what he wanted – loved power, loved being strong whilst others were weak. I didn't like him. I didn't know anyone who did either, though he managed to charm the ladies whenever it suited him.'

'Did Dr Rutherford work on the transports?' I said.

Dr Gunn licked his lips with a blackened tongue. I held the spittoon for him while he dribbled a stream of saliva into it. 'Yes,' he said, wiping his lips with the back of his hand. 'We both did.'

'Who had the camera then?'

'He did.'

'Where you on the same ship?'

'There was only one surgeon per ship.'

'Where did you meet?' I said. 'In Australia?'

He nodded. 'Newcastle.'

'And what ship was Rutherford on?'

'Different ones,' he said.

'Before you won his camera, I mean.'

'I can't remember.'

'Was it the *Norfolk*?'

Gunn smiled. 'The *Norfolk*,' he said. 'That's right – a long time ago now. Something happened – I don't know what. Nothing was ever made clear.'

'What?' said Will. 'What happened? To whom? Did it involve Dr Rutherford?'

'Oh yes,' said Dr Gunn. 'But I don't know what.'

'Think, sir,' I cried. 'What was it?'

Dr Gunn sighed and turned his head away. 'I don't know,' he said. 'I don't care either. Now go away.'

Angel Meadow Asylum,
18th September 1852

'It is therefore ordered and adjudged by this Court that you be transported upon the seas, beyond the seas, to such a place as Her Majesty shall think fit to direct and appoint for the term of your natural life . . . ' I have never forgotten those words. How can any who have been sentenced thus ever forget them? For my ordeal was set to continue: I was not hanged again – my escape was deemed providential – instead I was sentenced to seven years' transportation. My gaoler said the judge had refused to hang me for fear of the mob.

'Hundreds out of work,' he said, 'and they say we are the greatest manufacturing nation the world has ever seen!' He snorted. 'Hanging a pretty girl like you in front of that lot?' He shook his head. 'Your friends'd never stand for it.'

'I have no friends,' I said. 'They would gladly watch me die, thankful that it wasn't their own necks that were being stretched.'

'Pretty girl like you,' he said again, and he stroked my cheek. I bit his finger then, and he cursed me for being a hell-cat and slapped my face. 'A month in solitary and three months on a transport?' he said. 'You'll be glad of any kindness before long.'

At first I feared we were to be quartered on the hulks moored at Woolwich or Deptford. Once, when we were young, Goblin and I had gone out to see the prisoners from the hulks toiling on the docks. They were rowed ashore every day, to labour in full view of passers-by and spectators. I have never forgotten the stony countenances of the men as they worked breaking rocks and digging the earth. I knew men just like them in the Rents, had known them all my life, and yet I had never seen anyone in the Rents wear an expression of such suppressed rage and humiliation as I saw on those prisoners. I'd looked over at the hulks, huge rotten structures moored stern to prow. Even from the shore I could see that their barrelled sides were mottled with mould and slime. Their masts were cut to stumps and flapped with lines of washing, their hulls blighted with makeshift structures – platforms, galleries, and additional rooms – giving them a diseased appearance, like a row of bloated carcasses bobbing in the dirty waters. What horrors might lie within? I would never find out, for in the event I was taken to the Surrey House of Correction instead, as were all women condemned to transportation. I knew Goblin would not be so lucky.

At the House of Correction we were put in solitary cells so that we would have time to contemplate our sins. At mealtimes we were brought out, but we were made to wear a closed bonnet, the sides of which covered our faces so that we might not see our neighbour, nor talk to anyone. I had been told by the magistrate that I would have to endure three months of this, but we had hardly to wait three weeks before we learned we were to be taken aboard the Norfolk, *a transport ship bound for Botany Bay.*

I had never been on a ship before, had never been further than Prior's Rents, Mr Day's Blacking Factory or the House of Correction, and the prospect of leaving everything I was familiar with to travel to the other side of the world filled me with dread.

273

I was used to dirt and meanness and vice, and yet I knew another world existed – one of light and order and safety. I had dreamed I might one day escape to it – could I not read and write and keep accounts? Could I not speak like a lady and ape their fancy ways? I had only ever known London, and as bad as the Rents had been I had always had some hope. What hope might there be once I was trapped in the belly of a transport ship? I imagined a cramped and crowded space, pestilent and cruel, echoing with misery as it crossed the clamorous seas. What I was to find was a thousand times worse.

Chapter Nineteen

As we turned in at Fishbait Lane I sensed immediately that something was wrong. The door to the apothecary was open – not an unusual occurrence, especially if Gabriel had made some sulphur pills. If the room was not well ventilated the smell inside was like Hades itself. And yet I knew its windows intimately, and all the shapes and shadows beyond. Something was definitely amiss.

'Gabriel?' I leaped out of the hansom, the bag of camera plates I carried swinging against my legs. Behind me, Will struggled with the camera box.

The apothecary was in disarray. The poison drawer where I had concealed the skull was open, as were all the others along the wall. Jars had been taken down and set randomly about the place as shelves and cupboards were searched. Sacks of hops and burdock had been kicked aside, the baskets containing bunches of lavender, long strings of cleavers, dried plantain and chickweed had been pulled out and dumped one on top of the other. The shelves that contained my recipe and prescription ledgers, my books on anatomy and physiology, materia medica, botany and various pharmacopoeias, were ransacked, the contents flung across the floor in a fan of spreadeagled pages and trampled covers. My father's botanical notebook, which he had kept since he was an apprentice, lay face down, its cover bearing the unmistakable imprint of a dirty, street-soiled heel. Dr Rutherford's phrenology ledger was gone.

The place was still and silent, though I had the impression that it had not been so for long. 'Gabriel?' I said. 'Gabriel?'

I was answered by a moan from the back of the apothecary. I bounded over the books, almost slipping as my foot landed in a pool of spilled honey that oozed from an overturned pot. Gabriel lay at the back of the shop, pushed into a corner with his face to the wall. His hands had been tied behind his back with a length of the string I used to secure bunches of leaves before hanging them up in the herb drying room. One of the muslin bags we used for straining infusions had been pulled over his head and secured at the neck, his ankles bound over and over with string and tied with a length of it to his tightly secured hands. He whimpered, and tried to move but he could not. A red stain had seeped through the fabric of his hood. For all that he was tied so cruelly, and shoved into a corner, he had also been laid quite neatly upon some sacks. One of the lavender and lemon balm pillows I made for ladies overcome with the headache had been slipped beneath his head. The hood he wore was not a heavy sack, but was light and breathable. Altogether it was a most humane bondage.

Behind me I heard Will stagger in and dump the

camera down. In an instant he was beside me. Before us, Gabriel sobbed and moaned, his voice muffled and bubbling with snot. I pulled out my knife. The knots at his wrists and ankles told me nothing, but as I bent to examine them something caught my eye. Something had adhered to the muslin hood that covered the lad's head; something small but familiar. 'Quick,' I said to Will. 'Pass me the magnifying glass, the tweezers and a saucer.'

Gabriel made a muffled screaming sound and thrashed, as far as he was able, against his bindings. 'Lie still,' I commanded.

'Jem,' said Will, handing me the glass and tweezers. 'Can you not release the lad—'

'Another few seconds will not cause him any harm,' I murmured, bending close. 'If he was truly hurt he could not moan and fidget so. Keep still!' I snapped. 'We don't want to lose this in the mess and confusion,' and I plucked from his hood two small fragments and laid them in the saucer. 'Put them on the counter,' I said to Will. 'Now lie still, Gabriel, and we will have you free in an instant.'

I snipped through the string and held it up to the light, the magnifying glass still in my hand. 'The knots that secured his ankles are tight and strong,' I said. 'The ones at the wrists less so.'

'He has been trying to kick his legs,' said Will. 'The knots have become tighter.'

'And yet the evidence remains. The knots are tied more forcefully at the ankles.'

'So?'

I gestured to the pillow: 'And why not just leave the boy lying on the stone floor?' Then to the muslin hood: 'Why not use a sack to cover his head? There is one to hand right here, whereas the muslin has to be got from the other side of the room.'

'I don't know,' said Will. 'Did he know the boy?'

'He? Are you sure?'

'She?' said Will. 'Damn your riddles, Jem. You think it was a woman or a man who did this?'

'I think it might be both.'

Once his hands and feet were free, Gabriel curled into a ball, scrabbling his fingers at the hood that still covered his head. I cut the string that held it in place and gently pulled it off. His head was bloody, his hair matted, his eyes awash with tears. A gag – a length of torn muslin – pulled his mouth taut. When I saw his face I regretted my tardiness in liberating him. I untied the gag and cradled him in my arms. I could feel his shoulders shaking beneath my hands as he tried to muffle his sobs. 'You're safe now,' I said. 'We're here. Everything is well.'

'Everything is not well, Mr Jem,' he cried against my shoulder. 'They were here. They were waiting for me.'

'Shh,' I said. I rocked him in my arms. 'Let's see to you first.'

We steered Gabriel through the wreckage and sat him in my father's chair. Will put a blanket around the boy's shoulders, put the kettle on the stove top and poked the embers inside back into life.

'Let me see to your head,' I said. I filled a basin with warm water and added a few drops of tea tree essence, and a sprig of camphor. I found the bottle of iodine standing, untouched, on the counter – almost as though someone had left it out for me deliberately. I bathed his head as he talked, drying it gently and applying a balm, and some iodine, to the wound. It was a bruise, more than anything else, though the skin had broken and the blood had congealed in a black mass in his hair.

'Can you tell us what happened?' said Will, handing him a cup of tea.

'I came back from Sorley's and saw the mess—'

'Was the lock forced?' I asked.

'No.'

'Had you left the door unlocked?'

'No! No, Mr Jem, I swear it! I never leave it unlocked, never.'

'I know,' I said. I patted him on the head. The boy had many failings as an apprentice – he wasn't the brightest, he lacked initiative, he was lazy, greedy and slovenly by nature. But he was loyal; he had loved my father and had promised him that he would work hard – he'd meant it too, and he tried his best to be a good apprentice. The apothecary was his home, as it was mine and Will's, and it meant as much to him as it did to me. He was honest when it came to the important things, and if he had done wrong he would admit it. It was not impossible to open a locked door. All one needed was either the key, or the requisite skills. 'So they were already here?'

'Yes.'

'You didn't see them?'

'I saw the mess they had made and was going to go out to find you. I didn't see no one. Then they hit me.'

'"They"? Did you see more than one person?'

'No,' he frowned. 'But I heard . . . I heard you say.'

'Yes,' I said. 'I did say, didn't I?' I dabbed his wound with iodine. 'They aimed well.'

'What did they use, d'you think?' said Will.

I looked at the bruise at the back of Gabriel's head,

and the skin that had broken beneath his ear. 'Something long and heavy. Something hard, but softish too.'

'An iron bar!' cried Gabriel. 'Or a weighted cudgel. I'm lucky my head weren't stove in and me eyes and mouth stitched. Stitched ugly, like them doctors. It's all in *Vicious Dick*—' His face was pale and greenish. I pushed him back into the chair and slipped a cushion beneath his head.

'Rest now,' I said. 'I'll clear up.'

'You're sure there were two of them, Jem?' said Will in a low voice.

'Maybe. It's a strange mixture of violence and kindness. Someone did not pull the knots tight. Perhaps the same person who laid his head on a pillow, though it might take a stronger stomach to hit a lad over the head. And then there's this,' I said, picking up the saucer upon which I had laid the fragments plucked from Gabriel's muslin hood. I handed Will the magnifying glass.

He bent his head. I saw his knuckles whiten as he gripped the glass tightly. He stared at the fragment for a long time. When he looked up, his expression was troubled. 'Did you suspect this?'

'Of course,' I said. 'Didn't you?'

'Not for one moment.' He held up the tweezers. Between their silver pincers quivered a pale yellow stamen with a dusty saffron-coloured tip.

Chapter Twenty

Will and I tidied the place up as best we could while Gabriel dozed before the fire. When he awoke he said he felt much better. The afternoon was growing dark, though it was not yet five o'clock. I sent them out for some beer and a cold roast pheasant for our tea.

I was relieved when they had gone. I sank in my father's chair. My mind whirled with thoughts and images, from the present, from the past – Dr Stiven and Susan Chance, Dr Hawkins and my father. The skeleton of Dr Bain grinned down at me.

'What are you laughing at?' I said. 'D'you think you could do any better?'

The herb woman had been to us that morning and in addition to the mess our intruders had made there were sacks of hops and bushels of lavender stacked against the walls and beside the counter. I set the stove roaring, for the day had turned cold and damp and I wanted the place warm. I missed the herb garret we'd had at St Saviour's – that warm room, in the roof space at the top of the infirmary chapel where I had stored my botanical supplies. Everything had dried quickly, and I had had plenty of space for working. In our new premises we had to make do with the storeroom at the back. It was adequate, but not quite enough.

I was up a ladder against the high shelves when she came. Perhaps the sound of my own breathing distracted me, perhaps I was preoccupied with the questions in my head, but when I turned from the ladder and saw her there I was so surprised that I dropped the jar I was holding. Then I remembered that Mrs Speedicut had broken the clapper in the doorbell. No wonder the woman had been able to enter so silently. Aniseed spilled across the work bench.

'How long have you been watching me?' I said crossly.

'Since we first met,' she answered. 'At Angel Meadow the night Dr Rutherford was murdered.' The clock ticked as I waited for her to say more, to tell me what she wanted or why she had come. 'He is not my father, he is my stepfather,' she said suddenly. 'Though he insists that I call him "Father". I am one of his philanthropic projects.'

'I see.' Then, fearing this might not be enough, I added, 'And your real parents?'

'I never knew them. I'm not sorry about it. One cannot be sorry for something or someone one does not know.'

I nodded. I remembered saying something similar about my own mother, who had died as I was born. And yet the truth was quite the opposite.

Constance Mothersole ran her fingers across the face of the globe I kept on the counter top – I used it to try to teach Gabriel where some of our more exotic herbs came from though the lad was unable to grasp the distances I talked about.

'I would like to travel the world,' she said. 'Europe, America, Australia.'

'Why don't you ask your father?' I said. 'There is plenty of philanthropy to be had abroad, and all countries have ways of treating their mad. He might well be more open to the idea than you think.'

'Might he?' She looked about at the mess, her hands clasping and unclasping. 'The place seems very untidy. I would have thought you would have made more of an effort for me.'

'How was I to know you were coming?' I retorted.

'Because of the flowers I gave to you and Mr Quartermain.'

'Chickweed and corchorus? For itchiness and venereal diseases?'

'Oh, you're so prosaic,' she said. 'They mean far more than that.'

There was once a time when I might have known what such meanings were, for Eliza Magorian had enjoyed such playful use of herbs and flowers and I had loved her dearly. But she was gone, and so was my interest in such trifles. 'Perhaps they do,' I said. 'But I'm an apothecary, Miss Mothersole, not a lady who has nothing better to do than communicate in riddles and codes.'

'Well perhaps you *should* understand a lady's riddles and codes,' she retorted. 'How else might I say what I mean when my mother is watching? You might understand me far better – you might even have expected me – if you had bothered to find out what I meant.'

'If you had said what you meant I would not have to find out. But enlighten me, please, Miss Mothersole. What is the meaning of chickweed and corchorus?'

'Chickweed: "I would like a rendezvous". Corchorus: "I am impatient for your absence".'

I blinked. 'I didn't—'

'Yes, well, I guessed as much. And so I gave you a note too. Far more explicit.'

'When?'

'At Angel Meadow.' She laughed. 'Right under my mother's nose too. Oh, come now, Mr Flockhart. Don't be so arch with me. The card I gave you with the flowers pasted upon it. Did you not recognise them?'

'Yes,' I said. I pulled the folded card from my pocket. 'Pimpernel. Buttercup. Violet.'

'Pimpernel "Let us meet", buttercup "Today", violet "Five o'clock". It is five o'clock precisely.'

I sighed. 'Miss Mothersole—'

'You would like to see my notebook,' she said. 'Wouldn't you?'

'From the night Dr Rutherford was killed? Yes, I would.'

'And yet there are other nights, and other days.' She watched me, her expression guarded. 'I think you might find much to interest you.'

'Have you brought it?'

'No. I've nothing but myself for you today.'

'Where is it?'

'It's in the library at Angel Meadow.' She gave a faint smile. 'The best place to keep a secret is in full view, don't you agree?'

'Why, yes, I suppose that could be true.'

'I think you know that it is. Equally, the best place to hide a book is amongst books.' She licked her lips, and fell silent.

'Is there something else?' I said after a moment.

She picked up one of the spilled aniseeds and nibbled it.

'Well,' I said. 'It's a pleasure to see you, Miss Mothersole. But I must really get on—'

'There is also something on which I would like to ask your opinion.'

I motioned her towards the chair near to the stove.

'No,' she said. 'I cannot speak to you here.' She looked about. 'We must go somewhere private. I have locked the door but people may look in and see us. Where does this door here lead?'

'To the storeroom,' I said, mystified.

'Perhaps in there might serve. Is it private?'

The storeroom was small, warmed by the flue from the stove and from the bake house in the property next door. It was lined with shelves upon which were baskets full of dried herbs, leaves, seeds and petals. The walls were hung with bunches of calendula, feverfew and comfrey. I also stored our household linen there, as the spike lavender, rosemary and cedar deterred moths and made the bed sheets smell fresh. Constance Mothersole vanished into its cabin-like interior, her skirts whisking against the hop sacks and causing a basket of mallow root to spill its contents across the floor. I kicked them aside irritably and followed her inside.

'Miss Mothersole—'

She reached behind me and pulled the door closed. 'I must be private,' she hissed.

The only light came through a single narrow window high in the wall. Upon its ledge was a row of glass vessels containing various tinctures – St John's wort, sea buck- thorn, rosehip. The light filtered through them warmly, and I could not help but notice how pretty and clear-skinned it made her look. There was something on the girl's mind, for even in the dim light I could see a vein pulsing in her neck. With the door closed and the stove next door well stoked the smell from the herbs quickly grew heavy, drowsily floral with hibiscus and heliotrope. Beneath these I could smell the earthy, visceral scents of the green, low-growing plants – chickweed, plantain and burdock. Miss Mothersole's skirts pressed against my legs as she moved.

'My father,' she began. 'My father says that . . . that I'm not fit for a man. That I'll never make a wife. You have heard him yourself—'

'Miss Mothersole,' I said. 'I think you should leave that to the judgement of men other than your father.'

'I am not interested in the judgement of men.'

'Then you must trust to your own.'

She seized my hand. 'I am doing. That is . . . I wish to trust myself to *your* judgement. If you . . . if you could . . .'

I felt the blood rush into my cheeks. 'I didn't mean that *I—*'

'Shh!' She laid a finger on my lips. 'You must listen.'

I swallowed, feeling my birthmark pulse as I blushed to the roots of my hair. Her face was close, her finger warm as blood so that all at once a familiar feeling of fear and loneliness welled up within me; an aching desire for tenderness that I knew could not possibly be fulfilled. What did she want from me, this tall curious girl? Surely she could not want me for a lover. As a man I was ugly, as a woman I was hideous – tall and blighted, an abomination to be pitied and scorned, my birthmark an indelible mask behind which I hid my true self from the world. The only one person I had ever allowed to see behind it was Eliza. She was lost to me, but the need to be loved, touched, wanted, remained within me no matter how hard I tried to get the better of it.

'Mr Flockhart, my father says I will never make a wife. For my part, I hope I shall not for I could not bear to end up like my mother. And yet,' she hesitated. 'And yet I would like to *know*.'

The scents of the storeroom grew thicker, the air warmer, so that my skin prickled beneath my shirt. Once more I felt an aching loneliness. 'But I do not love you,' I said.

'I know that.' She leaned towards me. 'You're nothing like a man.' Her breath smelled of aniseed and apples. In the dim glow from the window her eyes were huge. In her expression I read kindness, and apprehension. But there was something else too. The pulse at her throat beat in time with my own. 'I see things that others do not. My father talks of the need for observation, and yet he sees nothing but himself, nothing of the world but his own place in it. But I? I see everything.'

'Miss Mothersole—'

'I see you,' she said. 'Like me, you watch and listen. You listen to me, here and now, and you don't object, you don't bluster and barge past and tell me to return to my father. Nor do you snatch what I offer as if it were yours for the taking. Why? Because you are not what you pretend to be.'

'You misunderstand—'

'No, I do not. We're the same, you and I. You're tired of your burden of loneliness and deceit, as I'm tired of my role as drab, loveless daughter. But I am *not* drab, not in my heart, nor in my mind. I will die an old maid, I know, and I'll never know the love of a man. But I would like to know the love of a woman.'

I said nothing. My feet seemed to have rooted to the floor. My heart in my chest was beating so hard that I was sure she might hear it. Could I give her what she wanted – whatever that might be? And what did I want? Love? Affection? I had those from Will. But did I not long for intimacy, for passion, for the physical touch of another? I did. Oh, I did.

She stood tall and straight before me, her arms long and slender. The legs beneath her dress would be lean and slim too, her waist narrow, her stomach flat and muscular. Her face was a perfect oval; her eyes a deep blue-grey, the dilated pupils lending her an extraordinary and luminous beauty. I could not believe that I had once thought her plain, that I had once looked upon her fair hair and composed features and thought nothing of her. I thought of how she endured her father's ludicrous orders and cruel remarks, and I felt humbled by her fortitude. And yet her replies had always been spiced with humour, so that although she spoke with every appearance of obedience she was, to anyone wise enough to listen, a woman who knew her own mind. What a companion she would make for anyone lucky enough to have her treat them as an equal. And now here we were, she and I. Were we not as much flesh and blood as men? Were they alone in having desires that demanded satisfaction?

I kissed her on the lips. 'In here?' I whispered. 'Now?'
She nodded. 'But fast. There's not much time.'
I tore my waistcoat and shirt off and tossed them aside. She unpinned my bindings, examining the manner by

which they were fastened. 'Does it hurt,' she said. 'To be wrapped so tightly?'

I shook my head, unable to speak as her hands brushed against me.

'I could do this too,' she whispered. 'I could live as a man. I am plain and unnoticeable, as tall and thin as you.' She pressed her hands to my breasts, crushing them against me. 'What freedoms it gives you!'

'It's a lonely road,' I said. 'There are few of us on it and our paths rarely cross.'

'Lonelier than the one I am on now?'

'It's a different loneliness. And there's always the fear of discovery.'

'So I own your secret?' she whispered. Her hands moved against me. 'I alone?'

I felt a pang of unease. 'I would be grateful if you would keep it out of your notebook.' I kissed her again then – I did not want to think about how casually I had just thrown away my identity – and worried at her dress with urgent fingers.

'Pull it down,' she whispered. 'It will never come off in time if you undo all the buttons.'

I did as she directed. The collar of her bodice was wide, and having managed to undo a few of the buttons I brought it down easily enough, so that her breasts and shoulders were exposed, rising from that a mass of navy blue fabric and white foaming underclothes as though she were a mermaid emerging from the sea. Her skin was pale and flawless and silky to the touch, her breasts small, as small as my own, soft and perfectly filling my palm. Standing beside her I opened my britches, took one of her hands and guided it between my legs. I could not stifle a cry – how long it had been, and how cold and lonely and without comfort I was.

My head cleared. I could hardly believe what I had done. What I was doing still, for there was Miss Mothersole, sprawling upon the bed of hop sacks, her face against my breast, her fingers between my legs. I pulled her hand out.

'What is it?' she said. 'I thought that was what you wanted?'

'I did. I do.'

'Then what—?'

'I have something for you too.' I knelt before her and pulled up her skirts – rummaging through the swathes of fabric and layers of petticoats, the folds of linen and lace. I found her at last, like a jewel buried within the soft and silky flesh of an oyster. I pushed her legs apart and buried my face between them until I drew from her a cry as sharp as my own.

Chapter Twenty-One

I had not been out at night on my own for a long time. Usually, if I was out after nightfall Will was with me, and I had to confess that I would have preferred it if he had been at my side. I had agreed to go up with him to the library at Angel Meadow the following day to find Miss Mothersole's notebook. Gabriel was still shaken, though he pretended he wasn't, and we did not want to leave him that evening. But I had been unable to sleep, and, eventually I had got up, dressed and slipped out, determined to retrieve the notebook and return home with it before anyone else was up.

The night was as black as molasses and choked with fog. The air tasted abominable, coating the inside of my nose and mouth with a poisonous layer. Something squelched beneath my soles and I felt a rat running over my shoes. I could see nothing – not where I was going nor where I had been. I had a lantern, though it offered me little illumination. The lamps in the street were no more than dim fuzzy orbs, and my own was hardly better, huddled within its squat glass prison as if in fear at the dark world that surrounded us. I hid my face in my handkerchief and hurried on.

The fog has a curious effect upon the senses. Unable to see, we have only sound – muffled and disembodied as it is – to keep us safe. Usually I paid no attention to the sound of my feet on the pavement. Now, they sounded a ringing declaration of my approach. My muttered curses echoed about me as if spoken by another, so that anyone standing still and silent would know exactly where I was, though I would have no idea at all where they might be even if they were right beside me.

I was passing St Saviour's church when I had the feeling that I was being followed. I stopped walking and held my breath – but there was nothing. Who might be out on a night such as this? I sighed at my own foolishness and suggestibility, and carried on. But there it was again – footsteps moving in time with my own; breathing, measured and controlled, coming from the gritty darkness somewhere behind me.

'Who's there?' I held up my lantern. But its feeble light could do nothing against the fog, and I could see only a dense sea of whirling brown particles, opaque as a jar full of smoke. No one spoke; no one strode forward out of the gloom or hurried past. I took a step back the way I had come, listening for . . . what? A sigh? The rustle of clothes or the echo of retreating footsteps? My eyes stared in my head, my ears straining. I felt the skin on my back grow chill, as if my flesh had been stroked by an invisible hand. All my instincts told me to move, to run as fast as I could away from that place – away from that invisible looming

archway, from the silent church hunched resentfully at its
foot, from the crowded, forgotten graveyard beyond the
wall. I had known St Saviour's Street my whole life, had
walked down it a thousand times. What had happened to
me, to the city, that I now felt so affrighted by it? The fog
was enough to unsettle the strongest of hearts but I walked
on, briskly now in the long fast stride I had inherited from
my father. Let anyone try to catch me, I thought. I could
outrun all of them, even on a night such as this.

A brazier in the shadow of the asylum wall gave off a
dim glow. Ragged figures huddled around it, coughing
and hawking. A chestnut exploded like a pistol shot and
a scrap of hot shell grazed my cheek. I held my keys close
in my hand, stifling their jangling with my fingers. Would
Pole be lurking in his burrow beside the door? I hoped not.
It had been after midnight when I'd left the apothecary,
I knew it could not be much later. I had left it until after
lights out so that I might reduce the chances of bumping
into anyone. I had never felt at home at Angel Meadow,
its associations were, for me, too brutal, too immediate,
to allow me any peace of mind while I was in the place.
Walking towards it I had felt a deepening dread, not for
fear of what I was about to do, but because of the utter
hopelessness the building represented to me. Cure, for
the most part, was illusory. Certainly some of the inmates
made a recovery, but in the main it was a prison for those
who could not be cared for anywhere else. I extinguished
my lantern, and unlocked the door.

Inside, the darkness was complete, for without Pole and
his lantern there was no light to guide me. Pole's den,
behind the door, was empty, the fire in the grate no more
than a small pile of clinker. I blew upon it, drawing from

the cinders a red glow. I plucked a taper from the earthen cup on the mantel and, certain that the building slept, re-lit my lamp.

I was no stranger to long, gloomy corridors, to reflections from windows that showed me my own crimson-stained face, to the creaking of floors and walls, or the almost-human sounds made by the wind. The fog outside showed black and gritty against the windows, the shadows from my candle jumping and dancing, so that I had the impression that something dim and formless was waiting just out of sight behind and ahead of me. As a child attending my father on his evening rounds about St Saviour's Infirmary I had seen terror in every shadow. My father had cured me of my foolishness by locking me in a windowless storeroom beneath the foul ward. There, with only a candle-end to light my prison, the shadows had loomed, the lumber of past generations – a headless skeleton, a stack of broken chairs, a pile of mouldering blankets – transformed into rearing terrors. Overhead, the sounds from the foul ward – the murmur of voices, the thump of footsteps, the dim sound of sobbing, retching, and spitting – had sounded in my childish ears like the ghosts of St Saviour's dead. After an hour, when my cries and shrieks had stopped, my father had let me out. The shadows at Angel Meadow were nothing compared to that. And yet something troubled me. Once more I stood stock still, my lantern held high, and listened. Around me the asylum held its breath.

The library was as dark and silent as a glove. Since the students had left to follow St Saviour's across the river it had seen far less traffic. Dr Hawkins and Dr Christie had their own libraries – in their homes and in the rooms they kept at the asylum. Dr Golspie had used it, but he had found its books to be stale and antiquated. The methods detailed between their pages were from a different world, he'd always said, a cruel world where treatments meted out upon the mad amounted to little more than torture.

'Look,' he had said to us. 'See the whirling chair? And Ramsay recommends cold wrapping and ice baths. Then there's the distaff. The chains and weights. The iron collar! Can you believe it? Even Rutherford wouldn't recommend such methods.'

Dr Golspie had removed some of the more alarming books altogether, so that here and there the shelves bore crooked gaps. The place smelled stale, of passed time and abandoned ideas. The floor creaked beneath my feet like the deck of a ship. I held my lantern high. The library was small, no bigger than the apothecary, but its walls were taller, lined with books, some accessed by a pair of thin ladders attached to the walls like rigging. A narrow staircase of wrought iron coiled upward to a mezzanine and a narrow gallery. Where would Constance have put her notebook? She had not said. Perhaps under 'M' for Mothersole? It was the most likely place, and she would surely not have expected me to look through every shelf? The shelves were inlaid with tarnished brass letters. I traced through the alphabet. Montague. Morton. Mosley—

I snatched a book off the shelf and flipped it open. Page after page of Constance Mothersole's small pencilled scribble proclaimed it to be hers. My heart beat against my ribs. I was certain, nearly certain, that I knew who had murdered Dr Rutherford, and who had murdered Dr Golspie too. I had little proof, other than my own deductions, and I had told no one, not even Will. For how

might I prove it? Without proof there was no certainty.
To accuse without evidence would simply galvanise my
opponent and I had to be sure, so sure. Within these pages
I might find what I needed to confirm my suspicions.

I took the book to the table, flicking through the pages
– 10th September, 11th September, 12th September – each
line was densely covered with tightly pencilled letters. I
should have taken it home, should have stuffed it into my
satchel and left that horrible place without looking back,
but I did not. What stopped me? Curiosity? Impatience?
Complacency? Whatever the answer, I remained where I
was, poring over those scribbled pages, my mind focused
on nothing but what Constance Mothersole had written.
I did not hear the door open behind me; I did not see my
assailant's face reflected in the dark mirrors of the library
windows, and I did not feel the stirring of the dry and
book-parched air as they drew back a hand to strike me
down.

At first I was conscious only of the sound of voices –
muffled and indistinct. Did I hear crying? I was not sure,
but I had the sensation of bobbing upon a gentle sea.
Then I jarred and jolted. I listened again. My head ached,
and I could tell from the way it throbbed that I had been
knocked out. But my head hurt on the inside too. I felt
groggy, almost drunk, my mouth as dry as if I had spent
the night drinking Sorley's ale.

I must have blacked out again, and when I came to once
more I could hear only one voice, at once comforting
and familiar. I felt my berth move, the motion leisurely,

rhythmic and soothing. I opened my eyes, but I could still see nothing, the darkness that surrounded me filling my eye sockets, my mouth, my nostrils so that I felt as if I might choke upon it. My head still throbbed, but this time I was less confused, and I recognised on my tongue the sweetish musty taste of chloroform. I tried to sit, but I could not. I tried to move, but still I could not. Fear scalded through me, and a scream rose and boiled in my throat. But I was bound and gagged, my eyes staring but blind, my mouth stoppered, my ears the only sense still in my possession. I felt myself tip and sway, heard again the dull intonation, then a wettish thunk and a sound like the scattering of seed or small stones. It sounded close, though I could not say how close, and it brought with it a damp chill and the smell of earth, of rotten flesh and worms. I heard the sound again, that dull thunk and a sound as if of scattered stones. I heard it again, and again, over and over but growing fainter, until in a short while there was nothing. Nothing in my ears but a terrible silence, and nothing in my eyes but darkness.

Angel Meadow Asylum, 18th September 1852

We left from Millbank, some two hundred of us, dressed in prison grey with what possessions we had bundled at our feet. One of the girls I had known in the Rents brought me one of Miss Day's dresses that I had kept well hidden – the other I let her have. I took the blue one, I was very clear about that, for I had sewn some of Mr Day's sovereigns into its bodice. I had done this well before Goblin and I were caught, for I am cautious by nature and wanted something should I need it.

It was at Millbank that I was to meet the man who was to make my life as much a torment on the other side of the world as it had been on this. We were shuffling our way up the gangplank, shackled together in twos, those ahead disappearing into the shady belly of the ship. Behind us, on the dockside below, something heavy crashed to the ground. The convicts who were still ashore, as well as those of us who were not yet aboard, stopped to look over at the commotion. A large box of some kind – made of a polished wood, with a rich patina and a brass eye projecting from one side of it, was lying upon the ground. Its owner was a thin man in a tall hat, long coat and white neckerchief. He carried a cane – I could tell by the swing of it as he shouted at the stevedore that it was weighted.

'If you have broken it I will flay the skin off your back with my own hands.' His voice was tight with fury.

I exchanged a glance with the woman to whom I was chained. 'Who d'you think he is?' she said. She grinned. 'Sounds like my da', though he's long dead.'

'I think he's the surgeon,' I said. 'See his bag?'

'P'raps it's not his.' She sounded hopeful. 'P'raps he's not on this transport.'

The man turned and seized the brown doctor's bag. He pushed his hat to the back of his head and looked up. His eyes were deep set, his cheeks sunken, his mouth an angry line. He stared at us, at my companion and me, and in his face I saw nothing but loathing and contempt.

The Norfolk *carried prisoners, both men and women, as well as free passengers, in addition to sailors and soldiers, so there were lots of us on board. I was used to crowds and small spaces, all of us were, but I could not believe how many hundreds of us were to be crammed inside that wooden prison. Some of the women said it had been a slave ship once, and when we were herded below into the terrible hutches where we were to spend much of our journey I could well believe it. We were berthed in two rows of bunks, double height, hard against the creaking hull of the ship. A narrow walkway ran in between, and iron gates divided our prison into sections. The place was airless and dark, noisy and stinking, so that many of us were sick straight away, for we were none of us used to the rolling, heaving movement of the waves. But there was little that might be done about it for the captain had his orders, and we were kept*

*down there, ironed to our berths, for many days until we had
left England far behind.*

*At last, after a week or more of being close quartered, we were
taken on deck, where we were lined up to be inspected by the
captain and crew, the soldiers and officers, and the ship's surgeon. This last was a man of some influence, the captain being
a rough man more interested in the seas and the wind than with
the well-being of his passengers, and concerned only that we got
to the Bay without mutiny or loss of life. He said as much, and
told us we might have a peaceful journey if we kept quiet and
caused no trouble. He showed us the cat – a fearful tangled whip
of knotted hide – and pointed to the triangle where we might be
bound, and the cramping box in which we might be crushed
should we choose to ignore his advice. Our transport was to last
one hundred days, the captain said, perhaps more but certainly
no less. He set out what was expected from us, namely – obedience and hard work. We would do the laundry, scrub the decks,
and lay down lime in the privies. If we behaved well we would
have exercise about the deck, as we would have our irons removed
once we reached blue water.*

*We settled into our tasks well enough. At first we were kept
under close watch; the convict men were put below decks when
we were up, and we went below when they were up. Once our
irons were removed we moved about more freely, and many of
the women took up with soldiers or sailors, or even the male
convicts. The free passengers were told not to mix with us, but they
hardly cared where they went and associated with whomever they
pleased. Rations were dull but adequate, and we were lucky to be
travelling on a ship that gave us a half-pint of port wine nightly.
Discipline was kept easily enough, for the threat of the removal of
this luxury was sufficient to make most behave themselves. We
were punished with irons, and the cramping box, the men with*

lashes too, though not above two dozen, and nothing like the two hundred or so we had heard about on other vessels, though the screams of the men as the cat cut away the flesh from their backs was pitiable nonetheless.

The weather grew warmer. How many days had we been at sea? I had no idea. Down in our bunks we were stifled – there was often no breeze at all, the only way for it to get to us was through the hatch, and yet when the hatch was closed it was thickly barred, and as impenetrable to air as any prison wall. The sun blazed down, the pitch dropping from the seams in the hull in burning black pennies. We longed for water, fresh water, our ration of two pints of warm putrid water a day the cruellest of jokes. And yet the opposite of this burning heat was no better, for in heavy seas the water poured down the hatch, so that those nearest were soaked to the bone, and all of us, by the morning, were crusted with salt and vomit.

Dr Rutherford spent much of his time in his cabin – he had secured a berth to himself, despite the cramped situation most others endured. What he was doing down there had become the subject of speculation. Some said he had animals – rats and birds – and that he experimented upon them at night. Others said he was dead drunk, or that he was dissecting the body of one Jane Calloway, a convict who had died even before we were a fortnight out, and whose corpse none of us had seen since. He showed no interest in the male prisoners, but stood watching us women as we went about out tasks or stood idling on deck. One day he had us line up before him. He went from one to another, taking our names, noting our convictions and measuring our heads with his metal callipers. He wrote everything down in his notebook. He was especially interested in those with the most violent and troubled pasts, though habitual thieves and prostitutes also fascinated him. These he took to one side. He had *set up his box – a camera was what he called it – behind a screen of canvas, and he positioned these particular miscreants in a chair and took their likeness.*

Then he came to me.

Chapter Twenty-Two

William knew that I had been sleeping badly, and when I did not wake early and join him for breakfast the next morning, he decided to let me sleep on. By the time he realised that I was missing from my bed, it was past nine o'clock in the morning.

'I was sure you'd gone to Angel Meadow,' he told me later. 'We were supposed to go together to find Miss Mothersole's notebooks, but I knew you for the most independent and inquisitive creature I'd ever met. If you could not sleep, what else would you do but carry on where we had left off the night before?'

Just as he resolved to go up to the asylum himself, he said, Mrs Speedicut appeared. She looked as though she had been sleeping on the floor somewhere for she was dirty and stained, with soot on her apron and straw in her hair. Mrs Speedicut admitted that she had 'fallen asleep at Sorley's', and Mr Sorley had left her where she lay. When he opened up the next day and found her still there he had kicked her out and sent her down to the apothecary with the bill. 'I gave her a mug of coffee, took her asylum keys, and went up to the place directly.'

By that time the air was clear, the black smoke that trickled from the chimneys streaking the angry sky like banners of tattered silk. London is rarely silent, the parish of St Saviour's – its tenements stacked together like rows of battered books, its houses divided and subdivided and filled to bursting with people – almost never so. There were always people about the streets, always noise and bustle, commotion and movement. And yet, Will told me, the road to the asylum was quiet that morning.

'I knew something was wrong,' he said. 'Even Angel Meadow was subdued, though there were people everywhere – attendants criss-crossing the hall, their strides purposeful, their arms full of swathes of black fabric, and groups of serious-looking men standing about waiting. Mrs Lunge had festooned the place with black crêpe, the banisters were sheathed with the stuff, the clock, and the portraits of asylum worthies had been draped in it.'

For a moment, he wondered what was going on. Mrs Lunge herself always wore black, so her garb was no more or less different than usual. But that day everyone else was dressed in black too. Then he remembered – today was the day of Dr Rutherford's funeral. A number of lunatics had been lined up to attend – men only, of course, and a white-faced Edward Eden stood sullenly at the end of the line. The serious-looking men were Dr Rutherford's colleagues – phrenologists, and men from the Mind and Brain Society. As Will arrived, the doors that led through to the mortuary eased open, and two attendants wheeled Dr Rutherford's coffin into the centre of the atrium –

the main entrance hall of the asylum. The presence of 'the casket' as Mrs Lunge kept calling it – a magnificent affair in polished mahogany and brass, paid for by the grateful members of the Phrenological Society – meant that everyone was suddenly distracted, and Will could pass through the crowds without anyone asking where he was going. No one was noticeable by their absence. He saw Pole buffing the mahogany lid of the coffin with a soft cloth. Dr and Mrs Hawkins were standing side by side at the foot of the stairs, Dr Stiven, once more in his wig, waited a little way from them. Dr Mothersole, a mountain of mourning flanked by his wife and daughter, stood with his huge bald head bowed, his chin sunk to his breast, a black handkerchief pressed to his lips.

'I am an emotional man,' Will heard him say to his wife. 'You know how deeply I feel, my dear. It is a curse, and also a blessing. Constance?'

'I am writing it down, Father,' Miss Mothersole intoned.

Dr Christie, his shock of white hair all the more dazzling amongst that sea of black-clad backs and shoulders, was looking at his watch, his manner impatient. He snapped it closed and blew a sharp blast on a whistle. The babbling lunatics sank into a nervous silence. Two of the more quiescent of them stepped forward, along with Dr Hawkins and Dr Christie himself, and two men from the Mind and Brain Society. They hoisted Dr Rutherford's coffin onto their shoulders and, led by an undertaker in a tall black hat who kept time with his staff upon the floor, stepped solemnly towards the asylum doors. Outside, a hearse waited. It was hauled by six black horses festooned in feathers and dark polished leather, and preceded by six mutes carrying tall crêpe-swathed staffs. The undertaker opened the doors to the hearse and Dr Rutherford's coffin was shunted inside, where it lay like a giant roasting tin inside a great glass oven.

The men filed out to climb into waiting carriages.

'Are you coming, Quartermain?' asked Dr Hawkins.

Without waiting for an answer he turned to Dr Christie. Will said he heard the two of them murmuring to one another about the day – the service was to take place at St Saviour's Parish Church, and Dr Rutherford was to be interred in whatever space had been found in the remains of the graveyard, his bones forever a-tremble at the trains passing overhead. Dr Christie was to read something appropriate from the Bible, Dr Hawkins was to say something about Dr Rutherford's work at Angel Meadow – Will had wanted to speak to Dr Hawkins but there was no time, and no opportunity, and all he could do was to follow him out of the asylum and blurt, 'Where's Jem, sir?'

'Not seen him,' said Dr Hawkins. He slipped on a pair of black gloves. 'I'm sure he's here somewhere. What do you think of "tenacious", Christie? Was Rutherford "tenacious"? Or "resolute". I'd prefer "stubborn", naturally, or even "obtuse"—'

Will slipped back into the asylum as Dr Rutherford's coffin was slowly driven away. Pole had vanished. Mrs Lunge was examining a ledger in which she kept a list of quotidian tasks, a group of maids and attendants standing in a semi-circle before her. Naturally women were not expected to attend the funeral, and Constance and Mrs Mothersole were standing with a group of women Will recognised as members of the Ladies' Committee. They were whispering together, and preparing to festoon the walls of the hall with swags of black fabric. They glared at Will with disapproval – should he not be on the way to St Saviour's with the other men to watch Dr Rutherford being put into the ground? Did he not want to pay his respects in person?

'Have you seen Mr Flockhart?' he asked them. 'Did any of you see him this morning?' But none of them had anything useful to tell him about where I might be.

'Perhaps he is in the library, Mr Quartermain,' Miss Mothersole said, her expression filled with meaning.

Will went to the library. Like me, he looked under 'M', but found only a gap where 'Mothersole' might be. Wondering whether I had taken the notebook already and was pursuing something I had found inside it, Will went to the next place he thought me likely to be – upstairs in Dr Rutherford's rooms. The door was open, and two men from the Phrenological Society were scaling the ladder that stretched up Dr Rutherford's wall of skulls and plaster death-masks. One of them had a large, cream-coloured cranium in his hands and was running his fingers over its contours.

Will ran back downstairs, calling my name now, uncaring who he might disturb or who might question his disrespectful behaviour. He went through the wards, through the dispensary, through the chapel, and the hall. Where previously the trestle tables had been set out with Dr Mothersole's art materials, now they stood as long dining tables, dressed in black linen and laid out with food and drink. Mrs Lunge stood still and silent, plucking at her tall collar and its glittering jet brooch as if trying to pull it higher. Maids and attendants scurried about her like mice.

Will went through to the anatomy museum, the teaching room, and into the cold and echoing mortuary. Where

Dr Rutherford and Dr Golspie had once lain side by side there was now nothing but an icy marble slab. Will swallowed and looked away. The stink of the place, he said, was enough to turn his stomach.

Next door, in the anatomy room, the air was curiously thick and damp, heavy with a smothering, moist heat that fogged the mind and snatched the breath. Will held a handkerchief to his nose to stop himself from gagging. Laid out on the table were half a dozen glass jars filled with a viscous whey-coloured fluid. Inside each floated a lump of flesh, a chunk of bone or an organ. They were new, Will could see that much, for they gleamed pinkly, and had not yet developed the bloated, waterlogged look of the long-preserved. On the far side of the room the fire roared and crackled. Upon it stood a large iron trivet, atop this was the source of the reeking, broth-like atmosphere: a huge copper-bellied cauldron, its sides crusted with a thick layer of ancient grease and soot. Its lid danced and trembled, belching hot breaths of meaty steam.

Will told me later that he had never seen an anatomist's cauldron before. A horrified fascination drew him onwards, a terrible fear at who, or what, might be inside that man-sized stock-pot. He had to look, he said, had to see for himself, to be certain . . .

In one swift movement Will reached forward and plucked off the lid. A cloud of fatty steam breathed into his face, and then cleared. The contents of the pot bubbled. For a moment he thought it might be nothing but clothes, stuffed into a giant copper washtub and set to boil, so that he almost laughed out loud with relief. And then something heaved up to the surface and swirled lazily; something thin and fibrous and gingery, its filaments waving and billowing like weed tugged by a gentle current. What was it?

Will reeled back, his hand to his mouth, and vomited onto the floor. 'I could not believe what I was looking at,' he told me. 'It was hair. A hank of hair. Who else but Rutherford had hair that colour? Yours is far paler – thicker and shorter too. And yet I had to look again. I had to have no doubt.'

He peeped into the pot once more. This time, something far worse than a hank of hair rose up to meet his gaze. It was no more than a glimpse but there was no mistaking that narrow skull, its top sliced off, the flesh stretched and flaccid as if it were two sizes too big for the bones beneath. A pale boiled eye rolled and glistened beneath a stitched and drooping lid.

I lay in the smothering silence. Tears stung my face, trickling sideways and filling my ears. I closed my eyes then. If I was to see nothing, I might at least be master of my own blindness. I tried to imagine light – the rising sun, the flame of a candle or the warm glow of a lantern. But my imagination failed me. I tried to shift my tense and aching limbs, but my bindings were too tight for any movement. I tried to scream, but my mouth was stoppered, my sobs muffled and impotent, so that I was reminded of those poor souls in the criminal wards at Angel Meadow, who had moaned and raved for a freedom that would never come. I heard my heart beating in my ears, and I forced myself to listen to its steady rhythm. Will will find me, wherever I am, Will will find me. But the rhythm was erratic, as if my heart were being stifled too. I opened my eyes. This was what death must be like, I thought. This was eternity, nothing but silence and darkness and a terrible clanging fear.

Into that silence came that rhythmic thumping once more. I thrashed against my bindings and roared behind my gag until my throat bled and I thought I might drown or choke. I fell silent then, my breathing shallow. My head felt dizzy, my chest tight. I knew what would happen when I had breathed in all the air. Had not my old friend Dr Bain showed me when I was an apprentice? He had caught a pigeon and trapped it beneath a bell jar. We had watched as the creature's flaps grew feebler, the longer it spent in that enclosed space.

'Will it die?' I had said pathetically. 'We can't let it die.'

'What's one pigeon, Jem?' he had replied. 'Are there not enough of the confounded things tormenting us with their showers of droppings that we should lament the passing of one? Look at the shoulders of my coat.'

'I know, but—'

He'd shaken his head. 'Such sensibility is of no use to us here. Yes, the bird may die, but it will die for science. A noble death. Look! You see what happens when it has used up all the air in the chamber? And yet—' The bird had lain motionless at the bottom of the jar. 'Open the valve. See what happens now?' I had done so, my eyes fixed upon that tattered pile of grubby feathers. But we had waited too long.

Of course, Dr Bain had insisted on running the experiment again, this time opening the valve as soon as the next pigeon was struggling. Naturally, it had revived. But I had not forgotten how we had suffocated that trapped and helpless bird. Once its air was gone, nothing could revive it. And so, as my head began to spin, the blood thumping in my ears, I knew what fate awaited me. I had no idea whether my eyes were open or closed, though I could now see flashes of light, as if stars were exploding in a silent cosmos hidden within my own head. I thought of my father and mother, of Eliza, and Will – all the people I had loved. I tried to conjure up Eliza's face, but instead there was my father once more. He was shaking his head.

'You didn't need those notebooks, Jem,' he said. 'You had everything that you required already. Trust yourself. Trust your own eyes and ears and they will tell you everything you need to know.'

I tried to speak, to ask what he meant, but I could not. My head felt as though it would burst; my chest as though a weight had settled upon it. Would I die here in this place, the voices in my head mingling with the roaring in my ears, the thumping of my heart shaking my whole being, as if it were beating its last in desperate laboured gasps? And the light! The light was so blinding that I could not look at it at all.

Will said later that he thought he was too late. When he wrenched open the lid of Dr Rutherford's coffin and hauled me out into the dazzling light – which was, in fact, the dismal grey of a drizzling London morning – I was as pale and limp as a corpse. He ripped the gag from my mouth, the rain misting my skin and mingling with my tears.

'If Rutherford was in the stock-pot, then who was in the coffin?' he said. 'That was my reasoning – am I not as fast and logical as you? All at once it was as obvious where you might be as if you had pinned a note to the cauldron itself. There had clearly been someone in the coffin – had I not seen six men struggle beneath its weight as they carried it from the asylum? I knew where Rutherford was to be buried, and so I came. I came faster than I have ever come to anyone. I had to dig like a dog in that filthy wet earth, for they had already put the coffin into the ground. And then there you were, bound and silent in that box – your face so pale, your birthmark – that beloved stain – the only thing that seemed still to pulse with life.' There were tears in his eyes as he spoke. 'I could not believe that you were dead, that I was too late and we would be parted so cruelly.'

I remembered how he had slapped my face as he pulled me out. 'Wake up!' he'd shouted. 'Wake up, you stubborn, pig-headed wretch. How dare you make me dig in this infernal graveyard yet again. Have I not had enough of the place that I must root you out of it too? Damn you, Jem Flockhart—'

I had felt the stinging blows. I had felt the rain, the cold, blessed rain, briny against my lips where it had mixed with his tears. When I opened my eyes I did not know where I was. I could not speak. I could not move. I saw Will smeared from head to foot in stinking St Saviour's mud. Beside him, Old Dick squatted, toad-like on the mound of sticky earth they had excavated from the hole. Will told me afterwards that he could hardly bear to look at me, that he had never seen a countenance etched with such blank and rigid terror. My hands, unbound, grasped his lapels as tightly as twigs that had grown through the fabric, my eyes so wide that he feared they might start from my face. I stared, and yet seemed not to see, my mouth open and screaming, but as silent as the ground from which I had been plucked.

I lay, raving, in my room at the apothecary. I remember kind hands pressing me back into the bed, Gabriel's anxious face, Will holding my hand. He would let no one see me but Dr Stiven, who prescribed me valerian and St John's wort and, when those failed, gave me bromide and opium. Was I mad? Perhaps I was. The lamp burned continually at my bedside. I would not have it moved, would not have it extinguished, but lay with my gaze fixed upon it, staring into its flame so that Will feared for my sight as well as my sanity. I did not eat; I did not sleep, for if I closed my eyes, the darkness sent me screaming back into the light.

Faces came and went, the faces of the living and of the dead. I saw my old room and St Saviour's, I saw Mrs Roseplucker's ravaged face and Susan Chance crouched on a pile of dirty straw. I saw Miss Mothersole, her notebook in her hands – she opened it before me and held it out, her finger pointing to the words she had scribbled across the page, words that had passed between two people – one of whom I knew to be innocent of all that had occurred, the other whose guilt, and complicity I had, until that point, been unable to attest: *Have no fear, we shall be more than a match for him . . . I have paid for my crimes thrice over, must I pay for them still? . . . Say nothing . . . Be as a stranger to me or all is lost.* I saw the hall at Angel Meadow on the night Dr Rutherford

313

was murdered. I saw faces I had once regarded with dispassion now filled with guilt and duplicity – Susan Chance smiling at me, her eyes sharp and black; Mrs Lunge, her fingers plucking at the large amethyst brooch she wore at the high collar of her dress, Dr Stiven – Joshua Milner – powdered and unsmiling at her side. I saw Dr Christie staring at Letty; I saw Pole and Edward Eden, both of them watching Mrs Hawkins, who stood tall and stately in the centre of the room, her jet beads glinting like eyes in the lamplight. I knew what had happened. I knew who had murdered Dr Rutherford, and Dr Golspie, and why. I tried to speak, to tell Will, but there was only Dr Stiven, and no words would come to me. He nodded and smiled and coaxed me back onto the bed. I felt a hand lift my head, felt the spoon against my lips and the burn of laudanum on my tongue. And then everything was black once more.

On the fourth day, I awoke to find that everything had changed. My head felt clear. I could look at the lamp without feeling it was an object so dear to me that I could not leave go of it. The night held no terrors. Constance Mothersole's notebook would have been destroyed by now, of that I was quite certain. I had read little before I was knocked out, but it had been enough to know whom I should be speaking to.

The following day we went back to Angel Meadow.

'Are you sure you are ready for this?' Will said as we walked up St Saviour's Street. 'Someone wants you dead. Someone substituted your body for Rutherford's and stuffed him into a giant cauldron. That someone is, in all probability, a resident of Angel Meadow.'

'I know that, Will, but we can't stop now. Besides,' I took his arm. 'You're with me now. What could possibly happen?'

'I've no idea,' he said. 'I'm no longer able to second guess anything that might happen in this horrible place.'

'But let us think about what we know, not what we might guess,' I said. 'That at least might lead us to some explanations. I was knocked out, but it was not a fatal blow.'

'Perhaps they were unable to kill you in cold blood.'

'You think we are seeing a sickening for murder? Evidence of a conscience?'

'Of sorts.'

'And why was I not stitched?'

'You were not dead.'

'Perhaps.'

'And if you might be stuffed into a coffin then why bother with such an elaborate ritual as stitching you up?'

'Perhaps getting me out of the way was all that was required?'

He shrugged. 'Maybe our attacker is not so systematic after all.'

'I quite agree. And perhaps whoever did this wanted to add further ignominy to Dr Rutherford by boiling him into broth rather than allowing him the dignity of a proper burial. And, not everyone might guess where I had ended up – at least not until it was too late.'

'We must also assume your attacker was a man.'

'Must we?'

'How would a woman drag you from the library to the dissecting room? How would she get you into Rutherford's coffin, how might she get *him* into the stock-pot? All this could only be the work of a man.'

'Or man and woman. Remember how we found Gabriel?'

'That's true.' He looked at me. 'Jem,' he said, 'What are you hiding? D'you know who did this to you? Who murdered Rutherford and Golspie?'

'I think I do,' I said. 'But I must be sure.'

We found Edward Eden outside, in the pigsty. He and two others were shovelling pig shit into wheeled boxes. It was to be spread about the asylum vegetable garden – what was not used would be sold. An asylum attendant was forking dirty hay out of the sty. I had seen the man before, and knew him to be a kind-hearted fellow. I asked if I might speak to Edward.

'If you're quick,' he said. 'We've a lot to get done here.'

Edward watched us approach, his face wary. He reached over and scratched one of the pigs behind the ears. Then he bent down and whispered something to it, pointing to Will and me. Usually he was pleased to see me, but today it was clear that he was reluctant to come forward, and he lingered beside the pig, glancing about warily, as though fearing someone other than the attendant might be watching. He had been this way – sullen, nervous and shifty – since he had found Dr Rutherford's corpse. Perhaps the sight of it had touched the fellow more deeply that anyone realised. That he had been falsely accused of murder, and incarcerated in the asylum's basement, had no doubt done much to render him distrustful and surly. The death of his friend and defender Dr Golspie had only made matters worse – and yet somehow I was convinced there was something else.

'Come along now, Mr Eden,' said the attendant.

Edward put his shovel aside and came towards us.

'Good morning, Edward,' I said. Then, hoping to draw him into my confidence by showing an interest in his favourite subject, added, 'How is your mouse today?'

'He's not well,' came the reply.

'How so?' I said.

'I don't know. But he will not wake up.'

'Where is he?'

Edward patted his coat pocket.

'May I look?'

Edward pulled out a small wooden box. It was the one I had given him. I took it and drew open the sliding lid. Inside, was a greasy mass of yellow stuff. A smell of decay and sour milk rose up. 'What's all this?' I said, trying to keep the disgust off my face.

'Cheese,' said Edward. 'In case he wakes up and is hungry.'

I pushed the cheese aside with my finger. Beneath it, the mouse lay stiff. 'Edward,' I said. 'He's dead.'

Edward snatched back the box and cradled it in his hands. 'He's sleeping. Look, there's much less cheese than before. He's eaten some and fallen asleep again.'

'It's fallen out,' I said, pointing to the ground. 'A dead mouse cannot eat cheese.'

His face sagged. 'But I looked after him well. I thought he was happy.' His face grew fearful. 'Perhaps he was poisoned. *She'd* do that.'

'Who?' said Will.

'Not telling.' Edward took the dead mouse from its box and held it to his cheek.

'Look here, Edward,' said Will, pulling another box

317

from his pocket. 'Here's something we bought out on St Saviour's Street. D'you think it'll do just as well?' It was identical to the one Edward held, only larger. 'Do you still have the mouse cage?'

'Dr Rutherford made Mr Pole take it away.'

'Well, let us get you another. You can put these inside.'

Edward's face was shining. 'Is it another mouse?'

'Two mice,' said Will. 'Both are white, so you will be able to find them in the dark.'

'Oh!' Edward took the box. The mice ran out as soon as he opened the lid and he seized them expertly by the tails and caressed their silky fur. One escaped, to run up the sleeve of his coat and around his collar. He laughed as its tiny feet tickled his face.

'Mr Connor.' He addressed the attendant. 'Do we still have my mouse cage?'

'Yes, Mr Eden,' said the man. 'Mr Pole put it in the outhouse.'

'Can you bring it up to my room?'

'I'm not sure as I should, sir. Dr Rutherford said—'

'I'm sure Mr Eden's father would expect it,' I said to the attendant. 'And he's been on the board of governors since Mr Eden was . . . sent downstairs.'

'We must bury Albion,' said Edward, looking sorrowfully at his dead mouse. He looked about. 'Over there.'

Will and I accompanied Edward to a straggling flower bed that ran the length of the asylum. The earth was thick with clay, the plants that grew there sickly and blighted. The north face of the building that overlooked us was black and moist and patched here and there with welts of slimy green mould. Edward looked about for a stick with which to loosen the claggy soil. He found what he needed and proceeded to jab at the ground with it, levering the earth until he could pull a clod of it up with his fingers. He dug deeper, wedged the mouse and its cheese-filled box in the earth, and raked the soil back over. High above, Dr Rutherford's windows looked out at us. The daylight was watery and yellow, the sun struggling to be seen behind a layer of dirty cloud. The asylum's windows reflected nothing, but yawned emptily, black and glittering.

'Edward,' I said. 'Who did you see that night?'

'I cannot say,' he replied. His face closed over and his expression became guarded once more.

'I think I know who it was,' I said. 'What if I whisper their name in your ear, and you can tell me whether I am correct? That way you have not told me, but I have told you.'

Edward hesitated. He considered my argument for a moment before concluding that it was a judicious arrangement. I cupped my hand about his ear and whispered a name.

'Yes,' he said.

'And if I tell you what I think happened that night, will you tell me whether I am correct?'

'Very well.' Edward opened his box and extracted the two white mice. They slipped in and out of his fingers, their noses quivering, their pink eyes bulging like drops of blood.

'You had Dr Golspie's keys, and you went up to Dr Rutherford's rooms.'

'I didn't know they were his rooms. I was lost. I came upon them by mistake—'

'Quite so,' I said. 'But you found Dr Rutherford all the same.'

'He was lying down.'

'You went over to him, and got blood on your hands when you tried to undo the stitches at his mouth.'

'Yes.' Edward put a fist against his lips, as if he hoped to stop the words from escaping. 'I wiped my hands on my handkerchief, but there was so much of it, on the floor, on my shoes—'

'But there was someone else in the room with him,' I said. 'Someone holding a skull. A small skull. You didn't see them at first because they were up the ladder against the wall of phrenology heads.'

'Yes,' whispered Edward. 'But then Albion escaped and ran to the shelves with the skulls – so many of them, rows and rows of them staring down at me. So many dead people! And at my feet Dr Rutherford too. And she was there, as if she was floating, floating like a ghost, all in white she was, and she had a skull in her hands—'

'She was not floating, Edward,' I said. 'She was merely up a ladder. And she was not a ghost, only in her nightdress.'

'She said . . . she said I would end up just like them – just like all those people – the ones whose heads covered the shelves in Dr Rutherford's room.'

'Why would you end up like them?' said Will.

'If I told anyone who I'd seen, of course. She said she would boil me in her pot until there was nothing left but broth and bones.' He looked at us in terror. 'Broth and bones, she said. And then she would put my skull on the high shelf so that no one would ever know me, and I would stay there for ever. But I've not said her name. I promised I wouldn't. She cannot say I told. She cannot boil me—'

'No one will boil you, Edward,' I said. 'You're quite safe now.' I looked up at those fathomless windows once more. A face stared down at us.

Angel Meadow Asylum, 18th September 1852

He said he had read all about me. He knew that I had been sent to the scaffold, but had survived. My crimes, he was convinced, were small in number, but far worse than those of many of my fellow prisoners. I was no sneak thief, no pickpocket; I was a murderer and an arsonist, a burglar and the daughter of a common whore. I told him I was none of those things, that I was the daughter of a seamstress, a victim of sorrow and the wickedness of men. I had done all I could to improve myself, I said, and yet here I was. I delivered my speech in my finest voice. I wrote my name down for him in my best copperplate handwriting – Catherine Devlin. He noted all this down and smiled, crinkling his eyes and pursing his lips. I thought he might prove himself my friend – Joshua Milner was a doctor and had been one of the kindest and most generous of men, would not Dr Rutherford prove to be the same?

How mistaken I was.

Some time after that we crossed the line – the equator. We heard that this was a time of carousing and jollity, that Neptune would enter the ship and anything might happen. I heard later that such rituals were quite usual, though I cannot believe that what took place on board the Norfolk was commonplace throughout the Bay Fleet. Perhaps I am simply naive.

That morning I was called to Dr Rutherford's cabin, where I found him holding my blue dress, the one I had stolen from Miss Day, and had brought all the way from England. His cabin was small, but grand and spacious compared to the stinking hutches below decks where we passed the night. There were no birds and rats cut into bits, and no dead bodies. I looked about for the corpse of Jane Calloway, but there was no sign of her anywhere.

'I want you to put this on,' he said, lifting the dress. He laughed as he spoke, and handed me a glass of rum. 'Your health, my pretty Miss Devlin,' he said. 'They say Neptune is coming amongst us today, will you not raise a glass to him?' His face was red from the sun, the lines on his long neck thick and leathery. I did not like the way he stared at me, and I refused his rum. He appeared unperturbed. 'Look,' he said, pulling open a door. 'I have a bath for you too.'

I have no idea where and how he produced an item of such luxury on board that stinking vessel, but behind the door, in a small room lined with polished wooden panels, was a canvas bath filled with fragrant water. 'Will you not bathe,' he said, 'and wash your hair in honour of the sea god?'

'Not while you are here,' I replied. He smiled at that and went out.

The water was cool against my skin, and I wallowed in it. I should have enjoyed it, but something made me uneasy. I could not say what.

When I came out I found he had taken my convict dress and left only the blue one. I was thirsty now too, for the day was hot and still, so I drank down the rum and water he had left for me. The blue dress looked neat and clean after my rough convict smock, and I put it on. Just as I was fastening my bodice, there was a knock at the door. Two women entered. I recognised them as two of the free passengers, a pair of trollops from County Kildare who were hoping to find work and new lives across the ocean. They had taken up with two of the soldiers soon after we left England and spent much of their time performing the offices of wives, though I could not see what good it would do them in the long term for I understood that the soldiers were already married.

The girls were drunk and giggling. 'Are you ready, miss?' one of them said as she came in. She dropped me an elaborate curtsey and sniggered.

'Ready for what?' I said.

'We're all waiting,' said the other. They laughed again. At the time I hardly noticed for I was filled with a raging thirst and I seized the rum bottle from the table where Dr Rutherford had left it and took a deep draught. They each took one of my arms and led me up onto the deck.

The sun was brighter than ever in the sky that day, so that it seared my eyes and made me want to lie down and sleep for ever. I felt thirsty again, and dizzy, and I took another gulp of rum, anything to assuage the dryness in my throat. The two women propelled me forward until we were standing in front of a tarpaulin that had been stretched across the ship's deck. It was tied to the foremast, and to the portside gunwale, so that it was raised at the corners to form a large canvas hammock. It had been filled with water. There were people all around – soldiers mostly, and some of the paying passengers, both men and women.

I recognised one or two of the most favoured convicts amongst them too. All of them were wet and laughing and drinking rum, and the heads of some had been crudely shaved. They cheered when they saw me led forward by those two drunken slatterns, and to my right a trumpet sounded.

A curtain of tarpaulin was thrown aside to reveal a man, a sailor, dressed in black with a piece of pale rope about his neck, in the crude semblance of a curate or parson. I noticed then that a packing case had been set up on the deck before him, a piece of netting draped over it, upon which were a few dead sea creatures – starfish, a sea urchin, a gull and two rotten fish. Still laughing, the two Irish girls marched me forward to stand before it.

'Who taketh this woman?' bellowed the sailor-parson.

'I do,' shouted a voice from behind me. It was rough with drink and lust and it made my blood freeze in my veins. From the crowd came the sound of laughter, catcalls and lewd shouts. My head was throbbing now, and I could turn it only slowly.

Dr Rutherford stood upon the deck, the crowd of leering faces at his back. He was in his shirt sleeves, the removal of his coat his only concession to the raging heat of the sun. At his side was the man who had claimed me. I did not know who he was, one of the sailors, I presumed. He was stripped to the waist, with a swab upon his head for hair, and another tied over his ears to hang down his face in the manner of a long, straggling beard. Upon his back he wore what looked like the skin of a sea creature – one of the sharks that followed us, perhaps, or a porpoise. It was bluish-grey in colour, wrinkled and dry and vile. Dead starfish had been tied into this hideous cloak; weed scraped from below the water line was draped over his shoulders and shells and more weed tangled into his hair and beard.

'Welcome amongst us, Neptune, Master of the Deep!' cried the

sailor-parson. There was more clapping and shouting. 'And who giveth her away?'

'I do,' said Dr Rutherford. He stepped forward, and smiled at me. That smile – how I came to loathe the sight of his thin cadaverous features. For here was no drunken reveller, out of his wits with rum and boredom. Instead, here was a man who was sober, fully sentient of what was about to take place and, in the name of entertainment, quite prepared to condone it.

'Then plight your troth, sir,' cried the sailor-parson, handing Neptune a bottle.

Neptune took a swig, then put the bottle to my lips too. I was so thirsty that I gulped it down – I could not help myself – the sounds of cheering and laughing echoing in my ears. I tried to speak, tried to ask what was happening, but I could not form the words. I wanted to sit down – I had to sit down or I would fall down. Hands took hold of me and propelled me behind another flap of canvas. A chair awaited me, and I was pushed into it. A ragged posy of weed and starfish and frayed rope was thrust into my hands. The sun burned my eyes, my throat screaming again for water, and even in my stupefied state I knew that Dr Rutherford had drugged me. But there was nothing I could do about it now for my limbs were unable to obey me, my hands felt as though they were made of wood, and my voice was dead in my throat. The stink of fish filled my nostrils till I thought I might be sick. I tried to look up, but the deck rose and fell before me. I saw Dr Rutherford tall against the sun; I saw his camera box, its brass eye trained upon me. I felt something hard grip the back of my head and my hands and feet were bound to the chair, the posy lashed to my hand when my fingers proved unable to hold it.

'Hurry up,' shouted Neptune. I noticed then that a thick rope-end was swinging heavily from his groin. He seized it between his hands and danced lewdly forward.

'Don't move, my dear,' said Dr Rutherford in my ear. His breath was sour, his long thin fingers cold as they brushed my cheek.

I did not move, I could not. I tried to clear my mind, but my head felt heavy and thick, and I could make sense of nothing. An eternity seemed to pass while I sat there, my head clamped, my arms and legs bound to the chair, the reek of that decaying posy wafting into my face. All at once I heard voices, counting down. Before me, standing beside the camera, I could see Dr Rutherford holding up his hand; a gold pocket watch balanced upon his palm shone in the sunlight, as though he were holding a living flame. He snapped it closed and there was a cheer. Someone released the vice that gripped my head, and unbound my hands and feet. Sea and sky lurched and wheeled in an arc above me, until I could not tell one from the other.

I fell, slipping from the chair to sprawl before the baying mob. The deck felt warm against my cheek; rough, but smooth with the passing of so many feet, and the smell of brine and tar was thick about me. A shadow fell across the sun, and I smelled again the stink of Neptune – rum and dead fish, dried weed and sweat. I felt my skirts being lifted, so that the sun was hot on my thighs. I heard cheering and clapping and lewd voices, and I felt a pain like a knife between my legs.

Chapter Twenty-Three

We would find Mrs Lunge upstairs, the porter said. She was expecting us.

'How does she know we want to speak to her?' said Will.

The porter shrugged. 'Not much goes on round here without her knowing about it.'

'I always knew it was the servants who had the key to all this,' I said as we climbed the stairs. 'I should have had more confidence, been more certain in my actions. But I could not be sure. And there is so much at stake. We could not make a false accusation—'

'Sure of what?' said Will. 'Of whom?'

'We will soon find out,' I said. 'Though I fear it'll lead to more harm than good.'

She was on the top floor, staring out of the window in Dr Rutherford's room, standing exactly where she was when I had looked up and seen her. Around her there was evidence of industry. Dr Rutherford's books and papers, his instruments, natural history collection, skulls and death-masks had been packed into boxes, for he had bequeathed everything to the Phrenological Society, and they were coming to collect it at the end of the week. The room looked bare, and yet still it was a small space for a doctor to spend so much of his time. He had owned a large house on St Saviour's Street, though he had rarely gone there, favouring instead the small suite of rooms at the top of the asylum.

'Why did Dr Rutherford choose to live in such a place?' said Will. 'There is not much room here, when all's said and done.'

'It was what he preferred, sir,' said Mrs Lunge. 'He said he had no use for lots of rooms. Said he'd been close quartered for many years and he would not leave it now.'

'Mrs Lunge,' I said. 'Why do you cry in the night?'

She blinked. 'I don't.'

'Mrs Speedicut heard you.'

'This is a lunatic asylum, Mr Flockhart. The place is rarely silent.' Her voice was quick and sharp, her words reasonable, but her face betrayed her, and I was watching. I saw her pupils dilate, saw the vein at her neck throb and her face become taut. I could not but admire her, for she mastered herself instantly, but in that single moment I knew I had glimpsed a different Mrs Lunge.

'Mrs Lunge, two men have been killed. Edward Eden saw you in Dr Rutherford's room with a skull – the same skull that went missing from the top shelf of Dr Rutherford's phrenological collection on the night he was murdered.'

I waited for her to speak, but still she said nothing. She stood without moving, her hands, for once, hanging limply at her sides. Her eyes were sorrowful, as if she were willing me to go away, to stop asking her what she knew. But I could not stop now, not when I was so close. And so I plunged on.

'You weep in the night. You were known to be close to Dr Rutherford and yet you showed no emotion whatever when presented with his mutilated corpse. How might these things be explained? How might I, or anyone, interpret them?'

Later, when I looked back on that last conversation I had with her, I realised that I had bullied her and I was sorry. I wondered whether this impatience, this angry aggressiveness – so against my usual calm and rational character – was the start of my own madness. Was I changing? Was I becoming someone other than who I wished to be, unable to control how I acted to others? All that I knew for certain was that I wanted it all to be over. I longed to walk away from Angel Meadow Asylum and not look back, for every moment I spent there had become a torture to me. And so I badgered her, dredging from my mind the most sordid of suppositions as to what she might be hiding: why might a woman cry in the night, a woman who had been known until very recently to have hung upon Dr Rutherford's every word. *Follows him around*, Mrs Speedicut had said. *Dr Rutherford said this an' Dr Rutherford said that . . . I've heard her cryin' in the night . . .*

'You and Dr Rutherford were lovers, weren't you?' I said.

She did not move. Her gaze darted towards the door,

as if she wanted to be free of the place as much as I. I remembered how stoical she had been as she stood within sight of his corpse. How could any woman remain unmoved at the sight of their dead lover? How she must long to show her true feelings.

'Mrs Lunge,' said Will. 'You must tell us—'

'He treated you shamefully, did he not?'

She closed her eyes at that and sank onto a chair. Her shoulders shook, so that I found myself amazed that anyone could have stored up so much grief for a man like Dr Rutherford. Had he been a better man than I had thought? I sat beside her. 'You have nothing to fear from him now,' I said gently.

Then she raised her eyes to look at me, and I saw that she was not crying at all, she was laughing. The sound rang out, mirthless and mocking. 'I didn't fear him,' she said. She looked at me pityingly. 'I hated him. I hated him, but I didn't kill him.'

'And yet you know who did,' said Will.

'Can you blame her?' she snapped back at him. 'I can't.' She jumped to her feet. 'Oh, I'm glad he's dead. Glad! I don't know why I let it happen, why I gave in to him. I knew all along that he had nothing to offer me. I knew he wanted someone . . . someone better than a gaoler, for that's all I was to him – he told me so often enough. I was lonely – of course I was. Is it only men who crave the companionship of their opposites, who ache for the physical touch of another? Am I supposed to lie in my bed, alone, night after night and be content? You will be disgusted, Mr Flockhart, and you Mr Quartermain, to hear me talk so, to think that someone like me might be flesh and blood beneath this shell of starch and silk.' She reached up and tore at her collar, ripping at the buttons that fastened it so high. Beneath the fabric I caught sight of a flaking red rash. She clawed at it frantically with her fingers.

'I understand more than you realise, Mrs Lunge,' I said.

'Do you?' She threw back her head, her collar open at her throat now, the eczema on her skin beaded with blood where she had raked at it. 'And so you will also understand how every time he came to me I said to myself that it would be the last. That every time he left me to return to his rooms I wanted to tell him to never come back, to leave me be. But I was weak. I said nothing. I despised myself for it. He never said he loved me. I knew he didn't, but I hoped he would come to. I hoped he might one day see—' Her hands flew to her throat, as if she felt his hands around it. 'Oh, why did I want such a thing from him? Why did I?'

'Because it seemed worse to be alone,' I said. 'Even though it was not.'

'He said he would come to me that night, but he didn't.' She flung herself back down into the chair. Her face was wild, her hair awry. Gone was the silent, pinch-faced matron, and in her place was a woman filled with passion and feeling. She clenched her fists. 'How often had he made me wait like that? He didn't care. It was me that it mattered to, not him; me who waited and wanted. So that night I got up and I went along to his rooms to tell him—

'But when I reached his door I knew he was not alone. I could hear voices. I recognised . . . it was Mrs Hawkins's voice. What was she doing up there at that time in the morning, and with him too! And so I listened. She was pleading with him. I heard what she said, heard all he had done to her.' Mrs Lunge covered her face with her hands. 'I didn't see her, I didn't need to but it was her, there is no doubt. And I knew she was speaking the truth. And how did he answer her? What was his reply? He laughed! Oh, John Rutherford was a vile man, Mr Flockhart. I knew it then, as I had always known it in my heart, and whatever feelings I had had for him turned to ashes right there as I stood listening at his door.

'I went back to my room, tried to think what to do. I waited for him to leave, hoping that he would go home that night. I could hear when he had gone for I know the sounds of the asylum as well as I know the ticking of the clock on my mantel – but he did not leave. I waited for the sound of his door closing but I did not hear that either. I slept a little. When I woke again it was two o'clock, and I did not imagine he would still be up. And so I went down the corridor to his rooms. His door was unlocked, the lamp still burning, just as I told you. And there he was, just as you saw him. She had killed him, Mr Flockhart. But I didn't blame her for it, I didn't blame her one bit and you shouldn't either. Ask her! She'll tell you what he did to her and you'll see. I vowed I'd not tell anyone what I'd heard, what I knew. Besides,' she threw back her head. 'I was glad, for I hated him then, hated him for who he was, for all the times he had humiliated me.' Her cheeks turned red. 'Oh, you don't know what he did to me. What I let him do in the hope that it would please him, that it might make him love me. I debased myself. Did he want to see how much I would take, to what depths of depravity I would sink? I hated myself, Mr Flockhart, but when I heard what he had done to Mrs Hawkins, well, I hated him one hundred times more.

'I decided then that I would keep her secret – I was determined about that, at least. Were we not sisters in pain and sorrow, she and I? Might we not help one another against the cruelty and viciousness of men? If I helped her I might harm him, even though he was dead, and I was more than glad to do it. Besides, she didn't deserve to hang for it. Had she not been through enough? But she wanted her baby so badly, no matter that it was only its little head that remained. He said it was his as much as it was hers and he would not hand it over. But I knew how to find it. I looked in his book – I had seen him poring over those ledgers often enough – and I took it. I gave it to her. I wrapped it up and I said I thought it was what she was looking for. I put my finger to my lips. She could hardly speak. She said she could never have another child, he had seen to that.'

'She is not pregnant?' said Will.

'No, sir. She never can be. He took that from her too.'

'But then Edward Eden came in just as you were retrieving the child's skull from the high shelf,' I said.

'Yes, sir.'

'You threatened him so that he would keep quiet.'

'Yes.'

I heard a movement at the door behind me. Pole! The fellow was always sneaking about the place, listening at doors and creeping along corridors.

'Step out, sir!' I cried. 'How dare you listen to what's meant for others—'

It was not Pole, though when I saw who it was, I wished that it had been.

The flower in his lapel that day was red, a loose and blowsy rose, large and heavy like furled velvet, as though he wore his own heart upon his coat. I had suspected for some time that Mrs Hawkins was not all she seemed – Mrs Lunge had merely confirmed it, and although I was not yet ready to accuse Mrs Hawkins of murder, I could not but think she was a very likely suspect. And her accomplice? I knew who he was, even if she did not.

'Dr Hawkins,' I stammered. 'I . . . we didn't hear you.'

'Clearly.' His voice was cold. 'And yet here I am. Is there something you wish to tell me? Or is it only meant for others?'

I felt myself blush crimson. I had known Dr Hawkins all my life, he had helped my uncle and my father; he had tried to help me too, and yet here I was, about to repay his trust and kindness by accusing his wife of the most terrible of crimes. I fell silent. I did not know how to answer.

'It is but speculation, as yet, sir,' said Will. 'I'm sure everything can be explained quite easily.'

'Dr Hawkins,' I said, 'you cannot allow Susan Chance to remain locked up for crimes she did not commit.'

'And my wife *did* commit these crimes? She murdered Dr Rutherford? Dr Golspie? She bound and gagged you and put you into a coffin?'

'But why, Jem?' said Will. 'Why would she do such things?'

'Perhaps we should ask Mrs Hawkins.' My words were reckless, and hurtful, but I had to press on. I had to know. If I had thought for one moment where my accusations might lead, that I was soon to be responsible for the most terrible pain and suffering, I would have chosen my words more carefully.

'I see you will not be stopped, Jem,' said Dr Hawkins.
'In that case we will find my wife and we will ask her what
she knows. But you must understand that our friendship
is at an end from this moment on.'

'But sir—'

'From this moment!' Dr Hawkins stalked out. 'She is in
the women's ward, with the Ladies' Committee, I believe.
No doubt she is planning her next attack.'

'Dr Hawkins.' I plunged after him. 'Ask her in private,
sir. Please.'

'She has nothing to fear. It is you who will be shamed
by this.'

'But what do you know of her, sir? How did you meet?
Can you truly say that you know everything about her
past?'

How could I explain my doubts, based as they were on
such slender but convincing evidence? For it was my firm
belief that it was Mrs Hawkins whom Dr Golspie had seen
in Dr Rutherford's broken mirror. Why else would Dr
Golspie have baulked at telling us who he had seen when
Dr Hawkins was standing right before him? I was certain
too that this knowledge had led to Dr Golspie's murder
– had she not been seen in Dr Golspie's stair? She had
given the name 'Susan', but even so unobservant a boy
as Billy Slater would have noticed that Susan Chance
was a cripple – the girl was unable to move without her
metal boot clunking on the stair. And yet he had said
no such thing. There was also the fact that Mrs Hawkins
was familiar with prison slang. 'Watch yer crabshells,
miss,' Pole had said as he swept the floor beside us. Mrs
Hawkins had stepped daintily aside straight away while
the rest of us stood our ground mystified. There was

also the tall concealing collar of jet beads she always wore at her neck, her pallor at the very mention of Dr Graves the anatomist, these things had crystallised into something meaningful only when I had discovered that the photograph was taken on a transport ship, when I had read in Miss Mothersole's notebook what she had overheard from the conversation between Joshua Milner and Mrs Hawkins ... *Have no fear, we shall be more than a match for him ... I have paid for my crimes thrice over, must I pay for them still? ... Say nothing ... Be as a stranger to me or all is lost.* The words were Mrs Hawkins's. Dr Stiven had pledged his silence, but at what price? Mrs Hawkins was a felon, there was no doubt in my mind. Where else might her acquaintance with Dr Rutherford come from but aboard a transport ship? It was Mrs Hawkins who was the woman in the picture. What might she not do to keep her identity a secret, to hide her past from her new husband?

'Dr Hawkins,' I said. 'Please sir, listen to me—'

He turned to me then, taking a breath to steady himself. I saw doubt in his expression, but his words remained faithful to her. 'I know what she's told me,' he said. 'And that is – that has to be enough.' He seized my arm. 'I'm aware that your mind at the moment may be ... overburdened. The murder of Golspie – I know he was your friend – your own recent experiences—' He cleared his throat as if he could hardly bring himself to remind me that I had been buried alive. 'That alone is enough to make anyone deranged, even temporarily. I can forgive you, but you must withdraw these accusations directly—'

But I was thinking clearly, and there was no doubt in my mind. I shook my head.

Mrs Hawkins and the Ladies' Committee were preparing to go outside and hoe the vegetable beds in the company of a selection of the more biddable asylum women. The chosen few waited about listlessly, blinking in the chilly sunshine or staring up in awe at Dr Mothersole, who stood at the window, bathed in a halo of golden light like some sort of over-fed celestial being. He was dressed in the costume of a Kentish yokel – a billowing smock of buff-coloured fustian, a blue neckerchief, and a drooping, wide-brimmed hat. Beneath this his legs were sheathed in the white stockings he favoured, while on his feet he wore a pair of working men's thick heavy boots. He held a hoe upright in his hand, like a halberd. Beside him clustered the ladies of the committee.

Dr Christie was standing beside the bookcase with his hands in his pockets. 'My dear fellow,' I heard him say. 'Can you not just sit down? All this gallivanting about – gardening, and handicrafts and dancing and whatnot. These women need rest, not excitement.'

Letty stood at his side, her finger in her mouth. She took his hand, but he shook her off with a shudder and stepped away.

'You really think any of them will benefit?' he said. 'I can hardly see that it is worth the inconvenience.'

'They need fresh air and exercise, Christie. Nature, sir. Air and earth – both help to soothe the raging beast or enliven the melancholic. Fatigue, sir, is the lunatic's friend, no matter what might ail him.'

'Well,' said Dr Christie, 'I suppose it's cheaper than all the bread and custard we feed them. They are as fat as

Shrewsbury geese! But I can hardly agree about the fresh air. It stinks out there today.'

In order to lead the exodus Dr Mothersole had unlocked the doors that led out into the asylum garden. The air that wafted in was laced with the reek of the vinegar works and the meat market, not to mention the usual pungency of the river. Out in the garden the watery sunlight illuminated dismal regiments of brownish-looking onions and leeks. Amongst them, Pole jabbed at the earth with a hoe, occasionally bending down and plucking a weed from the soil. He looked up as Dr Mothersole's voice boomed out, his face inscrutable.

Mrs Hawkins, I noticed, was standing a little to one side, her hand clasped to the jet beads at her throat. When she saw her husband march into the room, Will and me at his side and Mrs Lunge wringing her hands behind us, her face turned whiter still.

'What is it, sir?' she said to her husband. She smiled, but her face was waxy and mask-like, her expression wary. 'You're all looking terribly serious.'

'My dear,' said Dr Hawkins, 'we are here because . . . Mr Flockhart tells me . . . and Mrs Lunge—' His voice faltered. The doubt I had seen in his eyes now seized hold of his tongue. 'My dear,' he said again, his voice thick with emotion, 'you must explain.'

The room had fallen silent, every one of us watching Mrs Hawkins. A shadow moved behind Dr Mothersole, and there was Pole too, standing motionless in the open doors. For a moment Mrs Hawkins neither moved nor spoke. Her expression was blank, her gaze resting upon her husband as if she were still waiting for him to speak.

'Explain?' she said at last. She gave a short, brittle laugh. 'Explain what?'

'It's too late, ma'am,' cried Mrs Lunge suddenly. 'Oh, I tried to hide it. I tried to stop them but they would ask. It's him,' she cried, pointing at me. 'He's as much a devil as he looks.'

Mrs Hawkins took a step back. She seemed to dwindle, to shrink in stature, so that all at once I had the impression that I was looking at a girl dressed up in her mother's clothes, a child hiding within a carapace of damask and crinoline.

Mrs Hawkins glanced about at the grinning patients, the staring, judgemental gaze of the Ladies' Committee.

'Mrs Hawkins?' said one, as if she no longer recognised this half-crouched, hard-eyed version of the woman they had been told to love and respect.

Mrs Hawkins flinched. She looked into her husband's face, but saw, as I did, only wretchedness and sorrow, and she gave a sob. Oh, how I wished we had addressed the matter differently, in private, rather than under the disgusted looks of the ladies, the gibbering, grinning faces of the lunatics and the cold, fascinated, half-smiling gaze of Dr Christie.

Dr Mothersole glided forward. 'Dear lady—'

'Get away!' snapped Mrs Hawkins, lurching away from him. Her gaze darted left and right, searching the room for a means of escape. But she was in an asylum, and there was no escape for those who were not deemed fit to leave. I saw an attendant appear at the door. Dr Christie motioned the woman to stay where she was, though he could hardly tear his eyes from the scene unfolding before us. Mrs Hawkins saw the attendant too, and she became more agitated still. 'You promised,' she cried, staring at Mrs Lunge. 'You promised you would say nothing.' Her voice rang out wretchedly.

Mrs Lunge covered her face with her hands. 'I tried to help.'

Dr Mothersole was inching forward still. 'My dear Mrs Hawkins,' he crooned.

Mrs Hawkins started back, as if she had quite forgotten where she was, and when she saw Dr Mothersole's giant smock-clad form bearing down upon her she let out a yell and seized the poker from the hearth.

The ladies gasped.

'Who left that out?' cried Dr Christie. 'Pole?'

'Yessir,' muttered Pole.

'How many times must I tell you?'

Mrs Hawkins brandished the poker. Her hair was awry, her face smeared with soot and tears. The ladies clutched one another, the lunatics shouted and laughed. Dr Hawkins had neither moved, nor spoken. I put my hand on his arm but he did not even notice.

Events moved quickly. Mrs Hawkins turned around and about, searching for a place to run, but there was nowhere to go. At her back the fire hissed and crackled, tongues of flames shot out from between the coals, and the room grew hot and close. Still Dr Mothersole came on. 'Stand back, gentlemen,' he cried, as he saw Dr Christie move. 'The ladies are my forte. She will not harm me.' He opened his arms wide. 'Come to me, Mrs Hawkins!' and all at once he leaped at her.

Mrs Hawkins jabbed at Dr Mothersole's giant midriff with the poker, but it became tangled in the fabric of his yokel's costume and clattered to the ground. Pole sprang

forward and seized it, staggering back onto the hearth
to avoid Dr Mothersole's blundering boots. He looked,
for a moment, as though he were about to brain the
doctor with the poker, but Dr Mothersole surged forward
again, his meaty hands scrabbling at the air as he sought
to grab hold of Mrs Hawkins, and the poker swooshed
impotently by.

'Mr Pole,' I cried. 'You're making matters worse.'

Sensing victory, Dr Mothersole pressed forward. Mrs
Hawkins darted back so that he managed only to tear the
shawl from her shoulders. He knocked pins from her hair
and tore a ribbon from her dress; his fingers caught at her
throat and ripped away the collar of jet. Mrs Hawkins cried
out as the beads burst across the room in a hail of black
pellets. She writhed and squirmed in Dr Mothersole's
grasp, her hands clutched at her neck.

'Bring the strait jacket!' he bellowed. 'Christie! Now, if
you please, sir!'

Behind them, Pole raised the poker once more. This
time, it was quite clear who he meant to assault. I cried
out – and I saw Dr Christie and Will bound forward. And
then something happened, something more awful than
any of us could possibly have imagined. The fire gave an
almighty crack, and spat a fiery ember out from amongst
the blazing coals. It struck Pole's coat, catching in the folds
above his pocket, where it ignited the grease-impregnated
fabric in an instant. All the times he had wiped his hands
on his clothes after finding them sticky with boot polish or
been careless with the turpentine or formaldehyde, could
be counted in the size and speed with which the flames
consumed him. The poker clattered to the ground, the
shriek he uttered like nothing I have ever heard – like

nothing I ever wish to hear again. Mrs Hawkins and Dr Mothersole sprang away from him like scalded cats. The ladies and the lunatics screamed as Pole flamed before them, dancing and spinning, wrapped in a golden cloak of fire.

Angel Meadow Asylum, 18th September 1852

The place we had arrived at looked like paradise. The heavens were the brightest blue – a blue no Londoner has ever seen, so that it was hard to believe we all shared the same sky. Overhead, emerald birds wheeled and raced, as bright and joyful as our London pigeons are grey and wretched. Flocks of white doves settled in the trees, like hosts of angels, and everywhere there was greenness of a thousand different hues. The colours of the land and the sky were more vivid than anything I had ever seen, so that it was as though the whole world had been fashioned out of gemstones, cut and polished and set in a silver sea. We were used to dirt and squalor, to meanness, hunger and brutality, so that we hardly knew what to think when we climbed from our miserable floating prison and saw the gaudy world that awaited us. But life mocked us still, for we were to find plenty of what we were familiar with beneath those luminous skies.

I was granted a ticket-of-leave for good behaviour the moment we arrived – as were all but the most violent and furious of the women. You may ask why we were not locked away, but there was a shortage of women, and our ticket-of-leave meant no more than permission to work for a master, with our continued freedoms, such as they were, dependent upon church attendance and good behaviour. There was no choice and no dignity for any of us, and the manner in which our masters chose us was little better than a cattle auction. We waited on board ship, dressed in whatever clothes we had brought with us from England and which were not ruined and degraded by the journey. Men came from the town – those who wanted a maid, or a worker, or a wife – and picked whichever of us they wanted from the line.

I was taken by a merchant – he was a wealthy man and was given first pick of us. He had heard I could talk like a lady, could read and write and do arithmetic, and he paid a good price for me. I was lucky, but many were not. Those too old or ugly, too mad or troublesome to be either desirable or useful, were sent up river to the female factory at Parramatta: there was nothing there but violence, deprivation and misery. I visited the place only once. I saw the two women there who had watched me become Neptune's bride that day, though they did not recognise me. They were drunk, lolling in the gutter calling out in lewd language to the men who passed by. They were filthy and bruised, their faces puffy from the beatings they had received and the rum they had drunk. Did they ever think of home, as I did? I did not stop to ask them.

My master, James McKinley, was a Scottish merchant. He employed me as a housemaid, though when he had satisfied himself as to my honesty, he put me to work in his office. It was not long before my condition was obvious. But McKinley was a kindly gentleman – having him as my master was the only stroke of good fortune I had. He had come out as a free passenger some years earlier, and he knew what took place on board the transport ships. He never asked me about it, but said I might keep the child as long as it did not interfere with my work.

I saw Dr Rutherford about the town, now and again. He was known to McKinley, though he said nothing about what had happened on board ship. I too remained silent. I would not jeopardise my situation, would not be sent to Parramatta or have my ticket revoked. So I did as I was expected: I worked hard and I said nothing. The two of them had an interest in phrenology. Back home, McKinley had attended lectures by Combe in Edinburgh, and had his own collection of skulls, some of which – the skulls of aborigines – he had given to Dr Rutherford.

'Surgeon on board a convict ship?' I heard Dr Rutherford say. 'It will do for now, McKinley, but I have ambitions that lie far above and beyond. I am collecting the skulls of those who are slaves to their own base instincts, their own passions. Convicts and lunatics, natives, women and children – those are the forms that interest me most, and upon which I will forge my reputation.'

When my time came, McKinley called Dr Rutherford, though I screamed that I would not have him near me, that he was the devil himself and I would rather die than have him touch me. It was the only time my master raised his hand to me. He cut my lip with the back of his hand and bade me be silent, or by God he would send me to the barracks for the soldiers to use me as they chose. If he knew Rutherford for the man he was then he did not show it, and there was nothing more I could do.

Rutherford himself was singularly uninterested in me. He clicked his tongue as he opened his doctor's bag. 'I know what you are, my dear. McKinley has spent too long here to know a whore from a lady, though it's not for me to enlighten him. You should thank me for finding you so comfortable a situation.'

And so, my baby was brought into the world by the man who had watched while its father had raped me. I was determined that I should hate it. I imagined it having fish scales for skin, its hair strips of stinking weed, and when he handed me the bundle I would not look, not at him, nor at the child – a boy, I was certain, who would be born to violence and arrogance just like all men. But something in the baby's silence tugged at my heart. It had no choice who its parents were, no responsibility for the wicked deeds that had brought it into the world. I pulled back the blanket.

She was white as milk, and raven haired, like me. Her skin was smooth, flawless and perfect, her face peaceful, innocent of the cruel world into which she had arrived. I held her to my breast fiercely then, resolving to do all I could to care for her, to make her life better than mine. I stroked her cheek, and it was as soft as down and cool to the touch. She opened her eyes and stared straight at me.

He – I can hardly bring myself to write his name – was watching in silence. 'You must sleep,' he said. But I did not want to sleep. I did not want to let go of her, did not want to close my eyes with him still in the room. But I did sleep, for I could not fight it, though I slept with my baby at my breast, my arms close about her.

When I awoke she was gone. I asked where she was, my baby girl, but my master shook his head. 'She's dead, Kitty,' he said. 'Don't you remember?'

I said nothing, though I remembered that I had stroked her cheek, that she had been cool, cooler than she should have been, new-warm with my own blood. I remembered too that she had been still and quiet in her blanket, and I wondered whether it had been in my imagination that she had opened her eyes and looked at me. I asked him once more where she was, could I see her, but he only shook his head again and said the same words. 'She's dead.'

I never saw my baby daughter again. I asked after her over and over again, though I knew she would never come back to me. I wanted to bury her, to put her in the bright soil of her birth-land and allow the hot sun to keep her warm – not for my daughter the cold and putrid earth of St Saviour's. But my master shook his head, and said that it was better if I forgot. That it was too late. That Dr Rutherford had taken her, Dr Rutherford had her now.

I never saw Dr Rutherford again, until I came to Angel Meadow. I heard he had returned to England and had quitted the Bay Fleet, but I did not know where he had gone. My master never mentioned him once he had left Australia – acquaintance out there depends upon proximity, and neither had reason to maintain contact with the other over such a distance. I worked for McKinley for two more years. He married me then, though I did not love him. As a wedding gift he gave me a necklace to wear to cover up the scar – a pink ring about my neck that the noose had left – so that my past might be hidden from both of us.

After another year he decided to take me back to Edinburgh. I was on a conditional pardon by then, free, yet not permitted to leave the colony. But McKinley had many friends; it was always his intention to return, and so getting me onto a ship bound for Home was no hardship. We arrived in London at the same time as the cholera, and my husband died of it before he even reached his native town.

James McKinley was a good man, and I will not speak ill of him. He left me well provided for. But I was afraid that should anyone realise that I was neither fully pardoned nor officially free to return to England they would send me back, for as far as the law was concerned I was still a convict. And so I went to France – I had started a new life once before, might I not do it again? I had no friends there, but it was easier than I thought, for I had money enough to manage, and as a widow in command of some fortune I was able to acquire acquaintances easily enough. It was in that capacity – as an English widow of independent means – that I met Dr Hawkins.

Chapter Twenty-Four

I looked up at her, once I had finished reading. 'You're wondering whether I have told my husband,' she said. 'I have not. When I came to London with him and found Dr Rutherford here at Angel Meadow, I hardly knew what to do. I was afraid that he would betray me – to my husband at least – and yet I had never forgotten my daughter. Whatever Dr Rutherford had done to me when she was born I do not know, but I had never conceived again, and the need to know where she was, to get her back, overwhelmed me. My mind seethed with questions – what had he done with her? Was she really dead? Why had he taken her? And, I cannot deny it, somewhere at the back of my mind was the hope that she was alive. I *had* to know.

'That night, I took my husband's keys and I went to Rutherford's rooms. You have heard what Mrs Lunge had to say. It's all true. Dr Rutherford told me that my daughter was dead, and that he had her skull in his collection. Even then he taunted me, for he would not say which it was. And, Mr Flockhart, you are correct; it was me who Dr Golspie saw in the mirror, for I appeared behind him just as the mirror shattered. But I stepped behind the screen, so that when he turned I was gone. After Dr Golspie left, I confronted Dr Rutherford. He threatened to tell my husband who I was, to tell the magistrate that I had broken the conditions of my pardon. And he said that he would never give me my child's remains, that they were as much his as they were mine and they had become a part of his scientific collection.

'I left him then. I did not know what else to do. Should I tell my husband everything? I could not. And then Dr Rutherford was found dead – it was a murder straight out of Prior's Rents, as though time had contracted and vanished, and I was once more in that thieves' kitchen with Goblin, listening to my mother's tales, once more in Knight and Day's blacking factory, crouched over Mr Day's dead body.' She frowned. 'You know that Mrs Lunge gave me my daughter's remains. You know, too, that I buried her in St Saviour's churchyard. How did she come to be in your possession? It was well after midnight. No one saw me.'

'The sexton saw you,' I said. 'You cannot put anyone in the ground at St Saviour's without Dick the sexton knowing about it. He and I are old friends. How did you know we had found her?'

'Dr Stiven. He helped me to retrieve her from you.'

'You also went to see Dr Golspie on the day he was murdered, didn't you?' I said.

'I knew he would be sure to remember what he had seen in the mirror. I wanted to explain – I was certain he was a good man, that he would understand. But when I arrived he was dead. I was frightened. I didn't know who had done it, though I knew it wasn't me. I took the key and locked the door. When I saw the boy on the stair, I grew more frightened still. So I said that Dr Golspie was out, but that when he came back he was to tell Dr Golspie that Susan had called.'

'You were prepared to send an innocent woman to the gallows?'

She looked at the floor, her expression wretched. 'I didn't know that. I went to see her. I wanted to explain . . . but the sight of the place, the smell, the noises.' She covered her face with her hands. 'I could not bear it. I could not go back there, not again. I did not kill Dr Golspie. I did not kill Dr Rutherford. For all I knew it might well have been Susan – had she not already killed a man? Did she not have a sentence to serve for that crime?'

I thought of Susan Chance beating her head against the asylum wall, her eyes wild, and her face dirty and bruised. She had been released immediately, but whether we were too late to save her mind had yet to be seen.

'I did not murder Dr Rutherford or Dr Golspie,' she said again. 'And if it was not Susan Chance then I do not know who it was.'

After a moment I picked up the sheaf of paper upon which she had written her story. 'I'd like to show this to Dr Hawkins,' I said. 'He has a right to know. And there's also Dr Stiven – Joshua Milner. He used to know Dr Hawkins and would be pleased to put the past behind him. What you have written should help him achieve that, at least.'

'But you know I didn't kill Dr Rutherford.'

'Yes.'

'Or Dr Golspie.'

'Yes. I always knew.'

'Then why did you lock me down here? Why did you pretend—'

'Because I could not see how else I might get the truth from you.'

I sat with Dr Hawkins while he read his wife's story. He was silent throughout. Occasionally he drew breath. More than once he wiped his eyes. When he had finished, he went and stood with his back to us at the window, the confession upon the desk. After a moment or two he returned to his desk, took up the manuscript and tossed it onto the fire. 'I would be grateful if my wife might return to me as soon as possible,' he said.

'And Joshua Milner?'

'Dr Milner,' he hesitated, as if choosing his words with care. 'I wonder if he might consider a permanent appointment here at Angel Meadow. I will arrange it with the governors. Please tell him that he might leave off his . . . his embellishments if he so wishes.' He looked at me. 'And Pole is – was – the perpetrator of these crimes?'

'It seems so.'

'But why?'

It was Will who had tried to save Pole. While the rest of us had looked on in horror, frozen and unmoving, Will had leaped forward, tearing off his coat and flinging it about the blazing figure. Pole, oblivious, had screamed and thrashed as Will wrestled him to the ground, shouting at him to lie still. At the sound of his voice Dr Christie and I had jumped forward, and between us we had rolled the burning man in the hearthrug. Will's hands had been badly burned. My hair was singed and all our faces were black with smoke, our eyes and mouths moist and vivid in our sooty faces. Beneath our hands, Pole lay silent. Smoke seeped in lazy wreaths from around his neck and ankles.

We had carried him to the infirmary, but when we unrolled the rug we could all see that it was impossible to save him. Dr Christie and I had dressed the man's wounds as best we could, but we could not remove his clothes, for they had adhered to his flesh so closely that to try to pull them away would have brought him further agonies. And yet I still had questions in my head that remained unanswered, so that when Dr Christie took Will to dress his hands I had leaned forward and whispered in his ear.

'Who are you, sir?'

His eye, the one that was always clouded and pale, shifted between his scalded lids. 'I am Pole, to you,' he whispered.

'And to Mrs Hawkins?'

'To her I am Goblin.' He closed his eyes. Tears seeped from them to run down his blistered face. 'My name is John Godolphin. My mother's name was Pole.'

'Does she know who you are?'

'She does not. Not now, though I knew her once, a long time ago. Rutherford—' his voice failed.

'What about him?'

'I knew what he'd done. On the *Norfolk*. And after.'

'How?'

'Word gets out in a place like that.'

'You murdered Rutherford and Golspie?'

354

'I had to protect her. I said I would. I would not have her sent back to the gallows. To the Bay.'

'And she never knew who you were?'

'Thank God she did not. But I had to protect her. I said I would.'

'And me?'

'You?' He sighed. 'I could not. I could not kill in cold blood. Not again. And yet I must protect her. I said I would. Oh God! God!' He begged me for water then, and I held a glass to his cracked and blackened lips.

By the time Dr Christie had returned with the laudanum, Pole was dead.

I returned to the apothecary to find Will instructing Gabriel in the use of the camera. The paper had been prepared, the camera was balanced on its tripod and the herb drying room set up as a temporary darkroom. Will's hands were heavily bandaged. I had changed the bandages that morning and his skin looked as though it was sure to heal, in time.

'Someone else has taken over the plans for the House of Correction,' he said, brandishing his bandaged paws. 'I can't work with my hands like this. I must say I'm not in the least bit sorry.'

'You want to be in this picture, Mr Jem?' said Gabriel.

'Gabriel's picked it all up rather quickly,' said Will. 'Look, we took a picture of Mrs Speedicut with her pipe. She changed her apron especially, and wore a newly washed cap. Who'd have thought she'd be so vain?'

He handed me a small square of paper bearing an

image of the tubby old woman. The shades of light and dark gave her a dignity she lacked in the flesh, and her new apron gleamed white. Behind her, the bottles and jars of the apothecary shelves were ranked in neat and well-ordered lines. To posterity, Mrs Speedicut would appear a model of dignified matronliness – a far cry from the drunk and stained slattern I knew her to be. I propped the picture up against the clock on the mantel. 'I will have a frame made for it,' I said. 'We're unlikely to see such a vision of cleanliness and decency ever again.'

'Come along, Jem,' said Will. 'I'd like to have one of you too – both of us together. I'll sit here.' He sank into a straight-backed chair positioned in the light from the apothecary window. 'You stand beside me.'

And so I did as I was told, standing still and silent while Gabriel bustled about behind the camera. Its wooden box was scuffed, and spotted with water – perhaps from its many months at sea and its journey around the globe. I found that I did not mind having my picture taken – what I did mind was having it taken using Dr Rutherford's camera. Mrs Hawkins had sat before that steady brass eye, numerous other women too, whether they had wanted to or not, and the thought made me uneasy.

The picture was a good one: Will and I side by side, he sitting straight-backed, a book open upon his knee 'to give me an intelligent look,' he'd said, his precious stove-pipe hat on the floor at his feet. Beside him I saw a tall thin man, narrow shouldered, with smooth cheeks and a pensive gaze. His face wore a mask of discoloured skin, as though someone had tried to paint over his features, though his eyes stared out from behind it fearlessly. He looked sad and watchful. Perhaps I should try to cultivate a more cheerful demeanour, I thought.

I put the image beside Mrs Speedicut's on the mantel and, following instructions, took one of Gabriel and Will together. But the thing unsettled me, no matter that I told myself that it was nothing but wood and glass and brass, that it was not a wicked object in itself.

'I think you should sell that camera,' I said. 'We have no room for it here and Gabriel has enough distractions as it is.'

'I've already offered it to Dr Christie,' said Will. 'He's interested in physiognomy. He says it will be a useful addition to admissions and case notes at Angel Meadow, especially as he intends to use the wet collodion method, which is much faster. Dr Hawkins agrees.'

'You can't carry it up there with your hands like that.'

'Dr Christie is coming to collect it tomorrow.'

I looked at the camera. I did not know why but I could not rest until it was out of my apothecary. 'I'll take it up there now.'

I still had keys to Angel Meadow, and they jangled in my pocket as I lurched up St Saviour's Street with Dr Rutherford's camera. The asylum was not far, though by the time I reached the place I wished I had taken a hansom. I went in through the main entrance. The governors' pictures were still swathed with black crêpe, though I noticed that two attendants were beginning to remove it. I nodded to the porter and said I was looking for Dr Christie.

'I think he's in the ladies' main ward this morning, sir,' came the reply.

The porter unlocked the door for me. 'I must return these keys to Dr Hawkins,' I said. 'I'll leave them with you when I go.'

I walked through the asylum, unlocking doors and locking them behind me. How had Pole borne the sound of keys and bolts after so long a prisoner? Had he not longed for freedom, for air and solitude? And yet he had chosen to inhabit a place that was little more than a prison. He must have loved Mrs Hawkins very deeply, the bond between them, in his eyes at least, something to be honoured until death. I heaved the camera into my other hand as I walked down the long corridor towards the women's ward. Up ahead I could hear Dr Mothersole's voice raised in song. Despite the booming of his speaking voice, his singing voice was unexpectedly high-pitched. It blended with the voices of the ladies and the strumming of the lute. He stopped, and I heard the quavering sound of the pan pipes.

I looked in at the sitting room as I passed. The walls were black with soot and there was a grubby smear where the hearthrug had been. The room smelled of smoke. No wonder the Ladies' Committee had chosen to sing in the dining hall instead. There was only one person in the sitting room, standing over by the window, staring out as if waiting for somebody. Letty. Poor thing, I thought, she must be waiting for the ladies. She enjoyed the singing usually. I went in to speak to her.

Letty was holding her doll to her cheek, and she rocked to and fro as she stared out at the garden, making a low crooning sound. I laid my hand upon her arm. Perhaps the combustion of Pole had upset her. Just because she was no longer able to show her emotions did not mean she did not have any.

'Letty,' I said. 'Would you like to come through to the singing?'

She turned to face me. Her mouth was open, her gaze unfocused, the doll cradled against her breast. The doll had been made for her by Mrs Speedicut out of rags, and it was Letty's most beloved object. She had had more than one, but loved them so much that Mrs Speedicut often had to conduct repairs, or make a new one – both of which she did with surprising graciousness.

'Come along, Letty,' I said. 'Let's take dolly, shall we? Dolly loves the singing.' And I reached out and gently took hold of the doll. Letty yielded it without demur. We had always got along well enough, she and I. I looked at the doll – and my heart leaped into my throat.

'Letty,' I stammered. 'How . . . ' I could not speak. The face of the doll was not how I remembered it – button-eyed and rosebud-lipped. It was not what it had been at all, but was changed, grotesquely altered in such a way that I almost dropped it to the ground. Its button eyes were missing. Whether they had been ripped out by accident or intention I could not say, but they had been replaced by two uneven crossed stitches. The mouth too was obliterated, covered over by six, long and crooked sutures. I took Letty's hand. Between her fingers she held a bodkin, a length of coarse black thread through its eye.

Why had she done this? She had not seen the bodies of Dr Golspie, or Dr Rutherford. She had not read Mrs Roseplucker's lurid stories, nor spent her time in Prior's Rents. Not as far as I knew, at any rate. And yet, what did I really know about Letty? Where did she come from? Who paid for her board? Who were her family? I did not even know her full name, for we all called her 'Letty'.

'Come along, Letty,' I said gently. I took her hand, the camera abandoned in the middle of the floor.

Dr Mothersole was still singing when Letty and I arrived at the dining room. Miss Mothersole appeared at my side.

'Good morning, Mr Flockhart,' she said. Her voice was low, and urgent, but bubbling with happiness. 'I have asked my father if I might travel to America to inspect their asylums and report back to him and he has agreed! As long as I take a companion, he says. Of course, he cannot spare my mother, so I am to ask Mrs Lunge. Dr Hawkins says it will do her good and she is much more amiable since we discovered the truth about Mr Pole, and Dr Rutherford. What do you think of that? It was your suggestion. Are you not pleased? Mr Flockhart—?'

'Miss Mothersole,' I said. 'I congratulate you. But I need to speak to Dr Mothersole rather urgently. Can you divert him?'

Miss Mothersole vanished. I saw her emerge amongst the crowd of lady visitors and, when there was an interlude between his singing and his quavering notes on the pipes, she whispered in her father's ear. Dr Mothersole was modestly dressed that day in a black topcoat over a shimmering embroidered silk waistcoat that looked as though it had been made out of bluebottles. He came over to me while the ladies continued.

'Dr Mothersole,' I said, keeping my voice low in the hope that he might do the same. 'What is Letty's real name?'

'Letty? Why, her name is Leticia Forbes.'

'Leticia Forbes,' I said. I had heard that name

somewhere before, I was certain. But where? So much had happened in so short a space of time that I could not remember. I closed my eyes.

I saw in my mind the whirling figure of Pole, the fire that consumed him burning orange and blue, his coat smoking black at it gave itself up to the flames. I saw the brightness of the lantern that had sat at my bedside after I had been dug from the earth, the candle at its heart radiating a spectrum of white and yellow. I saw Will holding the camera, the sunlight glinting off its newly polished brass eye, and Dr Christie with his glittering pocket watch held between his fingers. He pinged it open and snapped it closed, pinged it open and snapped it closed, making the reflections from its glass face dance in silver circles about the room. And the words upon it, the words on the back of his watch that I had seen a hundred times and thought nothing of came into my mind. *To Dr John Forbes Christie, from the Association of Medical Officers of Asylums and Hospitals for the Insane* – My eyes flew open. I recalled my remark about Dr Christie's waistcoat, you wear an embroidered waistcoat ... *The work is poorly executed ... Would any man wear such a garment if he did not feel compelled to do so out of love or duty? ... A sister is the most likely explanation.*

'Dr Mothersole,' I said. 'Is Letty's full name Leticia Forbes Christie?'

Dr Mothersole nodded.

'His sister?'

'Yes.'

'You knew?'

'Of course. But professional courtesy forbade me to speak of it to anyone else.'

'Did Dr Rutherford know?'

'I doubt it. Christie asked for my discretion. Two doctors' signatures were required for her admission, Christie's and mine. As far as I am aware he told no one else. But what bearing might it have upon you? Or anyone?'

I snatched hold of Letty's doll. 'Nothing,' I said. 'Until I saw this.' I thrust the savagely darned doll into his face. 'Can you explain it?'

Dr Mothersole's flabby cheeks turned white. 'Why . . . no,' he stammered. 'No, I cannot.'

'Well,' I said. 'Let us see whether Dr Christie can.'

I found Dr Christie in the mortuary. He had his jacket off and was bending over a glass jar of formaldehyde. 'Hello, Flockhart,' he said. 'I wondered when you would come.'

'Your sister sent me.' I put the darned doll on the dissecting table.

Dr Christie wiped his hands. He held up the glass jar he had been looking at. It contained a pale slice of what looked like pickled cauliflower. It had a fatty, softish look to it. 'This is a slice of Dr Golspie's brain,' he said. He put it back onto the table and picked up another. 'This is a slice of Pole's brain. And this,' he pointed to a third jar. 'This is from the brain of Dr Magorian. One doctor, one felon, one madman. They look exactly the same – size, colour, weight, the differences are minute. Even the microscope shows us nothing. What evidence do we have of disease? Not a single thing. How can we help if there is nothing to see? It is the problem posed by the mind – when it is sick, diseased, we cannot detect where the problem lies. We cannot act – treat, or excise – what we cannot see.'

'But how might you define a diseased mind?' I said. 'Is Miss Mothersole's mind diseased because she wishes to read, to write, to learn, to travel? Or Susan Chance's, because she does not behave as we would like her to?'

He smiled. 'Or you, because of who you are and who you pretend to be?'

'Who I am is irrelevant here.' I was right – for once. Who others were was more significant than the role I was playing.

'Rutherford was sure we could intervene, was sure we could slice out the problem once we had agreed whereabouts in the mind it lay. I disagreed. He determined to show me he was right, and so he used my sister.' He put Pole's brain down on the table. 'He was wrong – wrong to experiment on her, and wrong in the way he was thinking. I was at the House of Correction when he did it so I was not here to stop him.'

'Did he know Letty was your sister?'

'He did not. I didn't want anyone to know.'

'Dr Mothersole knew.'

'Oh, he's no trouble. In fact, he suggested it. He knew my father, knew what had become of him. He would not have told anyone.'

'But you must have hoped for a cure. When all's said and done wasn't Rutherford trying to help?'

'John Rutherford helped no one but himself,' said Dr Christie. He sighed. 'The hereditary malady. You know what it's like, Jem, to labour under such a sentence. My father. My sister. Every day I asked myself whether it would also be my fate.' He picked up the doll. 'She used to enjoy the needle. Before Rutherford saw to it that she would never enjoy anything ever again, though as you pointed out, the results of her handiwork were less than proficient.'

'You were fortunate that Pole was here to conceal what you had done.'

'I didn't need Pole!' snapped Dr Christie. 'I managed well enough. Indeed, it is his fault that—' He stopped.

'That what? That I am standing here accusing you of Dr Rutherford's murder?'

'I had the matter perfectly in hand.'

'You intended to make it look as though Susan Chance had killed Dr Rutherford?'

'Quite so. I knew about Bess Bodkin from the records at the House of Correction. It was something Susan Chance alone was bound to be familiar with. I had no idea that Hawkins's wife would also be from the Rents, and Pole too.' He shook his head. 'I was unlucky there!'

'But to kill a man?'

'What of it? It is not such a difficult thing to do, not to a man in my profession. And using Rutherford's own damned phrenological callipers was rather poetic justice.'

'And Letty saw everything?'

'Yes. I took her with me and told Rutherford who she was. I told him that when she came to Angel Meadow she was troubled – angry and erratic – but nothing we could not manage. But she became his experiment. He thought only of his reputation, of how he might further our understanding, of how phrenology had something to offer medical science after all. Phrenology is for fairgrounds and quacks. It has no place in medicine and my sister deserved better. I put her here to keep her safe and Rutherford as good as killed her.'

'And after you told him who she was?'

'He laughed! He said that perhaps madness *was* hereditary if I was such a goose that I could not see the value of his work. He offered to put my name on his paper! The paper describing what he had done and which he was to submit to the Mind and Brain Society. He said that I had sanctioned the procedure simply by putting her into Angel Meadow in the first place.' Dr Christie's face had turned white with fury. 'And so I seized the callipers that lay on the table and I drove the point of them through his head.' He laughed. 'I wonder whether they went through his "organ of arrogant stupidity" for he would have had a very large one. Then I sutured his mouth closed – to deflect attention onto one who was already guilty. Susan Chance would end up either on the gallows or in an asylum, which was where she belonged anyway. Leticia watched,' he went on. 'Then I took her back to her ward.'

I remembered what Pole had said while he waited to die: *I had to protect her. I could not have her sent back to the gallows.* He had killed Dr Golspie to prevent him from telling us that he had seen Mrs Hawkins in Dr Rutherford's mirror. He had stuffed me into the coffin to prevent me from reading Miss Mothersole's notebooks in which Mrs Hawkins was implicated. And yet these actions were based on Pole's erroneous belief that it had been Mrs Hawkins who had killed Dr Rutherford.

'Pole only killed Dr Golspie,' I said. 'Though he used the same method, his handiwork was far clumsier. And yet we had all assumed that he had killed Dr Rutherford too.'

'I have no idea what Pole was thinking,' said Dr Christie. 'But you didn't kill Dr Golspie?'

'No.'

'Nor bury me alive?'

'No. Of course,' he said, 'as Pole is dead and has already shouldered the blame for everything, and your dear Susan is released, perhaps you might show some compassion?'

'I should let you go? Say nothing?'

'Exactly.'

'I cannot.'

'You will be sending me to hang.'

'You killed a man.'

'A man whose crimes speak for themselves.'

'Dr Christie—' I faltered. Could I really send a man to hang after all that I knew about execution? I thought of my father, of Mrs Hawkins. Who was I to condemn a man to such a death – for Dr Christie would end his life on the gallows, there was no doubt. I did not disagree that Dr Rutherford's actions had demanded retribution. But to kill him in cold blood? Was that justice? What had been Dr Rutherford's crime against Letty? Ambition? Curiosity? Should all doctors who made mistakes and errors of judgement in the quest for knowledge be condemned? His behaviour on board the *Norfolk* was no worse than many who had gone before and after. Did it demand his murder? And yet, was I not glad to have one less petty tyrant in the world? I was; I could not deny that either.

'Are you any better than Dr Rutherford, or Pole?' I said. 'I don't want to send you to hang, but nor can I let you go.'

'They are the only choices.'

'There is one other.' I took out my watch. It was the one my father had given me before he was hanged, the one his own father had bought for him when he had finished his apprenticeship. It was not unlike Dr Christie's, only my father's was engraved with the words *Jeremiah Flockhart, Licentiate of the Worshipful Society of Apothecaries—*. I pinged it open, the way I had so often seen Dr Christie ping open his own, balancing it like a golden clam-shell between my fingers. I pressed it again and in the back of the lid another compartment opened. Inside was a small fold of paper.

'I have this,' I said. I plucked out the tiny packet. 'It's for when I feel that I have become more like my father and my uncle than I would wish to be. Death won't be painless, but it will be quick.' I laid the fold of paper on the table between us and pushed it towards him. 'It is against the laws of men and God, but the decision rests with you.'

I felt as though I were rising up from a deep pool. I had no thoughts, only that I was warm, and comfortable. I could hear sounds, but they were familiar and restful – a low, swirling, rattling sound, and a rhythmic, gentle grinding. I let them lull me. For a moment I could not recall what they were, but as I surfaced I recognised the sound of pills rolling in the silvering box, and the grating of the pestle and mortar. I opened my eyes

I was in my father's chair, my stockinged feet on the footstool, my shoes warming beside the stove. Someone had placed a cushion of lavender and hyssop beneath my head and tucked a blanket around me. A small saucer of rose geranium oil evaporated on the stove top.

'Hello,' said Will. His sleeves were rolled up, and he was holding the silvering box in his bandaged hands. Beside him, Gabriel ground nigella seeds: I could smell their rich, woody spiciness rising from the bowl. The apothecary was warm and cosy, the lanterns aglow, the bunches and baskets of herbs adding to the heavy, earthy scent of the place. The ranked bottles of powdered root and leaf glittered on their shelves, the dark wood of the mahogany drawers below them rich and burnished. Gabriel had dusted, and the place looked neat and well-ordered, just the way I liked it.

'You've been asleep for ages,' said Will.

'How long?'

'Since you came back from Angel Meadow.'

I recalled how tired I had been, exhausted after all that had happened, all we had endured. I remembered sitting down before the stove, my head in my hands. But after that—

'Five hours,' said Will. 'I made you more comfortable. Would you like something to eat? A cup of tea? How're you feeling?'

'Better,' I said. I sat up. 'Five hours?'

'At least. Dr Hawkins came down. He was glad to see you sleeping; he said not to wake you. He's taking Mrs Hawkins abroad for a while. Dr Mothersole and Dr Stiven are to superintend the asylum.'

'And Dr Christie?'

'He didn't say. He said we should consider some time away too.'

'I cannot,' I said. 'Though I'll be glad not to go up to Angel Meadow again.' I made as if to stand up, but Will pushed me back.

'Rest,' he said. 'We can manage without you.'

'Course we can,' said Gabriel. 'I've been doin' without you for days. What's another few hours?'

I pulled the blanket up to my chin. I felt warm and drowsy. 'I might doze again,' I said. 'Just for a few more moments.'

'Did you give Christie the camera?'

'Yes.'

'And? Does he know what to do with it?'

'I'm sure he will do what's right,' I said. I had not told Will that I had a half drachm of arsenic hidden inside my watch – so that I could choose the time and place of my own death rather than await the one that fate might have in store for me. But then there are always some secrets that are best kept to oneself.

The gentle rhythm of the silvering box started up again. I closed my eyes, and slept.

Acknowledgements

There are many people who, in different ways, have helped me to write this book. I would like to thank them here. First and foremost, as always, John Burnett has listened to me talk about *Dark Asylum* for twelve months or more, and has read drafts and commented on my work with his usual skill and insight – John, how would I manage without you? Similarly, three other writer-friends have been invaluable with comments, corrections, and enthusiasm for the project: Margaret Reis, Olga Wojtas and Michelle Wards. This book is far better because of them.

I must also thank my amazing multi-tasking mother, Jean Thomson, who is awaiting my appearance on Radio 4, my sister and most loyal supporter Anne Briffett, and my lovely boys, Guy and Carlo, who have watched me drive away to East Lothian on three writing retreats this year – I'd never have finished without their patience and understanding (and willingness to endure an untidy house and some badly cooked meals). To Penny Cunyghame and Barbara Mortimer, loyal friends who have looked after my boys and given me the time and space to work on many occasions, I offer my love and gratitude.

Other friends have been more kind and generous than they realise, and their confidence in me and kind words about my work have been a great source of encouragement, notably Paul Lynch, Helen Wilson, and Paul Morgan – who leaves no text unanswered (especially valued during a dark and windy January in Gullane). Adrian Searle has been one of the best pals a writer could have, and has championed my work wherever he goes – once again, Ade, I'm in your debt. Thanks is also due to Charlie Hopkinson for information about photography, and Dr Gayle Davies at Edinburgh University for sharing her reading list about madness. Any mistakes in the interpretation of that information are mine alone.

As ever, I am super-grateful to Jenny Brown, my fabulous agent-friend, as well as to Krystyna Green, Tara Loder, Florence Partridge, Amanda Keats, the mysterious but brilliant copy editor I know only as Una, and all the marvellous people at Constable.

Finally, I owe a different type of thank you altogether to Trevor Griffiths, who has listened to me go on and on about this book, and made me laugh and forget all about it too.

This book was completed with the generous help of Creative Scotland.

Author's note / Bibliography

I was guided in the writing of this book by the first-rate work of others. Richard Barnett's *Sick City* (Wellcome Trust, 2008) provided me with a varied survey of the health of the city. Mike Jay's *Emperors of Dreams* (Dedalus, 2000) was an invaluable source of information about the history of cannabis use. Once again, Kelly Grovier's *The Gaol* (John Murray, 2009) and Wendy Moore's *The Knife Man* (Bantam Press, 2005) gave me fascinating insights into the workings of eighteenth- and nineteenth-century penitentiaries and post-mortems respectively. Lisa Appignanesi, *Mad, Bad and Sad* (Virago, 2008); Catherine Arnold, *Bedlam and Its Mad* (Simon and Schuster, 2008) and Sarah Wise, *Inconvenient People* (Bodley Head, 2012) provided the ideas and inspiration behind the various asylum doctors, patients and practices found within this novel, whilst an exhibition at the National Museum of Scotland, and its accompanying book *Photography: A Victorian Sensation*, by A. D. Morrison-Low (NMS, 2015),

372

was an excellent guide to the history and application of early photography. Finally, surely no one could write about convict transportation without referring to Michael Cannon's *Perilous Voyages to the New Land* (Today's Australia Publishing Company, 1995) and *The Fatal Shore* by Robert Hughes (Harvill Press, 1987) – a marvellous and moving book that everyone should read. I was lucky to find such a wealth of excellent histories upon which to draw. Of course, any mistakes that lie within the pages of this novel are mine alone.

Author Q&A

Do you have a particular process for writing a book or does it vary?

I have to write about my characters – who they are and how they might think and behave – before I can really get a sense of where things are going. The location of my stories is important, too, so I try hard to get this right at the outset. I've come to accept that writing the first third of a novel is the trickiest part for me. It's always the bit I re-write the most – setting out the people and the place, as well as a suitable crime. After this, the rest seems to follow much more easily.

In terms of the physical process of writing, I always write longhand at first, with a particular type of fountain pen, in a particular type of notebook. I have three fountain pens – two with broad nibs for speedy writing, one with a fine nib for editing my printed manuscript. I write longhand because I can't touch type. Using a pen means I can write quickly, I can doodle if necessary (I do a lot of doodling), and I'm not distracted by the internet. The pens are important. A biro is no use – all thin and slippery – it has to be proper ink. If I don't have my pen, I can't go on. My notepad has to be A4 in size with thick pages and widely spaced lines. Thin lines and cheap paper are an abomination. Once the pen and the paper are right, anything can happen.

Is there a particular place where you prefer to write?

I write anywhere. The notebook and fountain pen habit is useful here. I'm quite short of time due to life commitments other than writing, so being able to whip out a pen and paper at any time and place is the only way to make progress. I wrote much of my first novel on the number 23 bus on the way up to work. I've written in coffee shops whilst waiting for my sons to finish judo or sitting by the side of the pool during their swimming lessons. I've done it standing up beside the stove while the steam from a pan of boiling pasta wilted my paper. That said, I have two places that I love: the National Library of Scotland (if anyone sits in my favourite seat I lurk nearby until they go away), and a little hideaway I know by the sea in East Lothian. It's there that I really make progress, though the isolation and long days at the desk are hard going. It's great – but also terrible. Like lancing a boil.

Where did the idea of Jem come from?

I wanted a principal character who would be a strong woman, one who could go anywhere and do anything without having to apologise for her gender. Disguise seemed

375

the best option – anything else seemed unconvincing, especially given what I knew about Victorian patriarchy and the exclusivity of the medical profession. There was a real-life example, too: James Miranda Barry was a woman who had disguised herself as a man in order to read medicine at Edinburgh University. She qualified with an MD in 1812, several decades before any women were officially admitted there. Barry worked as an army surgeon all her life and her sex was only revealed *post mortem.*

The cross-dressing woman is not a new phenomenon in literature, but how else might a woman in the 1840s be free to do as she pleased? How else might she be educated as well as any man and able to speak her mind on any subject she chose unless her true identity was hidden? And how would it feel to be placed in this role by a parent – which is what happens to Jem – rather than choosing it for oneself? How might she reflect on the lot of women and her position as an impostor amongst men? I thought these might be interesting ideas to write about.

I gave Jem a red birthmark across her face to add an extra dimension of disguise, and also to give a tangible focus to her feelings of loneliness and isolation. When I started the Jem Flockhart books, I was suffering from a painful and unsightly skin condition known as Red Skin Syndrome. It lasted throughout the whole time I wrote the first book, though I was given some medication to help (it also helped all my hair to fall out, thereby exchanging one distressing situation for another). Despite the red skin, which affected my face badly, I still had to go out and about. I noticed people would look at me twice – a casual glance at a fellow human being quickly followed by a stare of horror and pity at the red mask that covered my face. They never saw the person beneath. I decided to use the red mask – but without the physical pain that I had endured – for Jem. I thought it would give her something to hide behind, something that she depended on for concealment, but also something she hated. Now that I'm mostly recovered when I'm writing about Jem and her birthmark I have to remind myself how isolated I felt at that time. But Jem is a strong character, and she now has Will as a confidante and friend, so things are not as bad as they once were for her either.

What is it about this particular time period that appeals to you?

I wanted to set my books in a period of history that was rich with new discoveries (chloroform, theories of disease causation, the birth of photography), but which had yet to realise the potential these discoveries might have. The late 1840s and 1850s were perfect for this: surgical procedures might take place under anaesthetic in 1850 which would have been impossible to attempt two years earlier. It was also a time of rapidly changing attitudes – towards the mentally ill, towards cleanliness, towards how we understand human anatomy and the interconnectedness of the body. And diseases of the mind as well as the body were endemic. Medicine is at the intersection between life and death; those who practise it are prey to rivalry, ambition and arrogance. It seemed the perfect mixture for trouble.

The wider urban environment, which I believe would be truly shocking to us today, was also a source of fascination and horror. Massive population growth, a general lack of sanitation and the development of dirty industries and the pollution they created meant that mid-nineteenth century cities were, quite literally, sinking under their own waste. I picked London because it was so huge and its problems seemed so insurmountable, though any large city would have been just as bad. These were dirty and difficult times. Using the sights, smells and textures of the metropolis as an essential part of the books was something that came easily. To miss them out, or make little attempt to capture their impact on daily life, would be to paint the wrong picture.

What are you working on next?

I'm working on Jem and Will's next adventure. It's set in the docks, on a floating seaman's hospital that occupies a rotting hulk – a decommissioned man o' war. There was such a hospital moored at Greenwich during this period. I've dragged it up-river for my story and filled it with menace and terrible deeds.